The B...

An Anthology of Erotic Writing by Women

The Best of Black Lace

Edited by
KERRI SHARP

First published in 1999 by
Black Lace
Thames Wharf Studios,
Rainville Road, London W6 9HA

Typeset by SetSystems Ltd, Saffron Walden, Essex
Printed and bound by Mackays of Chatham PLC

ISBN 0 352 33452 5

Contents

Introduction

*T*he *Best of Black Lace* is a sample of the diverse materials that we've published over the past couple of years. I've chosen not to include material from the earlier titles in the series as it is not necessarily reflective of how the imprint had developed. Also, a lot of the very early titles are long out of print, and extracts have already been taken from earlier books to make up previous anthologies such as *Modern Love* and *Past Passions*.

What we have here, then, is a selection of work from authors who have been prolific over the past couple of years – writers like Zoe le Verdier and Juliet Hastings – and women whose work is notable for its unusual slant or who have helped to shape the Black Lace series as it is today. Kristina Lloyd and Emma Holly fit into this category. Their clear writing style, grasp of contemporary language and fully rounded characters have meant that the Black Lace series has stayed ahead of the competition. While other publishers are resting their long-standing imprints, we're gaining strength in the market.

We've amended our guidelines over the past year so that they are less strict in terms of storyline, but we've also waged war on erotic clichés. We've revamped the covers to make them brighter, more colourful and upbeat, and the *Sugar and Spice* and *Wicked Words* compilations have revived the erotic short story format. Our changing editorial policy has resulted in a lot of new authors coming forward – authors who never considered writing for us before – whose work is stunningly original. Many of these people have come to our attention through submitting short stories, or making us aware of their websites.

As I write this introduction our very own website is going online at www.virginbooks.com where we will have complete booklists, synopses of all the stories, and erotic features. As we're always commissioning a year ahead, I can assure our readers that the year 2000 will be the best Black Lace year yet. There are some titles coming up which stand out as being really special and very different from anything we've published before. Watch out for *Cruel Enchantment* (March), *Hard Corps* (June), *Animal Passions* (June) and *Primal Skin* (July). I suggest that anyone who thinks Black Lace books are 'Mills and Bonk' should read these titles!

Also published this month is *Sex Magic* (Virgin £9.99). For all the witchy women out there who want to know the secrets of successful seduction using the best Eastern and Western techniques, this is the book for you. Check out the recipes for tried and tested aphrodisiacs and unique sensuous oils guaranteed to capture and enchant the lover of your dreams. Full of wonderful womanly wisdom, *Sex Magic* makes an ideal present for a best friend – or a very special treat for you.

Kerri Sharp

September 1999

The Transformation

Natasha Rostova

The Transformation is set in San Francisco, and is the story of three women at a sexual crossroads in their lives. The first extract in this anthology focuses on Lydia, senior editor for a style magazine, whose interest in Nicholas – a certain unkempt-looking intellectual bookstore owner – is a mile short of the kind of men she usually goes for. Nicholas has been celibate for ages, but the attentions of his flirtatious assistant reawaken his earthy desires. Meanwhile, Lydia is in denial and is trying to fix him up with her best friend, Cassie.

The Transformation is Natasha Rostova's second Black Lace book. Blending fairytale themes with contemporary situations, it's a heartwarming story of three close friends living in America's most liberated of cities. Natasha's other Black Lace book is *The Captivation* – an historical erotic novel set at the time of the Russian revolution.

The Transformation

'Here it is.' Nicholas Hawthorne took a book from the high shelf and grabbed a handkerchief from his pocket. He wiped a thin layer of dust off the book cover, sneezed, and stuffed the handkerchief back into his trousers. Tucking the book under his arm, he descended the ladder.

His customer, a distinguished, grey-haired man wearing a suit and bow tie, held out his hands eagerly. 'Well, my boy, I'm delighted. I never thought you would have this. Poor old Hendrik van Loon is difficult to find nowadays.'

'Let me know if there's anything else by him that you're looking for, Professor,' Nicholas said. 'I'll be happy to do a search for you.'

The professor looked down at the book, stroking his hand lovingly over the cover.

'Olive will ring it up for you.' Nicholas glanced towards the front desk, hoping to find his flirtatious employee actually working rather than filing her fingernails.

Olive was a student at the local university who had convinced him that her major in English literature made her an ideal candidate for a part-time position as a sales clerk. Nicholas suspected that the sight of Olive's abundant cleavage rather than her knowledge of literature had played more of a role in his hiring of her. He now paid a

3

daily penance for letting his hormones dictate his business decisions.

'Olive,' he called. 'Professor Martin has a purchase.'

Olive looked up from her careful nail filing and snapped her gum. 'Okey-doke, boss. How's it going, Professor?'

'Fine, dear, fine.' Even the professor's gaze slipped down to the generous valley revealed by Olive's low-necked sweater.

Nicholas sighed and adjusted his tortoiseshell glasses. One of these days, he was going to hire a friendly, little old lady who wore lace collars up to her neck, smelled of camphor, and whose last sexual experience had taken place during World War Two.

He turned and climbed back up the ladder to rearrange the books and fill the hole created by the professor's purchase.

'He's gone, boss.' Olive called from below.

Nicholas looked down at her from his perch, only to discover that she was standing next to the ladder. She was a pretty, plump blonde girl with a mischievous sparkle in her blue eyes, which were currently upturned and gazing at him. 'Good, Olive. Now, if you could please finish doing the inventory on the history section, I'd appreciate it.'

'Sure thing.' She didn't move.

Irritated, Nicholas shoved the books back into place and descended a few steps. 'Olive, when I give you a job, I expect you to do it.'

'I know.'

Nicholas immediately realised his mistake in pausing halfway down the ladder, as Olive was now at a perfect eye-level with his crotch. Worse, she was staring directly at it.

To his horror, he felt his penis start to swell with arousal. His position gave him a full view of the tops of Olive's creamy breasts, which only served to remind him how long it had been since he'd been with a woman. He could see the hard points of her nipples pressing against the front of her sweater. The deep crevice created by her full mounds fairly begged to be filled with the length of a hard cock . . . Oh, damn. Nicholas winced and gripped the sides of the ladder as his trousers tightened further and his penis began to throb. Mentally, he told himself to get off the ladder, but he couldn't seem to move.

Maybe because Olive's gaze was fixing him to the spot. Her blue eyes lingered on the growing bulge at his crotch as she snapped her gum. She lifted her eyes to him, a small smile playing about her full, red lips.

'You know, boss, I've been thinking that you should put together an erotica and sexuality section,' she remarked.

Nicholas swallowed hard, willing his body under control. 'Um, erotica?'

'Uh-huh. Erotic classics like the stories of the Marquis de Sade, *The Story of O*, some of that fabulous Victorian smut.'

'We have some of that.'

Olive's eyebrows lifted. 'Do we? Where?'

Anything to get her away from such close proximity to his groin. 'Over in the fiction section.'

'Hmm. Maybe I can be in charge of organising certain titles into a specific erotica section.'

'Great. Why don't you go get started?'

'OK.' She didn't move, but her gaze slipped back down to his erection. 'Some of that Victorian erotica is pretty hot, don't you think?'

'I wouldn't know.'

'You mean you've never read it?'

'No.' Nicholas's hands tightened on the ladder. This was insane.

'Pity. Maybe I'll have to read some to you sometime. It's quite raunchy, all that repressed sexuality suddenly bursting forth in these amazingly orgastic scenarios.'

Nicholas coughed and sought to regain his composure

and his position as her employer. 'Olive, this is highly inappropriate.'

'Your trousers don't seem to think so.' With a wicked little grin, Olive lifted her manicured hand and pressed it against the protrusion in his pants, her fingers cupping and caressing it.

A layer of perspiration broke out on Nicholas's forehead at the sensation of the luscious pressure. 'Olive –'

'Relax, boss. I'm supposed to be helping you out here. I mean, you're not paying me to file my nails now, are you?'

She winked up at him and took the zipper of his trousers between her fingers, slowly pulling it down. The raspy sound filled the air. Nicholas looked hurriedly towards the front door. There were no customers in the store, but someone could walk in at any moment. A shudder of excitement ran through Nicholas's body, and his fingers dug into the ladder when Olive slipped her hand into his open fly and began fondling the length of his penis.

'My, my, you really are the big boss, aren't you?' She grinned.

'Olive . . .' For the life of him, Nicholas knew that he would never be able to stop this, not when Olive's warm fingers were touching his cock and easing it out of his trousers. His heart began to pound violently, his breath escaping him in rapid gasps.

Her expression both hungry and aroused, Olive murmured a series of low sounds of approval as the length of Nicholas's erection came into view. Her tongue flickered out to caress her lower lip. Nicholas nearly lost control at the delectable sight, his entire body suddenly aching for the sensation of her pink tongue on his cock. Olive's fingers wrapped around his bursting shaft, and she squeezed him lightly, drawing her cupped hand up and down the length with slow, sensual movements.

'What a waste to hide such a magnificent specimen

under those baggy trousers you wear,' she murmured, her eyes gleaming as she traced the thick veins on his penis, rubbing her fingers over the hard knob.

Oh, Christ. The sensation and sight of her fondling was almost more than Nicholas could stand. He'd been relying on his own devices for longer than he cared to remember, and a perfectly luscious woman now appeared to be enraptured with his cock. He stared down at her, gripping the ladder so tightly he thought the wood would crack and splinter under the pressure. His glasses fogged.

'I'll bet you taste just delicious.' Olive smiled up at him before she leant forward and encased the head of his penis between her pouty lips.

Nicholas drew in a sharp breath. The feeling of her hot, wet mouth slowly enclosing him was an exquisite torment. His entire body pulsed with need. With an expertise he could not help but notice, Olive began to slide the length of his penis into her mouth as her other hand dipped down to caress the tight sacs between his legs. She rubbed her fingers over the crinkly skin, creating such a rush of sensation that Nicholas fairly trembled. Heat prickled along his skin, and he had to gasp to draw in a breath. Pressure built at the base of his cock, signalling an imminent orgasm, and he managed to croak out Olive's name in warning.

Olive's tongue licked up his shaft, dipping into the indentation at the tip as she slowly pulled away from him. Her pale skin was flushed with arousal, blooming a lovely reddish colour on her cheeks. She looked up at him, her breath emerging in hot, little bursts to torture his aching penis.

'Would you like to fuck my tits, boss?' she asked, her voice husky and raw.

Nicholas stared at her, stunned that she had fairly read his earlier thoughts. His throat worked as he tried to formulate a reply.

'I see you staring at my breasts,' Olive said, slipping one

hand down to finger her hard nipple through her sweater. 'Nice, aren't they? I've been wondering what you think when you look at them. Don't you imagine what it would be like to thrust your cock between them?'

Nicholas could hardly breathe. Sweat trickled down his back, and flames seemed to encase his entire body. His cock was so hard it hurt.

'Come down a step.' Olive's fingers moved to the buttons of her sweater, and she began to unfasten them, revealing her breasts clad in a bra that seemed too small to contain her abundant flesh. The sight was a glorious one, and Nicholas descended another step in a daze, his penis jutting out in front of him like a rigid pole.

'One more.' Olive reached out to tug his trousers down his legs, then slipped out of her sweater and reached behind her to unfasten her bra clasp.

Her breasts spilled out like gorgeous, ripe fruits, topped with round, pink nipples that jutted forth. Nicholas nearly came right then and there, and only the thought of burying his cock between such delicious breasts reined in his control. He stepped down another rung, his chest heaving as Olive took his oiled cock in her hand and guided it between her breasts.

A shiver of pure sensuality rippled through his body as Olive cushioned his erection between her warm, resilient flesh. She cupped her hands underneath her breasts, her fingers stroking her nipples as she pushed them together to create a deep valley. Nicholas thought he could have quite happily died right then and there. His shaft pulsed and throbbed against Olive's hot skin, burrowed in total, sensual pleasure.

Still gripping the ladder to maintain his balance, Nicholas drew back slightly and began to thrust his penis back and forth between Olive's breasts. She gave him a slow smile, pressing her globes even tighter around him. Nicholas's entire body tensed with sheer excitement. God, it was amazing, her voluptuousness totally wrapped around a raging erection, surrounding and immersing it as if in imitation of a more intimate kind of enclosure.

'That's right, lover, fuck them hard,' Olive urged, bending to lick at the head of his penis as it appeared in sporadic, rapid thrusts between the crevice of her cleavage. 'Ah, you have no idea what it feels like to have such a thick, long cock moving between my tits.'

Nicholas's mind spun with sensation and heat. He worked his hips back and forth with an increasing rhythm, unable to take his eyes off the sight of his shaft thrusting back and forth between Olive's breasts. The luxurious friction of Olive's soft skin and his cock increased his intense arousal, and the intermittent lick of her wet tongue nearly drove him over the edge.

Pressure seemed to envelop his entire body, centring in the aching swell of his penis, and then he could no longer stand it. With a pained shout, he rammed his cock upward, feeling Olive squeeze her breasts tighter around him as jets of semen spurted out on to her creamy flesh. Pleasure wracked Nicholas's entire body, making him shake with the intensity of it all.

'Jesus, Olive.' He could barely catch his breath.

She smiled up at him again, reaching up to slide her fingers over his moist penis as it began to soften and slide out of the warm valley in which it had been so happily nestled. Nicholas closed his eyes and leaned his forehead against the ladder, his chest heaving.

'I knew you'd been wanting to do that,' Olive said. 'I've been wanting you to, you know. That and much more.'

Nicholas opened his eyes and looked down at her. 'You have?'

'Mmm.' Olive began rubbing the damp trails of his seed into her breasts, making her skin shine with his arousal. 'I had a feeling you were a sexy man, boss. I mean, you're a complete nerd, but I knew something was simmering underneath all your geekiness.'

Nicholas gave a hoarse laugh. 'Thanks. I think.'

He pulled out his handkerchief and handed it to her, but Olive grinned and shook her head, still stroking her glossy breasts. 'Semen is good for the skin, you know. Lots of protein.'

'Olive, you're a very wicked girl.'

Olive laughed. 'Yeah. Lucky for you.'

'Hello?' The bell heralding a customer's entrance into the store tingled suddenly, making Nicholas start.

He turned and stared over the bookcases to the front of the store, horrified to find a man and woman standing there. Belatedly, he remembered his appointment with a photographer from a fashion magazine.

The man spotted him over the shelves and lifted a hand. 'Zack Donovan from *Savoir Faire*,' he called. He began making his way towards them.

'Wait!' Nicholas shouted.

The abruptness of his command made both the man and woman stop. Nicholas realised that the bookshelves hid his state of undress, but he and Olive would never be decent in the time it took the couple to cross the store.

'I'll be with you in a minute,' Nicholas called. 'Help yourself to some coffee. It's right by the door.'

'Great.' The man and woman exchanged looks over his odd behaviour, but Nicholas didn't care what they thought as long as they didn't try to approach him right now. Quickly, he descended the ladder, adjusting himself and zipping his pants.

Giggling, Olive slipped back into her bra and sweater. 'Imagine if they'd come in five minutes ago,' she whispered, her eyes sparkling. 'They would have seen you thrusting your hips like a wild man.'

'Thank heavens for small favours,' Nicholas replied, embarrassed by the mere thought of such an incident.

Olive glanced down at his groin. 'Well, I wouldn't call it a *small* favour,' she said.

'Olive, behave yourself.'

'Sure, boss. For now.' She gave him a saucy wink and

headed off to greet the couple, the luscious swell of her hips swaying.

Nicholas took a deep breath, straightened his glasses, and tried to regain his composure. He would have plenty of time later to think about what had just happened, but now he had a meeting. He walked to the front of the store, where Zack and the woman were waiting near the coffee machine.

'I'm Nicholas Hawthorne, the owner of the store,' he said, holding out his hand. 'This is my associate, Olive.'

'Lydia Weston, senior editor of *Savoir Faire*.' The woman took his hand and gave it a firm shake, then turned to greet Olive.

She was a striking, sophisticated woman with a cool, dark gaze, and attractive features made all the more elegant by the rather imperious way she carried herself. Her eyes slid from Nicholas to Olive, taking in their flushed features and rumpled appearances with a keen perception that made Nicholas hugely uncomfortable.

Quickly, he turned to Zack and shook his hand. 'I understand from your message that you want to do some photography here.'

'That's right,' Zack said. 'Your store has a great atmosphere for a line of clothing we're going to highlight.'

'And we're looking to do more shoots on location around the city,' Lydia Weston added. She glanced around the book-filled store, and Nicholas suddenly wished he had taken the time to straighten up and do a little dusting.

'Sorry, Ms Weston, we've been doing an inventory so it's kind of a mess.'

Lydia Weston's gaze went back to him. 'Call me Lydia, please, Nicholas. Your store is lovely. Reminds me a bit of an old library or a gentlemen's club.'

Nicholas was embarrassed by how pleased he was at her compliment. 'Thanks. Um, do you want to just look around?'

11

'Yes, we'd like to take some preliminary photos and see if this will work for us,' Zack said.

Nicholas frowned slightly. 'Then after you're finished looking, we can talk about whether or not your fashion shoot will work for me.'

Lydia Weston looked at him for a moment. A hint of something appeared in her eyes, and Nicholas didn't know if it was admiration or annoyance.

He blushed anyway. 'I just mean I don't want to inconvenience my business.'

'Of course not,' Lydia replied smoothly. 'We would never think of intruding.'

She nodded at Zack, and the two of them began browsing around the store and discussing the possibilities of a shoot. The sound of Zack's camera clicking echoed through the store.

Nicholas let out his breath in a sigh. Lydia Weston was obviously a sharp woman who had picked up on the fact that he and Olive had been engaging in a tryst. For some odd reason, the thought annoyed him, although he didn't think that his irritation was based on embarrassment. No, it was more the idea of Lydia Weston thinking that he was the kind of man who got off on regularly banging his employees during business hours.

'Well, they're very avant-garde, aren't they?' Olive had resumed her position behind the counter, and she gave Nicholas a grin. 'They seem like the kind of people who might have joined us.'

Nicholas shook his head. 'Olive, you're unbelievable.'

'So I've been told.'

'Would you please act professional right now?' Nicholas said. 'I'd prefer that people don't think this bookshop is a front for an orgy club.'

'Hey, now, there's an idea,' Olive said.

Nicholas gave her a dark look just as the bell rang to announce the entrance of another customer. Relieved, Nicholas turned his attention to the customer and soon became engrossed in a discussion of first editions of Stein-beck novels.

He spent the next hour with several customers, but was constantly aware of the presence of Zack Donovan and Lydia Weston as they meandered about the store and discussed lighting and locations. After the last customer left with three books, Nicholas approached Zack and Lydia.

'If you'd like to talk, I have some free time right now.'

'Perfect,' Lydia said. 'We love your store, and we'd love to use it for one of our shoots. Unfortunately, we'd like to do the shoot during the day, and I see from your schedule outside that you're open seven days a week.'

'Yes, but I'm willing to be flexible as long as I have adequate prior notice.' Nicholas wondered why Lydia Weston looked as if she were dissolving into an apparition, and then he realised that his glasses were fogging up again. He took them off, wondering why he was getting so warm, and cleaned the lenses on his jacket sleeve.

'Maybe we can discuss dates.' He replaced his glasses on his nose, glancing up to find Lydia looking at him strangely. 'I'm sorry, is there a problem?'

She shook her head, seeming to pull herself together. 'No. No problem. Is there a quiet place where the three of us can sit down and talk?'

'My office is in the back. I'll bring coffee.' He gestured to the door at the rear of the store and returned to the coffee machine. 'Olive, please call me only if it's urgent.'

'Sure, boss. Urgency is my speciality.'

Nicholas sighed as he walked to his office with the coffee. Clearly, his relationship with Olive would never be the same again.

Lydia crossed her legs and took a sip of coffee from the recyclable paper cup Nicholas Hawthorne had given her. She glanced around his cluttered office. A small desk with a computer sat in the corner, and the rest of the space was filled with file folders, inventory sheets, and books.

13

An entire leather-bound collection of Greek and Roman authors was stacked on the floor, and the walls were covered with photographs of famous authors.

She liked it. The place had a comfortable, intellectual atmosphere, not unlike Nicholas Hawthorne himself. She let her gaze settle on him. He was wearing corduroy trousers, a wrinkled linen shirt, and an old suit jacket that had holes in the lapel and elbows. His shoes were a scuffed pair of loafers that looked a hundred years old. His dark hair, badly cut and ruffled, brushed his collar. His face was obscured by a pair of tortoiseshell glasses and a scraggly beard. However, Lydia had been quite surprised when he had removed his glasses and revealed beautiful, dark eyes, thickly lashed and with well-arched eyebrows.

She wondered just what he had been doing with that lush associate of his. They had both looked as if they'd been exerting themselves quite heavily. Lydia suspected that they hadn't been hauling books around.

Nicholas looked up suddenly to find her watching him. A charming flush rose to colour his cheekbones. 'Um, do you want more coffee, Ms . . . I mean, Lydia?'

Lydia glanced down at her nearly full cup, not wanting to hurt his feelings by telling him how awful the coffee tasted.

'No, thank you. I'm trying to cut back on caffeine.' She placed the cup on the desk and leaned forward. 'Nicholas, we're willing to pay you well for letting us invade your space for a day. Of course, we'll have to move some things around, but everything will be put back. We will need you to temporarily close the store, but the compensation will be worth it.'

He was staring at her lips as she talked. Then, he nodded. 'Yes. Yes, I can see that.'

Lydia felt as if he had touched her lips rather than merely looked at them. She lifted her fingers to her lips, aware of an odd tingling sensation. 'Good,' she murmured, telling herself she was being utterly foolish. 'Then it's all set. We'll plan for a week from Monday.'

She rose and extended her hand. 'Thank you for your time, Nicholas. We'll be in touch.'

'Would you ... um ...' Nicholas's voice trailed off as another flush covered his face. 'Would you like to have dinner sometime?'

Lydia was startled. 'Dinner? With you?'

'Yes.'

Lydia could only imagine what it would be like going out with Nicholas. She didn't consider herself to be incredibly shallow, but as the senior editor of a fashion magazine, she did have standards. Standards that not even this odd sexual attraction could overcome. 'No, Nicholas, I'm afraid that wouldn't be possible.'

'Oh. All right.'

Lydia tried to quell the discomfort that rose in her stomach. She looked at Zack, who was barely repressing a grin. 'Come along, Zack.'

They said their goodbyes to Olive, who gave Zack a wink, and returned to Zack's Mercedes.

'Can you even believe he asked you to dinner?' Zack said. 'The nerve!'

'Stop it, Zack. He was just being polite.' Lydia settled into the leather seat. 'Good scouting, by the way. I like the idea of finding obscure places for photo shoots.'

'Yeah, those obscure places give the proprietors some privacy as well.'

Lydia looked at him. 'What does that mean?'

'Oh, come on. You know that Nicholas fellow was shagging his yummy little piece when we walked in.'

Lydia frowned at Zack's crudeness, discovering that she didn't like the idea of him knowing what Nicholas had been doing. It was one thing for her to speculate, but quite another for Zack to do so.

'Zack, he was standing on a ladder.'

Zack shrugged and eased the powerful car out into the

15

traffic. 'Maybe she was giving him a hand job or a blow job or something. You saw them, Lydia. They both looked pretty ravished, and two of her buttons were undone.'

'You're overreacting. You have a one-track mind.'

'Do I?' He grinned at her devilishly.

'Yes.' Irritated, Lydia crossed her arms and stared out of the side window. An image of Nicholas Hawthorne and Olive indulging in a hot quickie while standing up against the bookshelves appeared in her mind. It was not an image she liked.

'I don't know what she would see in him, frankly,' Zack continued. 'I mean, he looks like he just crawled out of a hole.'

'That's enough, Zack.'

Zack looked at her. 'Are you coming back to the office with me, or do you want me to drop you off at home?'

Lydia glanced at her watch. Four in the afternoon was usually far too early for her to go home, but she didn't relish the idea of returning to the office. For some reason, she was restless. 'Leave me at home.'

Zack manoeuvred the car through the streets to Lydia's stately home in the posh Pacific Heights section of the city. He pulled up in front of the Italian-style mansion and stopped the car.

'Want me to come in with you?' he asked suggestively.

'No.' Lydia retrieved her briefcase from the backseat. 'Tell everyone at the office I don't want to be disturbed unless there's an emergency.'

'OK.' Zack leaned over to kiss her cheek, but Lydia pulled away so that his lips brushed her hair.

'We'll talk tomorrow about the shoot,' she said. 'Thanks for driving.'

She hurried away from the car and went into her house, feeling an immediate rush of relief at being back in her sanctuary. She had made a point of decorating the home with warm antiques and paintings to give it an elegant but welcoming atmosphere. Her decor, enhanced by the bay views at each of the four levels, also made the house a perfect place for entertaining.

The housekeeper had gone for the day, leaving the faint scent of furniture polish in the air. Lydia dropped her briefcase on the foyer table and kicked off her shoes as she headed up the plush, carpeted staircase to her bedroom.

After checking her answering machine, which contained three messages from Molly in dire need of advice for her debutante ball and one from her friend Cassie asking her to dinner this weekend, Lydia stripped off her suit and went into the bathroom. She turned on the shower and glanced at herself in the full-length mirror as she waited for the water to warm. She was proud of her body, liking the way the lean lines of her curved hips complemented her full breasts and large nipples, and the way her shaven mons left nothing to the imagination.

Stepping into the shower, Lydia tried to let the tension of the past few weeks wash away. She pumped a generous amount of bath gel into her palm and stroked it over her abdomen and breasts, swirling the tips of her fingers around her hard nipples. Another image of Nicholas Hawthorne and Olive came into her mind, only this time it wasn't disturbing, but arousing.

Warmth flooded into the area between her thighs as she imagined what Olive's pretty plumpness would look like naked. She could picture it in her mind's eye, the two of them, Olive and Nicholas. Olive's leg would be wrapped around Nicholas's thigh as he pushed her up against one of those rickety, old bookshelves, pumping his penis into her as he bit at her voluptuous breasts. Olive's nipples would be hard and rosy, rubbing against Nicholas's hairy chest as her body shook with each subsequent jolt.

Lydia bit down on her lower lip, smoothing the bath gel over her belly and dipping her fingers between her legs. Her labia were moist with arousal, her clitoris tingling at the light brush of her fingertips. She wanted to bury her fingers deep inside her body, but she forced herself to take her fingers away. With slow, deliberate caresses, she stroked the gel over her firm, rounded buttocks, sliding her fingers into the crevice between her cheeks. Her body began to feel hot and languid, her mind filled with images of Nicholas and Olive thrusting and pumping against a backdrop of literary genius and leather bookcovers.

What would they sound like, she wondered, thinking of Olive's clear, pure voice when she had spoken to them. Her voice would deepen with passion, certainly, becoming a low purr in Nicholas's ear. And what would he say to her while he was sliding his hands under her luscious thighs, opening her fully for his penetration?

Yes, you're hungry for it, my Olive, hungry for the feeling of my long cock inside that sweet little pussy of yours. Come on, I want to hear you moan and beg. Tell me how much you want it, tell me . . .

Lydia shivered, her blood throbbing at the thought of Nicholas Hawthorne murmuring such lewd phrases. Her skin was hot as she stroked gel over the curved length of her legs, then rotated luxuriously underneath the shower spray to rinse her naked body. She reached out and turned off the shower, then grabbed a towel from the heated rack. She wrapped the towel around herself and went into her bedroom, her sex aching with the need for release. She took her vibrator out of a drawer in her night table and switched it on, then stretched out on her bed and let the towel fall open.

Ah, God, she couldn't remember the last time she had been so aroused by a fantasy. Letting her eyelids drift closed, she pictured them again, the slick slide of Nicholas's hard penis stroking in and out of Olive's spread channel. His tight balls slapped against the young woman, evoking the wet, delicious sounds of sex. Olive's breasts shook and bounced with the force of his thrusts, her high cries of pleasure spurring him to thrust harder, faster, deeper.

Lydia parted her lips and moaned, stroking the phallus

over her breasts and nipples, over her belly to the painful centre of her need. Her damp skin prickled with cold, but the air only served to heighten her senses and her arousal. She slipped the dildo between her legs, her body jerking with pleasure at the feeling of the vibrations against her velvety folds as she slowly began to push it into herself. Longing pulsed in her blood, colouring her skin with the reddish flush of passion, evaporating the lingering droplets of water on her body.

'Oh!' She arched her back, thrusting the vibrator in further, revelling in the sensations against her inner walls, sensations that trailed along every nerve ending. Her loins constricted with the advent of pleasure.

Nicholas was now lifting Olive's legs over his arms, spreading her so far apart that Lydia had a clear view of the thick root of his penis, well oiled by Olive's abundant juices, slipping back and forth. He stroked his fingers over Olive's swollen clitoris, eliciting a cry of ecstasy from the woman as she clung to his shoulders and received the full extent of his frenzied plunges.

Lydia grasped the base of the phallus, stroking it in and out of her body with increasingly rapid movements. Her hips pumped wildly to match her strokes, her mind filled with the sounds and sights of Olive and Nicholas fucking in the bookshop. He thrust into her again and again and again, making her sob with rapture and orgasm after orgasm until a burst of intense colours exploded in Lydia's body.

She cried out, shoving the vibrator up into her body and clenching her muscles around it as she succumbed to the vast, intense wave of her climax. And then suddenly, it was no longer Nicholas and Olive in her fantasy, but Nicholas and Lydia, and she was riding out her pleasure on his penis with his broad hands gripping her thighs and his hot breath on her breasts.

* * *

'Lydia, I have some of that wine you like.' Cassie stood on tiptoe to reach into her cupboard. She was dressed in jeans and an oversized shirt that made her look even more petite. 'Cabernet from the Hundred Acres vineyard in Napa.'

'Love, you know you don't have to buy wine for me,' Lydia said in dismay, aware of how expensive the wine was. She knew Cassie didn't make much money as an English literature professor, and she didn't like the thought of Cassie wasting her money just to please her.

'I know I don't.' Cassie began peeling off the cap of the bottle and flashed Lydia a quick smile across the threshold that separated the kitchen from the sitting room. 'But I like to.'

Lydia returned her smile, forcing herself not to say anything and hurt Cassie's feelings. Cassie had refused to let her bring anything to dinner, and the delicious scents of pesto and tortellini drifted from the kitchen.

'Did you find out about that research grant?' Lydia asked.

'Not yet.' Cassie poured wine into two glasses and came into the sitting room. 'I should hear by the end of the semester. If I get it, I'll have enough money to travel to London for research. Hopefully for an entire year.'

She handed Lydia one of the glasses and perched on the edge of an overstuffed chair. Lydia thought that Cassie looked extremely comfortable in her surroundings. Her friend lived on the second floor of a two-storey, Victorian building on the fringe of Russian Hill, a lovely, bright place with bay windows and hardwood floors. Molly, being the premiere shopper, had helped her decorate it with good-quality, inexpensive furniture and prints. Both Lydia and Molly would have loved to have helped Cassie out more financially, but they knew that Cassie's pride would never allow it. Even now, Lydia had to bite her tongue to prevent herself from suggesting that she fund Cassie's research trip to London.

'What's happening with that men's issue of the magazine?' Cassie asked.

'I have most of the staff writing stories already,' Lydia replied. 'That really is a wonderful idea, Cassie. Zack is even looking forward to photographing some male models.'

Cassie grinned. 'Maybe he's not quite as straight as you thought.'

Lydia chuckled. Cassie was probably right, but as long as Zack could still satisfy her, then she didn't particularly care about his extracurricular activities.

'Well, he gives me fantastic orgasms, so that's all I'm concerned about.'

Cassie was quiet for a moment. 'Lydia?'

'Hmm?'

'You're sure you're not just using Zack to, you know, fill a void?'

Lydia gave her a wicked smile. 'Of course I am, darling. He fills it quite nicely.'

A becoming flush coloured Cassie's cheeks. 'No, that's not what I meant. I mean, don't you think you're using these men when you're really looking for a soulmate?'

Lydia groaned. 'Good Lord, Cassie, the last thing I need is a soulmate. I'm a busy woman with very little time for a man. A satisfying fuck works for me just fine.'

'Maybe you're just trying to convince yourself of that,' Cassie said quietly.

'Cassie, I'm not like you,' Lydia snapped. 'I don't harbour dreams of romance and living out my old age with some decrepit man by my side.'

'All right, I'm sorry,' Cassie said. 'It's none of my business.'

Lydia sighed. She hated arguing with Cassie. 'I didn't mean to snap at you. I just don't like having my sex life put under scrutiny.'

Cassie reached out to refill their wine glasses. 'What about that fashion shoot you mentioned on the phone?'

'You mean the one at the antique bookshop?' Lydia took another sip of wine, relieved at having the subject changed. 'I went there with Zack on Thursday to meet with the owner. He turned out to be an interesting fellow.'

'Interesting how?'

'Well, he's extremely unsophisticated and appears quite homely at first,' Lydia said. 'But he's very intelligent. I was eavesdropping on him when he was talking to customers, and his knowledge of literature is vast.'

Cassie looked up. 'Really?'

'You and he could probably find a million things to talk about,' Lydia replied, realising that she was rather disconcerted by the thought.

'What does he look like?'

'Like a dishevelled, absent-minded librarian who sleeps in his clothes and fixes his glasses with masking tape.'

Cassie laughed. 'Not really.'

'Yes, really.'

'So, did he agree to let you use his store?' Cassie asked.

'Yes. We're doing the shoot on Monday.'

'Can I come? I'd like to meet him.'

'You're sure you'd want to? It's terribly boring to sit around and watch a fashion shoot.'

'I'd love to. I don't have classes on Monday. And I'm always on the lookout for a good bookshop. I won't get in the way.'

'No, I know you won't.' Lydia mentally chastised herself for being so reluctant. Heaven knew that she would never be interested in someone like Nicholas Hawthorne, but Cassie might find him fascinating. 'Of course you can come. I'll come pick you up.'

'Great.' Cassie smiled and padded back to the kitchen to check on the tortellini.

Lydia left around one in the morning, promising to pick Cassie up at eight on Monday. She drove back home, thinking about Nicholas and Cassie together. They might work quite well as a couple. They both adored literature, and Cassie was never picky about the way a man looked. Lydia stopped at a red light and bit thoughtfully on her thumbnail. Yes, they might work quite nicely, Nicholas and Cassie.

Continuum

Portia Da Costa

Spanking. The very word sounds naughty. And this is what Joanna gets plenty of when she is invited to spend some time at the house of Louise and Major Walker. This is the first step in a continuum of strange experiences. Drawn into a chain of sexual coincidences, like Alice in a decadent Wonderland, a world of adult fun is soon laid before her. Someone has arranged for her introduction to perversity, and Joanna suspects it's someone from her workplace. Is it Kevin Steel, her flirtatious colleague, or could it be the super-suave Halloran himself – MD of her company?

Either way, Joanna is about to get a good seeing-to in this extract from *Continuum*. As you'll see, the Major wastes no time in initiating her into his special world of punishment games.

Portia Da Costa is a mistress of adult fiction with a pervy twist. The author of seven Black Lace books: *Gemini Heat*, *The Tutor*, *The Devil Inside*, *Gothic Blue*, *The Stranger*, and *Shadowplay*, she is a prolific and enthusiastic erotica afficionado.

Continuum

Joanna didn't drink a great deal that afternoon. The magazines and books Louise Walker brought out, in abundance, were so absorbing that the wine remained forgotten.

The pictures were a revelation. It seemed that if the journals of perversion and punishment were to be believed, there were women like Louise – that was, those who were aroused by being punished – in every walk of life, and on every social stratum. All over the country – all over the world, even – women were baring their bottoms and allowing them to be thrashed.

And not just women. There were men who enjoyed being chastised too. Joanna entertained a fleeting fantasy of making Halloran bend over his own desk while she lashed him. Wouldn't that just teach him to play games with her life! If, that was, he was the one who had sent her to the Walkers.

Louise had claimed she had chores to do inside, and had left Joanna alone with her reading.

It must be the vulnerability, the submission, thought Joanna, staring hard at a flamboyantly posed photograph of a young woman bending over a kitchen table, her plump bottom offered naked to the lash.

The picture was crude in some ways, nowhere near as well composed as those in the magazine she had studied on the train yesterday, but there was something in the angle of the body, and in the fact that only the victim's buttocks were uncovered, that made Joanna tingle in the pit of her belly. Involuntarily, she put herself into the place of the model. She could almost imagine the wooden table against her belly, and the coolness of the air as it flowed across her bare skin.

A man would come into the kitchen. Not the undistinguished, slightly overweight nonentity in the picture, but someone dark, mysterious, and commanding. Trying to conjure more from the image, she expected to see Halloran, but the face of her unknown master wouldn't form. He was simply Everyman; tall, handsome and strong. He carried a strip of leather, coiled around his fingers, but then allowed it to hang loose as he took his place behind her.

Looking to the photograph for prompts, Joanna tried to envisage her own bare rump, instead of that of the sagging, sluttish young woman in the picture. Her own backside would be finer, its shape pert and well-toned; its nakedness more alluring. She saw the pallor of her skin there; the pout of her sex, where it nestled in plain sight, at the junction of her thighs.

Would she be as aroused, when the time came, as she was now? Lying on the sun lounger, reading and wondering, she suddenly wished again that she had allowed the masseuse to follow through on that final offer. Frustration then had primed her for an even greater degree of yearning now. Inside her cotton panties, her vulva was a river, its engorged banks overflowing with desire.

Did she dare touch herself? The state of her body seemed to command it, just as surely as the master – in the magazine – ruled his slave. Her hostess was busy inside, preparing something delicious and elaborate for dinner no doubt, and there was nobody else around. It would be simplicity itself just to ease up her skirt, slip her hand into her pants and rub herself.

Joanna turned the page, saw a girl kneeling on a wooden form in what looked like a mocked-up schoolroom, and her decision was made.

The picture had captured the young woman just after a blow had fallen, and her face, turned to the side, was contorted in pain. But it wasn't this that was so exciting. It was the fact that even though a set of clear weals was visible on the girl's rear cheeks, she was still curving her back and lifting her bottom towards the cane that had struck her. She was suffering, but, despite that, she wanted more.

Staring intently at the girl's attitude, and at her marks, Joanna tugged at the fullness of her soft, flower-printed skirt, and raised it to the tops of her thighs. Still cataloguing the nuances of the image – the girl's tense thighs, her gleaming vulva – Joanna slid first one finger into the leg-opening of her panties, then two, working them quickly through her sticky pubic hair.

'Yes!' she whispered, finding her clitoris. It was a swollen, taut knot beneath her fingertips, and her whole sex flexed as she began her favourite rhythm. Closing her eyes, and still rubbing, she saw herself on the wooden classroom form, her body naked, her bottom raised, all her muscles tensed in readiness. She had no idea quite what the pain would feel like, but just to hold the position in preparation for it was enough. Beneath her fingers, her clitoris leaped and she orgasmed strongly.

The spasms were fierce, and as she lay gasping – and enjoying the way the ripples seemed to tumble in on themselves, like a hot syrupy wave – she realised with some shock that a familiar man-shaped shadow had fallen over her.

'I see you're enjoying our magazines,' observed Major

Walker calmly, dropping his lanky frame on to the adjacent lounger. His eyes, thankfully, were hidden behind a pair of opaque sunglasses, which made the fact of what he had clearly just seen a little less mortifying.

But only a little. Joanna could say nothing – nothing at all – but, to her horror, she did emit a moan, and her fingers still moved wilfully inside her panties.

The moment seemed frozen, etched indelibly in time, completely unreal yet palpably happening. Her sex was still pulsing; she still felt exquisite pleasure. When it began to ebb, she turned away, her face doubly crimson with both shame and her climax. Reluctantly, she withdrew her hand from beneath her skirt.

After another unnatural pause, she felt her companion reach forward and take her wrist. Although she still couldn't look at him, she felt him lift her fingers towards his face, then felt the waft of his breath against their tips. He breathed in deeply, then laughed. Joanna sobbed, still speechless with guilt and embarrassment.

'I suppose this would make a perfect beginning,' observed the Major, his voice urbane, knowing. 'I could accuse you of being a dirty little girl and suggest that I punish you accordingly.' He paused, making Joanna quake as he brushed his lips against her musky fingertips. 'Or would that seem too contrived to you?' he asked.

'I-I don't know,' said Joanna, finding her voice at last, and hearing tones that were made husky by sex.

'I've used flimsier excuses,' replied Major Walker wryly, his fingers smoothing hers to relax them. 'And had them taken deadly seriously.'

'By Louise?'

'And other women,' he said, releasing her hand, 'Women who share – shall we call it – our "interest".'

'Did you know them beforehand?' Even though she still couldn't look at him, Joanna felt curious. Her intense need to know was still with her.

'Sometimes . . . Though not always,' he said slowly, as

if reminiscing. 'Sometimes, I've found myself spanking a woman I've never met before. Either she's offered herself to me at a party, or a smaller gathering, or she's been sent.' Significantly, he fell silent, and seemed to be listening to the soft swish of the lawn sprinkler nearby, and the chatter of the birds in the drooping alders at the bottom of the garden.

'You mean like me?'

He said nothing, but she sensed the question didn't perturb him.

'Do you know who's behind this? Who it is that's set me up?' she persisted.

'Louise is supposed to have dealt with that side of things,' he said, his voice giving the impression that he was trying to sound impatient, and perhaps a little testy, but that somehow that, too, was another contrivance. Maybe he really was impatient? Impatient to get her pants down and start spanking her?

'Why keep asking questions, Joanna?' he said suddenly, 'Don't you like mysteries? Does everything have to be explained? Accounted for?'

'It's my job,' she said, feeling a surge of defiance, 'to analyse. To account for things. To know the whys and wherefores. The causes and effects. I can't help doing it; it's what makes me what I am.'

'Well, if it's understanding you're after – ' He paused, slid off his sunglasses and looked at her very directly. His eyes were filled with the same fire-like intensity that had pervaded Louise's expression earlier. ' – I can help you. You know that, don't you?'

'Yes,' she said, her heart full of butterflies, her head full of fear and trepidation.

'But "yes" in what sense?' he asked, his voice so soft she had difficulty hearing him.

'In every sense,' she said, feeling a safety net slip away from underneath her.

31

'Come on then,' he said crisply, rising to his feet and holding out his hand to her.

Joanna took it and let herself be helped up and led into the house.

'We won't be long, my dear,' said the Major to his wife as they passed the kitchen door. Joanna looked into the light, airy room, and saw Louise, in an apron and with floury hands. The other woman smiled complicitly, then ran her tongue slowly over her lower lip as if expressing a hunger.

'Don't worry,' she called out to Joanna. 'He knows what he's doing.'

Which is more than can be said for me, thought Joanna, as she realised they were going upstairs to her bedroom.

'Has anyone ever seen to you before?' Major Walker asked as the door closed, and they were alone in Joanna's room.

She was puzzled for a moment, then understood. 'Seeing to' didn't mean sex in this context, but was yet another term for punishment. It had a vaguely benign sound to it, invoking a sense that a spanking might be thought of as a therapy of some kind. Something beneficial that might be performed on someone you cared for.

She shook her head.

'Wonderful!' The Major's voice was full of warmth and genuine happiness, 'There's nothing nicer than an initiate. A tender, untouched bottom.' He crossed to the windows, and drew the curtains slightly. 'There, that's better. Subdued light might make things a little easier for you.'

It was like the first time you found yourself in a bedroom with a new lover, thought Joanna and, on reflection, she supposed that was exactly what it was. Eroticism, but expressed in a different way. For an instant she thought of Kevin, remembering what had happened the first time she had been with him. That certainly hadn't been an average occurrence, either. What would it have been like, she

wondered, if he had wanted to smack her bottom instead
of to lick her sex, then fuck her?

'Are you quite here?' queried Major Walker, shaking her
from her thoughts. He had removed his jacket and folded
it neatly over the edge of the bed and, as she regarded
him warily, he sat down on the edge of the mattress – his
body sternly masculine against the softness of the Victorian chintz.

'I'm sorry,' said Joanna, aware that, subconsciously, she
was already halfway into her rôle.

'What were you daydreaming about?'

'About a man I've been seeing,' she admitted.

'A man you've been having sex with?'

'Yes.'

'What were you doing? Imagining that he was the one
who was going to spank you?'

'No! Yes! Sort of.'

'Well, you'd better come over here, then,' the Major said
evenly, 'I'll soon focus your attention for you.' When she
reached him, he took both her hands and made her stand
before him, like a recalcitrant child before its guardian.
'Look into my face first, Joanna,' he instructed her. 'Make
sure you know who it is who is going to punish you.' He
paused; looked thoughtful. 'I'm sure this man will get his
turn soon enough, as will others, I suspect. Many others.'

What others? I'm only going to try this the once, she
wanted to say, but couldn't, knowing that it might not be
true. She felt his hands around hers like a pair of steel
bracelets, felt his eyes boring deep into her soul.

'Now, my dear, dear Joanna,' he said, his voice strong
yet somehow also coaxing. 'Let's have you across my
knee.'

He wasn't rough, he wasn't forceful, and he didn't even
seem to push or pull her at all, but, almost before the
words were out of his mouth, Joanna was face down
across Major Walker's lap. In the first few seconds she felt

unsafe, with her weight precariously distributed, but then, with a clever shift of his thighs, he steadied her.

He patted her back in a gesture of reassurance. 'There, now; let's see what we've got, shall we?' His voice was warm, almost avuncular, and it regressed Joanna to the days of her childhood. Or at least to a version of her childhood. There had been no spankings in her home, and none necessary. The only discipline had been that which she had imposed upon herself, a regimen purely figurative, not physical.

Beginning to shake, she felt her thin skirt being lifted away from her legs and her buttocks, then folded neatly at her waist, out of the way.

'Lovely,' murmured the Major, touching her once more, his fingers drifting meditatively across her bottom cheeks. He seemed to be testing the firmness and resilience of the flesh he was about to belabour, assessing its sensitivity and its likely tolerance of suffering. She caught her breath when his fingers hooked the elastic of her knickers and began to tug it over her buttocks to uncover her. 'Lovely,' he whispered again, the task completed.

Joanna stared fixedly at the carpet just inches from her nose, concentrating on its elaborate Gothic lily design as if it were a mandala containing the secret of all existence. It was either that or laugh – or perhaps cry – at the predicament she found herself embroiled in.

'Ludicrous' was the best word to sum up the situation. She was face down over the knees of a man she hardly knew, waiting to have her bottom smacked. It was like a scene from an inferior 60s farce, and the sooner they started, the sooner the whole silly business would be over.

'Are you going to get on with it, then?' she enquired tartly, twisting around to glare up at her would-be chastiser.

His eyes twinkled in the subdued light, and his puckish smile gave his face a younger look. 'Certainly,' he said, and then commenced.

The first slaps were gentle, little more than pats, and strangely sensual. For a moment, Joanna wanted to laugh, thinking how foolish she had been to be frightened, when the sensations were more pleasant than painful. The acute arousal she suddenly felt was disturbing, though, and involuntarily, she began to work her hips and sigh.

'Are you enjoying yourself?' enquired the Major, catching her with a stroke that was real this time, and much harder.

'Yes!' she gasped. The pain had taken her by surprise.

'I see.' Almost contemplatively, he caught her with another heavy spank. 'How about now?' He hit her again, twice in quick succession this time, and with increasing force.

'Yes!' she cried defiantly, her bottom-cheeks stinging.

The blows continued, in a stately, even tempo, getting sharper and sharper each time they fell. He was hurting her now, making her bottom jounce and smart as he covered its whole surface in a methodical circular pattern.

'Are you still enjoying yourself?' he asked again after a couple of minutes, continuing to smack her with relish and vigour.

Was she? She couldn't tell any more. Her buttocks were glowing, throbbing; pounding with the hot blood that raced through her beaten tissues. It *did* hurt, more than she would have thought possible, yet she still couldn't give a simple answer.

'No!' she yelped.

A resounding, square-on spank hit her right on the join of her left buttock and her thigh.

'Yes!' she cried wildly as its impact resounded through her, then was lost in the shock of the next blow. He had caught her on her right side with a perfectly matched stroke, exhibiting an artistry she admired despite the pain.

'I don't know,' she finished, choking in horror at her own pathetic tears.

Why am I crying? she thought, while the spanking went

on evenly and inexorably. All through her life, she had been brave, tough almost; not one to fall apart in times of stress. Least of all when it was inflicted by a man.

Yet she couldn't help herself. The shame and ignominy of her position, the pulsating inflammation in her buttocks. These were upsetting her, but they didn't explain her sobbing. The weeping, she realised, came from an anger within her. She was furious with her own weakness, and confused by it. She was cross because the pain had turned her on.

But I'm not a submissive! I'm no man's slave, no weak and wimpish bimbo who gets off on being dominated and exploited. So why is my sex all wet and running again? Why am I aching more between my legs than I am in my buttocks? Why do I want this man so much, this stranger who is old enough to be my father?

As if aware of her every thought, Major Walker suddenly paused in his unrelenting rhythm. 'Are you all right, my dear?' he enquired, his hand resting caressingly upon her, its heat matching the heat it had created.

His hand must hurt too! The sudden thought amused her, shook her out of her self-pity and confusion.

'Yes, I-I'm okay,' she said, keeping quite still lest her movements reveal her passion. She really did want Major Walker, she realised, but there was also Mrs Walker to consider. It was a moot point as to whether allowing a man to fondle her bottom and spank her could be classed as seducing him, but allowing him to penetrate her was fairly unequivocal. She would feel truly guilty if she bedded Louise's husband.

'How do you feel?' the Major persisted, leaning closely over her. She could feel the brush of his well-pressed shirt against her soreness. 'Tell me honestly. No white lies.' His lips were almost touching her ear, and his hand, which was still against her buttocks, flexed and gripped.

A fresh jolt of sensation rippled through her; a new heat from his clasping of her bottom. Sinking into her vulva, his fingers made her gasp, and ripple there, too. She felt her labia engorge and her clitoris jump and stiffen.

'Joanna,' the low voice prompted as the fingers plagued her.

'It hurts!' she keened, her breath catching as his hold tightened and his thumb-tip brushed her anus. Trying to shift her hips and get away, she felt herself being poked in the abdomen by the bulge of his erection, then heard a ragged gasp as she moved herself against it.

The Major did not lose his composure, however, and his voice, when he spoke again, was quiet and calm.

'That isn't all though, is it?' he said silkily, his thumb relocating against her tender rear portal. When she didn't answer he pushed insistently against it.

'When you allow a man – a Master – to spank you, Joanna, you must yield all to him. Surely you realise that?' he went on reasonably. 'Half measures could be construed as fickleness. Wantonness. Entrapment.'

'But – '

'But what?' The pressing thumb seemed a mile wide now, and twice as determined. He was working it against the tight muscle ring, rocking it insistently.

'I only agreed to a spanking,' she hissed, her jaw clamping tightly as the thumb went right inside her and his fingers spread out across her bottom cheek, curving inwards to create four foci of heightened pain.

'I said I'd help you, Joanna. That I'd see to you,' he purred. 'I don't recall either of us setting any limits.'

There had been limits, of course, but neither she, nor Major Walker had set them, Joanna realised. The boundaries of what could and could not be done to her had been decreed by an outside agency, the same unnamed controller who had sent her to the Walkers in the first place.

Was it Halloran? Or was it Davidson? It could be either, or both, or neither one of them. There could well be some other figure who stood beyond them, wielding his – or her

– power from the shadows. Someone she hadn't yet encountered. Someone whose dictates had made the Major contain himself.

After her spanking, Major Walker had urged her back on to her feet again, with his intruding thumb still lodged inside her body. She had been deeply ashamed at how pleasurable that had felt, and had turned away from him to hide her scarlet face.

'You're very aroused now, aren't you, Joanna?'

The question had been redundant. She had revealed herself completely throughout the spanking, and during its interstices. Her visible wetness, and her sensuous moans had been too conspicuous to mistake. Her skirt had dropped back down around the site of the insult now, but her heaving chest and her erect nipples still betrayed her.

So why then, when her arousal was so evident to both of them, did she find it so impossible to admit to it?

'Joanna,' he had prompted softly, tightening his grip upon her body. His thumb moved inside her, making her groan aloud with desire, while his nails raked the redness of her bottom.

'Yes! All right! I *am* aroused!' she proclaimed defiantly. 'Can't you tell?'

'So what is it that's made you aroused?' he enquired, ignoring her bravado. His free hand settled just above the tangled bunch of her panties where they rested at her knees, then slid up and around to touch the soft hair at the juncture of her thighs. 'The spanking? Or what I'm doing now?' He wiggled his thumb and at the same time sought her clitoris, working his fingers through her sticky pubic bush.

'I don't know – both!' she gasped, as his fingertips found their target. When he started rubbing her, she swayed and almost fell.

The strokes that passed across her clitoris were light and shallow, and diabolically teasing; yet they seemed to rebound off the obstruction in her bottom. The presence of

Major Walker's thumb managed to both agitate and pacify her at the same time, setting a torch to something that was already dangerously sweet. Without thinking, she bent her knees to improve his access.

'Oh, yes ... Yes ... Yes ...' she chanted, her excitement growing, but, as her orgasm loomed, he withdrew his hand from her quim.

This retreat seemed to hurt more than the soreness of her buttocks did. 'What's wrong?' she demanded, her voice a strangled squeak. 'Why have you stopped? Oh God, I need to come ... Why have you stopped?'

'You must ask for what you want, Joanna,' the Major said quietly, his thumb rocking. 'Say "please"; it's merely a matter of simple good manners.'

Suddenly, Joanna's mettle was stung. He was enjoying himself, the bastard. He had broken their unspoken ground rules, and was subjecting her to a gross indignity. And, on top of that, he expected her to plead with him!

'Go to hell!' she said, trying to shake herself free and only making matters worse. His rigid thumb jiggled in its lewd, dark niche, making her almost choke with reluctant pleasure. At the same time, he dug his fingers into her bottom cheek.

'Temper, temper,' he chided, using his crude grip to turn her sideways and pull her back against him. His lively, bulging hard-on was a brand of fire against her and, hissing with fury, Joanna tried to hit out and force him to release her.

'Will you stop that?' he said suddenly, his voice calm yet menacing. For a moment, she seemed to see him clad in khaki, his fine eyes narrowed beneath his dapper officer's cap, his aura of command complete and unrelenting. Her body went limp, and she dropped her hands to her sides.

'That's a good girl,' he said, still holding her but no longer so fiercely. 'Now I want you to reach around and unfasten my trousers, if you will? I'm feeling a little uncomfortable, although I expect you've already noticed that?'

Not as uncomfortable as I am, thought Joanna, as she swivelled round – still speared – and obeyed him. It was impossible to look her captor in the eye, so she concentrated on the area of operations, watching her own hands as they negotiated his clothing. She fumbled a little – never having had to undress a man under such duress – but soon she was easing his erection from the fly of his white briefs.

And a handsome erection it was, too. Major Walker sported a stand more vigorous than many of the younger men she had had sex with. His shaft jutted proudly from the opening of his flannels, its rosy tip swollen and shiny with clear juice. She was just about to fondle it, when he caught her hand in his.

'No no, that's not what I want this time, young lady,' he said genially, directing her hand downwards. 'Pull your skirt up for me again, will you?'

Again, one half of her wondering why she was suddenly so compliant, she obeyed him, lifting her thin cotton skirt to her waist.

'There, that's it. Now hold it up with one hand – ' He paused, then slung his free hand around her, pulling her close to press his penis against her thigh ' – and use the other between your legs, the way I did.' Already breathing heavily, he leaned his head against her arm.

What an odd tableau this must be, thought Joanna dreamily, as she began to slick her clitoris. A middle aged man and a younger woman, half entwined, yet not fucking; each rubbing themselves to pleasure in different ways. There was something almost tender in the way Major Walker held her, his silvered head resting against her body; a feeling quite at odds with other aspects of their pose. His thumb still plugged her, its mass rude and thrilling in her rectum, and his prick jerked and plunged against her thigh. With each thrust it rubbed against her pulled-down panties. In wordless submission, she leant inwards to increase the friction.

Between her own legs, the fires were burgeoning too. It was difficult to masturbate the way she usually liked to, but the awkwardness and constriction of her position seemed to enhance the sensations. Her quim aflood, she swirled her clitoris in tiny ragged circles, then cried out when a sudden climax claimed her.

The pleasure was brief and sharp, spiked by her throbbing bottom and the living bung inside her and, as it began to fade, she felt the Major coming too. His penis jumped against her body like a captive serpent, and after a second or two, warm semen kissed her thigh. As it trickled over her skin and on to her panties, he sighed and hugged her to him, slipping his thumb out of her bottom to hold her better.

Sitting up now, on the high old bed, Joanna looked down it towards the spot where her disciplinarian had sat earlier, and where she had stood, like a helpless plaything, between his thighs. When pleasure had run its course for both of them, Major Walker had given her a chaste, almost paternal kiss, then – whilst refastening his trousers – he had suggested she take a rest before dinner. Joanna wondered if he knew just how much she needed one.

What had happened here in this room could not be glossed over. All parties in the house were aware of her spanking, even the one who hadn't participated. How on earth could she face the Walkers over dinner after this? Slipping down on to her feet, Joanna hoped – no, more than hoped – that Louise was accustomed to such arrangements. Things could be awkward if this was some sort of lapse on the Major's part.

Joanna unbuttoned her skirt and let it slip to the floor to join her panties. She moved to the elegant cheval glass in the corner of the room, and studied her reflection. She was completely naked below the waist and, pivoting like a dancer, she presented her bottom for inspection.

41

A veil of pink lingered where the Major had smacked her but, to her surprise, it was already fading.

An expert, eh? she mused, reaching around and running her hands sensuously over her slightly glowing buttocks. There was still a transient, almost ghostly tingle in the flesh there – a faint warmth that was erotic when she fingered it. On an impulse, she raised her hand and brought it down in a fierce slap across the already punished area, then yelped like a scalded puppy when hot pain flared once again.

Why do I like this? she wondered, admiring the increase in radiance. The heat, and the simple fact that she had smacked herself had made her feel aroused once more and, when she parted her legs and touched her vulva, she found it wet.

It doesn't make sense, she thought, still entranced by her own lewd reflection: her long legs, her sticky thighs, her bare and pink-tinged bottom.

'It doesn't make sense,' she repeated aloud, beginning to stroke herself slowly, almost absently, making a slicking noise with her own flooding wetness. With her left hand, she landed another slap against her buttocks, hitting the other cheek this time, and caught her breath as her arousal ramped up sharply.

'Oh God,' she moaned, slapping again, and speeding up her rubbing. Her movements were clumsy and uncoordinated now, but still effective. Tension was building in her sex, and she was getting wetter and wetter – and it was the renewed heat in her bottom that was doing it. Sliding, half falling, to the floor, she felt the soft carpet beneath her face as she contorted. 'Oh God,' she whimpered again, and kept on smacking and rubbing in graceless hunger.

As she orgasmed, she dug her nails into her pain.

Savage Surrender

Deanna Ashford

There's something very sexy about sword and sorcery stories, full as they are of warrior queens, beautiful servants, magical kingdoms and exciting battles. In this extract from *Savage Surrender*, the feisty young Rianna is desperate to persuade her father that she should take over as Protector of Harn – their homeland. He says a woman cannot be given that privilege and instead promises her to Prince Sarin, notorious ruler of a neighbouring land.

Rianna will be a fine gift for Sarin, and hopefully discourage him from attacking Harn. His taste for decadent amusement knows no civilised bounds, however, and his desire to push young miscreants to the extremes of depravity is known and feared throughout the kingdom. Rianna's none too pleased about this, and is determined to emerge triumphant and escape her fate en route to Sarin's castle, despite the fact that her father has entrusted Rianna's care – and virginity – to the odious Chancellor Lesand – Sarin's right-hand man.

Savage Surrender will delight any reader who appreciates a distinctly adult flavour to sword and sorcery. It's essentially a story about Rianna's quest for pleasure and justice, and it's full of battles and punishments and lots of earthy sex. Deanna Ashford's new Black Lace book is *Doctor's Orders*, an altogether more contemporary setting but no less explicit.

Savage Surrender

'This journey seems endless,' Rianna grumbled as she stared out of the window of her conveyance. All she could see was mile upon mile of flat uninteresting grassland stretched out either side of the road.

They'd left the castle of Nort almost five days ago, and for the last two days they'd been traversing the southern plains of Harn, which were virtually uninhabited as the soil was unsuitable for cultivating crops.

To ensure Rianna's comfort on the long journey to Percheron, Lord Sarin had arranged for a special conveyance to be constructed. A tiny house had been built atop a flat bedded wagon, containing both travelling and sleeping quarters for his bride. The house was a little cramped but luxuriously appointed, with a bed for Rianna, a folding bed for her maid, and padded benches to sit upon while on the road.

'We have many days of travel ahead of us, my lady,' her servant Jenna said in a suspiciously sulky tone.

Veba had fallen ill just before their departure and was deemed too unwell to travel. Rianna's father, Gerek, had asked Jenna to travel in Veba's place. In the normal course of events Jenna would have been honoured to become Lady Rianna's personal maid, but she had made it clear she had no wish to leave Gerek. Angered by her pleading

45

words, Gerek had bluntly ordered Jenna to accompany Rianna, insisting that there was no one else he could trust to care for his daughter.

'Far too many, Jenna.' Rianna peered out of the window, curious to know why her conveyance had come to an unexpected halt. 'I wonder why we've stopped. It is too early for the noonday meal.'

'Doubtless we'll be moving again soon,' Jenna replied distractedly.

'I will have no more of this.' Jumping to her feet, Rianna moved to the rear of their wagon. 'I will ride for a while. It will be good to have some fresh air, as I am unused to being so confined.'

Pushing open the door, Rianna sprang on to the rough road, which was little more than a track of hard-packed earth. She soon spied the reason for their unexpected stop: behind her conveyance was a wagon piled high with baggage; some of the contents had worked loose, and servants were clustered around the wagon trying to secure the load.

'My lady, is something amiss?' A sallow-faced youth, one of the servants from Percheron assigned to wait upon her, approached and bowed respectfully.

'Have my horse saddled. I wish to ride for a while.'

'Chancellor Lesand has not issued orders allowing you to ride, Lady Rianna. It would be safer for you to remain inside your wagon,' the youth stuttered.

Rianna frowned and tapped her foot impatiently. 'Do you dare to question my orders?'

'No, my lady.' He bowed again and added ingratiatingly, 'I will have your horse saddled immediately.'

As he left to do her bidding, Rianna took a deep breath and looked around her. The day was warm, with a slight breeze moving the sweet-scented air. The grass was a lush green, spreading as far as she could see, but in the far distance she could see a range of mountains, their high peaks reaching up to the clear blue sky.

She thought of her father, as she had often these past few days. She missed him desperately. Her unhappy musings were interrupted by a familiar whinny. Glancing in the direction of the sound, she saw the servant leading Freya towards her. The mare seemed restive; she had not been ridden since the day before they had left the castle of Nort. Freya wore one of Rianna's favourite gifts from Sarin – a saddle and reins of tooled red leather, liberally decorated with gold.

'It appears we are both impatient for our freedom.' Rianna patted the mare's nose. 'A long gallop will do us both good.'

She sprang lithely into the saddle, arranging her skirts so that her legs were discreetly covered down to her lower calves, exposing only her long, beige suede boots. Rianna had decided not to wear breeches, thinking the Chancellor might disapprove of such immodest garments.

Spurring Freya forward, she guided her on to the grassy plain and urged her into a canter. The mare needed no prompting as her nostrils caught the smell of freedom. They galloped across the flat plain towards the distant mountains, warm air caressing Rianna's face. The ribbon holding her hair loosened and her long locks streamed out behind her. She laughed joyously, feeling free and exhilarated, the throbbing of Freya's hooves reverberating comfortingly in her ears.

When she had ridden some distance, she slowed her mount and glanced back at the caravan, knowing it would be unwise to stray too far from the protection of her military escort. A mounted man-at-arms, wearing the Chancellor's black and red livery, had followed her, but he was discreetly keeping his distance to ensure her privacy. Rianna was not surprised, knowing the Chancellor would never have allowed her to ride alone. There was little chance of bandits in this barren area, but there could be dangerous wild animals such as bears or wolves.

Ignoring her unwanted escort, she urged Freya into a

canter again. However, the ground became rougher, scattered with many large stones. Fearing for her palfrey's well-being, Rianna turned and rode back towards the caravan. The long line of wagons had begun to move again and Rianna decided to ride alongside them.

Over the last couple of days a number of merchants had joined the caravan, feeling safer to travel to Percheron under the protection of Chancellor Lesand's soldiers. There were now at least six new wagons within the train, but there was also an unfamiliar and very odd-looking conveyance at the rear which Rianna had not noticed before. It appeared to be a heavy metal cage bolted on to a flat bedded wagon. Mounted men-at-arms, wearing a distinctive gold and black livery, surrounded the wagon. Rianna's curiosity was aroused. She wondered if they were transporting some rare beast back to Lord Sarin's private menagerie. But judging by the thickness of the bars, the creature had no chance of escape, and there was little need for it to be so heavily guarded.

She guided Freya forward until she was close enough to see what was inside the cage. To her disappointment she saw nothing but a pile of straw. However, a most unpleasant odour wafted towards her and she wrinkled her nose in disgust.

'My lady . . .' The soldier, who had been following her, manoeuvred his mount forward to ride beside her. 'It is not safe here. It would be best for you to ride at the front with Chancellor Lesand.'

'First tell me what kind of savage beast is in that cage.'

He gave a gruff laugh. 'Savage maybe, my lady, but no beast. It is a man – a prisoner.'

'What prisoner could deserve such barbaric treatment?'

The smell was stronger now. A stomach-churning mixture of sweat, stale urine and excrement.

'He deserves nothing better,' the soldier said dismissively. 'The more he suffers the happier I will be.' There was pure hatred reflected in his tone.

'Have you no compassion?' She saw the straw move. A grubby arm became visible, the wrist heavily manacled and chained.

'Not for him,' he sneered.

Rianna wondered what terrible crime the man had committed. Her father was a hard man at times, but even he would not have imprisoned someone in such foul conditions. Angered and disgusted by the prisoner's predicament she decided to raise the subject with Chancellor Lesand. Spurring her mount forward she rode to the front of the caravan.

Chancellor Lesand, riding a beautiful honey-coloured horse with a cream mane and tail, was heading the caravan accompanied by his captain of the guard, Feroc.

'Lady Rianna, it is good to see you.' Lesand smiled warmly. 'The ride has put a welcome colour in your cheeks.'

'Indeed it has,' she agreed, slowing Freya's pace so that she could ride beside him. 'But the malodorous smell has turned my stomach.'

'Smell?' Lesand enquired, raising his finely arched eyebrows. 'To what are you referring, my lady?'

'The prisoner in the cage at the rear. No one, however wicked, should be confined in such dirty conditions.'

'It is not your concern,' he said curtly, his charming manner dissolving in a moment. His expression hardened. 'Just content yourself with the knowledge that the captive deserves no better.'

'What is his crime?'

At first Chancellor Lesand did not answer. However, after a long uncomfortable pause he replied. 'The prisoner led an unsuccessful revolt against his sovereign, Lord Sarin. Many soldiers were killed in the battles. When it was clear he had lost he fled, intending to take refuge in the eastern kingdoms and seek their aid in raising another army to fight Lord Sarin. But we captured him before he could cross the border.'

'But is it necessary for him to be chained and caged?'

'Since then he has twice attempted to escape, so total confinement is very necessary. Lord Sarin has issued orders that the prisoner be taken in chains to Percheron in order to answer for his crimes.'

'Surely the cage can be cleaned, and the prisoner allowed to wash himself. The smell, I assure you, is quite disgusting,' she said with a determined tilt to her chin.

'I cannot agree to even that,' Lesand said stonily, his mouth set in a thin line.

'Then I fear it will prove impossible for me to continue my journey. The wind has turned, and the smell enters my conveyance, making me feel most unwell.'

'I am sorry, my lady,' he muttered.

'Yes. I shall insist on stopping to rest. It may even become necessary for me to return home.' She stared at him with calm determination, wondering if he would be willing to give in to her demands.

'You appear most resolute.' He smiled tightly.

'Compassion fuels my resolve.'

'I would venture to suggest that you try to quell such conduct in future, my lady. Lord Sarin does not welcome such forward behaviour from the ladies of his court. His decisions are never questioned – and his will is absolute.' Lesand awkwardly cleared his throat. 'However, at present, I am prepared to make concessions, purely to ensure your continued comfort and well-being. I have no wish for the prisoner to fall ill and die; Lord Sarin would never forgive me.'

'So you will agree to my demands?'

He nodded gravely. 'Indeed I will.'

'I am obliged to you,' she said with a sweet smile.

By mid-afternoon the caravan had left Harn and entered the northern reaches of Percheron. Rianna was at last in the land of her betrothed. Now she felt there was no turning back. The flat, barren plains had been replaced by

gently undulating countryside, thick with brightly coloured wild flowers. Here in Percheron, even the sky seemed
a more vivid shade of blue.

They stopped close to a lake surrounded by trees. It was
late afternoon, and all the travellers were pleased to have
a few extra hours of rest and relaxation. Normally, they
did not break their journey until dusk was falling.

Chancellor Lesand had promised Rianna that the prisoner would be allowed to cleanse himself, and that the
cage would be scrubbed out with hot water and strong
vinegar to kill the terrible odours. Rianna was determined
to ensure he kept that promise, so she decided to check on
the captive's situation herself.

Leaving Jenna to her own devices, Rianna walked
through the trees to the edge of the lake. The water looked
cool and inviting, prompting Rianna to cast off her clothes
and plunge into the blue-green depths. However, she had
other matters to attend to at present. Lifting the skirts of
her green silk gown, she made her way through the trees.

Lesand had told her that the soldiers escorting the
prisoner were members of Lord Sarin's personal guard.
They were camped in a clearing a short walk from the rest
of the caravan. Rianna cautiously approached the camp
site, taking advantage of the shelter provided by the trees
and bushes. She stopped behind a leafy bush covered in
glossy green leaves and trumpet-shaped pink flowers, and
peered surreptitiously into the clearing.

The door of the prisoner's cage was wide open and the
foul-smelling straw was being raked out to be burned. But
where was the captive? She looked around. There were a
number of soldiers waist deep in the lake laughing and
splashing each other, while two soldiers stood apart from
the others, in slightly deeper water, each holding the end
of a heavy chain. A head broke the smooth surface of the
water between them. The prisoner stood up, water streaming from his body, and shook his head, causing his long
hair to flap wetly around his face.

Rianna could hardly believe her eyes. She had expected a pathetic, malnourished creature, not this magnificent male. He was taller, far taller than any man of Harn, and broad-shouldered, with the finely-honed physique of a warrior. Every inch of his golden-skinned body was covered by hard muscle. He was strikingly handsome with the features of a true nobleman; his nose was straight, flaring slightly at the nostrils, his mouth wide and full-lipped. She wasn't close enough to make out the colour of his eyes, but they were an attractive almond shape which added to the piquancy of his good looks. His long hair was at present darkened by the water, but she guessed when dry it would be a pale golden-blond.

Impatiently, the two soldiers tugged at the captive's chains which were attached to heavy manacles on his wrists. It was clear the prisoner's ablutions were at an end. He waded from the lake, following the soldiers towards the bank.

As the prisoner slowly emerged from the water, a sudden heat scorched Rianna's cheeks. His escorts wore black woollen breeches, now dripping wet, but the captive was totally naked. She had never seen an unclothed man before, and could not tear her gaze from his superb body. The rippling muscles of his chest were covered by a sprinkling of golden hair, descending like an arrow towards his flat stomach, and leading her eyes downwards to his groin. The hair grew much thicker around his male parts, placing emphasis on the loose sac of flesh fronted by a thick phallus, the skin of which was a few shades darker than that on his body.

She watched his limp manhood sway enticingly as he strode forward, and her knees began to feel weak. Forcing her gaze away from his male organs, she re-examined the rest of his body. Droplets of water lay on his chest, gleaming damply in the late afternoon sunshine. There were a number of large bruises marring his smooth flesh, and two half-healed wounds, both red and inflamed. One cut deeply across his left upper chest and shoulder, the other extended from his groin to lower thigh. If left unattended, Rianna feared they would putrefy and spread poison through his magnificent body. She decided to ask the Chancellor for his permission to tend the captive's wounds. The Chancellor would surely agree, as he wanted this man alive and fit enough to face Lord Sarin's punishment.

The soldiers escorting the captive found amusement in tugging roughly on his chains. Once, he stumbled and almost fell, but regained his balance, moving with far more grace and dignity than the soldiers, whose sodden breeches clung unflatteringly to their scrawny legs. The prisoner was led towards two trees placed about ten paces apart, and stationed between them. The soldiers attached the chains leading from his wrist manacles to the trees at about shoulder height and pulled them tight. The captive's arms were jerked apart, allowing him to move no more than a pace forwards or backwards.

Leaving the prisoner, the soldiers moved away to dry themselves and dress. Soon the sun would set. It was becoming steadily cooler as the afternoon heat diminished. A light breeze sprung up, wafting lazily through the trees to brush the captive's damp flesh. He shivered slightly, but there was no sign of discomfort or concern on his face, his expression calm and aloof.

The other soldiers moved from the water. As they dressed, two of their companions, who'd not bothered to bathe, approached the captive. They began taunting him, but he ignored their shouts and raucous laughter, staring stoically ahead.

Frustrated by his lack of response, the soldiers began to poke and prod the prisoner.

One jabbed his stomach, while the other tugged at his pubic hair. At last the prisoner reacted, and snarling angrily, he leapt at them. His chains prevented him from touching the soldiers, but they still jumped fearfully back, far out of his reach. They stared at him nervously as he strained against his constricting chains. Even in his fury he was beautiful, thought Rianna. Each twist and turn emphasised the perfect lines of his muscles, the magnificence of his male physique.

An ugly, thickset man, wearing only a piece of cloth wrapped around his waist, secretly approached the prisoner from behind, and grabbed hold of his hair. The prisoner was clearly the stronger of the two but, taken by surprise, he was unable to prevent his head being jerked brutally back, thrusting his hips and sexual organs into prominence.

The other soldiers crowded forwards, joining their two comrades, cheering loudly as the thickset man ran a meaty hand over the prisoner's chest, pinching his copper-coloured nipples until they hardened and deepened in colour. The captive struggled fruitlessly, his face contorting in disgust as the meaty hand moved lower. It closed around his penis, jerking it upright. A few well-placed pumping strokes caused the organ to stiffen. The prisoner's cheeks reddened in shame, and for a moment he closed his eyes, unwilling to witness the spectators' lewd amusement.

'So much for pride, barbarian,' the thickset man sneered as he let go of the captive and stepped back a pace.

The prisoner's tense mouth softened with relief, but it was clear his humiliation was not at an end. Urged on by shouts of encouragement from the crowd, the thickset man grinned, and ducked under the taut chain stretching towards the left tree trunk. Then he moved to stand in front of the captive.

'My pride has nothing to do with this,' the prisoner replied in a voice choked with fury.

'It is said that pride goes before a fall, barbarian. You have fallen far for a noble lord, haven't you?' the soldier jeered. Chuckling menacingly, he unfastened the cloth around his waist and let it drop to the ground. His stubby penis was dark red and partially erect. He curved his hand around the base of the organ and crudely pumped it up and down until it stiffened and grew hard.

The prisoner looked at him with disdainful disgust, then pointedly turned his head away to stare calmly into the distance.

'Look at me,' the thickset man growled. 'See what is in store for you.' The prisoner did not respond, and his tormentor tensed in fury. 'By the gods, you *will* look at me.'

He reached forward and cruelly pinched the captive's penis. The prisoner didn't even wince, although it must have been painful. Rianna clenched at the silk skirt of her gown, crumpling the fine fabric in her hands as she waited to see what would next befall the helpless captive.

'Pray tell me, what is there to look at?' the handsome warrior asked caustically. 'Only a pathetic creature, clumsily attempting to pleasure himself.'

'Then I order *you* to pleasure me.' The soldier gave a leering grin. 'The men will loosen your chains. Then you will fall to your knees and take me in your mouth. Refuse and you'll be punished.'

'Why should I refuse?' The prisoner smiled contemptuously. 'Your paltry cock will be easy enough to sever with one quick snap of my teeth.'

A red flush of humiliation flooded the soldier's cheeks. 'Better still, I'll have you chained down, your buttocks spread wide. I'll plunder your arsehole until you beg for mercy.'

'Do it, Rorg!' the watching soldiers shouted excitedly.

Rianna was horrified. Surely they wouldn't stoop to such degradation, but she feared it was possible, judging by the ugly mood of the crowd. Her palms felt sweaty, her knees weak. She was appalled, but there was another much darker emotion lurking deep in the pit of her belly which urged her to stay and witness what would happen next.

'In no time at all you'll come to enjoy such sweet agony,'

55

Rorg taunted, placing his hands on his hips and pushing his pelvis forward to emphasise his stubby penis. It stuck out from his body almost at right angles, twitching obscenely as he took a swaggering step forward.

'Try it,' the prisoner growled half under his breath.

Rorg was so intent on entertaining his watching colleagues that he forgot just how close he was to the captive. He failed to see the prisoner lunge forward, straining each muscle and sinew to its fullest extent as he lifted his leg and kicked Rorg hard in the groin.

Rorg made a high-pitched squeal like a stuck pig, the sound immediately silencing the raucous shouts of the crowd. Then he crumpled to the ground, clutching vainly at his wounded sex. He lay at the prisoner's feet, moaning and twitching pathetically.

The prisoner grinned challengingly at his audience, but his satisfaction was to be short-lived. A number of soldiers surged forward, two dragging Rorg away, while the others grabbed the prisoner and rained down blows on his helpless body. Being totally outnumbered, he made no attempt to resist, perhaps resigned to his ignominious fate.

'Stop!' an authoritative voice commanded. 'That's enough. Do you want to anger your sovereign lord?' A man with a long, ugly scar down one side of his face, wearing the uniform of a sergeant, stepped forward and threw a pile of chains at the prisoner's feet. 'Confine him properly this time.'

Immediately the soldiers did as ordered, clamping the manacles around the prisoner's ankles, then attaching the chains to the base of the trees, forcing his legs wide apart like his arms. He was now entirely at their mercy. Rianna shivered as a soldier stepped forward and placed a whip, made of thin strips of plaited leather, in the sergeant's hand.

'Rorg was one of my best men.' The sergeant tapped the whip menacingly on the palm of his hand.

'If he was one of your best, then I pity you,' the captive

said defiantly. 'Any one of my soldiers was worth ten of him.'

'But you still lost the battle,' the sergeant sneered.

'There will be many more.'

'Not for you, slave.'

'I am no slave, I am Tarn of Kabra. Sarin may take my freedom, even my life, but I will never be his slave.'

'It is *Lord* Sarin to you,' the sergeant jeered. 'And do not try to deceive yourself, Tarn, you are his slave.'

'I have never bent my knee to him and I never will.'

Rianna admired the prisoner's brave defiance. Kabra, a land to the east of Percheron, had been conquered by Lord Sarin many years ago. Obviously Tarn was a nobleman of Kabra who had urged his people to rebel. Rianna began to feel even more sympathy and pity for Tarn, as members of the nobility captured in battle were usually treated with respect.

'Your foolish pride will be your downfall, slave. You must be punished for your insolence.' The sergeant tapped Tarn's phallus with the handle of the whip. 'A measure of pain, carefully applied, can stir the senses even of the most determined.'

'Do your worst, I'll welcome the agony. It will remind me that the soldiers of Percheron are cowardly scum,' Tarn said with bravado. 'Beat me senseless, kill me, I care not.'

'I'll not give you the pleasure of dying. My aim is purely to humiliate, to help you understand what it feels like to be a lowly slave. Today you will take the first step towards total and absolute submission.'

Even from this distance, Rianna thought she detected a faint quiver at the corner of Tarn's mouth. She knew that a true warrior would not welcome enslavement; far better to die a glorious death in battle.

'If I were not chained I would crush you with my bare hands,' Tarn replied defiantly.

The sergeant laughed and took a step closer to Tarn,

watching his chest rise and fall, his breathing a shade faster than normal. 'Admit how scared you really are. Tell me, what does it feel like to be so totally helpless?'

He grabbed hold of Tarn's scrotum, cupping it roughly, before slowly squeezing it until a flash of pain crossed the prisoner's features. Satisfied by Tarn's first real sign of discomfort, he curved his thick fingers around the captive's phallus and pumped it vigorously.

Tarn's expression remained calm, but his body tensed, his powerful thighs trembling slightly. Even in his stoic dignity, his inner shame was a tangible entity. However hard he tried, Tarn could not blot out the lewd shouts of encouragement from the watching soldiers. Neither could he prevent his body from automatically reacting to the unwanted touch. His dignity and self-respect were slowly and surely being dragged away from him.

He tensed, clearly trying to control his body's responses, but his resistance was useless. The rough stimulation was causing his phallus to harden, the skin on his cock rolling back to reveal the moist, purple glans. Rianna could not tear her eyes from the rigid stem crowned by the swollen bulb.

A faint shiver passed over the firm muscles of Tarn's stomach, revealing his inner humiliation, as the sergeant stepped back and grinned with cruel satisfaction.

'You'll learn, slave,' he growled, ducking between the chains to move behind the prisoner. 'You no longer have any rights over your own body. You do whatever you are ordered. That includes offering your arse if you're told to.'

Grabbing hold of Tarn's buttocks, he pulled them roughly apart. Tarn winced as the sergeant touched the tender flesh ring surrounding his small nether mouth, then rudely probed the tight opening. Despite the chill of approaching night, sweat beaded Tarn's brow. He jerked and clenched his teeth as the stubby finger penetrated his anus, grazing the tender interior.

'You're tight, but you'll soon become accustomed,' the

sergeant growled, slapping Tarn on the rump as he thrust his finger deeper into the virginal opening. 'When I move my finger thus, the sensation becomes almost pleasurable. I wager that in no time at all you'll be begging me for more.'

'Never,' Tarn hissed, despair fleetingly distorting his handsome features.

'You know Lord Sarin only too well. He'll soon find a way to destroy your wild spirit. Try to envisage what punishments he has in store for you, traitor.'

Stepping back a pace, the sergeant cracked his whip. There was a roar of approval from the crowd which made Rianna shiver apprehensively. The mood of the men was ugly, and she dare not move from her hiding place and go for help. She wasn't even certain that Chancellor Lesand would put a stop to Tarn's punishment. He had displayed no sympathy for the captive.

Tarn's cheeks were flushed with humiliation. His full mouth quivered, then hardened determinedly as he readied himself for the first cruel sting of the lash.

Rianna waited, riotously disturbing thoughts crowding her mind, unfamiliar notions that bespoke a darkness in her soul that she had never known existed. She was filled with the sudden, quite inexplicable need to remain and witness Tarn's pain and humiliation.

The sergeant drew back his arm, and the ugly sound of leather hitting flesh broke the expectant silence, evoking a low sigh of pleasure from the watching crowd. But the blow was far softer than Rianna had expected. She knew the lash must have hurt Tarn, but there was no tearing of flesh, no drawing of blood, just a raised pink weal snaking over the golden skin of his right shoulder.

He didn't respond at all to the blow, his expression remaining aloof and disdainful. But that was not what the crowd wanted. Their disappointment showed in their faces. They were all desperate to gain satisfaction from witnessing Tarn's agony.

More blows followed, the lash hitting Tarn again and again, leaving a criss-cross pattern of weals across his back. Soon Tarn began to jerk in rhythm with the blows, his body automatically pulling away from the caressing sting of the whip. Beads of sweat broke out on his forehead; the cords in his neck stood out. Only the tightness of his cheek muscles betrayed his discomfort. As the beating continued without mercy, he clenched his fists, straining against his chains until the metal shackles cut into his wrists and ankles.

The sergeant began to aim lower so that the thin strips of leather painfully stroked Tarn's buttocks and upper thighs. His skin afire, he sucked in his breath. His belly grew concave, while tremors ran down his muscular thighs.

Rianna was enraptured, along with the watching soldiers, as they witnessed Tarn battling to overcome his pain. Glorious in his distress, Tarn took a deep shuddering breath. The soft noise sent a dart of fire straight to Rianna's lower belly. Her legs grew weak, her groin full and heavy. A strange heat gathered between her thighs, and moisture seeped copiously from her sex, while her breasts seemed to swell in her tight bodice. She longed to pull Tarn's broken body into her arms and kiss away his agony.

The strands of the whip curled around Tarn's hips, the tips stroking his muscular stomach. Oddly enough his phallus was still hard, the shaft engorged. Rianna recalled what the sergeant had said about pain stirring the senses. She'd not believed it possible but, as she watched, Tarn's manhood appeared to harden even more. The exposed head grew darker, the skin stretched until it was shiny, while a tiny bead of moisture oozed from the tip.

Rianna shuddered, still overcome by a myriad of conflicting emotions, as the lash continued to deliver a caressing agony to Tarn's helpless flesh. There was a pronounced air of sensual excitement invading the clearing. It hung over the leafy glade like a dark palpable entity. The soldiers, open-mouthed and slack-eyed, were all intent on Tarn's writhing form. Some were red-faced, tense and breathing heavily. Others were openly massaging their cocks over their woollen breeches.,

An insistent pulsing heat permeated Rianna's groin. She was consumed by the need to feel that magnificent organ thrusting deep inside her. Filled with hungry desire she stared at Tarn. Almost unconsciously she clenched her fist and pushed it between her upper thighs, putting pressure on her wanton sex.

The lash embraced Tarn's body, stroking the shaft of his penis. It jerked, beating a rapid tattoo against his rigid stomach. Then the leather tips of the whip touched his balls. He groaned, and there was an accompanying gasp from the crowd. Again the lash snaked mercilessly over his sex, and he bucked against his constricting chains, trying to escape from the sweetly tearing agony.

Tarn's discomfort only served to increase the pressure in his penis, and it hardened into a rod of iron, standing out from his groin straight and proud. The glittering dewdrop at its summit grew larger, until it broke free and rolled slowly down the domed head. In unison, one sparkling tear slid damply down Tarn's taut cheek. He groaned harshly, drawing back his lips in a shameful mixture of pain and pleasure. He was well aware that his humiliation would soon be complete. He was steadily losing the battle with the contradicting demands of his own flesh.

'No,' he gasped, trying to deny the inevitable. He moved his head from side to side. His hair, darkened by perspiration, flapped lankly against his shoulders. The skin on his cock looked ready to burst. His sweat-soaked body tensed with sweet agony, his swollen veins visible under his golden skin. For a brief second he froze, looking like a statue of some warrior-like god carved out of solid gold.

Giving a harsh laugh, the sergeant dropped the whip and thrust his work-roughened finger deep into Tarn's anus. Tarn threw back his head and yelped, his muscles straining to breaking point. Then a creamy jet of seed spurted from his cock, followed by another and another.

Rianna gasped, pressing her bunched fist up towards her sex to relieve the throbbing pressure. An unfamiliar spasm of bliss consumed her completely. She shivered with pleasure as she experienced a climax for the very first time. The sensation astounded her, its aftermath leaving her spent, weak and exhausted.

She looked back at Tarn. He sagged between his chains, a thin trickle of semen running down one leg. His entire body trembled and his head was bowed in shame. It appeared his humiliation was complete. As the soldiers loosened his chains, he sank to his knees, immune to everything but his own despair. His arms hung limply at his sides, while his sweat-soaked locks tumbled untidily over his face.

The sergeant grinned and grabbed hold of Tarn's sodden hair, jerking his head back until his face was visible to all. It stood out luminously pale in the gradually darkening clearing. His lips were bloodless and two spots of livid colour stained his cheeks.

'What say you to resistance now, Tarn? Lord Sarin will find you all too easy to subjugate,' the sergeant said gleefully.

Thrusting a booted foot in the prisoner's back, the sergeant forced him on to the ground. Tarn pressed his face into the thick grass, making no attempt to struggle, totally overcome by his despair.

Tarn did not see the crowd of soldiers part to allow Rorg to step forward. He moved painfully, obviously still in some discomfort from the blow to his groin. Reaching Tarn, he bent to pick up the whip, and stood over the prone form of the captive. He trailed the sweat-soaked leather strands across Tarn's fiery flesh and gave a low, menacing laugh.

* * *

Rianna ran as fast as she could through the woods, and into the clearing where the rest of the caravan was camped. She had to find Chancellor Lesand – only he could put a stop to the prisoner's continued misery.

'Chancellor,' she cried out in agitation.

Lesand, who was standing in the middle of the clearing conversing with Captain Feroc, turned. 'My lady,' he said with concern as he moved swiftly to her side. 'What is amiss?'

'You must help,' she stuttered.

'Are you unwell? You are flushed. Perhaps you have a fever?' He put a cool hand to her hot damp forehead. 'I'll summon your maid –'

'No,' she interrupted, clinging on to his arm and digging her fingers into the sleeve of his black velvet robe. 'I am not ill, just distressed. I was walking in the woods, when I came upon Lord Sarin's soldiers abusing the prisoner.'

'Abusing?' Lesand frowned.

'They whipped him, and they . . .' she faltered, blushing deeply. 'I cannot say . . . it was so degrading.'

Rianna lowered her eyes, unable to forget the vision of Tarn writhing and straining against his chains. Neither could she forget the wrenching pleasure she'd experienced from witnessing the humiliation he was forced to endure.

'Go, Captain Feroc, put a stop to it now!' Lesand ordered.

Beckoning to two of his men to accompany him, Feroc ran swiftly through the trees towards the other encampment.

'Calm yourself,' Lesand said in a soothing voice as he guided Rianna towards her wagon. 'You must distress yourself no longer.'

'But you don't understand, we must help the poor prisoner,' she said anxiously. 'Not only was he hurt by the beating, he had other, more serious wounds.'

'Now, now, my lady.' Lesand placed a comforting hand

on her shoulder. 'Feroc is my most experienced officer. He will deal with the matter.'

'Please let me offer my services. I'm skilled in the art of healing.' Like all chatelaines, Rianna cared for the medical needs of the servants and soldiers in the castle of Nort. She had also been taught much about herbs by Jenna's mother.

'There is a military surgeon in the caravan. Feroc can call on him. Now, I wish to hear no more on this matter.' Lesand's voice took on a harder tone. His dark eyes were cold and pitiless as he looked down at her. 'Your soft heart does you great justice, Lady Rianna, but the prisoner does not deserve your sympathy. My only concern at present is your own well-being.'

Rianna bit back her pleading reply, knowing it would be to no avail. 'A short rest, Chancellor, and I'm certain I will be fine.'

Lesand looked around the encampment. 'Where is your maid? She should be here, waiting to attend you.' Jenna was nowhere to be seen. Lesand sighed impatiently and beckoned to his personal body servant. 'Baral, you will attend to Lady Rianna.'

Baral approached and bowed to Rianna. With his soft features and large dark eyes, coupled with his slim, slightly built frame and long dark curly hair, Baral would make a very attractive woman. The gentle, pretty young man had a sweet, clear singing voice. In the evenings Baral often entertained the travellers with his lute-playing and songs. Rianna had noticed that Lesand treated him more like a friend than a servant.

'My lady, it is an honour,' Baral said.

Just as he was about to help Rianna up the steps of her wagon, Jenna arrived looking flushed and rather dishevelled as she strolled leisurely through the trees ringing the camp site, accompanied by one of Lesand's soldiers. She clung attentively to the young soldier's arm in an intimate manner. It was the first time Rianna had seen Jenna look happy since they left the castle of Nort.

'Jenna.' Lesand's icy tones rang loudly across the clearing. 'Come here, girl.'

Jenna stiffened and shot a glance in the Chancellor's direction. Lifting her crumpled, grass-stained skirts, she hurried towards her mistress.

Pink-faced and embarrassed, Jenna bobbed a brief curtsey. 'Lady Rianna, Chancellor Lesand.'

'Where have you been?' Lesand demanded to know. 'Your mistress has need of your services, while it appears that you are more interested in spending your time with one of my soldiers.'

'I was just taking a breath of fresh air,' Jenna lied. 'I've been but a few minutes.'

Lesand glared at the soldier. 'Be gone, man,' he growled. 'And you, Jenna, take this as a warning. Your task is to care for Lady Rianna, not to be off trifling in some lewd manner with my men.'

Jenna paled and looked at Rianna for reassurance. 'Forgive me, my lady.'

'Now take your mistress inside and attend to her needs.' Lesand smiled tight-lipped at Rianna. 'No more worries now, rest easy. We'll speak in the morning. Baral, come,' he ordered.

As Lesand strode away, followed by Baral, Jenna took hold of Rianna's arm, guiding her up the steps and into the privacy of their house on wheels. 'What is amiss? You appear upset, and I've never seen the Chancellor so angry.'

'Neither have I.' Rianna was certain that Lesand's fury did not solely stem from Jenna's shortcomings. She felt it also had something to do with Tarn. 'I was upset by something I witnessed while walking in the woods.'

'You must rest,' Jenna said, leading her mistress to one of the narrow benches. 'You appear overheated. Let me cool you down.'

Rianna sat on the padded seat, while Jenna gently bathed her face with cool, perfumed water. 'My head aches a little,' Rianna complained, feeling suddenly very weary. 'Take out the pins and let down my hair.'

Jenna deftly removed the pins and uncurled the long braid from Rianna's crown. Then she loosened the silken locks, fanning them around Rianna's shoulders and down her back. 'May I ask what you witnessed that upset you so?' Jenna enquired, unable to contain her curiosity any longer, as she brushed Rianna's shining red-gold hair with smooth, restful strokes.

Rianna needed someone to confide in, and she could trust Jenna's discretion. 'You remember I told you about the prisoner in the cage at the rear of the caravan? I took a walk to the other camp site, merely to see if the Chancellor had arranged for the cage to be cleaned out as he had promised,' she confessed haltingly. 'The prisoner was in the lake washing. Curiosity prompted me to linger and see what the poor man looked like.'

'Was he handsome?' Jenna asked.

'Yes, amazingly so. Taller and far more well-favoured than any man of Harn,' Rianna said, colouring at the thought. 'They chained him between two trees, then whipped and abused him most terribly.'

'Why did you not leave?' Jenna asked, unlacing the back of Rianna's gown and sliding the bodice down to her waist.

More colour invaded Rianna's cheeks. 'I could not. I don't understand why . . .' she faltered. 'The prisoner's distress and the degrading things they forced him to endure moved me in the strangest manner.'

Jenna gave a soft laugh. 'You felt aroused, excited. It's not unusual to feel so, my lady. I've experienced the same emotions when watching some handsome miscreant being punished with a whipping.'

'You have?' Rianna said in surprise. 'But the prisoner is

66

no rough peasant, he is a nobleman. The soldiers' intentions were to humble him as well as to punish.'

Just speaking of Tarn made Rianna's breasts throb and her breathing quicken. Eager to be rid of her tight-fitting garments, she stood up and let her dress fall into a shining pool at her feet. Her shift felt impossibly restrictive, as it seemed to crush her breasts and rub enticingly against her rock-hard nipples. She hoped that Jenna didn't notice the way the tiny nubs stood out, lewdly distorting the fine silk of her undergarment.

'A nobleman,' Jenna repeated, lifting Rianna's gown and smoothing the shining folds before placing it in the storage chest. 'He is far more than that, my lady. Mircon, my soldier friend, told me that the prisoner is Tarn, the only son of the King of Kabra, and heir to the throne. How can so proud a prince reconcile himself to becoming a slave? Mircon says that is the fate Lord Sarin intends for him.'

'How can Lord Sarin allow a prince to be treated so cruelly?' Rianna asked. 'They did the most horrendous and degrading things to him.'

'While you stayed and watched,' Jenna reminded her.

As Jenna drew Rianna's shift up and over her head, the maid's cool fingers briefly brushed her over-sensitive flesh. Rianna shivered, finding the contact surprisingly pleasurable.

'I could not tear my gaze from him,' Rianna confessed, feeling conscious of her naked body. 'The whipping must have hurt, but the lash did not tear his flesh. There was no blood. It was purely to subjugate and humiliate . . .' She wanted to tell Jenna all that she witnessed and how aroused she felt, but she could not bring herself to voice the words.

'We all have a place of darkness within our souls.' Jenna slipped the finely embroidered, muslin night-gown over Rianna's head. The fine fabric fluttered downwards, gently caressing Rianna's febrile flesh. 'Watching pain being inflicted on a handsome warrior can be a potent spice to the senses.'

'I would never have believed such feelings possible, if I had not experienced them myself,' Rianna murmured.

'There are clearly many things you have yet to learn,' Jenna said with an understanding smile. 'Perhaps after all it is better that I accompanied you and not Veba. That dried-up old crone doesn't even know what it's like to bed a man.'

Rianna did not like the way Jenna spoke about Veba. She loved the old woman; however, she knew that in many ways Jenna was right. Veba was a spinster, with old-fashioned and restrictive views. Jenna was probably far more knowledgeable about matters of the flesh. 'Are you very experienced?' she asked shyly.

Jenna chuckled. 'I have known a number of men, if that is what you mean. You may ask me anything you want about the opposite sex, Lady Rianna. I'm certain to be able to provide you with a well-informed answer.'

'Anything?' Rianna asked, sitting down on her narrow bed.

'Anything,' Jenna confirmed, smiling affectionately at Rianna. 'I'll be happy to tell you about ways to pleasure a man. You'll no longer be a total innocent when you go to your husband's bed. But our discussions on this matter must cease now and continue on the morrow. Please, you must rest, I don't want to incur Chancellor Lesand's anger again.'

There was a multitude of questions Rianna wanted answered, but she knew Jenna was right – there was plenty of time for such discussions on the long journey to Aguilar, the capital city of Percheron. Rianna lay down on her bed, and smiled up at her maid as she covered her with a sheet. 'Thank you, Jenna.'

'Rest easy. I'll return later to see if you want anything to eat,' Jenna said, before she left the wagon.

With her head still full of images of the handsome

warrior naked and in chains, Rianna eventually fell into a restless, dream-filled sleep.

Rianna's slumbers were disturbed by a sudden noise. 'Jenna, is that you?' she queried.

'Yes.' Jenna moved closer, striking the tinderbox to light a small oil lamp. 'I'm sorry to disturb you, my lady, but Chancellor Lesand wishes to speak with you urgently.'

Forcing herself into full wakefulness, Rianna sat up and brushed the tangled strands of hair from her face. 'It's the middle of the night, is it not?'

''Tis way past midnight. The Chancellor says he has urgent need of your healing skills.' Jenna handed Rianna a blue velvet cloak. 'No time to dress, wear this.'

'Who's ill?' Rianna asked, pushing her feet into a pair of velvet slippers as Jenna wrapped the cloak around her. 'Have you my bag?'

'It is outside with the Chancellor's servant,' Jenna replied. 'And I do not know who is ill. The Chancellor did not choose to confide in me.'

Rianna hurried down the steps of her wagon to where the Chancellor was standing with his servant. Baral was holding aloft a lantern, and at his feet was Rianna's bag of instruments and potions.

'I apologise for disturbing you,' Lesand said, appearing rather agitated. 'There was no other I could turn to. Your maid assures me that your healing skills are well-known in Harn.'

'I'll do what I can to help. Who is unwell?' Rianna asked.

'During a struggle with his guards, the prisoner received a blow to the head. He's been unconscious for hours,' Lesand explained hurriedly. 'The military surgeon who accompanies us can do nothing for him, so I crave your assistance. Baral will escort you, Lady Rianna, if you would care to examine the man.'

Concern for Tarn made Rianna decide she did not want

to delay a moment longer. It was dark, no one would see she wore only a night-gown under her cloak. 'Of course, Chancellor. I'm ready.'

Baral picked up Rianna's bag. 'This way, my lady. Take care you do not trip on the rough ground.'

She followed him from the encampment and into the eerie darkness of the wood. Rianna had never been in a forest at night. She jumped nervously when she heard the distant scream of an unknown animal, and was relieved when she caught sight of the flickering flames of a campfire.

Three soldiers were sitting hunched around the fire, while the rest of the men appeared to be asleep, leaving Tarn unguarded. Unconscious, he lay on his stomach, close to the wagon that bore his cage. A rough piece of striped fabric was thrown over the lower half of Tarn's prone body, but there was nothing between him and the rough ground.

'Baral, I will need blankets for the prisoner,' Rianna said.

'Yes, my lady.' Placing the lantern and bag close to the prisoner's head, Baral moved over to speak to the soldiers by the fire. Meanwhile, Rianna examined Tarn's back. The flesh was red and angry, criss-crossed by raised scarlet weals. But there was no blood, no broken skin. The damage would heal swiftly and leave no disfiguring scars.

Opening her bag, Rianna took out a small clay pot containing a soothing ointment made of agrimony, rosemary and lavender oil. She spread it thinly over Tarn's damaged flesh, admiring the strength and hardness of the muscles under his skin. She had almost finished when Baral returned with the three soldiers, although she'd not yet lifted the strip of blanket to anoint Tarn's bare buttocks.

Under instructions from Rianna, the soldiers laid a blanket on the ground. She covered the top half with a clean cloth to prevent the rough fibres from sticking to the ointment on Tarn's back. Then she ordered the soldiers to lift him on to the blanket.

Tarn was a heavily built man, and a dead weight while unconscious. The three soldiers grunted in exertion as they lifted him and placed him atop the blanket. They decorously draped the piece of striped fabric across Tarn's hips to conceal his sex from her view. Then they insisted on putting manacles on his ankles and tethering his chains to the wheels of the wagon. However, because of Rianna's pleadings, they did not replace the manacles on the prisoner's wrists.

'You may leave,' Baral told the soldiers, who resumed their places by the campfire.

Rianna examined the wound on Tarn's head. The gash extended from his left temple deep into his scalp, surrounded by a matted mass of hair and congealed blood. She cleansed the gory mess with a cloth dampened in boiled water mixed with vinegar. The wound was bad, but the bone underneath appeared undamaged. Rianna's gentle probing fingers found no sign of a fracture, but even that did not ensure Tarn's survival.

'Is it bad?' Baral asked, unable to bring himself to look closely at the wound. 'The sight of blood sickens me.'

'It's hard to tell. I've seen men recover from worse, while others, with far less serious wounds, have died. Where the head is concerned, anything is possible.'

'Can you help him at all?' Baral stared sympathetically down at Tarn.

'A tisane of comfrey and valerian, mixed with mallow and borage will calm his blood and help relieve internal swelling,' she said thoughtfully. 'After that we will have to wait and see. Baral, will you go and seek out my maid, Jenna, and ask her to brew such a potion. In the meantime, I'll tend to these other wounds.' Rianna took a sharp silver scalpel from her bag. 'See here, on his shoulder.' She pressed an area of puffy, purplish-red flesh which bordered both sides of the long half-healed gash. 'There are bad humours here that have to be released, lest they drain into his blood and poison him.'

Baral turned pasty white. 'I'll find Jenna at once.' He smiled weakly. 'Will it trouble you to be left alone with the prisoner? I could call the guards.'

'No.' She looked down at her unconscious patient. 'What harm can he do me, Baral?'

'What harm indeed,' Baral agreed, moving quickly away before Rianna could use the scalpel.

Rianna worked with swift expertise, draining and cleaning the infected wound on Tarn's shoulder. Then she packed it with a healing unguent and covered it with a clean dressing.

Now she had but to examine the wound in Tarn's groin. She looked down at the unconscious warrior. He was quite the most beautiful man she had ever seen. His face was angelic in repose, the features bold but finely drawn. She wished she could see the colour of his eyes, now shaded by long dark lashes. She guessed they would be blue or grey because his hair was a pale shade of gold.

With the tips of her fingers she touched his mouth, easing it open a little. The lower lip was a little fuller than the upper, while his teeth were white and even. She trailed her hands down his corded neck to the firm planes of his chest. His heartbeat was regular, not thready, his breathing slow and even. These were good signs and she hoped with every fibre of her being that Tarn would recover.

Under the smooth, unblemished flesh, lightly tanned by exposure to the sun, his body was a mesh of strong, powerful muscles, honed to perfection by his life as a warrior. She continued her examination, her fingers brushing his nipples: two small dark nubbins surrounded by flat circles of copper. There was not even the faintest hint of a bulge at his belly; it was tight, iron-hard and infinitely appealing. Drawing her breath inwards, Rianna allowed her fingers to travel lower. Gently, she eased aside the striped fabric covering his groin. There was a dusting of pale blond hair on his lower belly, gradually thickening into the golden triangle of curls that covered his pubis. She couldn't resist staring at his male organs. Tarn's phallus was nestling limply atop the bed of curls and behind it lay the sac of flesh which held his seed of life.

The skin of his manhood was a shade darker than that of the rest of his body, darkening even more at the domed tip. The organ was far from small, but she still found it difficult to understand how it could grow so impossibly large. Who would imagine that this curved, defenceless instrument could stiffen until it was much longer and thicker than the handle of the Great Broadsword of Harn? She recalled the phallus as she'd seen it earlier in the day – taut and shiny, a huge purplish bulb at its tip, poised and ready to pump spurts of creamy seed from his body.

Once again she felt the unquenchable fire burst into life, deep in the pit of her stomach, knifing through her feminine parts and filling them with lust. She could barely imagine what it would feel like to have Tarn's phallus thrusting deeper and deeper inside her, the smooth skin of his cock shaft polished to slick perfection by the copious dew of her own body.

Rianna recalled the feel of Lesand's fingers inside her, checking her virgin status. She'd never believed the experience could be so pleasurable. But what if those long thin fingers had been replaced by Tarn's huge rod of flesh? Would the pleasure increase or would it prove to be painful?

Sternly reminding herself that she had a task to perform, Rianna focused her thoughts on Tarn's well-being. She looked at the long sword gash extending from Tarn's groin to half-way down his thigh. It was still a little inflamed but the wound appeared clean. She judged it to be mending well. All it needed was regular applications of soothing unguent.

Rianna spread a thin layer of healing ointment along the line of the wound. On finishing, she wiped her fingers, then rewarded her labours with another glimpse of Tarn's sex. The skin on the shaft of his penis looked wrinkled and rough. She touched it with the tip of her fingers, still finding it hard to comprehend how the organ could grow so swiftly. Surprisingly, the surface felt smooth and velvety, much like the skin of a ripe peach. She stroked the shaft, watching curiously as it slowly expanded. Before it straightened and hardened fully, she weighed the organ in her hand. How odd to spend one's life with this always hanging between one's legs. How much neater was a woman's body with everything tucked securely inside.

The head of Tarn's phallus was protected by a thick hood of skin. As she stroked and rubbed the shaft it grew larger, and the collar of skin slowly rolled back to reveal the tip of the expanding purple bulb that had so firmly imprinted itself on her fevered mind.

She was still marvelling at the amazing sight when she detected a slight trembling of Tarn's stomach. He gave a faint moan, and Rianna looked worriedly up at his face, but his eyes were closed and he still appeared to be unconscious. She glanced nervously over at the guards by the fire, fearful that they might be watching her intimately exploring Tarn's body, but they were all fast asleep.

Rianna was just about to return her attention to Tarn, when she felt a hand grab her wrist and jerk her forward. She fell across Tarn's chest, while arms, strong as steel bands, enfolded her.

'You've come to entrance me,' Tarn groaned. His sky-blue eyes raked her face, before he captured her lips with his.

As Tarn's tongue thrust between her lips, she gave a pleading moan. But as his searching tongue delved deeper, erotically exploring the moist crevices of her mouth, the fire in her belly blazed fully into life. She felt weak with wanting as she gave herself up to the sublime intimacy of his kiss. It was all she'd ever imagined and far, far more. Her heartbeat increased, turning into a helpless tattoo as she felt pure desire invade every nerve and fibre of her being.

Rianna forgot that Tarn was a captive, forgot that he was a stranger to her. She welcomed Tarn's touch as he ran his hands feverishly over her body. He stroked her lush curves through the fine muslin of her night-gown. His hand was so large it easily imprisoned one full breast, kneading and squeezing the sensitive mound of flesh.

She shivered with pleasure as Tarn's searching tongue continued to probe her mouth ruthlessly, his kisses and caresses wreaking havoc with her senses.

'Sweet faerie of the forest,' he murmured against her hot cheek. 'Bless you for coming to help wash away my shame.'

'No,' she gasped, but his ears were deaf to her pleadings as his searching fingers slid inside the loose neck of her night-gown. He stroked her nipple, pulling and squeezing the engorged nubbin until she cried out with the joy of it.

He kissed her again, with ruthless passion, enmeshed in a fantasy of his own making, prompted by the fevered confusion in his brain. One hand continued to fondle and stroke her breasts, while the other fumbled with the filmy folds of her night-gown, pushing the fabric away from her legs. Rianna's body felt boneless, her pudenda hot and moist. She wanted to open her legs and beg him to quell the slippery heat in her sex. She gasped as Tarn's hand moved up her thigh. His fingers slid higher to stroke the red-gold curls of her pubis and tenderly caress the engorged lips of her vulva.

Reason returned to Rianna in a sudden rush of heated concern. If she allowed Tarn to continue she would lose everything, and if anyone discovered her perfidy, Tarn would suffer even more, perhaps be put to death.

'No,' she wailed, trying to push his searching hand away from her sex. 'This must not be.'

Her struggles proved useless. Tarn was far stronger than her, and still totally enmeshed in his feverish fantasy.

Ignoring her protestations, he whispered soft words of love in her ear while the tips of his fingers slid between her legs to caress her sensitive, inner flesh. Fighting the urge to give up the battle and allow Tarn to continue on their mutual voyage of discovery, Rianna flailed her arms. Agitatedly she struck out at Tarn, unthinkingly catching his shoulder wound with the heel of her hand. Tarn groaned in agony, his hold on her lessening for a moment.

'Please stop,' she begged entreatingly. At last she managed to tear herself away from him and sit up. Pulling her cloak together with shaking fingers, Rianna struggled to contain the violent lustful urges that still consumed her inflamed flesh.

Tarn's arms fell limply to his sides as he stared at her in confusion. But a measure of rationality appeared to have returned to his mind. 'Who are you?' he asked hesitantly.

'I'm no faerie come to succour you,' she said, her breath still coming in nervous gasps. Rianna's skin was afire, and her wet sex throbbed. She fought the need to throw herself back into Tarn's arms and beg him to continue. The urgent desire he aroused in her refused to diminish and lust still simmered in her heart.

'Then I've not died and gone to heaven,' he groaned, closing his eyes as he put a shaky hand to the wound on his head.

Tarn's cock was hard and fully erect, standing out at right angles from his prone body, a gleaming pearl of moisture crowning its bulbous tip. Rianna glanced over at it and blushed, realising how close she'd come to losing control and with it her precious virginity. Filled with embarrassment, she draped the striped fabric over Tarn's groin, but his erect organ held a portion of the fabric lewdly upwards, like the pole of a tent. Not knowing quite what to do next, she looked back at Tarn's face.

'You're certainly beautiful enough to be a forest wraith,' he murmured in confused bewilderment.

'I came to tend your wounds . . .' She hesitated, uncertain whether to use his name.

'Tend my wounds, sweet lady?' he questioned. Tarn's eyes were the deep blue of a clear summer sky. Briefly, they clouded with pain as he tried to move his head. 'Ye gods, my head aches,' he muttered.

'Lie still. You've been unconscious for many hours.' She touched his forehead with trembling hands. His skin was now warm and slightly clammy. 'And you're a little feverish.'

'I've been insensible for that long?' Tarn gave a brittle laugh. 'I'm certain that swine Rorg must have suffered more. I hit his sex so hard he's unlikely ever to be able to father a bastard ag–' Tarn faltered, two spots of his colour appearing on his cheeks. 'Apologies, sweet lady, my words were crude and unnecessary.'

'Not unnecessary,' she said gently. 'Rorg deserved his fate.'

Tarn did not appear to realise that she knew who, and what, he was talking about. 'Lady, you must excuse my untoward behaviour . . .' he stuttered. 'To kiss and fondle you like that was unpardonable.'

'Your brain was fevered from the blow to your head.' She smiled tenderly. 'You did not know what you were doing. In your inflamed imagination you believed me to be some spirit of the forest come to claim you as her own.'

'I must have been dreaming most vividly,' Tarn said weakly. 'I could have sworn I felt gentle hands caressing me in the most intimate manner.'

Now it was Rianna's turn to blush. 'I was tending the wound close to your groin,' she said shyly. 'In my haste and concern it is possible I mistakenly touched your phal . . . touched you intimately,' she said in embarrassment, stumbling awkwardly over her words.

'I should be grateful that you showed such concern for my welfare.' Taking hold of her hand, he pressed it to his lips. 'I thank you for your kindness, sweet lady.' Tarn tried to lift his head but he grimaced in pain and perspiration broke out on his brow.

'No,' she pressed him back down. 'Your head wound is bad, and you must lie still for some time, until I deem it safe for you to move.'

'I will do as you say,' he said, attempting a shaky smile. 'What is your name, sweet lady?'

'Rianna.'

'And how came you to be on this journey? Judging by your unusual colouring, you are not from Percheron. I've never seen hair of such a glorious hue.'

'I'm travelling to Aguilar to be married,' she told him.

'Then you are the noble lady who is to wed Lord Sarin?' Tarn asked in harsh surprise. 'The daughter of the Protector of Harn.'

'Yes,' she confirmed a little uneasily. The cruelty inflicted on Tarn made her wonder even more about her future husband. She could only hope Lord Sarin knew nothing of Tarn's mistreatment.

'Sarin.' There was derision and abhorrence in the way Tarn spoke her bridegroom's name. 'How could your father sacrifice you to such a man?'

'It was necessary for the protection of my country,' she replied, 'lest he try to conquer Harn like he did Kabra. Fate has set my path, just as it has yours.'

'I made my fate, no one else had a hand in it. I brought about my own demise.' Tarn smiled wryly. 'Who would have thought the Prince of Kabra could fall so low?' He saw the apprehension and fear she felt reflected in her eyes. 'Do not be concerned, Lady Rianna. My situation is far different from yours.'

'We are both captives in our own way,' she admitted uneasily. 'Though my prison is far more comfortable than yours.'

His expression softened as he lifted a hand to touch her pale cheek. 'My hatred of what Sarin has done to Kabra colours my opinion of the man. He can be captivating and

charming to those he admires. Sarin worships beauty and
you are lovely enough to turn the head of any man. I'm
sure he will make you a fine husband.'

'You speak as if you know him well.'

'Very well,' Tarn confirmed. 'After he conquered Kabra,
I resided at his court for a number of years. He treated me
as a friend, a brother even; we were very close. I hear he
was devastated when I chose to lead the insurrection in
Kabra. Now he despises me as a traitor to our friendship
as well as to Percheron.'

'Then I fear his plans for you will be harsh,' she said
sadly. 'But do you not think that if he once cared for you
he will temper his judgement with mercy?' She blushed
awkwardly. 'I'm certain he would not approve of his
soldiers abusing you as they did. The soldier, Rorg and
his sergeant deserved any injuries you gave them.'

All the colour drained from Tarn's face and his features
contorted in distress. 'You saw?'

'Yes,' she admitted, unable to meet his anguished gaze.
'When I discovered what terrible living conditions you
were forced to endure, I persuaded Chancellor Lesand to
allow you to cleanse yourself. I wanted to ensure he kept
his promise so I came to this encampment and I uninten-
tionally saw what they did to you.'

Tarn turned his head miserably away from her. 'I cannot
believe you witnessed my humiliation,' he said, his voice
cracking on the words.

'But it was not your fault.' She was filled with infinite
pity for the suffering of this handsome prince. Tentatively
she stroked his taut cheek. 'Do not blame yourself, Tarn,
for what others inflicted upon you.'

'Say no more,' he groaned. 'If only I could find a way to
erase the feel of those hands from my flesh.'

Leaning forward, she kissed his cheek with sympathetic
understanding. 'Let me help you,' she whispered, her
warm breath brushing his face. 'Please look at me, Tarn.'

Slowly he turned his head. Rianna was so agonisingly

79

close to his trembling, vulnerable mouth. She wanted to kiss those soft lips, inhale the breath from his body and help wipe away his pain. Resisting the temptation, she smiled tenderly at him.

'Rianna,' he murmured as he stared deep into her compassion-filled green eyes. 'Such a beautiful name, but nowhere near as beautiful as its owner. No mere mortal has ever been so lovely or so tender-hearted.'

She placed the palm of her hand on the hard planes of his chest, feeling the agitated beating of his heart. 'Tarn, you barely know me.'

'I know all that I need to know.' He covered her hand with his. 'Earlier, when I said I felt you touching me intimately, I was not dreaming, was I?' he asked entreatingly.

She couldn't lie to him. 'No, you were not dreaming,' she said shyly. 'Before you, I had never seen a naked man. I was admiring your body. You're beautiful also, Tarn.'

'No, I'm not, I'm tainted,' he said in disgust. 'Forever befouled.'

'Not forever.' She ran her fingers over his chest, feeling the hard muscles tremble beneath her caressing touch. 'I could wash away your degradation and make you whole again.'

'Please,' he begged as her hands trailed lower to tantalisingly stroke the iron hard planes of his stomach. 'Help me.'

She slid her hands under the fabric covering his groin, savouring the heat of his golden flesh, the springiness of the curls covering his pubis. Tarn's phallus was still partially engorged, but now lying prone against his stomach. She touched the velvety skin of his shaft, feeling it jerk excitedly. 'I'm inexperienced in these matters,' she whispered as she ran the pads of her fingers slowly down the side of his rod of hot male flesh.

With a trembling hand, Tarn pulled the striped fabric

away, exposing all of his sex to her view. 'I ache for you, sweet Rianna,' he pleaded.

Cautiously she curled her fingers around his shaft, feeling the glorious power of his manhood throbbing gently beneath her fingertips. Then, unsure what she should do next, she recalled the sight of Tarn chained between the trees and the crude pumping motion the sergeant had employed when he'd forced Tarn's unwilling phallus into life. Using gentle, less vigorous strokes, she began to mimic the movement. At once, she felt Tarn's cock begin to harden, and she heard him give a soft, encouraging moan.

The sound pierced her body like a sword, travelling deep to the pit of her stomach. Her womb throbbed. A sudden rush of moisture seeped from her sex, and coated her inner thighs. She was filled with the sudden need to be invaded and stretched by Tarn's rigid staff of flesh.

Trying to ignore her own desires, Rianna stroked his cock shaft, still employing smooth regular strokes. His organ grew rapidly until it was firm and hard. She slid her fingers higher, forcing the skin on his cock to roll back and expose the swollen purple head beneath. She milked the shaft with slow precision, until she saw a bead of moisture seep from the tiny mouth at its tip. Soon the collar of flesh ringed the engorged head tightly. It appeared to increase the pressure in the bulb; the skin of the plum stretched, becoming taut and shiny.

With her other hand, she caressed his trembling belly and the soft blond curls at his pubis. Then she stroked the smooth pliable skin of his balls, feeling them tighten and ripple under her gentle touch. Her innocent attempt to pleasure Tarn appeared to be working most admirably. He rolled his head from side to side as a soft, 'Yes,' drifted from his open lips.

Rianna wanted to kiss Tarn, to impale her throbbing sex on his iron-hard rod and feel him thrusting deep inside her feminine sheath. She pressed her legs tightly together and ignored the wetness seeping from her pudenda, instead taking pleasure from Tarn's steadily increasing excitement. Pumping and squeezing the stem of his penis ever harder, she disregarded the growing fire in the depths of her own sex.

The wrinkled skin of Tarn's seed sac hardened into two firm stones. A harsh groan came from Tarn's mouth as a shudder of pleasure traversed the muscles of his groin. His stomach tightened, his phallus jumped beneath her encircled fingers and his balls tensed. A great jet of creamy seed spurted from his cock head, followed by another and another.

Shivering with the strength of her emotion, Rianna looked up at Tarn's face. His eyes were closed and he was breathing heavily; he appeared to be at peace with himself.

'Sweet Rianna.' His lips curved into a contented smile. 'I adore you,' he murmured so softly it might have been but a whisper on the wind.

Glancing briefly in the direction of the guards to ensure they were still asleep, Rianna returned her attention to Tarn. Taking a cloth from her bag she cleaned the remains of Tarn's creamy emanations from his still trembling flesh. She took hold of the other blanket Baral had given her and gently placed it over him. Then she tenderly stroked his cheek.

'You must try and rest now,' she said, feeling a great affection for the handsome warrior. She had never realised how easy it was to give pleasure to a man. She stared at the handsome planes of his face, the tender vulnerability in his full lips. She was certain Tarn would recover from his injuries, but she feared for his eventual fate.

Suddenly, she was disturbed by the sound of movement behind her. Thinking it might be one of the guards, she turned her head. It was Baral walking towards her carrying a cup of the steaming potion.

'My lady,' Baral said anxiously. 'I'm sorry this has taken so long.'

'No matter.' She smiled tenderly down at Tarn, who had now opened his eyes and was staring up at her. 'The prisoner had but just regained consciousness. But the wound was as bad as I feared, and his brain is in total turmoil. He knows neither who nor where he is. Also he has a fever. It appears I will have to tend to him for some days yet.'

As she spoke, Tarn gave a faint, barely perceptible nod and closed his eyes.

Cooking up a Storm

Emma Holly

The Coates Inn Restaurant in Cape Cod is Abigail's pride and joy, but it's about to go belly-up and Abby needs to take drastic action to save it. Along comes Storm Dupré, a handsome chef who claims to have a secret weapon: an aphrodisiac menu that her patrons won't be able to resist. It certainly works for Abby, who gives vent to passions she has denied for years.

But does this playboy chef really have Abby's best interests at heart when her body means more to him than her heart? He's charming the pants off her, and Abby ends up behaving like a wild woman. But Storm's got a secret plan and some decidedly strange personal habits which are bound to come out sooner or later.

Emma Holly is one of Black Lace's star authors. Her fluid style and great characterisation are admired by all lovers of erotica. She specialises in power games with a human touch, and all of her novels are set in her native America. This extract is taken from *Cooking up a Storm*. Emma's other books include *Ménage* and *The Top of her Game*. *Velvet Glove* is due out in November 1999.

Cooking up a Storm

*A*bby ran the damp, soapy cloth down the counter, so lost in her thoughts she wasn't aware that she was lost. The stranger was more exotic than handsome. His jaw was too long, for one thing, and his mouth was unusually shaped. She touched her own, trying to re-create it in her mind. Yes, his upper lip was almost triangular. It looked temptingly soft. His nose was on the large side. It matched his jaw, but not his pretty blue-grey eyes. His clothes were expensive, but his hair was shaggy – shiny, though, so he must care for it.

He was a misassembled puzzle, she thought. His face made one want to stare, to figure out what made it so appealing. Of course, it didn't hurt that from the neck down he was drop-dead perfect.

She ran the cloth the other way, heedless of the soapy drips trickling to the floor. Out in the lobby, she'd caught him staring at Jack's photo as if he wanted to crawl inside. The expression of naked yearning disappeared the moment he caught sight of her, but it lasted long enough to brand itself on her memory. She knew it was stupid, but she couldn't suppress the urge to soothe him, as if he were an injured puppy rather than a full-grown man who probably ate women like her for breakfast.

He had that heartbreaker's look; that 'I can have any woman I want and I've proved it' look. Was he ever sexy, though! Just holding his elbow, she'd marked the heat of him, the sexual electricity. Her pussy felt swollen even now. Every so often it gave a little twitch of longing.

Ridiculous, she thought, crouching down to swipe a soapy puddle off the floor. Bill hadn't been gone a week. Her body ought to be in mourning, not panting after a man who probably wouldn't give her a second look. He probably went for fashion-model types who wore designer gowns to the grocer's, women who read the *New Yorker* and never got grease under their nails. If she had the least bit of sense, she'd keep her interest hidden and save herself some embarrassment.

Marissa's unexpected entrance made her gasp and jolt to her feet.

'One of the customers wants to talk to you about the chef's position,' she said.

A little shiver tickled the back of Abby's neck. She just knew it was him, Mr Sexy in the linen jacket. Heart thudding in her chest, she asked Marissa which customer she meant.

Marissa studied her fingernails. 'Shortish guy. Long hair.'

Abby pressed her lips together to hide her smile. The man had been of average height and his shaggy brown hair did hang to his shoulders, but Marissa had to be blind to think that description did him justice.

'Bedroom eyes?' she added, succumbing to her urge to tease.

Marissa shrugged. 'He didn't make an appointment. Want me to show him the door?'

'Of course not.' Abby pulled the soiled apron over her head and tossed it on to a stool. 'I'll talk to anyone who'll get me out of this kitchen.' She peered at her reflection in the door to the microwave. 'Lord, look at my hair!'

Marissa's disapproving stare seemed to follow her to the dining room, but she forgot it as soon as she saw him standing by the corner table, waiting for her. He'd taken off his jacket. He wore a grey silk T-shirt beneath it and snug black trousers. She could see every lean, curved muscle through his clothes. He must work out. Nobody's genes were that good.

He reached towards her with a beautifully shaped tan hand. She put her own hand into it. A tingle shot up her arm at his firm, dry grip. A tiny muscle in her pussy quivered and, a second later, her panties were wet. Good Lord, she thought, this man was dangerous.

'Thank you for taking time to see me,' he said, smiling down at her, but not very far down. 'My name is Storm Dupré.'

He had a slight, delightful accent – soft consonants, sensual 's's and half-swallowed 'r's. French maybe, she thought, which would go with his surname. As she stared, the corners of his mouth curled upward and he lowered his silvery-blue eyes, as if his smile were a secret he couldn't share. A fan of black lashes shadowed his sculpted cheekbones.

Abby shook herself. 'Abigail Coates,' she said, her voice embarrassingly breathy. Alarmed at the sound, she released his hand. Hers was damp. She dried it on her flowered skirt. 'Marissa tells me you're a chef.'

'That's right.' He pulled out a chair and gestured her towards it. 'Why don't we sit and I'll tell you what I have in mind.'

Though his tone was not overtly suggestive, Abby couldn't suppress a blush. She cleared her throat. 'Have in mind for what?' she asked.

He proceeded to tell her. New menus, he said, with fewer dishes per night, but more variety from night to night. He'd go over her old receipts, keep the most popular dishes and jettison the rest. He'd want uniforms for the staff, nothing fancy – black trousers and clean white shirts would do. Advertising was advisable or, at the very least, press attention for the change in personnel. He was an award-winning Californian chef; he was certain they'd find him newsworthy. He didn't see any reason why the Coates Inn shouldn't be a place people ate at all year round.

'And the portions are too large,' he said, holding her with his soft, burning eyes. 'I don't propose we switch to *nouvelle cuisine* but, when it comes to eating out, a little too much is just right. People should go home feeling pampered, not pained.'

Abby nodded, just as she'd been nodding all along. The man named Storm waited.

'Oh,' she said, jerking out of the warm, floaty place where his voice had sent her. 'That all sounds very interesting. I should warn you though –' she smoothed the edge of the table cloth '– I'm on a limited budget. I can only afford to pay the salary I promised for six months and, if we aren't making money by then, I'll have to let you go. If I do all the things you suggested, we'd have to turn a profit much sooner.'

He leaned back in his chair. 'Ah,' he said. The single syllable rang with foreign charm.

'Where are you from?' she asked, unable to restrain herself.

'Montreal,' he said, the word very Gallic on his lips. 'But I moved to the States when I was sixteen.'

A silence fell then, a repressive silence that did not encourage further questions. Abby fidgeted. She wondered if she ought to tell him the extra operating capital existed, but her sisters – who owned the restaurant in common with her – had dithered endlessly about freeing it up. Nervous, she looked up at him. His face gave nothing away, though in repose he appeared sad. The corners of his beautiful mouth turned down, as did his lambent eyes.

No, she told herself, family business was family business. It wasn't meant to be shared with strangers, no matter how alluring and competent they seemed.

Finally, the man sat forward and rested his forearms on the table. Perhaps he'd come to a decision. Abby held her breath. She realised she wanted to hire him. Looks aside, he sounded like the sort of go-getter she needed.

'I don't think money will be a problem,' he said. 'Tourist season starts at the end of June, yes? I suspect we'll be turning customers away before July draws to a close.'

'You do?' she breathed, captivated by his confidence.

He smiled the slow, close-lipped smile she already knew must be habitual. Again, he lowered his eyes. He smoothed the edge of the table just as she had, but the gesture was different when he did it – sensual, as if it weren't a table he was touching. 'I have a secret weapon.'

'You do?' she said again, then pinched her thigh for being such a ninny. She managed this place, for goodness sake. She had a business degree from a respected university. Her family counted on her to keep her head and make sensible decisions. 'I mean, I'd need to know the secret weapon before I hired you.'

'Have you eaten?'

She shook her head. 'I usually grab something after I've finished cleaning up.'

'Well you won't have to grab anything tonight.' His eyes twinkled with devilment. 'Tonight I will lay the secret in your hands.'

The delectable Abby Coates led him through the dining room and past the servers' station. She tripped twice on the wide pine floorboards and stammered when she tried to speak. Her flusterment, obviously the result of a budding attraction, turned Storm's cock to hot, pounding stone. She was enchanting, adorable, fresh as the first spring crocus. He could hardly wait to slide between her plump pink thighs and drive them both to completion.

He would wait, though, of course. He liked to prolong the process of seduction as much as possible. No afters without starters was his motto, even if the afters were ready to leap on to your plate at the first crook of a finger.

He nodded in approval at the spotless, well-appointed kitchen. Too many owners, tired at the end of a sixteen-hour day, left the mess until morning. He was glad see this woman shared his passion for cleanliness.

Clearly, she deserved a special reward.

Without asking permission, he walked into the unlocked storeroom; that would have to change, too, he thought, and pawed through at the materials on hand. When he found a bag of pine nuts, the decision was made.

'Angel-hair pasta with fresh fennel pesto,' he said.

She responded with a squeak. He knew the cost of the ingredients alarmed her. He silenced her protest with a level stare, one that said: Don't you think you deserve it? She backed down with a nervous smile.

He made quick work of the sauce, pouring boiling water over the tomatoes and throwing the fennel, garlic and basil into the food processor. He'd been cooking professionally since the age of sixteen – twelve if you counted his apprenticeship with Mrs Kozlakis, their neighbour in Montreal. At this stage of his career, preparation was more art than mechanics. He didn't measure. He didn't fuss. He always knew precisely what he was doing, no matter how many pots he had going.

The pasta he cooked *al dente*. He drained it with a flourishing toss better suited to a *Teppanyaki* chef. Showoff, he thought, but he couldn't restrain himself.

Abby had long since pulled a stool over to the workstation, where she watched his every move with wide-eyed awe. Her nipples had puckered like currants beneath her pink cashmere twin set. He knew some women thought watching a man cook was sexy. He was glad she was one of them, even if his trousers had grown uncomfortably tight.

He pursed his lips in amusement as he tossed pasta and pesto together. Should he warn her precisely how many aphrodisiac ingredients this fragrant dish contained? The pine nuts, the basil and the olive oil were loaded with boron, vitamin E and zinc, libido boosters all. The fennel contained trace amounts of estragole, a mild hallucinogenic. Moreover, if Mrs Kozlakis could be trusted – and Storm thought she could – the merest whiff of raw garlic was guaranteed to get anyone's blood pumping.

But perhaps it would be more scientific not to tell her. As he well knew, suggestion itself was a powerful aphrodisiac.

'*Voilà*,' he said, transferring a small, steaming mound on to a plate. With a twist of his wrist, the pasta settled into a beautiful, twining pattern. He garnished his creation with a sprig of fresh basil.

Abby applauded as he set it before her. To his amazement, he blushed.

'Oh, my.' She gazed at her plate. 'It's almost too beautiful to eat. I'm starving, though, so I will.'

She ate the way a woman should eat: slowly but with gusto, savouring each bite and occasionally moaning out her enjoyment. She'll sound good in bed, he thought, surreptitiously tugging the cloth stretched over his crotch. His cock was straining for freedom now, head up, shaft quivering. But it would wait – and thank him for it later.

'How do you feel?' he asked when she'd sucked up the last strand of angel hair.

'Wonderful.' She wiped her chin clean on a napkin. 'Almost glowy.'

Storm smiled at her. Her cheeks were pink, her lips red. She squirmed a little on her stool. *Bon*, he thought. Good. She's ready.

He stepped around the work island, coming close enough to hear the tiny catch in her breath. Reaching out, he eased a strand of falling hair from her face, his touch too light to brush skin. The hair flowed like silk over his

93

fingertips. Her lips parted. Her mouth was a perfect Cupid's-bow, plump and soft and small. His throat tightened with a hunger to plunge his tongue inside, but he kept his voice steady. 'Do you, perhaps, feel as you do when someone kisses you?'

The gap between her lips widened, shock and arousal causing her jaw to drop. 'I don't know what you mean,' she said.

'Don't you?' He moved his hands, let the palms hover an inch from her breasts, just close enough to bathe her nipples in their heat. Her cheeks went as red as plum tomatoes, but she didn't move away.

'You can't do this,' she whispered.

'But I am testing my secret weapon.'

'You intend to treat all my customers this way?'

Laughing silently, he lowered his head until his breath stirred the fine hairs at her temple. 'It's an aphrodisiac.'

'I'm sure it is.' She fumbled for his wrists, catching them in hot damp hands and pushing. 'But it's not exactly professional.'

Her innocence was priceless. Heart warming with amusement, he squeezed the hands that were trying so hard to push his away. 'The ingredients in the pasta are aphrodisiacs. I wanted to see if they really worked.'

'Oh.' She stumbled back off her stool and pulled her cardigan together at the neck. He saw from her face that he'd hurt her feelings, though he didn't know how. 'I'm sorry,' she said. 'I thought you were making a pass at me.'

Now he understood. He was happy her hurt was so easy to soothe. He crossed the distance she'd put between them and laid one hand, very lightly, against her cheek. The feel of her skin made his eyes slide shut for a moment. Her cheek truly was as soft as a baby's bottom. All over, he thought. She'll feel like that all over.

'I am attracted to you,' he said, watching the colour come and go in her face. 'But I would never make a pass at a woman I hope to make my employer.'

'What do you call this?' she squeaked. When he chuckled and dropped his hand, she looked down at her flat-soled shoes. 'I don't think it's a good idea, mixing business and –' she hunched her shoulders '– you know.'

'No,' he said very seriously, without actually agreeing.

'Besides,' she added, 'I'm not your type.'

'But of course you are.' He caught her nervous hand. She gasped as he tugged it slowly, gently towards his bulging crotch. He gave her plenty of time to pull away. She didn't. In truth, she seemed mesmerised.

'Oh,' she moaned as he pressed it home. He decided 'oh' was his very favourite portion of her vocabulary.

'Oh,' she said again, exploring him with a surprisingly strong hand. Her fingers wandered over his swollen balls, then up his thick, stiffened shaft. Icy-hot tingles spread out from his groin as her dainty thumb dragged up the nerve-rich under-ridge. *Mon Dieu*, her touch was incredible, far more arousing than he'd expected. When she reached his glans and pushed the cloth of his trousers into its pulsing curve, he had to gulp for breath.

'You're almost as big as Bill,' she murmured.

Caught by surprise, Storm barked out a laugh.

Abby immediately released him and covered her adorable mouth. 'I can't believe I said that. I am so sorry.'

He wiped a tear of amusement from his eye. 'That's perfectly all right. Size isn't everything.' He grinned at her wail of mortification. 'I take it you have a boyfriend.'

'I used to,' she admitted and scuffed the toe of one sensible shoe atop the other. 'Maybe I should take you to your room now. I mean, just take you to your room, not ... Oh, dear, I really shouldn't have done that, should I?'

He took her trembling shoulders in his hands and squeezed until she met his eyes. 'I'm glad you touched me. I enjoyed it very much and I hope you will do it again. However,' he added, as she bit her lower lip, 'the fact that you did commits neither you nor I to anything. As far as

I'm concerned, every stage of a seduction requires permission.'

Her eyes went so wide he could see the whites all around. 'Are you planning to seduce me?'

He swept his thumbs in a half-circle around her shoulders. 'If you give me half a chance.'

'I'm not sure I'm ready to be seduced.'

When he smiled, her eyes followed the curl of his lips. 'Don't worry,' he assured her. 'I prefer to move slowly, to anticipate each small concession: the touch of a hand today, tomorrow a kiss or a smile, the day after that a slow dance under the moon. Hunger is the best sauce, you know.'

She blinked, her thick golden lashes sweeping down and then up. 'You've done this a lot, haven't you?'

The comment threw him off balance, but he was careful not to show it. 'Once or twice,' he admitted because lying could only cause trouble down the road.

'Hah.' She swept loose tendrils of hair off her forehead. 'I doubt it's only been once or twice.'

'Experience can be a lovely thing,' he said mildly.

She cast a doubtful glance from under her brows. With a pleasant skip to his heart, he realised he was going to have a bit of a chase after all. But his smile must have annoyed her. She crossed her arms and set her feet like a diminutive member of the riot police. 'I don't believe there was anything in that pasta but good cooking,' she declared.

He spread his hands as if to say: have it your way.

'Do you want the job or not?' she snapped, as much as a woman with a voice like a kitten could snap.

'Absolutely,' he said, though he wanted much, much more than a job.

With a suspicious frown, she led him on a tour of the inn, her crisp demeanor intended, he was sure, to keep him at a distance. She pointed out the staff locker rooms, the herb garden and the entrance to the now-closed north wing. He'd be staying in the south wing, she said, along with the waitress he'd met earlier. The rooms weren't anything fancy, but he'd have his own bath and he could change the furnishings however he liked.

'And nothing leaks,' she added, as though that should be the deciding factor.

He looked around the cosy sitting room. 'I like it,' he said, and he did.

An adjoining door led to a bedroom and, from there, to a pleasantly spacious bath. The furniture was all 'found' items, big fat chairs and scratched secondhand tables. Only the upholstery was new, a cheery cream-and-navy check dotted with scarlet diamonds. Another landscape photograph hung in the sitting room, this one of herons flying over a flooded marsh. He could picture himself living here after he bought the place. He needn't reopen the inn, after all. If he could not make a good income from the restaurant alone, he wasn't the chef he thought he was.

'You should air out,' she said, striding by him to fling open the inside shutters and throw up the sash.

A rose-covered cottage sat across the way, no more than a stone's throw distant. Two storeys high, it had a sharp peaked roof and the trademark dark-grey Cape Cod shingles. Swimming with roses, it looked like an illustration from a fairy tale. Its topmost window was lit against the coming night. A sight to welcome a man home, he thought, with an old hitch in his chest. In its own way, the cottage was as seductive as the inn.

'Who lives there?' he asked, coming to stand beside her.

For one telling moment she was silent. 'I do,' she said, and stalked from the room.

Storm unpacked, first his clothes, then his toys. Both bags were equally large and equally well organised. He set his personal massage oil on the small drop leaf table in front of the sitting-room window. The oil was his own recipe – a blend of sandalwood, cedar and other aromatic essences.

Much lighter than most people preferred, but effective for him.

He placed his favourite Delft blue saucer on the warming tripod and poured a pool of golden oil into it, making it a private act of grace. The flick of a match lit a small bayberry candle, which he nudged beneath the dish. At once scent rose in the air, sweetness and spice. His thigh muscles heated. His shoulders relaxed.

For a moment, he contemplated pulling out his bondage straps, perhaps the leather cuffs with the Velcro fasteners. He'd noticed a bentwood chair in the bedroom. He could secure himself to it with no trouble. His balls tightened eagerly at the idea and, as a result, he discarded it.

He did not intend to spill his seed tonight, not yet, and perhaps not at all. His passion for bondage was deep and secret. Always he indulged alone, preferring not to bare his vulnerabilities to an audience. The only people who knew of his hobby were the teenage girlfriend who'd given him his first taste, and a psychiatrist he'd consulted briefly when various childhood ghosts rose up to haunt him. Both the shrink and the girlfriend had made their natural exits from his life. Only his love of rope and strap remained. He did not regret the predilection. He could not regret anything that stirred him to such an agonising pitch of desire. Given his purpose tonight, however, the bindings might prove too stimulating.

While the oil heated, Storm removed his clothes and folded them. He looked down the lean planes and curves of his body. He was harder than usual at this stage of the proceedings, angling up a bit. The old-rose colour at the root of his cock darkened towards raspberry by the time it reached the mushroom-shaped head. He was circumcised, which he regretted sometimes, though it did put everything on show. No doubt he was not as large as Abby's former boyfriend, but no woman had ever complained about his looks and he didn't think she would, either.

Smiling to himself, he placed a bath towel over the seat

of one of the overstuffed armchairs. He adjusted the storm
shutters until they covered two thirds of the window, then
turned the chair to face the narrow view. Dusk had fallen
as he made his preparations. A standard lamp with a
pleated parchment shade lit the room behind him. Though
muted, the glow would reveal him to any passerby. That
was to the good. Storm hoped he'd be seen. In fact, his
erection stretched a good half-inch at the prospect. He did
not, however, wish to be obvious about it.

He sat and sank into the chair's embrace, then dabbled
his fingers in the warming oil. Excitement crawled over
his skin as he gazed at the lone lighted window in Abby's
cottage. A shadow moved behind the glass, slim and
small. She was home.

Let her see me, he prayed. Let her sense the current
between us and welcome its rise. A single evening in her
presence told him she was his favourite sort of woman:
not a virgin, but virtually unawakened to her erotic poten-
tial. Deep down where the self hides its secrets he knew
she was hungry even if, on the surface, she merely wondered what the fuss was about.

Oh, love, he thought, how happy I'll be to show you.

He closed his eyes. He must not be caught watching her
watch him. She must believe herself alone and safe in her
voyeurism.

He lifted his hand from the oil and moved it over his
erection. Fragrant droplets rolled down his fingers. They
fell to the bobbing head, a warm, wet patter, then ran in
tickly rivulets down his shaft and over his balls. He pulled
his feet on to the cushion of the chair, narrow feet with
long, agile toes. For an instant, he imagined them digging
into her mattress as he pressed slowly inside her. Would
her bed be soft like her? Would it smell of lavender and
musk? Shaking off the image, he let his knees sag on to
the chair's plump arms. A cool breeze slipped between the
shutters and ruffled the hair around his anus. He was
completely exposed now.

He dipped his hand in the oil again and let fall another rain of drops. His blood seemed to thicken in his veins. With the smallest sigh, he cupped his scrotal sac and began to massage his balls.

Was she watching yet, he wondered behind his shuttered lids, and what would he wish her to see if she was? Something that would shock her a bit. Something that would capture her attention and refuse to let it go.

He dipped his second hand in the oil and curled it into the furrow between his cheeks. Anal play excited him almost as much as bondage, but the risk was worth it. He would like her to know this about him, for the day when she changed from tempted to temptress.

Blowing his breath out lightly, he circled the puckered ring of muscle, then pushed his left middle finger firmly inside, down to the webbing. His thumb he centred over the Jen-Mo spot, an acupressure point midway between his anus and scrotum. Thus poised to halt ejaculation the moment it threatened, he willed his hand to stillness. The two pressures, on his perineum and in his anus, were pleasurable but not unbearably so.

And now to begin, he thought. With his right hand, he grasped his oily shaft, thumb on top and two fingers enclosing the ridge. He pulled upward, easing his grip as he approached the head, tightening it as he neared the less-sensitive root. Despite the precaution, his arousal spiked quickly. He couldn't help but think of her watching; couldn't help imagining how her hand would feel performing this service, small but strong, gentle but curious.

The image was too powerful. He had to back off. He lightened his strokes until his touch barely skimmed the surface of his cock. Even so, his skin stung with sensitivity, especially the drum-tight surface of the head. He felt a drop that was not oil roll down the glans. He forced himself to breath deeply, slowly. When that didn't calm him, he let go altogether.

Relax, he told himself. You've done this hundreds of times. You are not going to lose control tonight. He breathed in. He breathed out. He took hold of his shaft and resumed the massage. This time he allowed his stroke to rise only to the flare of the head. *C'est mieux*, he thought, better.

Just as he was congratulating himself, a bird took flight in the grassy space between the inn and the cottage. He started at the flurry of wings. Adrenaline flooded his bloodstream. He almost opened his eyes. Had Abby's appearance at the window alarmed the bird? Was she truly there? His excitement level surged so abruptly he had to administer a bracing pinch to keep himself from going over the top.

After a short rest, he began masturbating again, then stopped again. Four times, he repeated this pattern, each time rising more swiftly towards the point of no return. Thoughts of Abby disrupted his usual control: her soft pink lips tugging at his nipples, her thick, sun-bright hair sweeping his groin, the arch of her neck as she climaxed – all figments of his imagination but so vivid he realised tonight could be no demonstration of stamina. He must end it, and quickly, or he'd never be able to restrain himself.

Soon, he promised his clamouring cock. He was so hard now he had to pull the shaft back from his belly. He pumped harder, his fingers tight, almost rough. He gave his sensation-starved glans the attention it wanted, enclosing it with fingers and thumb at the top of every pull. His skin was hot and slick, his veins popping in tiny ropes of blue. Ah, it felt good. He never wanted to stop, but his balls were rucking up in preparation, his thighs burning. His anus quivered round the finger that pierced it. He should stop. This second, he should stop.

He squeezed out one more pump. His seed seemed to boil inside him. Out, it wanted out. One more stroke, he pleaded, risking it, loving it, but then his limit was reached. His orgasm was a breath away, a looming pressure, an ache. The first contraction fluttered. He dug his left thumb into the Jen-Mo point, halting his seminal fluid just as it exploded down his urethra.

A single, scalding spurt escaped the tip of his cock, then stopped as he increased the pressure of his thumb. He uttered a curse he couldn't hear over the roaring in his ears. Then he came in earnest – hard throbs of sensation, an orgasm slowed to quarter speed and cranked to quadruple intensity. His cock twitched with each contraction but emitted no more fluid. He came, for one minute, then another. His thighs jerked closer to his chest. He gasped for breath, his body dripping sweat. He flung his head against the back of the chair. He wriggled the finger that nestled inside his anus and came again.

Dieu, he thought, his brain reduced to one-syllable words. God. Sweet.

The contractions diminished, the sea of pleasure calming. He sighed and opened his eyes. He looked out the window towards the cottage . . .

And saw a slender shadow dart behind a curtain.

The memory of his pleasure haunted her. She lay in bed in her T-shirt and panties, with the covers shoved to her waist, and she remembered.

He'd been completely exposed. He'd pulled his feet on to the navy cushion and thrust his knees wide. She'd seen the dark pucker of his anus, and the finger he'd pushed inside. He'd opened his legs like a woman who wants to be filled, and yet she'd never sensed anyone's masculinity more forcefully. She'd been quivering with awareness, dripping with it.

He'd stroked himself. He'd oiled the stiff, thick rod so that it glistened in the lamplight. He loved his own cock; she knew from the way he touched it. He'd lingered, he'd teased, starting and stopping, starting and stopping, until she'd pressed her thighs together on a sharp throb of sympathetic longing.

Her fingers had twitched. She'd wanted to touch his swollen flesh herself, but even more she'd wanted him to come; wanted to see his hard shower of seed. That tiny jet had not satisfied her. She'd wanted fountains, oceans. Instead, he showed her that long, dry, bone-shaking convulsion. The length of it distracted her from her disappointment, and awed her. She'd thought it would never end. She'd thought she might come herself just by watching.

In all her life, she'd had two lovers: a boy in college and Bill. Nonetheless, she knew this wasn't ordinary male behaviour, neither the ritualistic auto-eroticism, nor the orgasm that wracked his body like an electric shock and refused to let go. How long had it lasted? Two minutes? Three? Had she ever seen anything like his transcendent, tormented expression?

Storm was different from other men.

Abby slid her hands down her body and cupped her panty-covered mound. She'd worked herself to three hard orgasms since she'd fled behind the curtain – three, and felt as if she'd had none; she was that hungry. This wasn't like her. Once had always been all she'd ever wanted. Had he put something in the pasta?

'Nonsense,' she said aloud for the reassurance of hearing the word. She'd watched him prepare the meal. There was nothing in that dish that wasn't perfectly ordinary.

No, his exhibition had done this to her. He'd opened his eyes at the end. Had he seen her? Had he meant for her to see? But what sort of man masturbated for an audience? A dirty old man with a raincoat, she thought. Except it wasn't like that. She couldn't say how it was different, only that it was.

She clenched her hands in front of her mouth. Maybe it was different because he'd known she wanted to see. But how had this stranger known what she hadn't known herself? Frustrated, Abby flopped on to her side. This isn't like me, she thought. This isn't me. She turned off the lamp with the fat red roses on the shade. She was exhausted. She needed sleep. But Storm followed her into her dreams.

They were waltzing on the beach under a crescent moon. She didn't actually know how to waltz but she swooped like a feather on the hard, damp sand. As they turned, her gown fluttered, filmy and white with a touch of innocence – like Clara's nightdress in the *Nutcracker* ballet. Like a true prince he danced her through the foamy edge of the waves. He smiled at her and didn't drop his eyes. She wished she could see them better. The dream was misty.

'I can't feel you,' she complained.

He pulled her closer, his palm pressing the small of her back. He was naked. 'Is that better?' he asked.

She squirmed, wanting to brand herself with the whole, hard imprint of him. His hip brushed her hip, his chest her breast. But the sensations wouldn't coalesce.

'It's not enough,' she said.

'Don't worry.' He brushed a wisp of hair from her face. 'Tonight I will lay the secret in your hands.'

She started awake and bit back an unladylike curse. Her body throbbed as though he'd teased her to the edge of satisfaction and left her hanging. The dream seemed so close, so vivid, she could almost hear the echo of his final words.

She shivered and hugged herself, then stiffened at a sudden sense of wrongness. The room was dark. The moon lit the other side of the house. The nearest illumination was the security lamps at the front of the inn. She listened, but heard nothing except her own quickened breathing and the waltz-like sweep of the curtains on the floorboards. The curtains were satin printed in large pink and yellow roses. Their hems pooled on the floor the way the Victorians used to favour, to prove they could afford more than just what they needed.

What had Storm said? 'A little too much is just right.' But how much was too much, and did he mean sex as well as food? Her pussy swelled, heavy and warm.

Something was different. The window was open. She'd left it open, but had she left it open so far? Had the breeze picked up since she went to bed? Was that why the curtains billowed out that way?

The sound made her think of sheets rustling, of making love to a stranger, slowly in the dark, without a word, just push and pull, push and pull, and throaty cries above the rustling of the sheets. She put both hands to one breast and pushed it back against her ribs. Her nipple was so hard.

A shadow detached itself from the shadow by the window.

'Pleasant dream?' it asked.

Abby's shriek was pathetic, a squeaky inhalation no louder than a mouse.

'What are you doing here?' she said, once she'd found her voice. She should have been outraged, or terrified. She was a little frightened, but it was a butterfly-in-the-stomach sort of fear. She knew the intruder's identity, of course. The way he moved gave him away: silent, confident, like an Indian rajah. He even smelt of India: sandalwood and other, more exotic spices, perhaps from the oil he'd used to rub his cock. In her mind she saw his hand again, squeezing up that thick column of flesh. She bit her lower lip.

'I thought you might want company,' he said.

I don't, she tried to say, but he was there, looming over the bed, and the words wouldn't come. Her body was melting, not just her quim, but her breasts, her bones, her tongue. She wanted company all right – his.

He pulled the light blanket down her body, then the sheet, like someone unveiling a work of art. Abby shivered. He laid his palm over her belly, pressing lightly through her T-shirt. Like magic, her shivering ceased. She was hot. His hand was hot. Was it normal to have hands that hot?

'May I remove this?' he asked, touching the hem of the cotton shirt.

She knew that if she said 'yes' to this, she'd say 'yes' to anything that might follow. But how could she refuse? She might never get another chance to sleep with a man like this, a man she'd wanted the instant she met him. Unable to speak, she nodded.

Even in the dark, he saw.

'Thank you,' he said, as though this didn't happen every day, as though he were someone who had to ask. He removed her T-shirt and panties, then folded both and laid them over the foot of the bed. Abby smiled. He was a neat-freak, she thought, liking him better for that small eccentricity.

'Tonight is for you,' he said, his accent even more wonderful in the shadowed hush, 'for your pleasure.'

'And not for yours?' she was bold enough to ask.

He growled. Really, she couldn't call it anything but a growl, soft though the sound was. The effect was delicious, like a finger trailing down her spine. Almost before she knew what he was doing he'd climbed on to the high tester bed. He crouched over her on hands and knees.

'I will definitely take pleasure in this,' he said. 'But tonight I wish to explore, not to experience, to discover what pleases you and what doesn't. For that I need all my concentration.'

'Oh,' she said, and wished she knew how to play his lush, verbal games, how to make him quiver with longing at the sound of her voice. It was probably too much to hope that he would stick around long enough to teach her.

Feeling wistful, as if this were already goodbye, she lifted her arms and lightly clasped his waist. His skin was warm and smooth, his flesh solid. He bent his head and kissed her, a slow, deep insinuation of tongue to tongue. After four years with Bill, kissing a man without a beard felt strange. Storm's lips were soft, his jaw shaved very close. He tasted faintly of anise, perfect for a woman with a sweet tooth. She moaned when he withdrew.

'No promises,' he murmured, the words tickling her lips. 'No obligations. Only pleasure.'

It sounded so appealing when he said it. 'No obligations. Only pleasure.' Hadn't she had enough of obligations, what with Bill and the restaurant and her sisters' children who were, face it, the teeniest bit bratty?

'Only pleasure,' she agreed, and felt him smile against her cheek.

Storm ran his hands down her body, one long sweep from shoulders to feet. She had the most incredible skin, smooth as silk, but not as fragile. More like velvet. The flesh beneath was soft and firm. He circled the gentle mounds of her breasts, then her belly. She tensed. A vulnerable spot, he thought, and bent to kiss it, gently, softly, until she relaxed.

Her legs were longer than he expected, and stronger. He lifted one foot and found a callus behind the heel. Perhaps she ran. That would explain the well-developed muscle of her thigh, the apple-firm round of her calf.

Her feet were small. The length of his hand covered her sole. He sucked a curled toe into his mouth and laved it with his tongue. She squirmed. Her musk rose in the air. She was silent, though, as if shyness held her cries inside. No matter, he thought. The other signs of her pleasure would read all the more clearly.

He kissed a path up her legs and parted her petals with his thumbs. Her sex glistened in the dimness, running like an open honeycomb. He inhaled deeply. Her scent swirled through his head, rich, sweet, and tinged with an exotic spice that was purely her own. That scent called to him, as if some celestial perfumer had designed her with him in mind. He was so hard his skin felt ready to burst. His testicles hung like stones in their drawn-up pouch. The temptation to eat her juicy peach until she begged for mercy was strong.

That, however, was a pleasure for another night.

He continued his upward progress, lips preceding fingers up arms, across shoulders. He found another sweet spot under her chin, a tender little pillow of flesh. He nuzzled it until her arms came round his back. Then he laid a trail of kisses to her breasts. The lightest touch of his tongue on her nipple broke her silence. Ah, her breasts were sensitive. One cry followed another as he suckled and plucked and nipped the sharpened tips. Her legs scissored on the mattress. Her hips thrust upward, seeking penetration. He had to lift his body to remove his half-crazed cock from temptation's path.

She whimpered at his retreat but he filled her with his fingers – just two fingers, for she was tight. Her warm, thick folds clung to his knuckles as he worked her, his thumb firm on her button, his mouth busy at her breasts.

'Please.' Her head thrashed from side to side on the pillow. She seemed unable to get where she wished to go. 'Please.'

He took her hand and placed it over his. She did not move. She seemed afraid to guide him. 'Show me,' he said, and kissed her full on the mouth.

Her tongue reached for his. She sighed, and then shyly she moved his thumb. She swept it from one side of her clit to the other, rubbing the slippery hood across the shaft. When he'd caught the motion she wanted, she pressed the back of his hand as if to say: a little harder.

Good girl, he wanted to say, but feared she'd take offence.

He brought her off three times, each hard and quick.

'Enough,' she gasped, though her body still squirmed around his fingers.

He let her rest for a moment, then sat back on his heels. 'I want to show you something.'

'I don't think I can stand any more,' she pleaded even as her sheath rippled and clung.

'One more special one,' he insisted, and curled a third finger into her body. After three orgasms, the swelling behind her pubic bone was unmistakable, a delectable, fluid-filled cushion. He pressed upward, slowly increasing the pressure until at the last he was lifting her weight off the bed.

'Oh, my God,' she said. 'What is that? That is so . . . oh, my God!'

He chuckled, delighted to be the first to introduce her to this pleasure.

'Abigail Coates,' he said, 'meet your G-spot.'

He covered her mound with his second hand and captured her clit between finger and thumb. She groaned. Lightly, he pinched the hood over the shaft and sleeked it up and down – not her motion, but one he thought she might like.

She did. Her hips struggled towards his hand. Her breaths came in aspirated moans.

'Please,' she said, completely beyond shyness. 'Make me come. Oh, God, I can't stand it!' Before the wail faded, her body bent up like a bow. Her sheath clenched tight. He pressed harder, within and without.

'Oh,' she cried, 'oh . . .' and spurted all over his hand.

It was over in five deep shudders. She sagged back against the bed. He petted her gently down before removing his sopping fingers. He was glad she hadn't realised she'd ejaculated. Some women got nervous about that, thought they'd lost control of their bladder. He could explain the difference to Abby some other night.

'That was incredible,' she said. 'I've never felt anything so intense. How did you know I could do that?'

He bent to kiss the tip of her nose. 'I make it my business to know.'

'Your business,' she said, a funny note in her voice.

'My avocation,' he clarified.

She seemed to like that answer better because she twined her arms behind his neck and pulled his head deeper into the kiss. Mm, she had a nice mouth, firm but pliant. He hovered over her, enjoying it, the tip of his cock throbbing painfully in time to his heart. He wanted to spill, needed to, but it would wait; just a little longer, it would wait.

Abby loved his tender exploration of his mouth, that one luscious point of intermingling. She wanted more, though. Every inch of her skin was hungry for contact. She wanted all of him to touch her. Most especially, she wanted to feel his cock. She wanted to feel what she'd done to him. She needed to know he was as hard now as he'd been when he was sprawled in that chair, rubbing himself the way he liked best.

'I want you touch me,' she said, the words bursting out, hot and impetuous.

He reached above her to turn on a lamp, a sudden and shocking exposure. She flushed as he drew back on to his knees, kneeling over her like a conqueror. His hands played lightly over her breasts. 'Where would you like me to touch you?'

Not where, she thought, I want you to touch me with your cock.

'Anywhere,' she said, and could have kicked herself.

He knew she was lying. He knew. He leant down and tutted in her ear. His hair, shaggy and smooth as silk, tickled her cheek. 'Tell me what you want, love. Whisper it in my ear.'

Oh, if only he hadn't turned on the light. But he kissed her eyebrow very gently and the courage came. 'Touch me with your cock,' she whispered.

A shudder coursed through him, a glorious, carnal shudder.

'Ah,' he said, and set his teeth to her earlobe, as though the tension inside him demanded immediate expression. His knees shifted. The heat of his groin approached hers. 'Where shall I touch you with my cock? Here?'

The satiny tip brushed from her knee to the top of her thigh. There it stilled, pressing softly, rhythmically against the valley that bordered her fleece.

'You're sticky,' she said, then wondered if that was the wrong thing to say.

He chuckled. When he spoke, his voice was rougher than before. 'I am overeager tonight.'

The admission, and the huskiness, thrilled her. 'Touch me all over.'

'With this?' He drew a curve around her belly with the hot, sticky head, then flattened the thick length of it over her hipbone. 'Or this?'

Abby rolled into the pressure. 'Yes. Both. All over.'

This time his chuckle was just an expulsion of breath. 'Want to test my limits, do you?'

'I want you to come.'

His cock jerked. 'Ah,' he said.

She loved that word in his mouth, a sigh of understanding and approval – and pleasure.

He said no more. He rubbed her with his velvet-wrapped hardness, up her thighs, around her belly. He rolled her on to her front and caressed her bottom, every inch of either cheek and then the crease between, with the head, with the shaft, with the soft-hard crush of his balls. He measured the small of her back, and trailed up the sides of her body until he could thrust once, slowly, into the pit of each arm.

Settling his knees beside her shoulders, he smoothed her hair backwards over her head, on to the pillow, and rubbed his cock along the nape of her neck. He probed each side, pushing along the underside of her jaw. Delicious, she thought, like having your whole body

111

fucked instead of just your pussy. She purred at the feel of it, then squirmed on to her back.

'I know what I want now,' she said.

His cock jutted directly towards her face, stiff but tremulous, vibrating with the blood trapped inside. She kissed the swollen cap of the head. Oh, it was so smooth and hot, like living satin. She licked it. It jerked under her tongue.

'No,' he said, and his voice was very low, very dark. 'Not that. Not until you know me better.'

She almost laughed. His cock was straining towards her lips, practically sitting up and begging. But that hadn't been what she meant to do, in any case. The sight of him had distracted her from her original goal. 'This,' she said, pushing her small breasts together to form a shallow channel. 'I want you to come here, where I can see you.'

'Ah,' he said, relief in the word this time. He lowered himself. His hip popped slightly and then he sighed as she embraced him with her breasts.

He thrust slowly but firmly, pacing himself. She tilted her head to watch. His cock and hips filled all her vision. He had tan marks on his hipbones. She guessed he liked revealing bathing suits. He'd look gorgeous in a little Speedo – even a thong. The hollows at the side of his muscular buttocks were well worth showing off. Even his pubic hair was beautiful. A wild thick growth at the base of his belly, it gleamed in tight black curls, as if he'd oiled it along with his penis. His balls rolled back and forth over her ribs as he thrust. She squeezed her flesh tighter, surrounding more of him. He gasped and braced his weight on his arms.

His strokes lengthened until he butted the softness under her chin, the little cushion he'd loved with his earlier kiss. He left his fluid on her flesh; he was dripping now, a clear sweet trail of eagerness.

'Come,' she said.

He choked out something she couldn't understand. Her hands occupied in holding herself around him, she lifted one knee and caressed the sweaty upper curve of his buttocks.

'Come,' she whispered. 'I want you to come all over me.'

'Jesus Christ,' he said, his accent so thick she almost couldn't decipher the words.

He pushed harder, faster. The friction burnt the tender skin between her breasts, friction and his own inner heat. She watched him watch his penis. The muscles of his face tightened. His skin went dark like an Arab's. She knew he was going to come any second, so she shifted her gaze to his cock. Like his face, it was darker and stiffer. The cap was red and shiny, growing even fuller as she watched. He moved faster still. A cry caught in his throat. He held his breath. The eye at the tip seemed to widen, darken, deepen.

Yes, she thought, yes, and he came, an explosive burst of white, hot against her chin, wet running down her neck and over her breasts as he pulled back and shoved again, still pulsing, each jet shooting strong and hard as though his entire supply must burst free in an instant.

Seconds later it was over. His arms shook from holding his weight. She stroked his shoulders and his elbows buckled. He eased himself on to her. He laid his head on her sticky breast. His eyes slid shut as she stroked his hair. He was easy to hold, not all that much heavier than her.

Sleep, she thought, even as she felt him fight it. She wanted him here in the morning, wanted him in her arms. Not likely, she thought, but she could pretend.

Forbidden Fruit

Susie Raymond

Beth is 38, and Jonathan is 16. They work in the same shop in the same small village and are both in their sexual prime. When Beth realises that Jonathan's spying on her in the staff changing rooms, she cannot believe it. Later, when she catches him playing with himself, she is so amused and aroused – and he is so embarrassed – that she suddenly finds herself having a lot of power over the young lad.

To Jonathan, Beth is so much more exciting than girls his own age. She's a sexy woman with experience and he has so much to learn. But Beth is aware that she's playing a dangerous game. If his mother found out what she was doing with her son, there would be hell to pay. The problem is, Beth's enjoying her evenings of secret lust with the fit young Jonathan. He's willing to do anything she asks, and at his age, is always ready for action.

With *Forbidden Fruit*, Susie Raymond has written a taboo-busting story of lust between an older woman and a teenage boy. And it's great. The naturalistic setting and fun-loving attitude of the characters make this a hugely enjoyable read. Susie's other Black Lace novel is *Taking Liberties* – where Beth is concentrating on her new career, and behaving just as badly!

Forbidden Fruit

*T*his must be the last time, Beth promised herself, as she bathed and dressed that Saturday evening. I'll just get him to entertain me once more, so that he is in no doubt about who's in charge, then I'll tell him that's the end of it, once and for all.

She was not really surprised when Jonathan turned up at her house slightly earlier than the first time. She had been ready for over twenty minutes herself.

'You know where the living room is,' she told him as soon as she had closed the front door behind him. There was no need for her to play at being the perfect hostess any more.

As she followed him down the hallway, Beth smoothed down her new black skirt and reflected that it was probably just as well that this would be the last time. Her bank manager would have a fit if she didn't stop splashing out on new clothes!

Without waiting to be asked, Jonathan sat down on the settee and stared up at her hungrily.

'Do you want a coffee?' she asked him as she pretended to ignore the way he was already undoing the buttons on her blouse with his eyes.

Jonathan shook his head and reached out to take hold of her arm. Before she could stop him, he had pulled her down on the settee beside him. He pushed her back against the cushions, placed one arm either side of her, and leaned forward to kiss her. His full body weight pushed against her so that she couldn't escape.

Beth closed her eyes and lay back, enjoying the feel of his lips against hers. When he pushed them open with his tongue this time, she did nothing to resist.

As he increased the pressure of the kiss, Jonathan moved his hands down on to her breasts. He ran his fingers across her nipples and she felt them spring up in response to his touch.

Beth whimpered softly, thrilled by the feel of his hands on her body. She imagined his penis growing harder and pushing up against his jeans. When he began opening her buttons, she still did nothing to stop him. She shivered with anticipation at the idea of feeling his hands inside her clothing and against her skin.

She jumped as his fingers slipped inside her top and began to caress her hardened nipples through the flimsy material of her bra. Her breasts were aching to be fondled. She was almost tempted to reach up and pull her bra out of the way herself.

Jonathan seemed to be shaking with desire. As he leaned over her, she could actually feel the hardness of his erection. He seemed even more turned on than last week by the feel of her breasts and the pressure of her lips against his. As he sucked urgently on her tongue, she shivered with pleasure at the sensation.

His hands visibly trembling, Jonathan slid his fingers down her stomach and into the waistband of her skirt. Beth moaned softly and raised her bottom slightly off the settee. Jonathan's excitement seemed to increase even more. As he pushed his hand down under the elastic of her panties, she noticed he was squeezing his own thighs together tightly as if to control himself.

His fingers made contact with the top of her pubic hair and he sighed with a mixture of success and anticipation. Beth flinched and Jonathan sighed again. Slowly, his fingers began to slide down into her panties. Beth stiffened. Any second now, he would be touching her there. He would feel how wet she was and know how excited he had made her. This wasn't what she had planned at all.

Reluctantly, Beth reached down and grabbed his arm. She pulled his hand up out of the top of her skirt and pushed him away.

'No,' she whispered. 'That's far enough.' In her excitement, her voice sounded much harder and angrier than she had intended.

Jonathan sat up guiltily, his excitement visibly receding. He stared at her in shock and confusion. 'What? Why?'

Beth wriggled out from underneath his arms and stood up. Her top gaped open and she saw his eyes lock on to her erect nipples.

'I definitely think it's time we had some coffee,' she suggested shakily. 'Stay here,' she commanded over her shoulder as she left the room. She certainly didn't want him following her again. She needed time to pull herself together.

Jesus! She had almost let things get out of hand that time. How could she possibly hope to control Jonathan if she couldn't even keep control of herself?

When she returned a few minutes later carrying two mugs of coffee, her face was still flushed and her eyes were unusually large and bright. She saw the look of disappointment cross his face as he noticed that she had rebuttoned her top.

Without speaking, Beth leaned over beside him to place the coffee on the table, careful to bend from the waist as she had practised. She glanced sideways to check his expression and smiled inwardly at the look on his face. She knew how high her skirt had ridden up.

'As I said the other day, I think that you are going to

have to be punished again, Jonathan,' she told him, as she straightened up slowly and sat back down beside him.

Jonathan gazed at her silently. When she saw the look of resignation on his face, Beth sighed with relief. She was certain he already knew what she was going to make him do. She was also certain that he would not be able to refuse her. However embarrassing it was to do it in front of her, his desperate desire was more urgent.

She had taken command again. She was back in charge of the situation. She was still scared at how close it had come to getting out of control. Just a few more seconds and she might have let him do whatever he had wanted with her.

Beth turned towards him and reached down to undo the button of his jeans. Using both hands, she started slowly pulling down the zipper. Jonathan closed his eyes.

Gradually, Beth peeled back the edges of his jeans as if she were unwrapping a birthday present. Excitedly, she examined the bulge in his pants. There could be no doubt about what she was doing to him.

'Lift yourself up and pull them down,' she commanded hoarsely.

With his eyes still closed, Jonathan obeyed her. His erect penis stuck up in the air in front of her, its shiny tip already wet. Beth marvelled at how hard he was.

Without taking her eyes off his erection, she raised her skirt and turned to straddle him so that she was perched across his knees, facing him, with one leg on either side of his thighs. She could feel Jonathan trembling at the silky touch of her stockings against his bare flesh. He opened his eyes and stared excitedly at the tantalising glimpse of her panties, just inches from his cock.

Beth raised herself and leaned forward to lift the bottom of his T-shirt. His eyes were now staring straight down the front of her top and the lace of her panties was just inches above his quivering erection. As if by instinct,

Jonathan raised his own buttocks and thrust himself upward.

Beth pushed him firmly back down on to the cushion and raised his shirt higher, forcing his arms up into the air as she pulled it over his head. She ran her fingers lightly down his chest, loving the way his skin twitched and fluttered at her touch. She sat back and ran her eyes over his erection again. Gently, she tightened the muscles of her own thighs so that she was pressed hard against him. Jonathan lay rigid, as though hardly daring even to breathe.

Slowly, Beth lifted one leg and climbed off him so that she was kneeling beside him on the cushion. She heard his sigh of disappointment. Hesitantly, as if half-afraid it might bite back, she reached out with one hand and closed her fingers round the shaft of his penis.

Jonathan drew a sharp breath and his cock lurched in her hand. Beth stared at it in surprise. She hadn't expected it would be able to move like that. It was almost as if it had a life and mind of its own. A strange tingling sensation ran down the back of her thighs.

Fascinated, she moved her hand slowly down the shaft until her little finger was resting against the soft pubic hairs around its base. Jonathan shuddered from head to foot, his face screwed up in a tight grimace. His cock twitched again.

The feeling of power returned and intensified. Beth felt exhilarated by the effect she was having on him. Her face intent with concentration, she moved her hand gently back up towards the tip then down again, trying to imitate the way she had seen him move his own hand.

Jonathan parted his lips and took a couple of deep, ragged breaths. He began moving his head slowly back and forth, his face twisted. Beth looked back down and noticed that he was clenching his thighs tightly together and rolling his hips from side to side as if he was desperate for a pee. She knew what that felt like.

Smiling with pleasure, she increased the speed of her pumping, using her fingers to squeeze him gently as her hand slid up and down the length of his cock.

Suddenly, his whole body went rigid. He raised his hand and placed it urgently over hers.

'No,' he whispered, trying to stop her hand moving.

Thinking he was trying to push her away, Beth instinctively tightened her grip, squeezing him even more firmly between her fingers and totally unaware of the devastating effect her vicelike grip was having on him. Hesitantly, she put her other hand down between his legs and began to fondle the base of his testicles as she had seen him doing.

Jonathan groaned again. His penis was twitching violently in her hands, obviously only seconds from exploding. Still she didn't release him. His whole body squirmed. He groaned even louder and Beth squeezed him again.

'Oh God, please,' he begged softly.

Shocked by his submissive tone, Beth relaxed her grip.

Immediately, a spurt of fluid burst out of him and flew up into his face. As Jonathan moaned with relief, the first spurt was rapidly followed by another. He reached down to grab himself.

With a strength she didn't know she possessed, Beth caught his hands and pinned them back to his sides, her fingers digging into his arms in her urgency not to miss what was happening. Jonathan sank back and let himself go. His muscles continued to tense then relax as each spurt tore from him and his chest grew damp and sticky with his spunk.

Finally, it was over. Jonathan slumped down against the cushions, totally spent. His bottom had slipped down over the edge of the settee and his legs were slightly apart. He began wriggling up.

'Lie still,' Beth commanded as she placed her hands on his chest to push him back. She wanted to see how quickly his erection went down.

Obediently, Jonathan stopped struggling. He closed his

eyes. As if he could feel her eyes watching his prick shrinking, he started to blush. Pushing himself with his heels, he renewed his efforts to sit up.

Beth lifted her hands off his chest and stared at the warm white come covering her fingers. She smelled its faint, not unpleasant, odour. She sighed softly, reluctantly accepting that it was all over.

'I expect you can still remember your way to the bathroom, can't you?' she whispered, as she stood up and headed out to the kitchen to wash her own hands.

Long after he had cleaned up and gone home, Beth sat quietly on the settee and sipped her drink. What had she been thinking of? There was no way that what she had just done to him could be considered a form of punishment. Worse, she had let him go without saying anything about her decision that it was time to put an end to the whole thing.

Beth squirmed guiltily and her face reddened as the vivid images of her actions raced through her mind. It was one thing taking it upon herself to punish him for his behaviour towards her – although, even then, if she were completely honest with herself, the way she had gone about it was somewhat debatable! She blushed deeper at the thought of him lying, half-naked, across her knee with his buttocks in the air and his erection pressed against her thighs. And, as for what she had just done to him . . .

The truth was, she had been indulging herself at his expense. Satisfying her own curiosity under the flimsy pretext of teaching him a lesson. The fact that he appeared to be enjoying the experience as much as she was, was no excuse. She had been shamelessly taking advantage of him. At her age, she ought to know better.

Beth sighed heavily. Why did it all seem so sordid and depraved in retrospect? When he was actually there with her, it seemed so natural and harmless. Like a teacher coaxing a willing student. Even if, in some ways, the student was more advanced than the teacher.

What a mess. Beth finished her drink and went out to the kitchen for a refill. What should she do now? Would Jonathan accept it if she just told him it was over, or would he make a fuss? Perhaps he actually believed himself to be in love with her. Young emotions could be so intense and the last thing she wanted to do was to hurt him. She wasn't ready to let him go yet, either.

They could hardly have a proper relationship though, could they? Beth couldn't help smiling at the idea of the two of them going out to dinner together, perhaps on to the theatre to take in a play.

No, whatever Jonathan might feel for her or she for him, she had to face the fact that their relationship could never be considered normal or acceptable. It would be far better just to finish it before it led to real trouble.

She decided that she would just say nothing. She could act friendly but distant at work and let things take their own course. He would get the message. Before long, he would find a girl his own age and forget all about her. She felt a sudden rush of jealousy at the idea of him with that young blonde girl she'd seen flirting with him at the local swimming baths. Her own Saturday evenings were destined to be pretty dull and boring from now on. Beth sighed again.

As Jonathan lay in his bed that night, his mind was going round and round in circles. What had he done wrong? Why had she suddenly become so angry with him? He had been so sure that she was going to let him have her properly. He had been certain that she wanted it as much as he did. He had felt the way she was trembling, seen the flush of her skin and felt how hard her nipples had become under his fingers.

Everything had been all right until he had tried to put his hands inside her panties. Despite his confusion, Jonathan shivered at the memory of the feel of her. He had never touched a woman there. God, he had been so close.

And, as for the way she had pleasured him like that with her hand! His cock jerked against the duvet and he put his hand down quickly to hold himself. Christ, the way it had felt when she had held him like that, stopping him letting go. He would never forget it. It was as if his prick had been about to burst wide open with the pressure. Why hadn't he known about that? Did all women know how to do that to a man? Holding it off until he had thought he would die with the agony and the ecstasy of it.

Why had she done that, but not let him have her? Perhaps he had been in too much of a rush. Maybe she had wanted him to move more slowly. Slowly! He sighed again at the thought of how close he had come. He wanted her so much.

As soon as he walked through the door of the shop the following week, Beth knew that she was in trouble. All her careful rationalising, which had seemed so obvious and logical at the time, had taken no account of the way she felt when he looked up at her hungrily and began undressing her with his eyes.

'Hello, Jonathan,' she said breathlessly, feeling immediately flustered by his eager gaze. 'There's a big stack of boxes out the back that Mr Bailey wants you to take care of this morning,' she added quickly.

Jonathan nodded. 'OK. I'll see to them in a minute,' he replied as he walked across to stand beside her. He looked around as if to make quite sure that they were alone then took her arm to pull her towards him. Beth stiffened.

'What do you think you're doing?' she hissed angrily.

Jonathan ignored her and began running his hands all over her body.

'Let go of me.' Beth pulled away from his roaming fingers and stared at him furiously. 'Don't ever do that again,' she shouted, her fear feeding her rage. 'Not here in the shop where someone might see us. Now, go and take care of those boxes.'

Jonathan smiled triumphantly and turned away to head out the back. Beth rested her elbows on the counter and struggled to get herself back under control. Things had got more out of hand than she had realised. How dare he try to grab her like that in the middle of the shop? A customer might have walked in and seen them. What if his mother had walked in? It might be a good idea to take care not to be alone with him at work for a while.

She decided that she really would have to give him a serious talking to. Do something to make quite sure he understood his position with her. When he came round to her house later, she would have to teach him a lesson he would never forget.

When she left the shop that lunchtime, she had another adult magazine in her shopping bag. There was an intriguing article in it about bondage that she was looking forward to studying more closely later. Coupled with what she had recently read at the library, one or two ideas were already forming in her mind on that subject.

By seven o'clock that evening, she was ready and watching for him out of the kitchen window.

As he opened the gate and strolled casually up the front path, Beth examined his face, trying to gauge his mood. She didn't like the hungry, almost cocky, expression in his eyes. It was the same expression he had worn in the shop earlier. Her own face hardened. No matter what happened tonight, she was determined that he would be left in no doubt who was the boss. After she had finished with him this time, he wouldn't even dare look at her in the shop without permission.

She opened the door at his second, impatient, ring.

'Jonathan?' She feigned surprise. 'I don't remember inviting you round tonight.' She suppressed a grin at the sudden look of insecurity on his face. That's it. Start as you mean to go on, she congratulated herself. She licked her lips and hesitated.

'Well, now you're here, I suppose you might as well come in.' She struggled to suppress another smile as the look of fear on his face changed to one of hopeful expectation.

As Beth led the way into the living room, she was very aware of him following closely in her wake with his eyes locked on the swing of her hips. She smiled happily to herself, knowing that she was looking good.

She was dressed, as last week, in her short black skirt and button-through jumper, and her hair was fluffed out around her face and hanging loose down her back. She knew that she had never looked more desirable. Let him look, she told herself. That was all he was going to do. If he thought she was going to give him any opportunity to take advantage of her tonight, he had another think coming. For once, she was going to have all the fun while he looked on.

She quickly stifled the panic already rising inside her and reminded herself of the effect of what she was going to do was sure to have on him. 'The power is all mine,' she muttered to herself. 'I am in control here. I can do anything I want with him.'

Jonathan hovered awkwardly in the middle of the living room. She could see that he was already feeling less sure of himself than the last time he had been there. The cold way she had greeted him had obviously had the intended effect. Now she needed to push her advantage before she lost it.

'OK. Strip.' Beth was standing by the settee, just out of his reach, with her hands on her hips. Her face was completely expressionless. She didn't want him to have any idea about what was going to happen to him until it was too late.

'I said, strip,' she repeated loudly, when he made no

move to obey her. She forced herself to look stern. Jonathan stared at her in silence, his eyes huge.

'Well? What are you waiting for? Or do I have to do it myself? I would have thought you were a bit big to need help undressing.' Beth found she quite liked the idea of doing it for him. She took a step towards him.

'What are you going to do to me?' he questioned, his voice high-pitched with apprehension.

Beth shook her head. 'Nothing,' she replied. 'I'm not even going to touch you.'

Jonathan cringed. Beth was certain she knew exactly what was going through his mind. He thought she was going to force him to do it in front of her again. Was he ever in for a surprise!

Wordlessly, Jonathan turned away from her and began to remove his clothes. The blood was already rushing to his face again. Beth smiled triumphantly and her eyes narrowed as she watched his outer clothing disappear. She would never tire of looking at his body.

Reduced to just his pants, Jonathan hesitated again. Beth looked down and noticed that, for once, he wasn't already hard. Perhaps the idea of stripping off completely while he was like that was more embarrassing than when he was ready. Did he fear that she would make fun of him?

'Everything off, Jonathan,' she whispered, excited by the sight of his red briefs against the tanned flesh. She remembered the thrill she had felt watching him harden in front of her on the stairs. She wanted to see that again.

With obvious reluctance, Jonathan pulled down his pants and stepped out of them. She noticed that he was careful to keep his head down and turned away from her. His penis and testicles hung down loosely between his legs, as if imitating his head and expression. As before, Jonathan moved his hands round to cover himself.

Beth turned her back on him and picked up a longish piece of cord that was lying, ready, on the settee. She moved towards him, took hold of his hands, and pulled them up towards her. Swiftly, she tied his wrists together securely.

'That should ensure that you keep your roaming hands to yourself.' She grinned as she reached round to pat him gently on the bottom.

Jonathan flinched at her touch and stared at her in confusion.

'What are you going to do to me?' he repeated, with a note of fear creeping into his voice. She saw his penis stir slightly as if remembering how good it had felt when she had taken him in her hand. She quickly suppressed her own sigh of anticipation.

Beth took his arm and guided him back slightly. Still holding the end of the rope in one hand, she climbed up on to the side of the chair and raised his arms. Jonathan twisted round so that he could watch what she was doing. His breathing quickened at the sight of her long legs almost level with his face. As she stretched up towards the ceiling, her skirt lifted so that he could see the tops of her stockings. He moved his head round to get a better look. She glanced down and saw that his cock had already begun to harden.

Beth looped the rope round a heavy hook fixed into a wooden beam that ran across the length of the ceiling. As he watched her, she tied the end securely to the hook.

'It used to hold a chandelier,' she explained conversationally. 'An old family heirloom of my ex-husband. I never did like it. This is a much better use for the hook.'

Beth climbed down off the chair and moved round so that she was standing in front of him. She looked down at his groin again and smiled happily at his growing enthusiasm.

Jonathan flushed and moved one of his legs round in front of the other, twisting his hip forward as if to try to cover himself. Beth laughed, fascinated to see that his penis seemed to be shrinking again as his discomfort increased. Well, she would soon do something about that.

Her own inhibitions at what she was planning seemed to subside a little at the sight of his obvious embarrassment. They were both nervous. It wasn't just her. If he could put up with all this for her sake then, surely, she could overcome her own fears?

Beth walked across to the doorway and turned the dimmer switch on the sidelights right down until the room was in semi-darkness. The centre lamp now illuminated Jonathan perfectly, almost as if he were standing under a spotlight. The shadows increased her confidence further. It was almost like the setting for a play: the two of them merely actors playing out their parts according to the writer's script. According to her script.

Beth turned back to face him and walked forward until she was standing about a foot in front of him. Trembling from head to foot with fear, she crossed her hands in front of her and took hold of the bottom of her jumper. Slowly, she began drawing it up over her head.

Jonathan drew in a deep breath and his eyes widened at the sight of her stripping in front of him. He stared greedily at her breasts, watching them change shape under the bra as she raised her arms.

Beth turned sideways to him. She bent forward from the hips, tightening all her muscles, then leaned over and placed the garment on the settee. She had already practised this in front of the mirror and she knew that she looked every bit as good as the models in men's magazines.

She straightened up and spun round slowly on her heels until her back was turned to him. She lifted one hand and undid the top button of her skirt with a flick of her finger. Gradually, she began undoing the zipper.

Jonathan drew another deep breath. He shivered slightly at the sound of the button popping open, then gasped as the zipper came undone.

Praying that she was doing it right, Beth wriggled her hips from side to side and slowly pulled the skirt down until it came free and fell in a heap at her ankles. She stepped out of it and pushed it aside with one foot.

She was now standing in front of him, clad only in her black bra and thong and a matching black suspender belt, stockings and high heels. The tiny strips of lace and nylon framed her round buttocks perfectly and the white of her skin was shockingly erotic against the black material. She heard him swallow. Slowly, she turned back round to face him.

Jonathan was standing completely still with his arms raised above his head by the rope and his face filled with longing. She looked down. His penis was sticking out in front of him, straight and hard, as if saluting her performance. As she watched, it twitched slightly, bobbing up and down as if caressed by unseen fingers. A rush of confidence flowed through her body, a feeling of such power and such control that her legs turned to jelly. A shiver ran down her spine and her final inhibitions vanished. She was in total control now.

Smiling provocatively, her lips parted, Beth placed her hands on her hips and moved towards him. She stopped in front of him and eyed him up and down critically, like a sergeant inspecting the troops. Jonathan stood to attention. She moved on, passing by and circling round behind him.

Jonathan twisted his head round, desperately trying to follow her with his eyes. Finally, he could turn no further. Quickly, he whipped his head round to the other side and she saw him wince at the pain in his shoulder and neck muscles.

Beth circled right round and then stopped in front of him again. She looked down at his groin. His penis was twitching rhythmically up and down as he involuntarily tensed and relaxed the muscles in his excitement. Beth felt an almost overwhelming urge to reach out and fondle it. She moved back a few paces and turned her back on him again. She could feel his eyes devouring her body.

Trembling with anticipation, Beth raised her hands again and unhooked her bra. As the back strap fell free, she held the bra in place over her breasts. Jonathan gasped again at the sight of the bare skin of her back. She could almost feel him throbbing for her.

Almost beside herself with fear and excitement, Beth spun round on her heels again so that he could see only her hands were preventing her bra from falling free. She slipped the straps off each arm in turn and lifted her hands to allow the garment to drop to the floor in front of her. Her breasts bounced free, their dark nipples already hard and erect.

Jonathan's body shook as if he had been slapped. He was staring at her bare breasts like a starving man eyeing a table set for a feast. His mouth was gaping open so that he seemed to be practically drooling. He leaned forward and strained against the ropes holding his wrists. His erection grew even harder and Beth could hear him moaning softly under his breath. She could clearly see the beads of perspiration standing out on his forehead.

Enflamed by his reaction, Beth began to circle him again, strutting proudly in her high heels with her breasts swaying delightfully at every step. Once again, she moved round to stand behind him and, once again, Jonathan twisted his head awkwardly so that his eyes were riveted on her bare breasts.

'Face the front, Jonathan.' To her surprise, the command was firm and uncompromising, betraying nothing of her emotions. Jonathan's head jerked round as if it were on strings. He reminded her of a puppet. Her puppet. She gazed downwards.

His buttocks were so tense and rigid that they looked as if they were made of porcelain. She experienced an almost irresistible urge to lean down and bite him, to watch him jump. She cupped one cheek in her hand and fondled it gently. Jonathan trembled violently and twisted his head back round over his shoulder. His arms strained against the bindings again.

'I said, face front.' Beth removed her hand and waited for him to turn away.

'You know I still owe you a spanking,' she threatened softly, and was delighted at the way his buttocks immediately stiffened and twitched as if he expected to feel the sting of her blow at any moment. She waited silently, revelling in the sight of his whole body tense with anticipation. Finally, she walked back round and stood just in front of him again.

Beth rested her foot on his thigh and leaned forward to begin undoing the suspenders holding up her stockings. Her breasts swung down in front of her, wobbling gently back and forth as she moved. Jonathan squirmed again. She realised that he had probably never seen a woman like this before.

Slowly, she began peeling one stocking off.

'Please,' Jonathan whispered desperately as he writhed from side to side against his constraints. His whole body was shuddering. His cock was as hard as she had ever seen it. He was shifting first on one leg and then the other, squeezing the tops of his thighs together as he desperately sought a way to rub himself.

She was certain that any inhibitions he might have about masturbating in front of her had vanished. Right now, judging by his expression, if he could only get his hands free he would have done it in front of a whole roomful of watching eyes. The extent of his desperation was intoxicating. She felt certain that if she so much as touched his penis with her own fingers he would come.

As if totally unaware of his plight, Beth finished removing her stockings and slipped her feet back into her shoes. She stood back up and slid her hand down inside the tiny triangle of lace covering her sex. She could feel the dampness of her own excitement on her fingers.

All her senses were heightened. She could feel a slight

breeze from the open window running icy fingers over her skin, hear the sound of the clock ticking on the far wall, and even smell the warmth of both their bodies.

Beth closed her eyes, ran her fingers through her pubic hair, and touched her clitoris with the tip of one finger. She jumped at the intensity of the feelings that immediately rushed through her. She raised her other hand and ran it across her nipples, sighing gently at the shivers of pleasure running down her spine. She opened her eyes again and examined his reaction curiously.

Jonathan was going wild. He was so aroused that he, quite obviously, didn't know what to do with himself. With a desperate groan, he strained forward again, moving his legs and hips from side to side as he twisted and turned in vain. His face was bright red and his eyes were bulging out of their sockets. His throbbing cock twitched and jerked in front of him like a wild animal.

Beth licked her lips and stared at him hungrily. She wondered if she dared bend forward and kiss its burning tip. Would he be able to contain himself?

'Please,' Jonathan whispered again. 'I can't, I want . . .'

'What do you want?' she teased him softly as her fingers began once more playing with herself. 'Tell me. Do you want this?'

As she spoke, Beth removed her hand and pirouetted round on her heels again. She raised her hands and began to peel down the back of her panties to reveal the curves of her buttocks. She turned back, placed her hands just below her navel, and lowered the front fractionally to reveal a few of her curls. She stopped and waited, then slid the material a little lower.

She couldn't believe how much she was enjoying herself. She would never have dreamed of doing anything like this for her ex-husband. Perhaps she should have. Maybe she still should.

As she lowered the material over her crotch, Beth continued to study Jonathan's response carefully. He just couldn't keep still. His whole body was juddering and twitching and his penis looked hot and swollen, as if it were ready to split open. She had never realised that it could become so dark and hard.

Beth bent her knees and slipped her panties down over her ankles. She stepped out of them and straightened slowly, then used her right foot to flick them up into the air. They landed against his chest and slipped down to brush his erection before dropping to the floor. Jonathan jumped and lunged forward, straining desperately against his bonds. His soft cry was full of desperation.

She stood facing him, with her hands on her waist and her legs slightly parted. Jonathan had stopped wriggling, his eyes now riveted on the dark shadow of her pubes. He almost appeared to have stopped breathing. Beth reached round and unhooked her suspender belt. It dropped softly to the floor so that, probably for the first time in his life, Jonathan was staring at a completely naked woman standing just a few inches in front of him. His whole body shuddered again.

'Is this what you want?' Beth whispered as she placed her hand on top of her mound.

Jonathan groaned loudly, a desperate moan of total frustration and anguish. His cock pumped up and down in the air and his thighs tightened. Suddenly, his face contorted and a stream of come spurted violently from his tip and flew up into the air. His orgasm was so powerful that the fluid shot across the space between them and landed on her bare leg.

Jonathan groaned again as spasm after spasm of come burst from him. He slumped forward with his chin resting on his chest and his eyes closed. His penis was still twitching, almost as if it wanted to spurt more, yet he had nothing left to give.

Beth walked across to the table and picked up a box of tissues. After she had wiped herself carefully, she picked up the dressing gown lying over the back of the settee and slipped it on. Although she was still tingling with desire, she felt a deep sense of satisfaction at what she had achieved. He had been so excited at the sight of her naked body that he had lost it, just looking at her!

Calmly, she walked over to the chair, climbed up on to the arm and untied him. Her gown gaped open, hiding nothing.

She climbed down again and quickly undid his hands. She suffered a slight twinge of guilt when she saw how red and chafed his wrists were from straining against the rope.

'I think you had better go and shower,' she suggested softly as she examined his damp, sweat-streaked body. 'I'll make us both some coffee.'

Ten minutes later, when he had still not returned, Beth felt her curiosity aroused. What was taking him so long? She tiptoed up the stairs, pushed open the bathroom door, and peered inside.

Jonathan was standing under the shower, facing her, surrounded by a cloud of steam. He had closed his eyes against the spray and he was soaping his chest with a damp sponge. She ran her eyes slowly down his body. God, he was gorgeous: so tall, so muscular. For a moment, she was tempted to slip out of her gown and join him. She shivered at the thought of how it would feel to wash him herself, to run the sponge gently across every inch of his exposed flesh.

Clearly unaware of her presence, Jonathan moved the sponge down between his legs and carefully soaped his genitals. As she watched, he dropped the sponge, and started to rub himself with his hand. His cock immediately began to stiffen.

Beth stared in astonishment. He was already aroused again! Even after what had just happened, he was already wanting more. It would seem that her friend Ann had been perfectly correct about the stamina of youth.

Beth felt suddenly irritated. Why should he keep having all the fun when she was still keyed up and unsatisfied? It was time she exercised her authority again.

She waited until he was really hard again and had begun to pump himself urgently up and down. God, she loved watching him do that. She took a deep breath.

'It's time you got dried off now, Jonathan,' she announced loudly as she moved into the room and picked up a bath towel. 'It's getting late. You should be off home before you get into trouble.'

Jonathan stopped pumping and opened his eyes. His cock stuck out straight in front of him again, hard and stiff. Beth feigned total indifference.

'Come on. Get a move on. If you are too late getting home, your mother might not let you out next week.'

She hadn't meant to say that. She hadn't consciously planned anything more than what she had just done. Wasn't she supposed to be putting an end to all this?

Beth shrugged, finally admitting to herself that she had no intention of putting an end to it. She was having far too much fun for that. Oh well, she would just have to think up something else to remind him who was the boss, wouldn't she? She waited for him to dry off and get dressed, amused by his obvious discomfort and his still half-erect penis.

Her loosely tied gown continued to gape, taunting him.

It was only after he had gone that Beth realised he had not tried to cover his erection from her gaze. In fact, he had actually turned round to make sure that she could see it. Was he finally losing his embarrassment in front of her and becoming too sure of himself? Or had he just wanted to show her that he was ready again?

It had been a good idea to send him home still not fully satisfied. As long as she kept him on his toes, maybe she would have less trouble keeping him under her control in future. She wasn't so sure about her ability to control herself.

The Hand of Amun

Juliet Hastings

Marked from birth with the symbol of Amun – greatest of the Egyptian gods – Naunakhte is taken from her village and made to enter a life of sensuality as a servant at the temple. She is both privileged and cursed; young men stand in fear and awe of her, but none may touch her for she belongs to Amun. But Naunakhte is ripe for love, and desperate for the feel of a man close to her.

This isn't her only problem. She has a rival in the form of Tiy, a petulant and beautiful girl who believes *she* is destined to be Amun's servant. Knowing nothing of the secret rites, Naunakhte is thrown into a strange world of intoxicating rituals and hostile strangers. This extract from *The Hand of Amun* describes her arrival at the temple, where she finds out for the first time just exactly what is expected of her.

Juliet Hastings is a prolific writer and historian. *The Hand of Amun* is often cited as being our readers' favourite historical Black Lace novel. Her other books are *Crash Course*, *White Rose Ensnared*, *Forbidden Crusade*, and *Aria Appassionata*. We're hoping that Juliet will continue to write for Black Lace into the new millennium.

The Hand of Amun

Naunakhte lay awake beneath the warm stars, gazing upward into the velvet sky. A great glowing moon hung above her, casting brilliant silver light across the sleeping village. On each flat roof of the close-packed houses on either side of the main street people slept, naked for coolness in the waxing heat. A cat yowled in the graveyard and cicadas whirred from every stone in the desert.

A great moth fluttered past Naunakhte's face, grazing her with its spotted wings and making her jump. She brushed off the insect and turned over, stretching out her long limbs under the single linen sheet. Sleep was far away.

That morning Akhtay, wife of Djutmose, had given birth to her third child. She had given her husband a strong healthy boy, but afterwards the bleeding had not stopped but worsened, and before the sun had set Akhtay was dead. Naunakhte and Akhtay were the same age. They had played together when they were children, making dolls from straw and clay, and had gone hand in hand to the Valley of the Tombs to take food to Akhtay's father, who was a master-mason. Five years ago Akhtay had

141

married Djutmose, and now she was dead.

'Great goddess Nut,' Naunakhte whispered, turning her face to the glittering sky. 'Lady of the sky, guide me. Send me a sign.'

She did not know what sign she sought. She only knew that she was strange; that no other girl in the village was like her. She was adopted. Her father Ammenakht and her mother Hatia had taken her into their house at the request of the high priest of Amun. Her mother and father loved her, but they seemed always to keep her at a distance, as if she were not quite real. And the high priest had said that the god Amun had ordained that Naunakhte should never marry. So one by one, at fourteen and fifteen years of age, her friends had married the young men of the village and gone to their husbands' houses to have children and grow old and die, while Naunakhte remained in the house of Ammenakht, puzzled and alone.

Until today Naunakhte had believed that she was accursed. Why should her friends have weddings, the status of married women, the love of their husbands, the sound of children in their houses, while she had nothing? She was nineteen years old now – almost too old for marriage in the village's way of things. Outcast; accursed.

But Akhtay was dead, and Naunakhte's other friends were growing old before her eyes, losing the youthful elasticity of their skin, spreading with childbirth and tiring with the cares of a household. Naunakhte was nineteen, but the men of the village still looked at her with admiration when they saw her dressed for work in a simple linen kilt. They admired her small, high breasts, round and firm as pomegranates, the suppleness of her narrow waist, the swell of her soft belly, the opulent fullness of her hips and thighs, the elegant slenderness of her calves, the high strong arches of her delicate feet. One or two of the bolder boys quoted love poems to her: *If only I were your laundryman, just for a single month, I would rejoice to wash out the perfume from your dress.*

They admired her. But none of them ever came near her, or tried to kiss her, or offered to take her to his house as his wife. She was set apart, taboo, forbidden by the word of the god Amun. And the god had set his mark upon her, for on her left arm, just above the elbow, there was a little birthmark. It was dark red and as long as Naunakhte's little finger, and it was the exact shape of an erect phallus, thickening at the base as if it were clasped by a fist. Nobody doubted that it was the sign of Amun. Naunakhte wore an arm-ring of gilded copper and enamel to cover the birthmark, because when it was on view the people of the village would stare and whisper. She hid it as if she could hide herself from her fate. What did the god intend for her? Was she cursed or blessed?

'Lady of the sky,' Naunakhte whispered, 'send me a sign.'

As she lifted her hands to heaven in the attitude of prayer, a vivid white meteor flashed across the blue basin of the sky. Another brilliant flash followed it, then another. Then there was nothing, only the glowing of the stars and the creaking cries of the cicadas.

Naunakhte's eyes opened wide. They were beautiful eyes, the shape of almonds, with long dark lashes, pure smoky whites and irises darker than polished ebony. She lifted herself on one elbow, gazing upward with parted lips, wondering what this sign could mean. She pushed back the sheet and rose soundlessly to her knees, then crossed her hands on her bosom in respect for the goddess. She felt her pulse striking within her breast as hard as the mason's hammer.

She had thought herself the only person awake, but she was wrong. As she knelt looking up at the sky she realised that her father Ammenakht was waking too. He pushed himself up from his sleeping mat with many grunts and gasps, for he was corpulent, and stepped with absurd delicacy over the body of his sleeping wife.

Naunakhte was very pleased to be distracted from the

uncomfortable thoughts which had filled her. She forgot her vigil and covered her mouth with her hands to keep in a giggle. She knew well what her father was about. Only three days ago he had got himself a new servant, a girl from Punt, the hot, strange land far to the south where incense grew. Pati was a pretty, round creature, with skin the colour of polished mahogany and woolly dark hair cropped close to her well-shaped head. Her bottom was large and succulent and moved most enticingly while she walked. According to Ammenakht she would help his wife around the house, but Hatia had not been convinced, and everyone in the family knew that the new servant was really intended as a concubine. Ammenakht had not succeeded in having her yet, but it looked as if he was going to put things to rights that night.

Moving slowly, so that her father might not notice her, Naunakhte leant across to the reed mat beside hers. Her brother Harshire slept there, Ammenakht's oldest son. Like his father, Harshire worked as one of the village scribes. He was twenty years old and ready for marriage, though he had not yet found the right girl. Naunakhte believed that Pati had caught her brother's eye too, and she did not want Harshire to miss the first encounter between the girl and her father.

'Mmph,' Harshire said as Naunakhte shook his naked shoulder. 'What – ' Then he saw Naunakhte leaning over him in the moonlight, one hand on her lips and the other pointing towards Pati's pallet, and he fell silent and pushed himself to a sitting position.

Ammenakht was intent on his task and had not noticed that his eldest children were awake. He tiptoed across the flat roof, like a hippopotamus manoeuvring its way through a papyrus field, until he reached the pallet where the new servant slept. His big belly swayed from side to side. Naunakhte saw with a quick thrill of excitement that beneath it his penis was erect, sticking up as stiff as the long thin palette in which he kept his pens and inks.

Ammenakht looked down for a moment, rubbing his hands together. Then he lowered himself awkwardly to the ground beside Pati, who was asleep on her belly, and shook her shoulder. She came awake with a protesting little squeak and rolled over, then gasped as she saw her master above her.

'Hush,' said Ammenakht, and he put his hand on the girl's breast. She gave a single wriggle which might have been of protest and might have been of pleasure. Then she sat up and smiled. Her white teeth flashed in her dark face.

Ammenakht lay down on Pati's pallet and tugged at her until she was lying half across him. He caught hold of her by her woolly hair and pulled down her head to kiss her. The girl began to giggle – little breathless, soft giggles as if she didn't quite believe that this was really happening. Ammenakht arranged her astride him, plump thighs spread across his bulging belly. Her back was towards Naunakhte and the full glistening moons of her backside gleamed as she shifted up and down, rubbing herself against her master's body with lewd determination.

'Ah,' Ammenakht grunted in satisfaction. He put his hands on the girl's back and ran them down from her shoulders to her buttocks, then pulled roughly. Pati gave a gasp and leant forward as he dragged the cheeks of her arse wide apart and thrust his fingers between them, exploring the lush moist folds of flesh and the dark inviting cleft thus exposed to the warm night air.

'By Seth,' whispered Harshire. Naunakhte turned to look at him in shock and disapproval, for it was both blasphemous and dangerous to swear by Seth, god of darkness, of chaos, of war and disorder. But she said nothing, because in the silver moonlight she saw that Harshire was fully aroused, his member thick and erect, its bulbous tip glistening wetly. He was clasping the stiff shaft in his right fist, and as she watched he began to masturbate, rubbing his closed hand strongly up and down, up and down, the swollen rod. His breathing turned into regular gasps, their rhythm aligned with the movement of his gripping fingers.

He took his penis in his hand. He made love to his fist. At once the words came back to Naunakhte, the story of how the god Amun had created the world with the spurting of his semen. She watched, entranced, as Harshire thrust harder into the clasp of his hand and breathed quickly through his gritted teeth. She had never seen a man do this before, and suddenly the story of the god came alive for her. She imagined Amun, great and mighty, beautiful and powerful beyond men. The delicate skin of her brother's penis slid up and down as he rubbed himself, and her mind pictured the god's penis, glowing with the life contained in it. Harshire gasped with pleasure, and she heard the god's sighs, strong as the winds over the desert.

A stifled squeal drew her wide eyes back to her father and the servant girl. They were in the same position – Pati straddling Ammenakht's belly and leaning forward to allow his mouth to suck at her dangling breasts – but now her father had three fingers thrust deep within the folds of the girl's sex, moving slowly, juicily in and out. Every time the fingers sank again into her moist opening she gave a long sigh, almost like a sob. Ammenakht's other hand was at the base of Pati's belly, rubbing and stroking.

Suddenly Pati twisted away, pulling herself upright. She reached behind her and found her master's penis with her hand, lying engorged against the folds of his stomach. Her fingers explored its length and then hoisted it upright, and without hesitation she guided its shining head between the lips of her sex, then sank down.

Harshire made a sound halfway between a gasp and a moan as Pati impaled herself upon Ammenakht's erect phallus. She twisted her head and leant back, tensing her belly and loins. Her hands clasped Ammenakht's spread thighs to give her purchase and she began to ride him, grunting as if she urged on a galloping horse. The soft dark flesh of her thighs and buttocks shook as she lifted and lowered herself upon her master's shining penis. For a moment Ammenakht held on to her hips, then he seemed to realise that she needed no guidance. His hands slid up her writhing body and found her heavy breasts. She moaned and flung her head from side to side as his fingers clasped her dark red nipples and tugged at them. Her body struck his with a soft, urgent sound, and she began to let out little shrill yelps in rhythm with her movements. Ammenakht squeezed and pinched her bouncing breasts, and the speed of her lunges increased to a desperate climax.

At last she let out an odd, strangled cry and arched backward, her mouth open, her eyelids fluttering. Ammenakht grunted and grasped her hips tightly and thrust his penis up into her with all the strength he could command; once, twice, and then he snarled and pulled her rigid body down on to him as if he wanted to split her in two.

Naunakhte was breathing quickly, as if someone were doing to her what her father had done to the servant. She licked her lips and looked at her brother just in time to see him bare his teeth in pleasure and clutch fervently at the jerking head of his phallus. White semen spurted from it, glistening in the moonlight.

For long moments there was silence, broken only by irregular gasps. Then Ammenakht gently rolled the girl off him, patted her flank and pushed himself to his feet to creep back to his own pallet.

If he believed that his adventure had gone unnoticed, he was mistaken. As he knelt down his wife Hatia's voice spoke, shockingly loud after the smothered silence of secret sex. 'Well, was she good?'

'Hatia!' exclaimed Ammenakht, his voice revealing his surprise. 'Whatever are you doing awake?'

'Listening to you copulating with Pati,' said Hatia acidly. 'What do you expect?'

Ammenakht lowered himself cautiously to the pallet and said in soothing tones, 'Don't be angry, my wife. Go to sleep.'

'Go to sleep? I shall not. If you had enough energy to make Pati squeal, husband, you can do the same for me.'

'Oh,' said Ammenakht. 'Ah, I don't think I could quite manage that, wife. I'm not as young as I used to be.'

Hatia's voice dripped irony. 'Well, Ammenakht, if you don't want me to tell the women in the marketplace that your papyrus reed is too soft to write with, you'd better think of another way of satisfying me.' She shifted beneath the linen sheet. 'Try putting that slick tongue of yours to another use.'

Naunakhte knelt a little more upright on her pallet, trying to see what her father and mother were doing. She frowned in puzzlement as with many gasps and groans of discomfort Ammenakht positioned himself face down between his wife's legs, his head buried between her spread thighs. Hatia gave a long sigh and rested both hands on her husband's head, stroking her fingers lovingly across the bald patch which by day was covered by a smart wig.

Silence fell again, broken only by the sound of lapping and Hatia's liquid moans. Presently her hands moved from Ammenakht's head to her breasts and she began to caress and tease her erect nipples. It was not long before she gave a great cry of delight and wrapped her thighs so closely around her husband's ears that Naunakhte was afraid her father would be smothered.

After a few minutes Ammenakht crawled grumbling up the pallet and fell flat on his face with a sound like a water melon being dropped from a height. Hatia whispered in his ear and kissed his cheek, then sighed. Soon both of them were snoring.

Harshire and Naunakhte, on the other hand, were still

wide awake. Harshire lifted himself half to his feet and hissed, 'Do you think they'll wake up?'

'Why should they?' Naunakhte whispered back.

Harshire grinned at her, a devilish grin. 'Because, sister, by Seth, I'm going to give that little witch Pati the screwing of her life. What's good enough for father is good enough for me.'

'But – ' Naunakhte began, but it was too late. Harshire was on his feet and moving silently across the roof to Pati's pallet. His sister pressed her hands to her mouth, astonished by his insolence. If her father awoke he would be furious. Such an insult!

Harshire had reached the servant girl's pallet. The girl's dark figure lay below him, sprawled in the abandon of sleep. Naunakhte expected Harshire to lie on Pati at once and thrust himself inside her, but he did not. He knelt beside her and then swung one leg over her, straddling her chest, his half-erect penis pointing towards her parted lips. Leaning a little forward, he caught hold of the girl's hair. She woke with a sleepy moan and without a word he pushed the head of his phallus into her open mouth.

Pati's eyes opened very wide. She made a smothered sound of protest, then suddenly seemed to realise what was happening to her. Protest turned to delighted acquiescence and she began to suck, her cheeks hollowing as she worked on Harshire's penis with tongue and lips.

No wonder she was delighted, because the phallus in her mouth was larger than her master's. Harshire was young and strong and his penis was splendid; thick and long and beautifully hard, like the penis of the ithyphallic god Min in the temple hieroglyphs. Pati sucked eagerly at the glistening shaft and lifted her dark hands to caress Harshire's sturdy thighs and muscular, taut buttocks. Naunakhte took a quick breath of shock, for she was sure that she saw one dusky finger wriggling its way deep between the cheeks of Harshire's backside, sliding into the little tight forbidden hole between them. Could that possibly be true? And if it was true, why was Harshire breathing hard and clenching his cheeks with what must be pleasure?

Pati had done well: Harshire's fine phallus was restored to full hardness. He kicked her feet apart, then caught her beneath her thighs and lifted her plump legs to wrap them around his waist. His lips sought hers and he pushed his tongue into her panting mouth to silence her, then without another word plunged into her to the hilt.

The servant girl had ridden her master vigorously enough, but all her efforts were as nothing compared to the shafting that Harshire gave her now. He had already spurted his seed once that evening and now he seemed tireless. Over and over again his thick rod drove into her and withdrew, glistening with her eager dampness, only to lunge again. Beneath him Pati gasped with helpless delight, arching her juicy hips up towards him to welcome his thrusts. He held her lush breasts in his hands and slid his full length into her with feverish strength, grunting as his hot swollen flesh was simultaneously soothed and maddened by her silky folds. Pati moaned and whimpered as her climax approached, but Harshire did not stop. He forced his mouth down on hers to smother her little quivering cries of orgasm and seemed to relish the sensation as her body tensed and shuddered beneath his and the velvety glove of her sex pulsed and tightened around his plunging penis. Then, when she was limp and helpless beneath him, he caught hold of her wrists and spread them wide apart so that her bouncing breasts were exposed to his gaze. He held her beneath him, pinned down like a slave, and worked his gleaming phallus to and fro, to and fro, until at last he gasped and drove himself into her and his fierce climax overwhelmed him.

Everything was very quiet as Harshire tottered back to his own reed mat and lay down again. The servant girl gave a little whimper of disbelief and delight, then subsided into slumber. Naunakhte slid down beneath her sheet and stared up at the hot stars, breathing fast.

Between her legs she ached; a dull, numb ache. She touched herself there, hesitantly, and felt that the tender petals of her secret flesh were moist and slippery and slightly swollen. They were so sensitive that even the lightest touch of her finger made her shiver.

She was ready for a man, ripe for love. She knew it was true. Whenever she heard or saw people in the act of generation it had the same effect on her. Even thinking about it had the same effect.

Thinking about it ... There was a man in the village whom Naunakhte desired. He was one of the medjay, the state policemen, and his name was Psaro. Psaro was of Nubian extraction. His skin was as black as charcoal and as smooth as polished stone, and his lips were full and red. He was beautiful, and whenever Naunakhte saw him she wondered what it would be like to be kissed by those full lips, to be pressed against that strong burnished torso. She thought of him now as she touched herself, hoping to bring herself to some sort of release from her frustration and misery.

But she was taboo, the prisoner of Amun's word. Psaro would never hold her, would never press his lips to her flesh, would never penetrate her with the ebony staff that hung at his loins. The god had forbidden it.

For a moment she was angry. She wanted to deny the god's command and assert herself; to seize her freedom at all costs. Her fists clenched and her jaw set. She was ready to swear by Seth and invoke the forces of darkness, if only she could be free.

Then, above her, another meteor streaked over the sky. Another followed it, and another. Naunakhte's eyes filled with tears as she watched the tracks of burning brilliance. How much more clearly could the gods reveal themselves?

The meteors ceased. 'Oh lord Amun,' Naunakhte

prayed, 'I beg you to release me from this life. If I am to be yours, mighty Amun, if you truly set your seal upon me when I was born, send another star. Let it fall from my right hand to my left, great god of life.'

And, in answer, a blue line of flame scored its way across the sky. It fell from right to left, and as it flamed and vanished the tears which stood in Naunakhte's eyes brimmed over and slid down her cheeks, brighter than the stars.

'Nakhte!' Hatia's voice shrilled up the hole that led to the flat roof. 'Nakhte, come down here at once!'

'You're in trouble,' said one of Naunakhte's smaller sisters, with satisfaction.

Naunakhte frowned. Her mother's voice sounded to her not angry, but afraid. She pushed her bundle of clean white linen, the family's working clothes, into the hands of the next oldest girl. 'Fold it carefully,' she said, then smoothed down the tight knee-length kilt which was her only garment and ran to the stairs.

As she descended she closed her eyes, but even so when she opened them again she was quite blind for a few minutes. The reflection of the sun on the white linen shimmered before her, dancing like red motes. At last, though, her vision cleared. The dark room where the family lived swam into view before her, and she gasped.

Psaro the medjay was standing there beside her mother, his head brushing against the roof, he was so tall. Naunakhte's heart began to flutter and thump. Psaro looked nervous. Uncomfortable. Could this be the answer to her prayers? Had Psaro come for her?

'Naunakhte,' Hatia said. Naunakhte jumped, because her family hardly ever used her full name. She looked at her mother and saw with a shock that Hatia was weeping. Tears left shining trails down her weatherbeaten face. 'Naunakhte, Psaro has come to take you away.'

'To take me away?' Naunakhte repeated. She took a step towards Psaro, her face revealing her vivid eagerness.

'To the temple,' Psaro said, looking at the ground. His deep voice was like the rumble of thunder over the desert. 'I'm sorry, Naunakhte.'

Suddenly Naunakhte felt cold all over. 'To the temple?' She pushed her hand through her thick black hair, pulling her braids awry, and looked beseechingly at Hatia. 'Mother – '

The street door opened and Ammenakht entered, puffing like a bull. He must have walked all the way from the Valley of the Tombs in the morning heat, an unheard-of exertion for a respected scribe. Naunakhte began to tremble. 'What's this?' Ammenakht demanded, between gasps.

'The high priest of Amun has sent for Naunakhte,' said Hatia, and Psaro silently held out to Ammenakht a small papyrus scroll. Ammenakht unfolded it and quickly scanned the writing. As he read his face changed.

'Naunakhte,' he said at last, rolling up the papyrus, 'I am afraid it is true. The god Amun has summoned you at last. You must go to the temple at once.'

So this was the meaning of the omen. This was why the god had answered her prayer. Suddenly Naunakhte was terrified of leaving the cramped little house where she had spent all her life. 'No,' she said, putting her hands to her face. 'I don't want to go.'

Her mother hugged her. She was smaller than Naunakhte by a head, but her embrace was still as comforting as it had been when Naunakhte was a little child. 'Hush,' she said. 'There is no use fighting the gods. You were only ever lent to us, Naunakhte. You have always belonged to Amun.'

'We must not delay,' said Psaro, making patterns with his toe in the sand on the floor.

Naunakhte began to weep. Hatia pulled the girl's head down on to her shoulder and said past her ear to Ammenakht, 'Get some of the children to find Naunakhte's best things. She must go to the god looking her finest.'

The boat soon pulled up to the temple quay. At a little distance the first pylon gateway of the temple loomed huge and awesome. Naunakhte walked between the medjay captain and another of the medjay until they reached the gateway. It stood open, guarded only by its holiness. No Egyptian would dare to trespass on such sacred ground. The captain led her through it and into the precinct of the temple.

A second gateway followed the first, and then Naunakhte stopped in her tracks and gazed about her, hardly able to believe her eyes. She stood in a massive hall, the largest enclosed space she had ever entered. The walls were decorated with painted sculptures of the gods and holy texts, and the roof was held up by a seemingly endless forest of columns, hundreds of them, some painted, some sheathed in gold. The columns were the shape of papyrus plants; smooth, thick stems capped with a bulbous tip. Naunakhte found her eye drawn to a representation of the god on one wall. He appeared as a handsome young man, naked and powerful, with a long, erect penis. The shape of his phallus irresistibly recalled the shape of the columns. Naunakhte stared at the image of the god, imagining her tender body ravished by his might, immolated by the flame of his ejaculation. She began to shiver uncontrollably.

'Is this the new girl?' A young woman's voice echoed back from the myriad columns and the coffered roof. Naunakhte jumped and pulled herself back to reality with an effort. Approaching her was a girl of about her own age, petite and no taller than her shoulder, dressed in a splendid gown of folded and pleated linen, like a noble lady's best dinner dress. The girl wore no wig, which was hardly surprising, for her own hair was a bright copper-gold, an astonishing colour for Egypt. As she drew closer,

Naunakhte saw that her eyes, which were painted with green malachite and black antimony, were brilliant pale green.

'I am Tiy,' said the girl, stopping in front of Naunakhte and looking her up and down. 'I am the chief handmaiden to the Hand of God. She has sent me to fetch you.'

'I am Naunakhte,' Naunakhte whispered, thoroughly cowed by Tiy's striking appearance and cool confidence, 'daughter of the scribe Ammenakht.'

'Is that what they told you?' asked Tiy, with arch superiority. 'You do have a lot to learn. Follow me.'

She turned her back and began to walk away. 'But –' Naunakhte protested feebly, 'my bundle.'

Tiy stopped and looked at the linen-wrapped bundle with distaste. 'What is in it?' she demanded.

'Another dress,' said Naunakhte timidly, 'and my kilt, and my eye paint.'

The pale green eyes examined Naunakhte again from head to heel. Naunakhte was a little irritated by Tiy's disdain, especially as she was wearing her best dress. It was made of fine pleated linen, closely fitted around her slender waist with two broad straps covering her breasts, and at her ankles it was embroidered. She had embroidered it herself.

'If it's no better than that one,' said Tiy at last, 'I would throw it in the Nile. But the servants will bring it, if you must. Now come with me. The Lady Hunro awaits you.'

Fighting down a surge of anger, Naunakhte hurried after Tiy through the multitude of columns. 'Who is the Lady Hunro?'

'She is the god's wife of Amun,' said Tiy over her shoulder, 'the Hand of God. Her husband is the Lord Merybast, the high priest. Don't worry about him, you'll hardly ever see him; he delegates the temple services and keeps himself busy with administration.'

Naunakhte raised her eyebrows. How could anyone whose duty it was to serve the god prefer to undertake tasks that could be discharged by a scribe? But she did not dare say this aloud, and in any case Tiy was still speaking.

'The Lady Hunro,' Tiy went on, 'is well past her thirtieth year. She will soon choose another to take on her titles. It should be her daughter, but she and Merybast have no children. So she will probably adopt someone and make her the Hand of God.' Tiy glanced around and met Naunakhte's eyes. Her smile had a brittle edge. 'People say that she is likely to choose me. It would be suitable. I have served a long time in the temple and I understand the rite. Also, I am attached to the chief priest, who undertakes the temple duties in Merybast's stead. His name is Panhesi. It would be convenient for all if Panhesi became Merybast's successor as I am intended to be Hunro's.'

Tiy's pale eyes shone. Inexperienced as she was, Naunakhte understood the unspoken message. She was not to interfere with Tiy's plans. She was surprised to hear of Tiy's attachment to the priest Panhesi, which seemed a rather worldly thing for the servants of a god. But there again, the high priestess herself was a married woman. Naunakhte adopted an expression of suitable meekness and followed Tiy into the labyrinth of the temple without another word.

They went through gateways and passages and at some point seemed to turn away from the main processional route into the temple. Naunakhte gazed from side to side, lost and puzzled. Tiy did not attempt to enlighten her. At last they came to a small closed door. Tiy knocked and said loudly, 'It is I, Tiy.'

The door swung open and Tiy led Naunakhte through it. Beyond it was a big room, pillared like the hypostyle hall but on a much smaller, more intimate scale. The floor was paved with smooth glittering stone and at one side the room was open to admit the sunlight. Beyond the portico lay a broad shimmering lake, green with waterlilies and flanked by ornamental trees. A woman in a long white dress was walking around the pool, followed by a little black slave girl carrying a parasol made of palm leaves. The smell of costly perfumes caressed Naunakhte's nostrils.

The room was full of women, mostly young girls like Naunakhte, although some were older. Some were sleeping; others were playing games, making music, or attending to their clothes and hair. They looked up when Tiy entered and one of them called out, 'The new girl!' and another sprang to her feet and ran out through the portico to the pool.

'Welcome,' said one of the girls, running up with a smile. 'I am Neferure. Welcome to the temple.'

'Thank you,' said Naunakhte, reassured.

Then all the girls in the room drew back and made obeisance as the woman who had been walking by the pool entered, stepping soundlessly with bare feet. Naunakhte bowed too, for she had guessed that this was the Lady Hunro.

The Lady Hunro was not tall, but she carried herself like a queen. She was curved and rounded in shape, with full breasts and heavy thighs beneath her translucent linen garment. Her face was high boned and haughty and her eyes were very bright. She was clearly a woman of middle years, but she was still beautiful.

'Naunakhte,' said the Lady Hunro. 'You are welcome.'

'Thank you, lady,' Naunakhte murmured.

The Lady Hunro took hold of Naunakhte's hand and felt it. 'Ah,' she said, 'hard fingers. You have worked, Naunakhte, in the village of the tombmakers.'

'Yes, lady.' Naunakhte was astonished by the softness of Hunro's hand. It was as if she had never known toil. She was suddenly afraid that she had failed a test, that she would be turned away like a peasant girl turned out of the kitchens.

'It is nothing,' said Hunro, looking Naunakhte up and down. 'Nothing, when compared to your beauty, Naunakhte. By all the gods, you are the image of your mother, and I never saw a woman to rival her.' Naunakhte gasped with astonishment and Hunro smiled. 'I was going to ask you to show the mark on your arm, to ensure that the scribe Ammenakht and his wife had not substituted a daughter of their own for the god's servant. But you are so like your mother that there is no need.'

'I will show you, lady, if you wish,' said Naunakhte. Hastily she pulled the gilded bracelet from above her elbow, revealing the small dark image on her golden skin. The temple girls pressed close around her, sighing with amazement as they saw the sign of the god on Naunakhte's arm.

'There,' said Hunro. 'I said there was no doubt.'

'Lady,' Naunakhte asked timidly, 'will you tell me about my mother? I know nothing of her.'

Hunro nodded. 'Ammenakht was told to keep it secret. I am glad he obeyed. I will tell you, Naunakhte, it is right that you should know now. But it is not a pleasant tale. Come and sit with me under the portico. We will drink a little date wine.' Then Hunro frowned as she noticed the dust on Naunakhte's feet and clothing. 'But you are hot and tired,' she said. 'Let the girls wash you first. Then I will tell you everything.'

At once the girls descended on Naunakhte, unfastening the straps of her dress and peeling the linen from her so that she was quite naked. Like all Egyptians she was unselfconscious about her nude body, and she helped the girls to strip her. The sooner she was washed, the sooner Hunro would tell her about her mother. Her real mother, the woman that nobody in the village had ever mentioned.

'Oh,' said Neferure with a smile, 'you are lovely, Naunakhte. The god will be pleased to see you play for him.' She shook her head, making the tiny plaits of her long heavy wig bounce and sway.

Naunakhte smiled in return, but as she turned to walk to the pool she saw Tiy watching her with an expression of distaste and anger in her shining green eyes. It chilled her so that she shivered.

'Come,' said another of the girls, 'let us wash you. You'll enjoy it!' And they flung off their clothes and surrounded Naunakhte and guided her down into the cool water of the lake. Glittering red fish darted away from them to hide beneath the shadows of the waterlilies. Naunakhte shivered afresh at the chill kiss of the water, and her skin came out in goosepimples and the dark points of her nipples lengthened and hardened.

One of the girls cupped the shining water in her hands and splashed it over Naunakhte's body. Another brought a phial of scented soap to cleanse her. A third began to rub the soap into her skin, coaxing away the dust of the road. Naunakhte had never smelled a scent like the perfume of the soap, like tuberoses and lilies and lotus flowers mingled with the essence of nard. She sighed with pleasure as the girl's fingers rubbed up and down her back, then slipped to the front of her body to cup and caress her breasts.

'Such lovely breasts,' whispered Neferure. She stood in front of Naunakhte and placed her hands gently over her erect nipples, rubbing with her palms. A spear of sensation lanced from Naunakhte's breasts to her belly, wakening the hollow aching feeling that filled her when she saw men and women making love. She took a quick deep breath and Neferure reached up and kissed her on the mouth.

Nobody had ever kissed Naunakhte on the mouth. For a moment she tensed, almost frightened by the unfamiliar sensation of Neferure's hot tongue probing between her lips. Then she was filled with a sudden rush of immediate, uncomplicated desire, acceptance of the pleasure which the kiss gave her and eagerness to have more. She pressed her body against Neferure's and moaned.

'Ah,' murmured Neferure, smiling as she pulled away.

'More in a moment, little lotus flower. Come and let us anoint you.'

She took Naunakhte's hand and led her out of the pool and into the shade of the portico. There she laid her down on a linen couch and knelt beside her, a jar of scented unguent in her hand. She poured a little of the fragrant oil into her palms and then set her hands to Naunakhte's body and began to glide her fingers across her soft skin, soothing and moisturising it and at the same time stirring Naunakhte to almost unbearable arousal.

Naunakhte had forgotten how much she wanted to hear the Lady Hunro tell her of her mother. She was conscious only of Neferure's hands moving up and down her skin, kneading her breasts, flickering over her swollen nipples, teasing at the delicate flesh of her thighs until she sighed and flung her head helplessly from side to side, rejoicing at these unfamiliar, delicious sensations.

She opened her eyes and looked up at Neferure. The temple girl was leaning over her with the heavy locks of her wig falling on to her naked shoulders and her face set in an expression of deep concentration. A tiny smile touched the corners of her mouth. She was beautiful, and the delicate, refined detail of her highly dressed wig above her simple nakedness was infinitely attractive. Naunakhte remembered how the men of the village used to draw little pictures on the scraps of limestone left over from their building – pictures of girls stark naked except for their luxuriant wigs, and she understood why they found this combination so alluring.

'That's right,' Neferure whispered. She had her hands on Naunakhte's breasts and was gently fondling her nipples, making them longer, stiffer, more sensitive. 'Yes, Naunakhte, yes. How beautiful you look.' And over her shoulder she whispered, 'Touch her there.'

Naunakhte closed her eyes and whimpered. Another pair of hands was fondling her thighs, moving them apart gently but very firmly. A long, slender finger coiled in the nest of dark curls at the base of her belly, then slithered a little further down.

'Ah,' Naunakhte moaned, for the finger was caressing her in a way that gave her such exquisite pleasure that she could not keep silent. 'Oh, oh, please.'

'Such a sweet blossom,' murmured another voice. The finger between her legs stroked and stroked at one particular place, and whenever it touched her she was pierced by arrows of the purest bliss. 'Pretty as a desert rose and glistening with dew. Ah, sweet.'

And now another finger was on her, sliding its way into her secret places even as the first continued to touch and caress that magic spot. No perfumed unguent was needed to make her slippery and soft, for the delicate flesh between her legs was already soothed and lubricated by her own fragrant dew. The pleasure that filled Naunakhte changed, becoming more urgent. Tension increased within her, making her moan. Every time the finger rubbed against her she wanted it to touch her harder, to soothe the unbearable emptiness that grew even as her pleasure grew. Her round hips lifted upward, a motion like the waves on the surface of the Nile. As if in answer the finger slid inside her. Pleasure turned suddenly to pain and Naunakhte cried out.

At once all the hands that touched her withdrew. She opened her eyes to see Neferure leaning over her, frowning in astonishment. 'Naunakhte,' she said softly, 'are you a virgin?'

Unable to speak, Naunakhte nodded. Everything was so strange. Was it wrong to be a virgin? How could she help it? The men of the village had never wanted her. It was not her fault.

The Lady Hunro appeared above her, smiling, and Naunakhte felt immediately reassured. 'Naunakhte,' she said, 'if this is true, it will be most pleasing to the god. But you are nineteen years old. None of us expected you still to be a virgin, when you have waited so long to enter your service, and you are so – ' She gestured with one soft hand at Naunakhte's still-quivering body ' – so easily aroused. But lie still, Naunakhte, until I discover whether this is true.'

'It is true,' Naunakhte whispered. But Hunro shook her head and held out her other hand. In it rested an object shaped like an egg, but made of sparkling white alabaster. 'Let us see,' said the Lady Hunro.

Naunakhte lay very still. Dragged from everything she knew into a strange and erotic place, she was uncertain of what she should say or do. She closed her eyes and tried to think herself away from where she was now. Her memory conjured up a festival at the village, when everyone took three days off work and spent the whole time feasting and drinking. They ate together under the stars, enjoying the good meat and fish which Pharaoh sent them, and drank the best beer and date wine in such quantity that most of them were paralytic. People played and sang and the villagers danced under the bright stars and laughed and went off into corners to make love to each other. All except Naunakhte, the strange one, the girl marked by Amun, who sat beside her little brothers and sisters, drunken and melancholy and alone.

Her mind shied away from the memory of her own strangeness. Now she was in Amun's own place, his temple, the seat of his power, and the lady who was the god's wife on earth was parting her thighs to make some arcane trial of her chastity. Naunakhte gave a little helpless moan as she felt Hunro's soft hands gently, delicately, exploring between her legs, fondling the place where she was liquid and melting with longing. The high priestess's touch reawakened all the hot desire that had filled her when Neferure had put her hands on her breasts and another girl had skilfully, dexterously fingered her vulva and clitoris. She bit her lip, trying to keep silent.

Then she felt something cool and hard pressing against her, pushing its way between the lips of her sex. It felt painful, wonderful. It was thick and it stretched her, making her want all sorts of contradictory things. She wanted to part her legs further, to close her thighs against the unexpected intrusion, to resist, to submit.

The pain grew and she let out a sharp cry. Then, as suddenly as it had come, the cool hard thing withdrew and the Lady Hunro's voice said, 'By Hathor, it is true.'

What could make the priestess of Amun swear by the goddess of love? Naunakhte opened her eyes and saw Hunro holding up the alabaster egg, examining its rounded tip. The smooth white stone gleamed with the slippery juices of Naunakhte's desire, and the pointed end was just stained with pink.

'Naunakhte,' said the Lady Hunro, 'you will be most acceptable to the god. And . . .' She opened her lips and delicately drew the tip of the alabaster egg between them, tasting it. 'And you will be most acceptable to me.'

Without another word the high priestess sank to her knees beside the couch on which Naunakhte lay. She kissed her soft rounded belly and the swell of her mound of love. Naunakhte made a sound of protest, sure that it was not her place to have the Hand of God thus worship her. But Hunro said, 'Naunakhte, the place of the women of the temple is to arouse the god, and to arouse me, the god's wife of Amun. Your beauty arouses me, Naunakhte. Be still.'

A soft hiss beside Naunakhte made her glance around. Tiy stood there, close to her, staring with malevolent anger in her pale eyes and repeating that cold vicious sound, a hiss like the hiss of a cobra as it prepares to strike. Clearly Tiy was most displeased that the high priestess found Naunakhte attractive. The hatred in her face struck Naunakhte with a chill of fear.

But then she forgot her fear, because the Lady Hunro's head had moved between her open thighs. For the first time in her life Naunakhte felt the warmth of a mouth caressing her sex, the softness of lips encircling her swollen clitoris, the warm prodding of a strong, hard tongue between the moist petals of her vulva. The pleasure was indescribable. She closed her eyes and leaned back her head and let out a long, breathy sigh of ecstasy. The tension that had filled her earlier had quite vanished. She was immersed in sensual joy, lifted to higher and higher planes of bliss by the steady lapping of Hunro's tongue. The sensations swelled and grew and Naunakhte's soft cries became sharper. Her hands gripped helplessly at the linen of the couch. And then Hunro caught her engorged clitoris between her lips and drew the tender bud of flesh into her mouth and sucked at it gently, her tongue thrilling against the tiny shaft, and Naunakhte let out a long dying wail and arched her back as her first orgasm blazed through her, soaking her in sensual ecstasy and shaking her to the roots of her being.

Presently she opened her languid eyes and looked up at the Lady Hunro with an expression of stunned amazement. 'Lady, I am sorry,' she whispered. 'Did I cry out? I didn't realise – '

Hunro smiled kindly. 'Naunakhte, little golden flower,' she said, 'I took as much pleasure in your cries as you did. All is very well, little one. Think of it as your introduction to the service of the god. There is great pleasure in serving the temple, Naunakhte, as you will find.'

The Lady Hunro got up from the floor by the couch, where she had knelt to caress Naunakhte with her mouth, and stretched. 'Now,' she said, 'come and sit by me, and I shall tell you of your mother. Girls, help her.'

She turned and walked away and the temple handmaidens hurried to help Naunakhte up from the couch. All except Tiy, who stood with her slender arms folded and her lips curling with disdain. 'Very clever,' she hissed, in a voice just loud enough to carry to Naunakhte's ears. 'Very clever, village girl. Who told you that the Lady Hunro finds innocents amusing? Don't worry. She will soon find out that you are a whore, just as your mother was.'

Naunakhte was shocked and furious. She was about to make an angry retort when one of the girls caught her arm and whispered, 'Don't argue with Tiy if you can help it, Naunakhte. She knows people. She can make things very difficult if she doesn't like you.'

In a tense silence Naunakhte met Tiy's eyes. They were bright and hard as green stones, gleaming with spite. After a moment Tiy turned away without another word and Naunakhte prepared to follow the Lady Hunro to the shady spot under a date palm by the shimmering pool. As she went she noticed how the temple girls looked at her askance, as if she carried bad luck with her. It was clear that they feared Tiy's resentment more than they hoped to befriend their new colleague. Was she destined to be alone in the temple of Amun as she had been alone in the village of the tombmakers?

'Don't argue with Tiy if you can help it,' Naunakhte repeated sadly to herself. 'What was there for me to help?'

'Come and sit by me, Naunakhte,' said the Lady Hunro, patting the cushioned seat beneath the spreading date palm. 'Bring us something to eat and drink,' she commanded one of the girls, who hurried to obey. The others settled down around them in the shade of the palm tree, excited at the prospect of a tale.

'Now,' said Hunro, looking at Naunakhte's face with a sober expression, 'where to begin? Naunakhte, do you know anything of your parentage?'

Naunakhte shook her head and regarded the Lady Hunro with all her attention. At last she would find out why all her life she had been different.

The girl brought a gilded dish laden with dainties, slivers of roasted meat, salted fish, honeyed dates and ripe figs. She set beside it a flagon of wine made from grapes and two cups. The cups were made of chased gold, with designs inlaid in blue enamel. Naunakhte had never seen so much luxury in one small space, but although the girl filled one of the golden cups and put it into her hand she could not drink. 'Please, lady,' she begged, as Hunro sipped her wine and enjoyed a bite of food, 'tell me everything.'

Hunro set down her golden cup. 'Well, little one,' she said, 'first, you must know that your father is Pharaoh, King Rameses himself.'

Naunakhte's hand closed into a tight fist around the golden stem of the cup. She felt first cold all over, then burning hot. The blood surged up into her face, staining her honey-gold cheeks with a scarlet blush. Around her the girls drew back, whispering and rustling like a bed of reeds at dawn. Pharaoh was a living god, and his children carried the blood of gods in their veins.

But Pharaoh's wives and concubines lived in the palace, and his countless children lived there too. What had Naunakhte done to be exiled? She gazed at Hunro, and now her face was beseeching.

'Seventeen years ago, Naunakhte,' the Lady Hunro went on, 'there was a plot against King Rameses. Some of his chief ministers plotted to murder him and put upon the throne a man they could more readily bend to their will.'

'To murder Pharaoh?' gasped the listening girls, horrified. To kill Pharaoh was more than treason; it was sacrilege.

'They chose a boy in his teens, the son of Rameses's favourite concubine, the Lady Tiy,' went on Hunro. 'He was your full brother, Naunakhte. You are the daughter of the Lady Tiy and King Rameses. She was the most beautiful woman in the palace, and she bore Rameses many children.'

Naunakhte was trembling from head to foot. She set down her wine, lest the shaking of her hands spill it.

'I remember the day the plot was discovered,' said the Lady Hunro, and now her eyes seemed to look beyond

Naunakhte and into the distance of the past. 'I was a visitor in the palace that day. They cried that there was poison in the king's drink. Everything was confusion. I heard later that they had taken the Lady Tiy and she had confessed to her part in the plot.' Hunro's eyes focused again upon Naunakhte. 'She was guilty,' she said softly. 'She had desired to be the mother of the new Pharaoh. She had carried the poison to Rameses with her own hand. The king could have had her executed by any means he chose, but he offered her the poisoned cup instead so that she might die with honour. By his order she gave the cup to her children also, not just her son, but all the children she had by Rameses, except you, Naunakhte.'

It was hard for Naunakhte to speak. She struggled with her shivering and at last whispered, 'I don't understand. Lady Hunro, why was I chosen?'

Hunro stretched out her hand and touched the mark of the god on Naunakhte's arm. 'When you came from the womb, Naunakhte,' she said, softly tracing the outline of the phallus shape with her finger, 'you carried this mark. The god Amun set his seal on you when Pharaoh's seed created you within your mother. The king did not dare kill you out of hand. He asked advice from the oracle of the god. It spoke clearly and said that you were destined to live and that you would be summoned when Amun desired it. So the king spared you, but he sent you out of the palace so that you would not be a reminder to him.' Her eyes softened. 'You see, Naunakhte, you resembled your mother, and Rameses had loved her. Her betrayal gave him great pain.'

So the god Amun had saved her life when she was not three years old. Naunakhte did not know whether to be sorry that she was the child of a wicked and treacherous woman, or pleased that she was the daughter of King Rameses, or in awe at the care that Amun had taken of her. At last she looked up with tears in her eyes and said, 'The god did not forget me.'

Now Hunro smiled. 'He did not forget. His oracle summoned you, and you are here. We must wait and watch to see what he has in mind for you now.'

Her smile became confiding and she stroked Naunakhte's cheek with her hand. The watching girls murmured again as they noted this mark of the high priestess's favour. Hunro's eyes darkened as she touched Naunakhte's smooth skin. 'Tonight,' she said, 'when night comes, we will offer you to the god. Beauty like yours will be most welcome to him. And in future, Naunakhte; in future, who knows?'

The Lady Hunro got up from her seat and stretched and yawned. 'It is hot,' she murmured, looking up at the burning noon sun above the screen of branches. 'I shall go and rest. We have much business tonight, and tomorrow at dawn you will attend me in the rite, Naunakhte. You should rest too. The girls will show you how things are here.'

She cast a fold of her white linen gown over her head and walked slowly away from the tree. Naunakhte watched her go, afraid to be left alone with these strangers. She looked around for the friendly face of Neferure, but could not see it. Instead she saw Tiy's bright hair and pale eyes, glittering with hatred.

' "In future," ' Tiy mocked, ' "in future, who knows?" What do you think the Lady Hunro has in mind for you, daughter of a whore and traitor?'

'My mother was not a whore!' Naunakhte protested, leaping to her feet with her fists clenched.

'She was,' insisted Tiy. 'Everyone knows it. You are no more Rameses's daughter than you are the god's. Your mother, my namesake, had taken his chief minister for her lover. They meant to rule together. You are the child of two traitors!'

'The Lady Hunro did not say so,' retorted Naunakhte, determined to keep calm.

'The Lady Hunro admired your mother when she was a

girl,' said Tiy scornfully. 'She would not like to believe ill of her. But we know, don't we?' She looked around, checking that the other girls were on her side. They shifted uncomfortably and would not meet Tiy's gleaming eyes, but not one of them spoke up to support Naunakhte.

'I know your plan,' hissed Tiy. 'You mean to usurp my place as the next Hand of Amun. It will not be so, Naunakhte, be certain of it.' Her face twisted with rage, losing its prettiness. 'I do not wish to resort to poison, as your mother did,' she snarled, 'but if I must . . .' The words hung in the air as Tiy turned and stalked away. One by one the other girls followed her. Some of them cast anxious glances at Naunakhte over their shoulders as they went, but all the same they followed Tiy.

Naunakhte stood in the shade of the palm, shuddering with anger and shame. What if what Tiy said was true? For a few moments she had believed herself daughter of Pharaoh. Was she now to find that she was the child not of one traitor, but of two?

It was too much for her. She sat down again on the cushioned couch and bowed her head as the tears came. She wrapped her arms tightly around her as if she could comfort herself.

Her right hand lay upon the mark on her arm. She opened her eyes and looked at it, and gradually her weeping ceased. Whatever the truth of her parentage, the god had not betrayed her. He had signed her before her birth and he had watched over her, and now he had called her to him. More than any man he had taken care of her.

She lifted her eyes to the sun. It glittered through the palm fronds and the remnants of her tears. 'Great god Amun,' she whispered, raising her hands in prayer, 'I will stay here, since it is your wish, whatever Tiy attempts against me. I am your servant, Lord Amun, as I was born.'

The memory came to her of the alabaster egg in the Lady Hunro's hand. It had slipped between the moist lips of her sex, opening her and filling her with fear and desire.

Tonight the god would be offered the gift of her maiden-hood. Perhaps Amun himself would take her, parting those same lips and this time not withdrawing but moving on within her, filling her, soothing her fears with his mighty presence.

'May it be so,' Naunakhte wished. She stroked the mark of the phallus on her arm and smiled at the sun. 'Oh Lord Amun, I am willing. Make me yours tonight.'

The Artist-in-Residence

Sophia Mortensen

This is light-hearted story of transgression within the confines of a religious seat of learning. The seduction of the pious always has a powerful erotic appeal, especially when the object of desire is a young and attractive man of the cloth. In this short story, Sophia Mortensen employs her knowledge of symbolist and pre-Raphaelite painting, giving her amoral heroine Caroline an advantage over the object of her desire – a trainee priest who's about to get a nasty surprise!

The Artist-in-Residence

Caroline had been artist-in-residence at St Joseph's college scarcely six weeks before the trouble started. It all began, as so many misdemeanours do, in the library. It was Friday afternoon and the pale November sun cast a watery light over the desks as assorted members of the clergy went about their business with silent efficiency. Caroline was sitting at a desk facing the entrance and was busy scribbling notes for her forthcoming paper on the role of women in religious painting.

A weighty, leather-bound encyclopaedia of art history lay in front of her, open at a section on Gustave Moreau. His work had captured her attention earlier that year, in the closing weeks of her time at art school. The sinister beauty of his Salome in *The Apparition* and the tortured, androgynous figures in his painting *The Suitors* excited in her a feeling that was positively voluptuous. The complexity of the work was mesmeric, the painterly skill impressive, but it was the women in his pictures which impressed her the most.

Not for Moreau the fluttering fairy creatures of Romanticism; Moreau's women were deadly beings whom it would be unwise to upset. They exuded a cruel majesty which Caroline aspired to. She sat admiring the colour plates, imagining herself in the role of Jupiter, dressed for nothing other than pleasure – but pleasure not given lightly.

How Caroline loathed having to wear respectable day clothes. Her postgraduate study at St Joseph's required conservative dress as this small, educational place of worship offered places only to those who chose to pursue a theological career. Caroline had worked hard for a placement in a religious establishment and wasn't about to put her aspirations in jeopardy by flouting their old-fashioned codes of conduct. To compensate, however, she had taken to wearing undergarments of unusual design. After having tried on a corset in a theatrical costumiers in London for her fancy dress graduation party earlier that year, Caroline had realised that her taste for garments of constriction was somewhat more enthusiastic than that of other girls her age. At twenty five, she was pretty and not afflicted by false modesty. Her waist-length chestnut hair, naturally shiny, hung like a glossy curtain down her back and when curled and pinned up to stunning effect looked beautifully sculptured. Her nicely-rounded form invited contemplation; while in no way skinny, her limbs were graceful and well proportioned and her breasts – although small – were immediately noticeable as pert mounds underneath her jumper. Most striking, however, was her face. Her dark eyebrows arched quizzically over deep-brown, heavily lashed eyes and her lips were full and rose-coloured, and looked as if they had been anointed with berry juice. Not for Caroline the countenance of the cynical art student, nor the insipid pallor of one who has spent too long in a darkroom. Her face exuded a healthy glow, and brightness shone from within her.

Her secret wardrobe was coming together quite nicely. With little to do at nights save more studying or venturing into town with students of a devout religious persuasion – who were, she thought, all unattractive – she would find sanctuary in her room by transforming herself from smartly dressed academic to tightly corseted mistress, experimenting with her hair and make-up and preparing for the inevitable day when –

Her reverie was interrupted as the arrival of a visiting party punctured the library's respectful silence.

'If you care to look, gentlemen, the library at St Joseph's boasts a collection of religious art books unparalleled in other colleges,' announced the elderly rector, his voice becoming louder as they approached the entrance. 'Feel free to browse, should any of you have an interest in religious art, otherwise we shall continue our tour along the main vestibule of the annexe.'

Several pairs of polished shoes creaked on the heavily varnished wooden floor and Caroline was forced to look up from her book. From where she was seated, she could spot Father Benedict addressing his troop, who were obscured from her vision by a ceiling-high bank of library shelves. He was an enthusiastic host and always showing parties of old clergymen around St Joseph's. She would probably be asked to give another lecture; to engage once more in gentle hyperbole with octogenarians. She sighed. To be surrounded each day by elderly and celibate men was nothing short of cruel. It seemed a shame that her postgraduate placement had to mean abstention from the pleasures of flirtation. During her undergraduate years, Caroline had indulged in games of lascivious courtship with enthusiasm.

She heard a voice; the first to engage in conversation with their host. 'And does the college have any paintings in its collection? Say, those of Burne-Jones or Holman-Hunt, perhaps? I've heard that some of the Pre-Raphaelite works are in private collections.'

It was then, with great pleasure, that Caroline realised her first impression had been very wrong. For the average age of the rector's visiting party was at least 55 years younger than she had predicted. She caught a glimpse of them through gaps in the shelves as they continued their stroll to the opposite end of the room. Who were they, this group of young men? Maybe they were other art students visiting St Joseph's for research purposes for their dissertations. But no. She'd already heard the rector ask them if they were interested in art. If they were from a visiting art school – as she had been, this time last year – that question would be redundant. She assumed they were all male, so it was unlikely they were students. Female art students outnumbered males by four to one.

She had to find out who they were. She swivelled around in her chair and waited as the party emerged at the other end of the room. They continued their walk towards her. As they approached, she noticed their clothes looked somewhat irregular for students unless – of course! Realisation dawned on her with great disappointment. They were trainee priests; young men sworn to the cloth.

The visiting party continued its tour of the library, crossing the room to look at some of the exhibits on view in glass cases, illuminated manuscripts and the like, all the while getting a running commentary from Father Benedict. Caroline carefully observed them from a distance. Ever aware of aesthetics, she noted with immediate approval, the appearance of one of them. At an age when young men are meant to be in their sexual prime, this poor chap was practising vows of celibacy. The sight of this beautiful young creature, clad in the sombre garments of his chosen calling, stirred feelings in Caroline which provoked an immediate response. She felt herself begin to moisten as impure thoughts flashed into her mind. The dew which soaked into her oyster-coloured silk knickers felt warm and viscous. If there was such a thing as a lust gland, Caroline's was working overtime. As her beauty lips engorged with desire, her gold labial piercing twisted itself around to gently graze her clitoris. She softly squeezed her legs together and wriggled on the seat. It would be enough to bring her off right there in the library, should she continue her hidden writhings while observing this delightful creature from a concealed distance – like some kind of academic voyeur. How old was he? she thought. No older than twenty-three, surely. His countenance resembled that of a petulant child. His expression would have looked more at home on a reform-school boy than an aspiring man of the cloth. His pale hair flopped forward over his forehead, his complexion looked baby-soft and on the end of his nose there rested a pair of round gold-rimmed glasses which added a curious intelligence to the petulance. The long black gown which covered his body from neck to feet concealed, she surmised, an athletic structure: a body which would never know the delights of a woman's ministrations, she pondered with regret.

They had finished looking at whatever it was Father Benedict was showing them and started to walk towards where Caroline was seated. She fidgeted, trying to remain impervious to the presence of the beautiful one.

'This is Miss Caroline Wardell,' informed Father Benedict, 'whose outstanding academic achievement in the subject of religious art has earned her a year's placement in our educational department. During your stay here, you may bump into Caroline in the course of your studies in the library, or in the chapel where she sketches the statues occasionally. Isn't that right, my dear?' he asked.

'Oh, absolutely. I'm already finding my time here most rewarding, Father,' she replied, squirming in her chair, fixing her gaze on the young blond man. She was scared to move from her chair. She felt so wet inside her knickers, she was worried that her skirt may have darkened and, if she stood up, this group of holy men would know her terrible secret.

Every pair of eyes was on her and all of them were male. Despite her concern about her overactive juices, she felt a curious sense of triumph. There is nothing like dominion to give one a sense of power, thought Caroline. Being the only young female in the building, she was unhindered by all-too-knowing creatures of the same sex. For men, Caroline had long been aware, were remarkably easy to affect and manipulate.

She found herself looking straight into the eyes of the object of her increasing desire. She had singled out the gorgeous one and had only a couple of moments by which to impress herself upon his consciousness. He certainly looked the most artistic of the group; the others looked somewhat gauche, ungainly and not at ease with themselves in the same way as he. Her agile mind decided to take a chance and, in the second before Father Benedict was about to announce their departure, she blurted out, 'Did I hear one of you ask something about Burne-Jones?' Without waiting for a reply she continued, 'My dissertation last year was on the subject of Pre-Raphaelite women.' She looked around at the whole group, so as not to be quite so obvious in her attentions. Luck appeared to be on her side. Her intuition rarely let her down.

'Yes,' came a quiet but assured reply from the young man. 'I find an exquisite sense of peace from contemplating the masterly skill of Pre-Raphaelite work and, well, it's something of an obsession of mine,' he continued, smiling shyly.

An obsession! Priests weren't meant to have obsessions, thought Caroline. The rest of the group seemed restless. They had obviously heard it all before.

'I see young Gregory has found something of an ally,' said Father Benedict, cheerfully. 'Come on, let us continue our tour. Gregory, we'll be heading towards the annexe for refreshments. Join us at your leisure.' And with that, the rest of the group dispersed.

Caroline was thinking fast. Her agile mind had not known such a challenge since attending her placement interview. With his colleagues out of the way, they were practically alone together. He was obviously a little nervous about this. Caroline realised it was time to take control; to work her charm with skill. 'I would very much like to show you what I've written on the subject,' she announced, 'if you were interested.' She took care to maintain a regal air. If it sounded like she was showing off, she didn't care. 'This term, I'm studying Symbolist allegory within religious painting,' she said.

She paused, placing her pen on her lower lip, making minute movements around its tip with her tongue. She was aware of how her every action was under scrutiny from her sex-starved audience of one. 'St Joseph's is wonderfully . . . equipped,' she added.

Caroline let her gaze wander from his eyes, and down the length of his body. She knew that under his priestly robes there was a pounding and delightful gift, waiting and wanting her to release it from its capacious covering. If only you knew what was happening between my legs, you wouldn't feel so alone, she thought. She cursed Catholicism and the guilty baggage which accompanied it. She wanted to introduce young Gregory to sinful pleasure. But she had to hurry. 'I would be delighted to tell you all about my studies for the particular paper I'm preparing. But do let me know if I'm boring you. I do go on sometimes.' She could tell from the young man's shaky hands and dry lips the effect she was having. She was so quietly yet so powerfully sexual when she wanted to be: when she needed to be.

'No. No, not at all,' said Gregory. 'I would be delighted to see your writing, especially your dissertation. I am always keen to learn new things about my chosen areas of interest.'

'Oh, me too,' replied Caroline. She arranged to meet him later, in the small church, where a practice communion was being conducted at seven o'clock.

Caroline couldn't face the boredom of another service and besides, she wanted time to prepare for her rendezvous. Once satisfied with her ensemble, she slipped her coat on and made her way to the chapel just before eight. She was slightly early. Trainee communion had finished and Gregory was folding the altar cloth with reverence. The others had left to prepare for supper and the chapel was silent. Caroline's entrance startled the young man. He whirled round, and stood aghast as a female image of the kind he had only dared dream of walked towards him.

Caroline was dressed very differently from how she had been earlier, in the library. Over a thin, cream silk blouse she wore a severe-looking and waist-clinching leather corset which pushed her firm breasts upwards and made them even more noticeable. Her skirt was long and dark and would have looked conservative if not for the fact that the buttons on the front of the garment, from her hem to halfway up her thighs, were undone and exposing a lot of leg. Gregory's eyes darted from her breasts to the uppermost area of her thighs. He could just see the lacy tops of her stockings and a tiny amount of flesh. Soft, warm, womanly flesh. He was so startled that his calculated, ritualistic tidying of the altar changed immediately to fumbling clumsiness. His pale hair flopped in front of his eyes and he could barely get up the courage to address her. After several drawn-out seconds of agonised silence, he managed to stammer a hello.

'You look nice,' he said, almost inaudibly, his nerves making him feel thirsty and weak.

'I feel nice, Gregory,' she replied, looking him straight in the eyes. She took the communion goblet from him and placed it back on the altar. She took one of his hands to her lips and gently kissed it, then allowed it to follow its natural course – towards her silk-covered bosom. His face reddened, his eyes were downcast and he was trembling.

'I have to wait for Father Richard,' he said. 'It's my turn to be in charge of the altar today and I'm being tested for punctuality and procedure. I think I'll have to decline your earlier invitation,' he stuttered.

Caroline could see he was worried but it didn't stop her from getting slightly annoyed at him for being so subservient to the priesthood; so in awe of religious doctrine. She was going to have to be firm if she was to get her way with this young man. 'It's not an invitation, Gregory,' Caroline said firmly. 'It's an order. I noticed the way you were looking at me earlier in the library.' She leaned closer and grabbed him by the arm, pressing him firmly against the altar. She slipped her right leg between his legs, trapping him with her thighs. With her right hand she lightly traced a path towards the centre of his body; an area as yet untouched by woman. She smiled as she felt his hardness and she moistened. 'You're supposed to be sworn to celibacy very soon, my dear. This could be your last and only chance to spend an evening in the company of a normal woman. Think about it,' she added, coquettishly. 'I won't tell a soul.'

'I'm not experienced. I ... I don't know much, well, anything really.'

'Don't worry. I do,' whispered Caroline into his ear. She continued to rub her hand along the dark cloth of his priestly robes. His penis felt huge and hot inside its confines.

In a moment of temptation too strong to resist, Gregory consented and allowed her to lead him from the chapel, around the back of the building, and up to the residents' rooms. The halls of residence were deserted, as was his place at the supper table. Caroline wasted no time. She marched him along the corridor and unlocked the door to her room. Although modestly furnished, it was lavishly adorned and reproductions of Symbolist and religious paintings hung on the walls. A large pencil drawing of Salome holding the head of John the Baptist featured over her bed and reproductions of Moreau's decadent couplings lit up the walls. A look of apprehension crossed young Gregory's face as he swiftly realised he had entered the chamber of some kind of Jezebel. But the pent-up desire of a catalogue of unreleased fantasies swirled around his head and, in the presence of such masterful command, he was powerless to resist.

'Take that ridiculous cape off,' she commanded. 'What's the point of dressing up if you're not allowed to have fun.'

'I've not met a girl like you before,' said Gregory. 'I think you're very pretty but I'm not sure I want to go through with this. To think that I've sinned in the house of God.'

'Oh shut up, and stop being pathetic,' said Caroline. She pulled him over to her dressing table and forced him to look in the mirror. 'Look at yourself. Look how attractive you are.' She took off his glasses and ruffled his hair. 'You'll not regret coming here, I assure you,' she said and eased him down on to the bed. She took her coat off and paraded in front of him. Then, slowly, she eased her skirt down over her hips and let it fall to the floor. She stood beside the bed and slipped her hand into her black, lacy knickers and began to touch herself. She was wet and excited although she maintained a calm exterior. She knew that her behaviour would have an immediate effect on the young priest, but if he were to leave now she couldn't bear it. She was too far gone in her arousal. She was going to have to play this very carefully. He lay on her bed, continuing to look nervous but unable to take his eyes off her.

'What do you want me to do?' he asked.

'Turn over,' she ordered.

'What? Why?'

'I said turn over,' she repeated, her irritation and desire inflaming her determination. Briefly he ran his hand over her leather corset. She could see he was fascinated by the material but was too shy to ask if he could touch it properly. She smiled and, once more, indicated for him to turn over. He obeyed, rolling over onto his stomach. As a precaution against him escaping, should he suddenly be consumed with guilt, she took a length of sash cord from the box of tricks stored under her bed and began to bind his hands together.

'Why are you doing this to me? I want to explore you fully. There is no need to tie my hands together,' he protested. But Caroline did not want to hear useless protestations and immediately gagged him with one of her scarves.

'Now you're going to be quiet as you have no choice,' she announced triumphantly. She pulled him up off the bed, wrapped her arms around him and pressed her body against him. He groaned softly, from behind his gag.

'I know that you are a filthy-minded young man because I can feel that you are in a state of excitement,' she said with relish, feeling the hot promise of his hardness through the dark cloth of his trousers. 'And I'm sure that Father Richard and Father Benedict would be most disapproving if they knew what you were doing now,' she continued. 'Indeed, you had better come up with a good excuse for your absence at dinner.'

Gregory whimpered a protest, but by now she had released his stiff prick from its confines and was working it with practised skill as she looked him fully in the eyes. It was a beauty indeed.

His gaze was averted; he couldn't bear to see his own arousal witnessed by someone else; a young, attractive woman at that. Oh the shame was too much to bear! His pious pretensions were dispatched to the realms of ridicule as he blushed and moaned and made pathetic attempts to struggle. Caroline snapped him out of his self-pity.

'I'm going to spare you your virginity and not demand that you perform for me,' Caroline said. 'For I have something even more exciting for you which I know you will like and I'll bet we both get lots of pleasure from.'

She eased him back down on to the bed, untied his hands then demanded that he kneel on all fours with his face turned to the wall. She took another scarf from her dressing table and blindfolded her errant charge. After a few seconds she returned and began to remove his trousers, gently easing them over his enormous hard-on. When they were pulled down to his knees it was then that the full horror of this shameful situation made itself apparent to young Gregory. As she applied a liberal amount of lubricant between his buttocks he knew his fate was sealed. He wasn't going to be made to fuck her. He was going to get a buggering!

Caroline was already wearing the strap-on dildo as she took up her position behind him. How wonderfully alive and powerful she felt watching this young supplicant in the throes of his debauching. His blond hair was getting very messed up each time she forced his face down on to the pillow. He still made small protests into his gag but he was as stiff as a pikestaff and not far from his release. With gentle coaxing she eased the solution into him with her finger, a centimetre at a time until he was sufficiently lubricated. Then, after taking aim, her latex appendage pointed at his virgin bottom-hole, she plunged her six inches into the trainee priest. He yelped in surprise and groaned with a mixture of discomfort, protest and shame; an unholy trinity of violation.

'I know you want to come, you little slut,' she teased, 'but not until I've give you a good seeing-to. You must be made to respect the female; to know her presence is divine and that she is beyond reproach. You can worship your Blessed Virgin all you like, but the devil woman is much more fun. And the words of the song are true, you know; she's going to get you from behind.' Caroline laughed and continued her thrusting.

The north wind puffed a cool breeze through the slightly open window and Caroline felt victorious. There was nothing she preferred to this moment. The shame – the dishonour of this obstinate would-be parson fed her with an energy she found revitalising. She was a champion of depravity at last! His young body, never before violated in this way, was hers for the next few moments. She intended to enjoy it.

Being forced to kneel on all fours, he was unable to give himself the release he craved so fiercely. Caroline sensed his urgency and – although a cruel temptress – was not so cruel as to not let him have his own pleasure. But his release would be in the form of his own debasement, she decided. She stopped lunging into him for a moment and whispered in his ear, 'If you promise not to yell, I'll let you have what you want.'

He nodded his head furiously and she knew she had him in her power. She untied the scarves from the back of his head and gently eased out of him. He turned around to face her; his cheeks crimson with embarrassment, his breathing fast and shallow. He found the courage to quietly ask, 'Please may I make love to you?'

'What?' Caroline exclaimed. 'Your impertinence is astonishing. To think that you have the gall to expect that I would allow you the indulgence of that which is only permitted in the sanctity of marriage! Oh no, my lad. I want to see your virgin sperm leaving your filthy prick.' She unstrapped the dildo and threw it aside then began to rub herself slowly through her knickers. Gregory's prick was straining and purple and she knew there would be little point in allowing him to fuck her. 'Play with yourself like you do when you're alone,' she ordered.

'How do you know I do that?' he asked, kneeling up on the bed.

'Just call it female intuition,' she replied. He clasped his hand around his huge penis and slowly began to work it up and down.

Caroline moistened her lips with her tongue and, as she watched him, felt her own arousal building to a point of no return. She had resisted the temptation to masturbate earlier, as she prepared herself for their liaison – and Gregory's inevitable fate. She often got really turned on when dressing up for sex – when the excitement was just too much. Sometimes, it was such a wonderful bother being a girl! She could feel her orgasm beginning to build in her thighs and spread quickly upwards to the centre of her being. She made Gregory watch her and slowed her movements to an almost unbearably enticing speed.

'Stop,' she commanded, grabbing hold of his hand. 'I want you to watch me come first. It's my privilege as your mistress for the night.'

Just a couple more gentle touches and her cunt exploded exquisitely, dancing inside her panties. She was coming, although the only obvious sign was the rapturous expression on her face. She threw back her head and gasped with pleasure. Gregory watched in fascinated awe. The pangs of guilt had long since abated and his whole body felt alive with new sensations. There was no going back. He had to experience what Caroline had just experienced.

'Please, please may I come now?' he pleaded, although he found it difficult to say the word.

'OK, Gregory,' she replied, gently. 'But keep your eyes closed and do it slowly. I'm going to watch every second of your most intimate moment.' There was one thing left for Caroline to do in order to complete the task she had set herself earlier. Still recovering from her orgasm, she carefully leaned back and took her camera out from underneath the bed. It was all ready, with flashlight in place and shutter speed correctly set. She concealed it behind her, in case the young priest would be tempted to open his eyes. 'Keep your eyes closed, my sweet. You look wonderful,' she said.

'I can't stop it, Caroline. I'm going to do it now. I'm going to come all over you. Oh blessed saints, forgive me,' he cried as he spurted his virgin tribute over her bed and on to his priestly robes. With all the skill of a wildlife photographer, she captured him at the Zen instant – the moment of his climax.

* * *

Ten minutes later, they lay together on Caroline's bed. She gently stroked his arm and he remained silent but content, his lovely hair tumbling over the pillow. So it was true what was written in those filthy magazines, thought Gregory. It really was as if flashing lights exploded inside your head when it happened. It had never been as powerful before, when he did it by himself. He wanted that feeling again. He turned to Caroline and whispered, 'Can I come to your room again? I'm here for another two weeks and I'd very much like to make love to you properly, if I may. I would also still like to read your dissertation.'

She smiled. Yes. She'd like that very much. Perhaps they would meet in the chapel after dark and slip into the confessional. She was already concocting fiendish plans. 'Oh I'll have to look at my diary, Gregory,' she said, feigning disinterest. 'You had better return to your room now, though. Sharing with the others, I think they'd notice if you didn't return at all.'

He gathered himself together, polishing his glasses and adjusting his trousers. He was already conjuring up untruths as to his absence at the supper table. It was no good. He realised that he was already on the road to unholy behaviour, even if he had retained his virginity. What a dilemma! He slipped out of her room after planting several kisses on Caroline's lips at her insistence. As he tiptoed down the corridor, he couldn't help grinning to himself.

Before retiring to bed that night, Caroline sat up, admiring herself in the mirror. Another one saved from a life of chastity she thought, smugly. And this time she would have something else to show for it. For her photographic evidence would provide the basis for a stunning new work to be unveiled in the church gallery on the presentation of her master's degree. I think I'll call it *Led Into Temptation*, she thought, smiling sweetly, unpinning her hair and allowing it to cascade around her shoulders.

A Dangerous Addiction

Zoe le Verdier

Married comfort. Friday-night dinner parties and salads dressed with balsamic vinegar. White fluffy pillows and suburban security. For three years Johnny's been happy with this. Then, one night, he realises he's been missing danger, adventure, and taking a risk. When he meets a tall, confident, fit woman called Nova, who drinks like a man and can chew him up for breakfast, he weakens – just once.

But once isn't enough. Johnny wants more danger, more excitement, and more thrills. And when he returns to the scene of his infidelity, she ups the stakes and brings along her husband. He's an expert in pain and he's known as the Marquis. And he isn't going to let Johnny off lightly.

This story is taken from Zoe le Verdier's first collection of short stories entitled *Insomnia*. *In the Dark* – her second, and just as varied – collection of cutting-edge shorts was published in October. She specialises in contemporary settings and relationships with a powerful subtext. Apart from writing numerous erotic short stories, she has also written three novels for Black Lace: *The Succubus*, *The Seven-Year List*, and *Undercover Secrets*.

A Dangerous Addiction

*H*e met her in a gay bar. His eyes were immediately drawn to her, although that was understandable, since he was the only staunchly straight man in the pub and she was one of only four women there, and she stood apart from them. She wasn't one of the sycophantic fag hags, cackling raucously at the jokes of the vicious queens and gentle queers. She sat alone at the bar, not bothering to turn around when she was jostled and nudged, her eyes glazed with boredom. He watched her drinking – she drank like a man – and something gripped him. It might have been lust, but it felt stronger, more sinister than that. It ran through his veins, quicker and darker and stickier than blood; it pulsed deep inside him, in time with the pounding beat of the music.

He pushed his way to the bar and looked at her while he waited to be served. She was beautiful in her selfish solitude. A beauty that scared him because, like a child wanting to pull the wings off an insect, he wanted to crush her. To stick his cock in her mouth and fuck her. The vision was disturbing but her thoughts precluded him and he wanted to invade her private world. He wanted her to look at him; to acknowledge his existence. To care whether he lived or died.

'Hello,' he said hopefully, then immediately wished he hadn't.

She turned and looked at him. She summed him up with eyes that fell quickly over his body, pausing at his shoes. They were nice shoes. He believed in spending a little extra on good shoes. It was always worth it. But she didn't look overly impressed.

'Can I buy you a drink?'

Her eyes narrowed. 'What do you want?'

'I don't want anything,' he lied. 'I was just offering you a drink.'

'You don't know me. Why on earth would you offer me a drink? Unless . . . Unless, of course, you're going to try and chat me up.'

I see, he thought. It's like that, is it? 'Well, would you mind if I tried to chat you up?'

'Didn't your mother teach you not to talk to strangers?'

'Yes, but . . .'

She smiled slightly. 'But what?'

'You're more attractive than the average stranger.'

'So you're willing to break Mother's rules? Talking to strangers can get you into trouble, you know.'

Her eyes flashed with evil. A stream of pure desire shot from his stomach into his mouth. 'Is that a promise?'

'It's a warning.' Her dark eyebrows flickered suggestively. 'I should also warn you that I'm married.' She gave him a look that didn't exactly say, 'Keep away, I'm married' – it said something else altogether. It said, 'Yes, I know I'm horny. I know you want me. I would have been very surprised and actually quite disappointed if you hadn't tried to chat me up.' At least, that's what he thought it said. But at the same time she lifted her hand and showed him the undeniable, solid-silver proof of her wedding ring.

'Is that why you drink in gay bars? To avoid all the men who would otherwise try and chat you up?'

'How do you know I'm not gay?'

She couldn't possibly be. Lesbians just didn't look like she looked. 'I thought you said you were married?'

'I could be married to a woman. Things aren't always what they seem, you know.'

'Are you married to a woman?'

'No. And I don't come in here to avoid being chatted up. I like being chatted up.' This time she gave him a look that said, 'Don't even think about it/I'll eat you for breakfast/Come and have a go if you think you're hard enough.'

He was confused. There were conflicting signals sparking and clashing in the muggy, nicotine-stained air. Back off. Come on. Try it if you dare. Johnny was out of practice with all these pre-fuck mind games – he'd been married for three years. His relationship with his wife was so comfortable; so easy. He hadn't considered flirting with another woman since his wedding day, let alone picking a woman up in a bar and dragging her into a back alley and pushing her to her knees and dragging his fingers through her long blonde hair and unzipping his flies and –

'So what's your excuse?' she asked, giving him a smile that derailed his train of thought.

He blinked several times. 'Sorry?'

'What are you doing in here if you're straight? If you *are* straight, that is,' she added, teasing him. 'Of course, you could be bisexual, which would explain why you're in a gay bar trying to chat up a woman.'

'I'm straight,' he said. 'Honestly,' he insisted, at her sneer of doubt. 'You can ask them.' He tilted his head towards the corner, to a quiet group of young men in very tight T-shirts. 'I work with that lot. They dragged me in here. I think they're trying to convert me.'

She didn't even bother to look round at them. 'You're definitely straight?'

'Definitely.'

She looked as if she knew better. 'You sure about that?'

'Very sure.'

Her small, sexy, cock-hungry mouth shrugged. 'Shame. Bisexual men are far more interesting.'

He was silent, and slightly surprised to be kicking himself for not being bisexual. What was it about her? She made him feel conservative with a big C. Since when had plain old 'straight' become so boring?

'So, are you going to try and chat me up, then?

'But you're married.'

'So are you.' She smiled sneakily, obviously pleased with herself and amused at having spotted his wedding ring.

'Just because a man's married, it doesn't mean he has to stop noticing other women.'

'And what about fucking?'

'Sorry?'

'Do you draw the line at noticing other women? Or do you fuck them too?'

Her aggression should have been a turn-off, but it wasn't. It was just frightening. He'd never felt such pressure to impress a woman – and such a need to get inside her knickers.

'Look at my wedding ring,' she invited, holding out her hand.

He took her fingers in his. Jesus. The sensation of holding a part of her body. Feeling her skin on his. The temptation to pull her off her stool, pin her down on the dirty, sticky floor and push up her skirt and fuck her, hard.

'Look at it,' she urged.

Her low, luscious voice wrapped itself around his neck and slowly squeezed. He wanted to close his eyes and roll around naked in the filthy thoughts that were turning his mind into a dirty, muddy swamp; but he obeyed her and looked. Her wedding ring was a flattened band of dark silver with letters engraved all around it.

CKMEFU

'Fuck me,' she said.

He looked up at her. 'Pardon?'

'That's what it says. On my ring.'

He looked down again. The letters rearranged themselves and punched him between the eyes. 'Your husband gave you a wedding ring with "Fuck me" engraved on it? Charming.'

'Don't you want to?'

'Sorry?'

'Don't you want to fuck me?'

He should have thought. Should have realised that this woman, whose husband had married her with a Fuck Me ring, was danger. But he didn't think.

Like a child inching his way towards the edge of the high-diving board, he tried to convince himself he could do it. Would do it. He counted to ten and then flung himself off. 'Yes,' he said, as the air whipped past his face and the force of the fall sent his heart jumping up into his mouth.

She stared at him for a long time, head tilted, eyes narrowed, summing him up. Assessing him. Deciding whether he was going to be allowed to fuck her. 'How will you do it?' she asked at last, as if this was the final question she'd reached in her mind. The final hurdle.

'How will I . . .?'

'Fuck me. How will you fuck me?'

Oh God. This was pressure. This woman had probably seen it all, done it all. What could he possibly offer that was going to shock or arouse her? How was he going to impress her enough to make her stand up and say, 'OK. Let's go'? What could he say?

The barman hovered meaningfully and she looked up, breaking the spell; saving Johnny from coming up with anything witty and/or devastatingly sexy – for the time being.

'What are you drinking?' Johnny asked.

'Southern Comfort.'

He smiled to himself. She could have been the poster girl for Southern Comfort – she'd have fitted in perfectly with its advertising campaign and the image of its drinkers as non-conformists. She certainly didn't conform to his usual idea of what was sexy. Up until now, he'd always gone for shy, small, sweet types – stereotypes of what he thought women should be. Women who wore pretty, flowery dresses and perfume and necklaces and delicate, strappy shoes with little heels and who looked adorably cute wearing his rugby shirt on Sunday mornings. Softly spoken women who flinched at the F-word and got positively upset at the C-word. Sensitive women. Gentle, girly women. She was none of those things. He watched her, her eyes lazily following the barman's movements as he served them, and he longed to see inside her head.

She nodded with casual familiarity as another drink was placed in front of her. She took a big, manly, greedy gulp – the sign of someone who needed a drink rather than enjoyed it – then turned back to him. 'Go on then. Tell me how you'd fuck me. I'm dying to know.' She licked her upper lip. 'Make me wet,' she challenged.

'I . . . I . . .' Oh God. 'Well, I'd . . .'

She grinned. 'Tell me what you thought when you first saw me. The truth.'

The truth? The truth was lurking in a dark place in his brain; hiding behind a door he didn't want to open. He couldn't possibly tell her what he'd thought when he'd first seen her. His mouth flapped. He swallowed air. She raised an eyebrow and waited.

'I, well, I . . .'

She drummed her fingers on the bar.

'I thought . . . I thought you were very attractive.'

'Is that all?'

'Yes,' he lied.

She thought about this for a moment. 'You didn't think about maybe sticking your cock in my mouth?'

She said the words very slowly, deliberately rolling them around on her tongue before letting them out. She left her mouth open in teasing invitation, and he couldn't help staring at her small lips. In his silence, he admitted that she was right.

'I'm right, aren't I? A lot of men want me to suck their cocks. Something about my having a small mouth, apparently.'

His mobile rang. For a while, deafened by the sexual storm raging between him and this woman, he didn't hear its shrill, insistent whining.

'It's my wife,' he said, after pulling the phone out of his jacket pocket and reading the number.

'Ignore it,' she challenged.

His brow dipped. 'It's my wife. I can't ignore it.'

She shrugged disinterestedly, as if this loyalty was a weakness on his part. He watched her talking to the barman as he spoke to his wife, and he wished he could hear what they were saying. They were laughing at some secret joke – laughing at him, he suspected – and he could barely concentrate on the instructions his wife was giving. 'Get home as soon as you can, darling. David and Penny are coming over for dinner then we're going to watch a video. Can you buy some French bread on your way home? Oh, and David will be driving, so you'd better get some mineral water too. Where are you? I can hardly hear you, that music's so loud. Have you been drinking?'

She slid from her stool. On her feet, she was as tall as him. Tall, for a woman. Imposing. Scary. She knocked his shoulder as she brushed past him and weaved her way through the crowd to the cigarette machine. 'Are you listening?' asked his wife. 'Yes,' he said, watching her hips sway; her long strides; her fingers tearing off the cigarette packet's plastic wrapper as if it was his skin. He promised his wife he'd be home in half an hour and put his phone back in his pocket.

'Your wife checking up on you?' she asked, getting back on to her stool. 'Does she know you go to gay bars and talk to strangers?'

'Does your husband know about everything you do?'

'My husband and I have a very trusting relationship. He lets me fuck other men. And I let him.'

Oh Jesus. Oh Jesus. If that wasn't an invitation, what was? He gritted his teeth and cursed his pretty, sweet, clever, loving wife and their happy, comfortable marriage which suddenly seemed too comfy – a bed so soft he couldn't clamber out of it; white, fluffy pillows choking him with mouthfuls of feathers; sheets so clean they'd been bleached of life. A freshly washed nightmare. He cursed dinner parties and friends he knew too well and Friday nights with bottles of wine and videos. He cursed the safety of it all.

She pulled out a cigarette, without offering one to Johnny. He slid closer and offered her a light. She held his wrist and lit her fag. She carried on holding his wrist and studied the inscription on the battered gold of his Zippo. 'To Johnny. Love, Rebecca.' She let go. 'Does Rebecca trust you, Johnny?'

He swallowed hard. 'She trusts me not to sleep with other women.'

'But sometimes you want to.' She sucked on her cigarette and exhaled a thought. 'I know the feeling, Johnny. Sometimes my husband just isn't enough. Sometimes I just want to stay out all night and have dirty sex with someone I've only just met.'

Oh. Jesus.

His phone rang again. Did Rebecca have radar? 'Yes?' he said, a little too forcefully, so that she asked what was wrong and told him not to get uptight, she was the one at home doing the cooking, all she was asking him to do was pick up a few things she'd forgotten, if that wasn't too much trouble. 'Half an hour,' he promised. 'No, I haven't left yet. I'm just about to. No, I won't forget the balsamic vinegar, I promise.'

He sighed and turned off his phone. What the fuck did she need balsamic vinegar for? 'I've got to go,' he said with heavy regret. 'I wish I didn't have to.'

'Don't then.'

'I have to.'

She shrugged. 'You don't have to do anything you don't want to.'

God, how he wished that was true. He spent his life doing things he didn't want to. 'Believe me, I have to get home.'

She blew smoke in his face. 'You just haven't got the balls to fuck me, have you?'

Probably not. 'I just have to get home.'

'OK. Go, then.'

Suddenly, he realised how little he meant to her. He knew that if she never saw him again it wouldn't matter – he would never occupy so much as a second of her thoughts.

She, however, would occupy long hours and days and sleepless nights of his. 'Can I call you?'

'What would be the point if Rebecca doesn't let you out to play?'

'I'd like to see you again.'

She stared at the fingers holding her fag, following the swirling smoke with lazy, drunken eyes.

'Will I see you again?'

'In your dreams.'

She turned away. He did something he shouldn't have done – he reached out and grabbed her wrist. He couldn't help himself, but as she looked down at his hand she withered his bones with her stare and he wished he hadn't done it.

'What do you think you're doing?'

'Sorry,' he said, uncurling his fingers.

'Go home,' she suggested. 'Go and shag your wife senseless.'

'I don't want to.' His voice was bleating. 'I want to shag you.'

'Then ring your wife and tell her you won't be coming home tonight.'

'I can't do that.'

'Then close your eyes and pretend it's me.' She glanced at him; in an instant his innards turned to charcoal: black, flaking, dead. 'It'll be the best fuck your wife's ever had.'

'But . . .'

'But what? I've made it pretty clear I'd have let you fuck me, and still you tell me you have to go home. Go then. I don't give a fuck, either way.'

She looked at him for what seemed like forever. Then she turned her back on him and began a low, private conversation with the barman, who was hovering again.

Johnny fought the urge to pick up her drink and throw Southern Comfort and glass and fury and frustration at the grubby wall, slammed some money on to the bar and slunk back to his friends to deliver their drinks and tell them he was leaving. He could taste anger in his mouth, even more flat and disappointing than his pint. 'Fuck,' he muttered, quickly swallowing his drink because he'd paid for it and didn't want it to go to waste. 'Fuck.'

He watched her. He had never experienced such a violent rush of sexual desire. He wanted to pull her long, blonde hair. He wanted to bite her lips. He wanted to fuck her, hard. Until it hurt. Until she cried. Until those wide blue eyes were forced to show surrender. She had the sexiest eyes he had ever seen.

She had a tattoo on her upper arm that he hadn't noticed before – a small green and blue butterfly. She had a streak of dark blue running through her hair, and her long fingernails were painted dark blue too, to match the short, dark-denim skirt that showed her muscular thighs and shapely calves. She had on heavy black leather boots and a thin leather collar around her neck. Her skimpy T-shirt was a pale blue that matched her eyes. The material was silky and incredibly clingy, and it seemed to Johnny that she wasn't wearing a bra underneath. Her tits looked lovely: pert and just too big to be a handful. He imagined them jiggling as she straddled him. He imagined biting on her nipples until he tasted blood.

She downed her drink in one, stood up and leaned over the bar to kiss the barman on both cheeks. Her skirt rode up as she bent forwards and Johnny felt the breath hovering in his throat, burning his insides like a mouthful of dry ice. He imagined those long, tanned, muscular thighs wrapped around his waist. Around his neck. Imagined his thumbs pressing into her flesh. Imagined them shaking – not trembling gently, but full-on shaking – at the force of his fucking. He imagined biting those thighs until they were spattered with dark red teeth-marks.

He blinked and tried not to think of those things. He watched as the barman – a queer so raging that his bald head and pierced tongue and thick moustache made Johnny's skin crawl – whispered something to her and she nodded, and when she turned there was a secret smile on her lips. He felt panicky as he watched her squeeze a path to the door, and suddenly, for the first time since the age of about ten, when he'd developed a fascination for catching butterflies and pinning their beautiful wings down and watching as they slowly gave up the fight for life and died, he discovered that violence lurked inside his mind.

Through the window, he saw her emerge into the sticky summer night. Like a wild animal released into the urban jungle, she blinked hesitantly. She looked up and down the pavement several times, unsure of where to go. Turning her back on the street, she sheltered herself from the world with a long drag of her cigarette while she ran her fingers through her hair. Then she looked directly at him. She smiled.

That was it. Fuck dinner. Fuck balsamic vinegar and

videos and David and Penny. Fuck Rebecca. He slammed down his pint, slopping a little on the already sticky table. 'Got to go,' he said to his friends.

But by the time he escaped from The Marquis, she was gone. 'Fuck,' he chanted. 'Fuck, fuck, fuck.'

He would never find her in the dark. His panic inexplicably grew into terror. He hunted for a flash of blue, without success.

He would have to go home, close his eyes, pretend his wife was the other woman and shag her senseless. He started walking to the tube.

Then he spotted her. She was on the opposite side of the road, standing at the bus stop. Laughing at him with her cold eyes. As he waited impatiently for a gap in the traffic he stared at her determinedly. He wouldn't let her get away a second time – not after that smile.

She languidly turned her head as he appeared at her side, breathless. Her self-assurance made him feel inane and childish and utterly stupid, like a spotty, pre-pubescent boy asking a supermodel for a date. 'Hello again.'

'Haven't you gone yet? Your wife'll be getting very anxious.'

'I . . .' What should he say? You smiled at me and I changed my mind? I'd like to fuck you now, if that's OK? 'I don't feel like going home, just yet,' he ventured, hoping he sounded rebellious and a lot braver than he felt. 'I thought maybe we could go somewhere where we can, er, pick up where we left off?'

She tilted her head and weighed him up. 'OK,' she said at last. 'Come on. I owe you a drink.'

He stood in the corner and she brought the drinks over. The Liberty was much quieter: a back-street pub populated with businessmen. When she spoke, her voice was hushed conspiratorially.

'What did you think of The Marquis, then?'

She pronounced it the French way – Mar-key – rather

than the English, Mar-kwiss. He thought nothing of it. 'It's
OK,' he said. 'Not really my scene, to be honest. But I'm
glad I went. I wasn't expecting to meet anyone like you in
there.'

She looked at him over the rim of her glass as she drank.
His penis thickened as he realised how beautiful her eyes
were. Wide, with thick, dark lashes that didn't match her
blonde hair. Pale-blue irises streaked with a darker, dirtier
blue. Pupils dilated. Did that mean she wanted him? She
looked directly inside his head, baiting him with silence.

'Would you like to see something?' she asked, not
waiting for an answer and knowing that he would want
to see whatever she chose to show him. A strange
expression lit her eyes. She backed herself into the corner
and pulled at his sleeve, moving him until he shielded her
from the view of the rest of the pub. She put down her
glass and turning her back, lifted her T-shirt.

Her skirt was slung low over hips that curved upwards
into a slim waist. Her skin was brown and luxuriant, but
damaged like a peach that had been repeatedly and cruelly
slashed with a blunt knife. Either side of the furrow of her
spine, her flesh was scarred with purple streaks of violence. Johnny became aware of the loudness of his heartbeat knocking at his hollow chest. She turned to face him
again and, letting her top fall, she eased up a corner of her
skirt. First, unavoidably, he saw the black lace edge of her
knickers, and dark tufts of pubic hair trapped beneath the
elastic; then deep, mottled wounds of green, brown and
indigo at the top of her leg. He saw a welt on her inner
thigh, recent and long: a raised strip of swollen, pink flesh.
Holding his breath, and without realising what he was
doing, he ran his fingers over the wound. Either side of
the welt her skin was cool, and so soft it made him ache.

His voice, when it eventually arrived in the smothered,
smoky atmosphere, was barely audible. 'Who did this to
you?' He grabbed her shoulder. 'Who did this? Tell me.'

'My husband.' She seemed slightly, insanely proud of this announcement.

She dropped her skirt. Johnny looked furtively around to see if anyone else had been watching, while she retrieved her drink and bathed in its amber glow.

He looked at her: at her bowed head, her golden hair swishing forward and hiding her shame; at the long fingers clutching her glass as if the alcohol could save her if she hung on tightly enough. And rage forced its way through his gritted teeth. He couldn't get his head round this, at all. Such a strong woman – how could she have let this happen?

'Is he sick?' The hand that held his glass shook slightly. Anger swelled at the back of his neck; worse, his penis thickened further. 'Is he sick?' he said again, not knowing what else to say. 'Why do you let him do this to you? Why do you stay with him?'

She lifted her head, moving in slow motion as if it was a tremendous effort. Her eyes were glazed. She had retreated from the present and moved back into her own, dark world. Her voice was calm. 'You wouldn't understand.'

'No, I don't think I would.' He shook his head. 'Explain it to me. I want to understand. I want to help you.'

'You can't help me. I don't need help. I need him.'

He cupped her elbow in his palm. He wanted to rip her T-shirt at its low V-neck; to suck her breasts. He wrenched his mind away from her breasts and back to what he was supposed to be thinking. 'You've got to get away from him.'

She swallowed the rest of her drink and shuddered as its fire hit her damaged belly. 'I don't want to. I trust him. He's the only man I've ever met who understands me.'

She ran out of the back door, into the darkness. For the second time that evening, Johnny abandoned his pint and ran after her.

He couldn't see her, which meant she mustn't be far

away. He felt sweat prickling over his skin with the muggy heat, and swirling confusion in his brain. He stumbled along the empty pavement behind the pub, desperate to find her, although he was no longer sure why.

She was hiding down the first dark alleyway he came to; hiding like a child wanting to be discovered. She stood with her forehead to the black wall, her palms spread against the bricks as if he was about to frisk her. As he approached her, he heard that her breathing was shallow and irregular. He assumed she was having a panic attack.

'Are you all right?' He placed a gentle hand on her shoulder.

She shivered and turned to face him.

He struggled to comprehend the look in her eyes – plea, test or warning? Ashamed by his overwhelming desire to fuck her, he felt responsible. 'Look, you must take my card.' He delved into his pocket. 'If you need any help, or you just want to talk, you can ring me any time. Promise me you will.'

She studied the card for a moment before pushing his hand away. 'Thanks,' she whispered. 'But I don't need any help.'

'I think you do,' he said. 'Jesus, I thought you said you and your husband had a trusting relationship?'

'We do.'

'I'm sorry. I don't understand. He lets you sleep with other men – and you let him hurt you?'

'He lets me sleep with other men but he punishes me for it, afterwards. It's the price I pay for my freedom.'

'I still don't understand.'

'You may never understand.'

'Jesusfuck.' He sighed at the empty hopelessness and the utter madness of the situation. Don't get involved, his common sense told him. But he already was. He was already addicted to this mad, dangerous, frighteningly sensual woman.

THE BEST OF BLACK LACE

For a long time, they stood in silence, looking at each other while her breathing slowed.

Then he kissed her.

Their lips matched. He had kissed women before whose lips had been out of sync with his. Their noses had bumped and they had banged teeth. They had stopped before he had wanted to, or wanted to carry on when he'd been itching to move on to the next stage. They had been forceful against his tenderness, or vice versa. But her kissing was fluent. As their tongues touched and he tasted Southern Comfort, he felt himself floating into insanity. He clasped her face in his hands. Her fingers moved over his back and he felt his cock, straining for release, pressing hard against her hip.

When they parted for air her lips shone with their saliva. She was smiling. 'Would you like me to . . .?' Her fingers moulded tightly to his balls.

'No.' He wanted it desperately. 'No.'

She pressed him against the wall and knelt in front of him. He groaned as she unzipped him. Guilt speared him because he had already envisaged this scenario, long before he'd had the right to. He forced himself to keep still and not to thrust into her, like he wanted to. Knowing what he knew now made the agony of his coming violent and quick. He pulled her up and held her, tasting himself in her mouth. He had never wanted to do that before, but it was different with her. He was surprised by the flavour.

'Your turn,' he promised. 'I want to do something for you.'

She jolted as if he'd hit her. 'No.'

He paused to zip his weeping cock back into his jeans, and she was gone. He'd lost her. He went home, closed his eyes and shagged his wife senseless.

Outside, in his garden, the man and woman who had followed him home lay on the grass with their fingers in each other's pants.

'What do you think?' asked the bald, pierced, mousta-chioed man.

'I think he's perfect,' said the blonde, blue-eyed, giggling woman.

'Think he'll co-operate?'

'Of course he will.' She closed her cruel fingers around his prick. 'He's dying to fuck me. I know his type.'

He groaned, partly with the sensation of his cock thick-ening in her grasp; partly at the thought of the man inside that house who was blissfully unaware of the two warped perverts lying on his lawn; and of what they had in store for him. 'Did you show him the whip marks?'

She smiled. 'He didn't know what to think,' she said. 'He had a hard-on and he was ashamed of it.'

'Oooh,' he cooed appreciatively. 'Shame. My favourite.'

'I thought pain was your favourite.'

'Pain and shame. I get the pain with you, but you're no good where the other's concerned. You're utterly shameless.'

She grinned and spread her legs as four of his fingers thrust inside her hungry pussy. 'Shameless,' she repeated in a grateful whisper, as if she'd just been given her mantra.

Johnny went back to The Marquis every night, but she never returned. The barman watched him suspiciously, and Johnny supposed he took him for one of those un-happily married, closet gays. His wife probably thought he was either having an affair or becoming an alcoholic. His boss assumed he had problems at home and told him to take some time off, after he made several mis-takes that cost the company minor expense and major embarrassment.

He hid himself in thoughts of her. In his lonely fantasy, he replayed their scene over and over again with the blind obsession of a trainspotter. He catalogued every moment and savoured every word. Sometimes he forgot a minute but essential detail and would have to rewind to the beginning again. Sometimes he would purposely omit a section, so that he could run back to the start and relive that amazing, earth-shattering, mind-altering first moment he'd seen her. Occasionally, he'd skip straight to the end, and his cock would twitch at the thought of her lips around him.

In a way, he didn't want to see her again. It was tempting to hold her in his memory, where he could gain access at any time. His fantasy could have been very satisfying, especially after he began to elaborate on reality, fucking her while he jerked off. It was almost perfect, apart from that look in her eyes: unresolved, incongruous. There was sorrow there, and the look of someone lost. But on top of that, there rested a layer of certainty which intrigued him. He had to understand it; had to find her.

Besides, she needed saving from her husband. Johnny saw every painful blotch in his mind, plotted clearly as if he had a map of her injuries that he'd drawn himself, and each day that passed without seeing her could only mean she was being subjected to some new and unbearable torture. The other man invaded his thoughts – a psychotic ogre who beat her mercilessly. Johnny imagined her being tied up and made to suck her husband's cock, which in his mind was huge and threatening and suffocating. (This thought aroused him intensely, and he hastily buried it like a guilty boy stuffing pornography under his mattress.)

He didn't see her for a month, and he began to fear the worst. He nearly went to the police station to report her missing, but realised just in time how stupid he would sound. He didn't even know her name. He became withdrawn, and his wife suggested they go to marriage guidance counselling.

Then one Friday night, just like every Friday night, he went into his local pub and she was there. She was wearing the same clothes she had worn the night he'd met her, but she looked very different. Her legs were just as he remembered. So were her hips, her waist, her back, her arms – he was immediately intoxicated by the sight of her skin – but her haircut had changed her appearance completely. Her hair had been long and blonde; now it was short and almost black, cropped and slicked down. It showed the length of her neck and emphasised the solemn shine of her eyes. Its severity shocked and excited him: it made her seem delicate and vulnerable and invincible and overtly, rabidly sexy all at once. The pain of his wanting her became unbearable as it honed itself into a white light that pierced his consciousness and made him feel dizzy. He felt jealous of the other people in the pub – other people sharing the space her glory shone in, and dulling her shine; other people touching her as they pushed past her to the bar; other people breathing her air; other men looking at her and wanting her, when she was his. He didn't even register the madness of this thought as he forced his way through the crowd towards her. He touched her shoulder and she turned.

'I've found you. At last.'

'Yes.' She didn't seem at all surprised. As if she'd known, during the torture of this last month, that on this Friday night, in this pub, they would meet again. Her calmness would have been unnerving if he'd thought about it for longer than a millisecond.

He motioned her urgently towards the pub's narrow hallway, watching her hips move as he followed her. They stood close. He felt uncomfortable, not knowing whether to touch her or not. Her lack of emotion when he'd confronted her had disturbed him and for a sickening moment he felt his fantasy drop away like his stomach on the Big One at Blackpool last summer. Perhaps she didn't want to see him. Perhaps she didn't like him. Perhaps she hadn't thought about him at all since that night. And why should she have done? Why would she be as obsessed as he was?

'I thought I'd never see you again,' he said, realising

that he had no choice but to let her know she'd filled his every waking thought, and most of his sleeping ones, even if he did make a tit of himself. He didn't care any more. 'I missed you. I couldn't stop thinking about you.'

'Why? What's so special about me?'

He wasn't sure. 'I've never met anyone like you.'

She smiled: not the sort of smile he'd expected. More of a twitching, struggling-not-to-laugh-out-loud smile.

Undeterred, he carried on. 'I looked for you in The Marquis, but you never came back. I went to that other pub too, but –'

'I thought about you too.'

Thank fuck for that. He smiled back: just the sort of smile she would have expected from a poor, obsessed, pitiful, weak, grateful and painfully heterosexual man.

But her attention drifted before his smile grew to full size. She pressed her fingers to her temples as if with sudden pain. 'I was late getting home that night,' she said quietly. 'You know. The night we met. My husband was waiting. He punished me.'

'Oh Christ. Are you OK?' But he knew before the question reached his lips that she wasn't.

Her eyes danced. 'I'm stronger than he is.'

He was confused. 'What do you mean?'

'Control is so hard to define, don't you think?' Her eyes narrowed. 'Do you recognise those moments when you're driving, and you suddenly realise you're not in control of the car, you're just this helpless human trying to control it, but in a second you could lose that control – in a second you could be dead?'

'Well . . .' Where was this all coming from? He'd only wanted to know if she was all right.

'If you can accept that realisation without fighting against it, it can be the most thrilling moment of your life. Sometimes it's the powerless who have the real power.'

He didn't listen. He should have done. He only felt his blood congeal as he lifted his hand and touched two fingers to her lips. He kissed her. His tongue slid tentatively on to hers.

Footsteps approached; little noises that became sharp as they emerged from the blurred hum of the pub. He pushed her further down the hall and into the ladies' toilet, locking the door behind them. They stared at each other for a while.

'What happened to your hair?'

'My husband liked it long. I cut it myself. I did it to piss him off.' She laughed slightly. It was the first time he'd seen her laugh. 'It was a very cathartic experience.'

'You used to be blonde.'

'It was dyed. This is my real colour.'

It suited her. Now her eyebrows and lashes matched her hair. Her eyes seemed even bluer. 'I like it,' he said.

'I'm glad.'

He touched her hair, her neck, her shoulder. He felt the tension in her body releasing as his fingers spread over the swell of her breast. The silky material of her T-shirt clung so tightly to her shape that he could see the outline of the tender flesh around her nipple, and he heard her sigh as he touched it. She bowed her head and her gaze followed his hand as it brushed over her, slowly exploring her. She was stunning. Every inch of her. The slope of skin beneath her shoulder, with its gently gathering curve gradually arching into a soft point; the underside of her breast where it met her ribs. The way her nipple hardened instantly beneath his touch into a peak that was obvious through the silk of her top. The way she chose not to wear a bra, so that he could feel the weight and shape of her without the usual impediments. It would have been cruel to keep those beautiful, tender, soft breasts trussed up with straps and wires. Cruelty reminded him of something – one of the thoughts that had haunted him since that night when they'd met.

Her body stiffened again as his hands slowly eased

downwards and felt for the hem of her skirt. Watching her face, he lifted it up.

'Don't,' she pleaded, but her eyes encouraged.

He looked down. As he had done countless times in his dreams, he recognised the sweetness of her thighs, but the map he had drawn for himself was obsolete. The old markings were gone, replaced by fresher, harsher wounds. The bruising had faded, the welt he had touched had healed, the scar still there but only faint. But beneath the pale pink stripe was a wound far more shocking. A fresh tattoo, messy like a child's first attempt with felt tips, scrawled across the top of her thigh. It was written large. There was no mistaking what it said. WHORE.

The skin around the word was swollen angrily in protest. He read it again to be certain, as if trying to translate from a language he was unsure of. WHORE. Embarrassed, he searched for the right words of outrage and comfort, but she shook her head.

'My punishment for being late that night,' she explained. 'He said that no man could ever want me after seeing it.'

The cruelty took Johnny's breath away. But also – although he denied it to himself like a murderer suddenly realising with blinding clarity that he was a murderer and he couldn't be stopped – it excited him. His groin throbbed. 'I want you,' he offered, praying the violence of his wanting wasn't in his voice.

She took a slow deep breath and released it. 'You do?'

'Yes.'

She pressed her lips to his ear. She might as well have kissed his prick, the effect her mouth had on him. 'Do you want to fuck me?' she breathed.

The shock gave him an immediate erection. 'You know I do.'

His skin felt cold when she pulled away. She shone with satisfaction. He forced himself to remain calm as he looked again at the obscenity that branded her skin. Then he looked beyond, at the black triangle of her knickers, and his whole body grew hot. Tremulously, he touched her. She felt warm. He traced the edge of her knickers and the backs of his fingers felt the intolerable softness of her inner thigh. He slipped his hand beneath the elastic and eased himself inside. Amazed at the effortlessness with which he entered her, he gasped. She was very wet. As he began to slide in and out, her tender pink flesh clutched at him, and her soft hairs brushed damply against the palm of his hand. He pushed another finger in alongside the first. She held on to his shoulder, steadying her body as every muscle quivered.

He touched her clitoris. She smiled slightly. He smiled back, dizzy with the pleasure glowing like an aura around her. She was captive to the pleasure he was giving her. He would make her come – feel her body give in beneath his fingertips.

She leaned against his shoulder and put her mouth to his ear again. 'Do you want me?' she whispered.

He didn't need to answer.

'Do you want to make me come?'

Yes. Yes. Yes. He wanted her. He wanted to fuck her, lick her, suck her, finger her hard until she came; until she cried out for him to stop. He wanted to know everything about her and to do everything to her.

'Do you want to hurt me?'

He froze, unsure why the menace in her voice frightened him and made him feel so guilty.

'Nova?' Someone banged on the door. 'Nova? Are you all right?'

'I'm fine,' she replied, looking at Johnny. It seemed a cloud had lifted from her face. She seemed amused by something. 'I'll be out in a minute.' She flicked her tongue across his lips. 'It's my husband,' she whispered. 'I'll have to go.'

'Don't go,' he begged.

She pushed his hand away from her pussy. 'I have to.'

He grasped at her arms. His desire was a fury inside. It panicked him. 'What did you mean, do I want to hurt you? I couldn't hurt you.'

She ignored him and unlocked the door.

He put his hand on top of hers, delaying her escape. 'When will I see you again?'

She shrugged.

Oh God. Do something now. Think of something. 'It's my wife's thirtieth birthday tomorrow. We're having a party. I want you to come. I have to see you again. Please say you'll come.'

'Tomorrow? I could make it tomorrow. My husband's working tomorrow night.'

'I'll get a friend to collect you here, at eight.'

'Fine.'

Again, that puzzling sureness, as if she had fully expected the invitation. He locked the door behind her and sat on the toilet with his fingers in his mouth, tasting her, repeating her name to himself over and over again as if it was a cure for this madness that was taking him over.

When he emerged she was sitting at a table in the far corner, with a man Johnny vaguely recognised, perhaps from his imagination – hard to tell where from, since he had his back to Johnny. For several long minutes he watched her, coldness clutching at his spine, his emotions swinging pendulously. At first he was lulled by her, falling into a semi-slumber as he studied her face; then abruptly he fell into panic that he couldn't speak to her, and his pulse raced irregularly. Once, she looked up and he suspended himself in her as they shared a smile; a subtle glance that acknowledged what they knew.

Nova's smile, however, did not acknowledge what they knew. It acknowledged her husband's fingers up her skirt and inside her pussy. Her husband's cruel fingers, discovering how wet she was.

'How much longer?' he asked impatiently.

'Not long,' she promised. 'Tomorrow night, and he's ours.'

The next morning, while his wife was out shopping for the party, Johnny rang his best friend, Phil.

'I need a favour, Phil. A big one. I'll do anything if you'll do this one thing for me.'

'What's going on, Johnny?'

'I'm obsessed with a woman called Nova.'

'What sort of fucking weirdass name is that?'

'Help me. Bring her tonight. Pretend she's your girlfriend.'

There was a long, long pause. 'Tonight is Rebecca's birthday party. Rebecca. Your wife. The woman you promised to love and cherish – remember her?'

'Please, Phil. I'll never ask another favour as long as I live. You have to do this for me.'

'Why on earth should I?'

'I have to see Nova tonight. I'll go mad if I don't.'

Another disapproving pause filled with disgust and disbelief.

'Phil, please. You know what it was like when you saw that woman on the tube. Like a thunderbolt, you said. Well, that's how I felt the first time I saw Nova. I can't stop thinking about her. Please, Phil.'

'Is she good-looking?'

'She's amazing.' His voice got sucked back into his lungs as his head filled with her, again. 'She's . . . I'd do anything for a night with her. Anything.'

'Even cheat on your wife?'

There was terror in his silence, as he realised the idea of cheating on his wife – the woman he'd loved for the last three years – didn't strike any sort of guilty chord inside him.

'You're not planning to fuck this woman at your house. Just promise me that.'

'I just want to see her.'

'I hope you've thought this through.'
'I have to see her.'

It was a mistake. He knew that as soon as they arrived together. Jealousy choked him as Nova was introduced as Phil's woman; he snapped at his wife when she commented on what a good-looking couple they made. He took refuge in brandy, which always made him ill and, mixed with the champagne he'd drunk earlier, gave him a headache that made him aggressive. He gulped down its warmth anyway, hoping it would settle his churning gut and numb his frightening passion. He wanted to be numb. His feelings for Nova were too fierce to control.

His eyes burned into Phil. Phil, the blond, lumbering, rugby-playing sloth. What the fuck did he think he was doing, parading round the room with his huge arm draped around her waist? Laughing at her jokes, eyes flickering over her cleavage. Bastard. You were supposed to bring her to me. Get your fucking hands off her.

She made it worse. She was playing the part of Phil's girlfriend with a little too much conviction. She barely looked at Johnny. She had a knife in his heart and she was twisting it. And enjoying his pain. When their eyes did meet he could tell she was taking a warped delight in this impossible situation. What the fuck was she playing at?

When the lights were turned out for the birthday cake, Johnny gave in to the brutal longing that was hurting his brain. He swiftly manoeuvred himself through his friends until he stood behind her. Singing filled the room, but he was immune to its simple jollity, and trapped by her proximity.

She was wearing a long, straight black dress with thin straps and no bra. Beneath its hem, mock snakeskin peep-toe sandals with four-inch stiletto heels peered provocatively at him and whispered, 'Fuck me hard.' I will fuck you, he promised, his eyes on the smooth, bare cups of her shoulders. Tonight.

Ignoring Phil, ignoring his friends, ignoring his wife, he eased his body closer to hers until he could smell the summer on her skin. He slid his fingers around her waist and pulled her backwards on to him. His cock, hard as it always was when she was near, nestled between the tight curves of her glorious arse. One hand slipped around to her front and he infiltrated the lips of her pussy through her dress, delighted to find her cunt bare and willing beneath the thin material. 'I want to bite your tits,' he mouthed to the back of her head. 'I want to hear you scream.'

The singing stopped and the lights came on. He pulled away from her and reluctantly went to kiss his inconvenient wife.

When Phil and Nova left, Johnny abandoned the party and followed them. Alcohol and envy made it dangerous for him to drive, trailing Phil's dark-green sports car instead of watching the traffic. 'He barely fits into that poncey car,' he muttered resentfully. 'Great big fucking oaf.' He strained his eyes for the back of her head, searching for clues in her movements. It surely wasn't possible that she had connected with Phil as dramatically, as definitely, as she had done with him. And yet they'd left together, with no more than a cursory, 'Goodbye. It was a lovely party. Thank you,' to him and Rebecca. She'd shaken his hand as if he was a stranger. 'But I want to fuck you,' he'd wanted to say. He'd almost wanted to see the shock in his wife's sweet eyes, and for her to know the sordid truth.

He watched them disappear into a doorway next to The Marquis pub, and as he searched frantically for a parking space, he knew that he would do whatever it took. This was where he had first seen her. This was his fantasy, not Phil's, and Phil had no right to be trampling across his tortured soul with his size-thirteen boots.

Johnny found the doorway. The buzzer said NOVA CAINE

& THE MARQUIS, but he thought nothing of it since he didn't need to use it. He should have thought. Should have thought. Nova Caine. Why did that remind him of the dentist? And she lived with the Marquis. Not Mr Caine. The buzzer did not say Mr and Mrs Caine. He should have registered these thoughts, but the front door was open and he thought of nothing but having her. He ran up the dank, gloomy staircase. At the top, another door was slightly ajar, and he pushed at it further until he could see.

If he had been more aware, he would have heard the soft, repetitive thud of the music from the pub downstairs, and the jumpy buzz of male voices. He would have realised she lived above The Marquis, and perhaps found this interesting, particularly bearing in mind the name on her doorbell. As it was, he was only aware of the dull red light; of the black strap of her dress, slowly falling from her shoulder. Of Phil's gigantic hand, cradling one bare breast. Of Nova's eyes turning to meet his: a challenge.

'Get out. Now,' he hissed at Phil.

Phil jumped. He looked to Nova for approval. She nodded. 'You'd better go,' she said.

Yes, he thought. You better had, before I kick your stupid head in.

'I didn't mean for this to happen. It just . . .' He looked confused, as if Nova had lured him here without him knowing what he was doing. 'I'm really sorry, mate,' Phil said quietly.

'You will be if you don't fuck off, now.' Johnny slammed the door behind his friend, feeling brutal – feeling scared by the force of his own emotions. 'What the fuck is going on, Nova?'

'Isn't it obvious?' She waited, eyes wide, lips open – mocking him. 'Would you like me to spell it out for you? Phil and I were just about to fuck.'

'But I asked him to bring you to the party tonight because I . . .' His head was spinning. 'I . . . I wanted to fuck you. You know I did. I thought you wanted me but you're laughing at me.'

He wanted to hit her. To make her feel as helpless as he felt. Her smile was so cold it made him feel sick. He sucked in air, trying to fuel his brain to make the words. 'What the fuck are you doing to me, Nova? You make me feel so . . .' He clenched his fists to show her.

She laughed, but her eyes were vicious. 'You don't have a divine right to fuck me just because you want to. You don't own me, Johnny. You're not my husband.'

He could barely breathe. A fist gripped his windpipe. 'I didn't invite you to my wife's birthday party so I could watch you flirting with my best friend.'

She shrugged. 'Then you shouldn't have asked your best friend to pretend to be my boyfriend. I was supposed to be with Phil, remember? What did you want me to do? Stand on my own all night and not talk to anyone in case it hurt your feelings? I liked Phil. I wanted to fuck him.'

The life was draining from his body. 'Are you doing this on purpose?'

'Doing what?'

Torturing him. Smiling at him as if it was all a joke. Sliding the other strap from her shoulder and letting her dress fall to the floor. Stepping out of it and standing there in only her fuck-me shoes. Sucking on the tip of her middle finger and rubbing it between her pussy lips. Driving him insane.

Her body was incredible; her perfection somehow heightened by the scars and marks and that tattoo across her upper thigh. She was like a statue, her marble purity made even purer by the dirty graffiti streaked across her. Or a fallen goddess. Or a kamikaze angel that had taken a dive into the temptations of hell and come up dripping with lust and carrying memories of the horrors she'd seen in her eyes. The light from the red bulb was coating her skin in the colour of desire. The air was full of tension and the smell of sex.

Before he knew what was happening, his thoughts became words. 'I want to fuck you more than anything else in the world,' he said. 'I've never wanted anyone so badly.'

'I know.'

Her finger disappeared all the way inside her cunt. His knees went weak. 'I lied to my wife to come here because I couldn't bear the thought of you with my best friend.'

'I know.'

'I think I'd have killed him if he'd slept with you.'

She nodded and sighed as she fingered herself. 'We're alone now, Johnny. What do you want to do to me?'

So many things. Where to start? He wanted to hit her; to slap her hard across the face and make her gasp and let her know the force of his anger at how weak she made him feel. He wanted to push her down on to the bed and fuck her from behind, taking her body for his own selfish needs and to hell with what she needed. But he wanted to see her face, too: to see her gratitude and watch the coldness in her eyes melt into pleasure. He wanted to hear her whimper. He wanted to make her come. He wanted to look inside her mind.

He drifted towards her. 'I, I . . .'

'Don't say anything.' She took his hand and put it where hers had been, cupped over her pussy. 'Just show me.'

He showed her. He slid his finger deep inside her cunt. She shuddered and sighed and he sighed too, knowing that at last she would be his, even if it was for just a moment.

He fingered her hard, rubbing her clit with the heel of his hand between long thrusts and making her squirm and cling on to him. Her nails dug into his arms and the pain spurred him on. He fingered her harder and quicker. 'Show me what you want,' she whispered.

He showed her. He fed her on her own juice, poking his soaking wet fingers into her mouth and letting her lick them, then rolling his tongue on top of hers and stealing the taste back again. He held on to her head and gripped her neck as hard as she'd gripped him, showing her how much he wanted this; how much he'd thought of it; how nothing else mattered but his hard, violent lust.

He grabbed her arm and pulled her over to the bed that was waiting against the wall. He turned her to face the wall, so she had her back to him, and jerked his knee into the back of her knee so her legs gave way. She kneeled on the edge of the bed with her hands on the mattress, her body open and vulnerable and waiting for him. Not bothering to undress, he just unzipped his flies. Standing behind her, he held on to her hips and plunged his cock inside her.

Her groan was full of anguish. He smiled at the sound and grimaced at the sensation of fillng her tight, wet, hot cunt. She deserved this. She deserved to feel as helpless as he'd felt every day since they'd met; especially tonight, when he'd had to watch her with another man. She deserved to be turned into a trembling, whimpering body. Nothing more. Just a body. A pussy. His pussy.

But she wasn't just a body. He didn't just want her pussy. He wanted her. He wanted to know that she was his. He pulled out and pushed her down on to the bed. Flipping her over on to her back, he kneeled over her sex-flushed body. He lowered his already oozing penis towards her open pussy. She bent her knees up and spread her legs in readiness. He looked down, saw the WHORE tattoo, saw the dark strip of her pussy hair, and plunged into insanity.

He watched her as he fucked her. She was silent, the only sound her breathing as with every stab of his cock he felt the short bursts of breath on his face. Her thighs were wrapped around his waist and he could feel her heels digging into his back. Her hands were on her breasts, squeezing and rolling her nipples. Her eyes were on him. She was waiting.

She smiled. The sight made his longing burst from his

cock and he thrust hard, wanting to flood her; wanting to stain her for ever with him; wanting to mark her like her husband had done. She hadn't come, but he didn't care.

He'd taken what he wanted. He should have felt relieved. But as she smiled he realised he was addicted. He didn't just want her for a moment – he wanted her every day and every night. He wanted to feed from her. He didn't want to ever go home; he wanted to exist in her shadow.

Detached from his own body, he suddenly saw himself for what he was: not a lust-fuelled man selfishly grabbing what he wanted, but a poor, helpless insect, blinded by her irresistible light and now slowly dying in her arms. He felt small and weak, and angry that she made him feel like that. And when she asked him, 'What would you do for me?', he answered truthfully, 'Anything.'

'How touching,' said a man's voice.

Johnny jerked his head around towards the voice. Another man was in the room with them – another man who'd stood there, silently watching, as he'd fucked her.

'Johnny, I'd like you to meet my husband, the Marquis.'

He flinched in fear and tried to pull out of her, but her thighs were incredibly strong and she wrapped her legs tighter around him and wouldn't let him move. He just had to lie there, his cock still throbbing inside another man's wife, while the other man looked on.

Johnny recognised him this time. He was the barman from The Marquis: tall, pierced in places he shouldn't have been, with a bushy moustache and a bald head. He had a broad, muscular chest that was bare apart from the huge, sprawling, bluish-green tattoo that covered his breasts. Gold rings hung from his nipples. He was wearing finger-less leather gloves. His legs were long and huge and heavy, and tightly wrapped in black leather trousers.

Johnny looked down at Nova. He could feel his face twitching as he struggled for comprehension. 'Your husband?' he asked. She smiled up at him. 'But he's . . .'

222

'Gay?' The Marquis came closer. Standing at the side of the bed, smiling as if nothing out of the ordinary was happening, he put a hand on Johnny's shoulder. 'Things aren't always what they seem, Johnny. You mustn't judge people by their appearances. I like men and women.'

What could he say? 'Oh.'

'If you judge on appearances, Johnny, you can get the wrong impression.' His cruel fingers – the same cruel fingers that had inflicted all that pain on Nova's skin – clasped Johnny's cheek. 'You can look at a man like me and make assumptions. Yes, I fuck men.' He leaned forward and whispered into Johnny's ear, brushing his skin with his coarse moustache. 'But there's nothing like pussy, is there Johnny? Blokes like you just can't resist pussy, can you?'

'I'm sorry. I'm sorry. I didn't know you were . . . I'm sorry,' stammered Johnny.

The Marquis wasn't listening. 'If you judged people on their appearances, you could look at a woman like my wife and make assumptions. You could look at all those scars and you could think that this woman is married to a cruel man. Is that what you thought, Johnny? Is that what she told you?'

'I . . .' Please God, let this be a dream.

The Marquis sat down on the bed. Johnny felt dizzy from too many emotions and thoughts that wouldn't mix. Here he was, his cock limp now inside her, while her husband sat inches away and stroked Nova's hair. This was too weird.

'Did she tell you that I punish her? That I hurt her? Did she tell you that whenever I know she's been with another man, I whip her until she begs me to stop?' He grinned, showing a gold tooth. 'Did she tell you that I carved the word "Whore" into her thigh to stop any man from ever wanting her again?'

Johnny was scared. More scared than he had ever been. More scared than before his finals or during his first job interview or just before he'd lost his virginity. More scared than when he'd been playing rugby and someone had stamped on his face and his cheekbone had broken and poked out of his cheek so he could see it out of the corner of his eye when he looked down. 'I don't know what's going on here,' he said, 'and I'm really sorry but I think I'll just go now and leave you to –'

'But did she tell you that she begs me to hurt her?' The Marquis paused for effect. 'You see, that's what I mean about judging by appearances. Such a beautiful woman, isn't she? Such a strong woman. You'd never believe it.' He stroked her cheek, ran his fingers over her neck and on to her tit. He pulled her nipple until her back arched slightly and she gasped. 'She's addicted to pain, poor girl. She likes to be hurt.' The Marquis winked salaciously at Johnny, as if they were sharing a secret. 'She likes to be treated like a whore.'

Johnny swallowed. He was scared shitless. He didn't want to be here, listening to this and sinking further into the nightmare. He didn't have a clue what was going on, and he wasn't sure he wanted to.

'Would you like to hurt her, Johnny?'

He looked from Nova to the Marquis. Both were grinning inanely at him, like a couple of teenagers urging the square kid in school to try a cigarette and knowing that he'd become addicted and smoke himself to an early death. 'What?' he said quietly.

'I bet you'd like to try it. I bet you'd like to pay her back for making you feel so helpless.'

How did he know that was how he felt?

'I bet you've thought about it already, haven't you? I bet you thought about hurting her the first time you saw her.'

He gulped down his guilt and tried to prise Nova's legs away from his waist. 'I think I should go now.'

'I bet you wanted to make her feel as helpless as you do.'

This was too bizarre. For the first time since he'd met Nova, he thought of his wife, at home, and the thought gave him the strength to fight his way out of Nova's grasp. He zipped up his flies and practically ran to the door.

But it wouldn't open. He spun round to find the Marquis standing on the bed and manhandling Nova. She kneeled up obediently and held up her hands. He cuffed them in the leather handcuffs hanging down from chains hooked to the ceiling. Johnny hadn't noticed those before. He hadn't noticed lots of things.

What he noticed now was that his fear was subsiding and being replaced by something far more terrifying. He should have been looking for the door keys, letting himself out, running away – doing anything but edging his way slowly back to the bed. Shuffling inch by inch across the floor, he watched – intrigued, bemused, exhilarated – as the Marquis unzipped his flies and brought out his monstrous cock. He watched as, with her beautiful, scarred back to him, Nova wriggled and moved her head from side to side to try and escape that enormous cock. He watched as submission shivered through her spine and her head was held still. The Marquis's fingers pulled at her hair and kept her where he wanted her while his hips began to thrust.

'See, Johnny?'

He saw things inside himself he didn't want to see. He felt his prick getting hard again and he was ashamed. But his shame didn't stop him from wanting her; it propelled him nearer and nearer to her and to the insanity in her eyes.

He stood by the side of the bed and watched that massive cock sliding in and out of her small lips. There was terror stretched across her face – her husband's cock was far too big, and was slamming far too hard against the back of her throat. The sinews in her neck were taut with fear and the strain of trying to get away from him. Johnny wanted to make her feel like that. He wanted to

225

make her feel like he'd felt. He was ashamed of his desire, but he wanted to hurt her.

She coughed and spluttered obscenities as the Marquis pulled out and shot come over her throat and breasts.

'See, Johnny? She's a whore. That's the only way to treat her. Like the whore that she is. Isn't that right, darling?'

He pulled her head up by the hair. She looked exhausted and excited and edgy, like a junkie. 'Hurt me,' she whispered hoarsely.

'Hear that, Johnny?' The Marquis raised one eyebrow. 'She wants you to hurt her.'

'I can't,' he said. Her skin was so beautiful. There were so many scars – so much pain already embedded in her flesh. 'I couldn't hurt her,' he whispered. But he wanted to.

'Hurt me,' she begged. The Marquis clambered off the bed and strode across the room. He picked up something that was coiled on a chair and brought it over to Johnny. It uncoiled and trailed along the floor behind him. It had a thick, smooth handle that he placed into Johnny's sweating hand.

'Hurt her,' the Marquis said.

Johnny looked from his hand to the bed. Strung up, waiting, Nova whimpered. 'I can't,' he said, incredulity in his voice. 'I can't do this.'

The Marquis stood like the devil at Johnny's shoulder, muttering all the reasons why Johnny could. 'Think,' he urged. 'Think of how she makes you feel. Think of what you wanted to do to her the first time you saw her. Think of how she flirted with your best friend and made you feel like she had your balls in her hand and she was squeezing them and digging her fingernails in. She was flirting with him on purpose, to torture you. She would have fucked him in front of you just to get a reaction. She wants you to hurt her. She's a whore. Hurt her.'

The tension in his guts shot into his hand. He gripped the handle tight, raised it behind his head and brought the leather tail whipping through the air. The crack was loud. Her cry was louder. Her whole body jerked with the shock. Immediately, a fresh red slash marked her skin and shame speared him. What was he doing? What was he thinking?

'Again,' she groaned.

He did it again, flailing the whip across her buttocks this time. Her arse cheeks quivered uncontrollably in reponse to the pain. 'Again,' she said, and he whipped the backs of her thighs, her shoulders, her waist, feeling his own lust curl around her like the whip's rasping leather tongue. At last, he felt release.

'She's a whore,' the Marquis said again and again. It was like a subliminal message that Johnny picked up and repeated. 'Whore,' he murmured.

'Yes,' she sighed, between yelps of pain.

'Whore,' he said, louder this time.

'Oh yes,' she moaned. 'I'm a whore. Punish me. I deserve it.'

He whipped her again and again. Her buttocks were his favourite; expansive curves of soft flesh just crying out for sharp punishment. The way they trembled after the whip's caress; the way he wanted to bury his cock between them.

'Whore.'

'Yes. Hurt me.'

'Bitch.'

'Whore. Hurt her. She's a whore. She wants this. Look at her. She's so far gone, the only thing she can still feel is pain.' The Marquis eased the whip out of Johnny's hand and pushed him towards the bed. 'Fuck her, Johnny. Fuck her hard, until she cries.'

Hovering on his shame, he moved to her side. He climbed on to the bed and kneeled up in front of her. Her eyes were full of the mad mindlessness of the addicted. Tears fell down her cheeks. 'Show me,' she whispered, her voice shivering like her body. 'I'm a whore. I'm your slut. Show me what you want to do to me.'

He unzipped his flies and moved closer. He ran his fingers through her tears, over her come-stained breasts and through her damp bush. Parting her pussy lips, he bent slightly to bring his penis to the mouth of her cunt. Then, holding on to her hips, he sheathed himself inside her.

He fucked her hard. He fucked her the way he'd wanted to that first time he'd seen her. He pumped into her like she was one of those repulsive moulded pussies they sell in sex shops; fucked her with as much respect. 'Whore,' he snarled, revelling in the freedom of this. He bit her neck until she flinched and pinched her nipples until she begged for him to stop it. At last, he had her where he wanted her. He felt the surrender flowing through her trussed-up torso.

But then the Marquis carried on where Johnny had left off. The whip screamed through the sticky air again and landed across her shoulders. Her eyes and mouth jerked wide open; her expression a frozen moment of fear. 'Fuck her, Johnny,' the Marquis said. 'She wants this. She deserves this.' Again, the whip. Again, the jolt of every muscle in her body. Johnny fucked her faster, forcing deeper, but he knew now that what her husband had said was true: the only thing she could feel was pain. She was numb to his prick and the desperation in his fingers as they clutched on to her. She was immune to pleasure. Her only pleasure was hidden deep within the pain.

All right. If that's what she wanted. He withdrew from her cunt and went over to the Marquis. He took the whip and returned to the bed. Standing up behind her, he unbuckled her hands and pushed her down on to all fours. 'Give me that,' he said to her husband, pointing at a tub of face cream on the table by the bed. He unscrewed the lid and threw it away, then scooped out a handful of the white goo. Slapping it between her open cheeks, he worked it into her anus, muttering all the while about how if she wanted it, she'd get it. Then, before her tiny hole had even got used to the width of two fingers, he pushed the whip's moulded handle into her arse.

She went rigid. He heard the breath being pulled into her lungs and could tell by the bunched muscles in her shoulders that her eyes and mouth were wide open again. He had her now: she was gripped by the agony. 'Do you like that, you whore?' He pushed the handle in and out. Her anus was distended unnaturally. His lust was distended so far it wasn't recognisable as lust any more. It had turned into anger. He was disgusted with her, kneeling there and letting him treat her like this, with her arse a mess of white cream and the whip trailing out of her hole. Her pussy lips were swollen and streaming juice and her clit looked painfully hard and red. One hand was busy with the handle but he raised his other hand and just touched her clit with his thumb. Spasms took hold of her.

He lost control. He slid one finger after another into her cunt until all four were inside her and his thumb was on her clit. He fucked her in both holes at once, both hands pushing in a rhythm that synchronised with her screams. He fucked her too hard, wanting to hurt her. He fucked her until her whole body shook, ravaged with the terror of having both orifices filled with friction. Her scream was shrill and loud and time slowed so much he thought the music downstairs had stopped. But it hadn't. Time had stopped up here, in this little room, while he'd made another man's wife give in.

Pulling the whip out of her arsehole, he pushed her down and flipped her over on to her back again. The Marquis got on to the bed and kneeled at her head, cradling her in his lap and holding on to her wild arms, keeping her still. 'Take what you want,' he suggested to Johnny.

That was exactly what Johnny was going to do. He pushed her legs apart. Drained by the force of his fingers, her knees flopped open. He was going to fuck her again now. He was going to fuck her again and again, until she couldn't take it any more – then he was going to do it again. He was going to leave bruises on her inner thighs.

'What would you do for me, Johnny?' she asked.

It took a moment for her faint, wisping voice to register. 'What?' he asked.

'What would you do for me?'

He didn't want to answer that. He filled his mouth with her soft breast and bit down hard until he felt that any harder and he'd puncture her skin.

'Tell me what you'd do for me,' she said, her voice a relentless echo in his mind.

He tried not to say the word, even silently inside his head, fearing that once he'd acknowledged it he'd be bound by it.

'You'll never be able to fuck your wife again, after this,' she warned.

'Shut up,' he said, putting the whip's slimy handle in her open mouth to silence her. She was completely helpless: her wrists gripped in her husband's huge fingers, her body pinned down by Johnny's, her gaping cunt waiting to be fucked and her mouth full. But she was the one who was smiling.

He slid his penis inside her. But it was too late. She was right. He'd never be able to look his wife in the eye again, let alone fuck her. After this – after her – normal sex would have as much effect on the yearning inside him as an aspirin would have on a madman. He knew he would crave more. Darker thrills. Deeper pain to inflict and be inflicted upon him. Life was never going to be the same again. He was addicted.

He would do anything to fill his craving. Anything to find the elusive high.

Anything.

And so, later that night, when she asked him to prove it, he lay down on his stomach and bit the pillow as the Marquis buggered him. As the sensation swung between shame and desire, excruciating agony and excruciating ecstasy, and a power surge electrified his body, he knew that life as he knew it was over. He was trapped in the dark side of pleasure. He would never get out.

Feminine Wiles

Karina Moore

Imagine having a life of luxury Californian style: private swimming pool, constant sunshine, housemaids and servants and a social whirl of exclusive parties. And then someone wants to take it all away from you. That's just what happens to Marissa, manipulative hedonist and stepmother to Kelly Aslett who, at twenty-five, is now entitled to claim her inheritance – including her late father's property where Marissa now lives.

Marissa is determined to hang on to her lifestyle by any means she can – even if crime becomes an option. With Italian-American friends in powerful places, Marissa sees no alternative but to make Kelly 'disappear'. That's if she can keep her scheming mind on the job. She's such a pleasure-seeker that she keeps getting distracted by all the attractive men she encounters: the swimming pool attendant, her lawyer boyfriend Larry, and a local traffic cop. However will she manage to carry out her dastardly plan?

This extract is taken from *Feminine Wiles*, Karina Moore's highly filmic story of greed, revenge, crime and lust. Her other rip-snorting action adventure is *Packing Heat*, which is reminiscent of a film noir, involving embezzlement, shady chaaracters and a desperate road trip to Vegas, all wrapped up in one steamy package.

Feminine Wiles

Nestling high in the hills, midway between Santa Ana
and the mountains, overlooking the valleys, David
Aslett had found the home of his dreams. The view and
the location were superb and the house, though fairly
modest by Californian standards, was a wonderful, Mexi-
can-style hacienda, with white stucco walls and dark
timber shuttering.

David Aslett's young widow, Marissa, was deep in
thought as she wandered barefoot along the rear terrace
of the house and down the steps towards the swimming
pool.

She lay back on a sun lounger, squinting up at the early
morning Californian sky, so blue it was almost navy.
Within minutes, the heat from the sun was burning her
through the fragile cotton of her robe but she was far too
preoccupied to move. Instead she reread the note she had
in her hand. It was short and to the point and when
Marissa had finished, she held it above her in both hands
and tore it, with perfect symmetry, down the middle. Then
she tore it again and again, letting the scraps of paper
flutter gently to the ground.

The note was from her stepdaughter, Kelly, giving the

date, time and flight numbers of her intended arrival from Paris. Not for the first time did Marissa curse her late husband for his folly in having a daughter. If it wasn't for Kelly, Marissa would have been set up for life when David went and died on her. She would have inherited everything. As it was, she was hardly destitute – David had left her a very generous lump sum in his last will and testament. But it was by no means enough. No sir. Not nearly enough. Not for a girl like Marissa!

She rested her head back, closing her eyes. What in hell was she going to do? The damn girl was due back soon. No doubt she would sign on the dotted line faster than Marissa could sneeze. And then what?

Marissa opened her eyes suddenly and raised her head to look around her. All this would be Kelly's, she thought, the familiar tide of hatred rising up inside her. She looked at the long, oval swimming pool, the surface of the water sparkling like diamonds; she looked at the lush, low palms dotted haphazardly around the manicured gardens, at the magnificent view sweeping down over the valley, at the distant blue of the ocean merging hazily with the skyline. She looked long and hard at it all, unconsciously clenching her fists. She'd be damned if she'd give it all up, just like that. Leastways without a fight. That's one thing Marissa never did: give up without a fight! Yes, she'd find a way. Someway, somehow.

Feeling much better, she dropped her head back against the cushion. The brightness made her screw her eyes up again and, ever fearful of wrinkles, she quickly shielded them with her hand. She was only 29, but she'd lived in the sun all her life and there was no way she intended ending up as a Californian prune.

She lay back contentedly, allowing her mind to drift. As she relaxed, a welcome heaviness began to gather, flowing through her body like a strong river current. It seemed that the source was that familiar, desirable ache deep in the pit of her abdomen.

Pity Larry isn't here, she mused, letting her hands wander idly down her body, resting lightly on the tied belt at her waist. Deftly, she undid the knot and opened up her short cotton gown. She was naked beneath.

Slowly, she trailed her hands across her flattened stomach, marvelling at the way it sent shivers through her breasts. It felt good and quiet out here alone. Pushing her gown further open, she spread her legs slightly, running opposite forefingers simultaneously along the tender skin at the edge of her mons and then back up over her hipbones, savouring the little thrills her own touch evoked.

As she stroked herself, writhing gently on the sun lounger, the soft material of her gown beneath her rucked up between her buttock cleft. She wriggled her hips up and down against it, delighting in the gentle friction as it stimulated the little, puckered mouth of her anus. Not wishing to satisfy herself too quickly, she withdrew her hands from her hips and, gripping the sides of the sunbed, she continued to rub her bottom up and down the ruck. She parted her legs a little wider, exposing herself to the hot morning air and pressed her buttocks down harder. Tendrils of excitement ran through them. She could hear the purr of an engine but it seemed so distant, so vague, that she ignored it, rather more concerned with the pleasures of her body.

Suddenly a vehicle door slammed. Unmistakably loud. Unmistakably near.

Quickly, Marissa closed her gown over her, belting it tightly around her middle. A moment later, a young man appeared round the side of the house.

Whistling softly, he strolled towards the pool. He was dressed in a ragged white T-shirt and faded denim cut-offs that ended just above his knees. He didn't seem to notice Marissa.

'Morning, Ray,' she called out.

The young man glanced up, startled. Seeing Marissa

reclining on the lounger, he grinned sheepishly. 'Oh, mornin', ma'am. Didn't see you there!'

'I'd forgotten it was pool day,' said Marissa.

'Yep,' grinned Ray. 'Every Thursday. Regular as clockwork.'

Marissa smiled, forming her lips into a silent 'Oh'. She watched as he began his cleaning routine, returning to his van several times to retrieve various pieces of equipment.

He crouched down by the side of the pool, dipping his finger into the water. His muscles moved nicely under his T-shirt and every now and again he smiled up at Marissa, flashing teeth that looked whiter than white against the deep golden-brown of his face. He'd gathered his dark blond hair carelessly into a little ponytail and it rested in the very attractive nape of a very smooth, sun-darkened, blond-fuzzed neck.

Marissa was strangely fascinated. Far from dissipating, her unfulfilled arousal seemed to be leapfrogging. Cute, she thought, moistening her lips. Not at all bad for a pool boy. How come she hadn't noticed that before?

She watched him some more as her mind ticked over.

'Ray,' she called out. 'I'm going in for some juice. D'you want some?'

Ray looked over, surprised. 'Er, yeah, sure. Thanks.'

Marissa sauntered into the house, making sure the thin cotton of her wrap was pulled tight across her buttocks. In the kitchen, she quickly poured some drinks, detouring into the hallway to glance in the mirror. She was startlingly pretty, with a dewy fresh complexion and perfect little button nose. Her big blue eyes stared innocently back at her and ribbons of soft, butter-blonde hair fell in layered waves past the top of her shoulders. She smiled happily at her reflection, briefly primped her hair, then grabbed the drinks and walked back outside.

Setting the tray beside her, she settled back on to the lounger. 'Ray. Juice!' she called.

Ray nodded and wandered over. He looked slightly

uncomfortable as Marissa handed him the glass, brushing her hand against his. He stood with his shoulders tensed, silently sipping his drink.

'Sit down, why don't you,' Marissa said softly.

'Uh, um, yeah. OK.' Ray sat on the ground adjacent to Marissa, pointedly staring at the pool.

'Is it cold enough?' asked Marissa.

'W-what?' said Ray, glancing up at her.

'The juice,' she said, flicking her eyes to the glass. 'Is it OK?'

'Oh, yeah, great.'

'That's good,' she said quietly, noticing how perfectly arched his eyebrows were. Casually, she shifted her legs, the smooth skin of her thighs revealed. She watched his face over the top of her glass with the surreptitious gaze of a skilled seductress.

'Rosita's off today,' she murmured, flicking out the tip of her tongue and licking at the frosted moisture round the rim of the glass.

'Yeah?' mumbled Ray, looking directly at her.

'Mmm,' she whispered. 'All day.'

Ray's eyes switched back in front of him. Nervously, he licked his lips.

Marissa smiled happily. 'Ooh, it's so hot,' she gasped, stretching up her arms, 'accidentally' tipping up her glass. 'Whoops!' she giggled, as a river of ice-cold, sticky juice trickled down the front of her gown.

Ray's eyes darted back towards her. He looked sort of startled, like a rabbit caught in the beam of a headlamp.

Marissa tugged at the sodden material. 'Darn it! Would you look at this!' she laughed, pulling the clinging fabric ineffectually upwards.

Ray's eyes were now frozen on her body. He seemed to have lost the ability to speak. Marissa shifted a little on the lounger. Then she shifted some more, the robe parting in an upside down V-shape to either side of her hips, still tightly belted at the waist. 'Whoops again!' she giggled, delightedly noting his reaction. He was staring intently at her exposed lower body, seemingly unable to drag his eyes away. He watched, mesmerised, as she rested her hand on her satiny stomach. 'D'you like what you see, Ray?' she teased.

'Uh . . . yeah,' he said, his voice cracking as he spoke.

'I do too,' she whispered, moving her eyes very slowly, very deliberately, down his body.

To her absolute joy, a sweet, faint flush darkened the even, golden skin of his cheeks.

'What're you waiting for, honey?' she purred, stroking the dark-blonde fuzz on her mons. She bent her legs at the knee, letting them fall casually apart, brazenly inviting.

Ray seemed rooted to the ground.

'C'mon, Ray,' she coaxed softly, sliding down the sun-bed until she was perched at the end. She spread her legs wide to either side. Her sex was now level with Ray's startled face and Marissa placed her thumbs and forefingers at right-angles at the tops of her thighs, framing the delicate, pink folds of her labia.

Ray flushed even deeper, his breath rasping and uneven.

'You know what I want, don't you Ray,' she crooned, her voice thick and syrupy. She lay back, waiting.

Ray looked incapable of movement. He cleared his throat noisily. 'Um, can I –?' His voice was so croaky he sounded as though a family of frogs had moved in.

'You surely can, baby,' purred Marissa.

Hesitantly, Ray placed his hands on her inner thighs, craning forward. Briefly, he glanced up towards Marissa's face, his own face a blend of delight and disbelief. Then, swiftly, he dipped his head and took her sex in his mouth.

Marissa gasped out loud as he ran his tongue with surprising dexterity down the sides of her clitoris, circling the centre of her pleasure. He started to tease the uppermost tip with little, darting flicks.

'Oh honey!' she gulped, raising her hips up, pushing herself towards him. Gently, he licked and sucked her, his confidence growing by the second. Her sex began to darken and swell. She dug her shoulders back into the lounger and raised her feet up on to the sides, sighing breathlessly at the excruciating pleasure he was giving her. Deliriously, she fumbled with her belt, undoing the tie and pulling her wrap fully open. She reached for her breasts and fingered her nipples, synchronising her movements with Ray's flicking tongue. A heavy swell began to rise up, spreading sensationally to her knees and chest. Marissa spread her legs even wider, pushing her feet hard against the sides of the lounger, her knees bent outwards. She raised and lowered her hips in a gentle, thrusting motion as Ray started to probe her greedily with his tongue, making it rigid, inserting it inside her.

Marissa closed her eyes, feeling the ripples of pleasure begin. She moaned continuously as he tongued her, lost in her own joyful waves, her body shaking lightly when she climaxed. Ray closed his lips around her clitoris, pressing down hard with his tongue, prolonging the reels of rapture till she dropped her weakened legs to the ground.

Dreamily, she looked at him. No trace of shyness now, she saw. He stood up slowly. His eyes were bright, boldly burning, uncertainty long gone. Taking in the curves of her body, he dispensed speedily with his clothing, pulling his T-shirt over his head and dragging off his cut-off jeans. His body was uniformly tanned and Marissa noted with satisfaction the spectacular jutting shaft of his penis, straining out from his hips. She pictured him over her, pushing up deep, deep inside her, filling and stretching her, sating her never-ending hunger. Not yet, she decided. She liked this boy, she wanted to take her time. 'Step over me, Ray,' she instructed.

Willingly, Ray complied, clearly eager for whatever she had in mind. He stood over her supine body, feet firmly planted to either side of the lounger. She took his hands and placed them above her head, so that his bending body was supported, then lightly she pulled his narrow hips towards her chest. Realisation flashed in his eyes, as she grasped each of her breasts and pushed them together, enclosing his penis within.

Excitedly, he dipped his hips back and forth, moving between the rich valley of her breasts, gliding slickly and easily amongst the beads of her perspiration. Marissa rolled her thumbs over her nipples as she pushed her breasts together, delightedly watching Ray's progress. His movements quickened, becoming almost frenzied. Panting unevenly, he thrust his hips back and forth with such long, fast strokes that the tip of his penis jabbed intermittently at the soft underside of her chin. Suddenly, he straightened, groaning loudly as he reached a swift, forcible climax, jaggedly spilling upon her.

Gasping, he stepped away, slipping down exhausted to the ground beside her. Their quick, short breaths seemed amplified in the still quiet of the morning, neither speaking as their bodies recovered.

After a while, Marissa reached down, feeling for Ray's hand. 'Shall we swim?' she asked gaily, shrugging off her gown which hung, fruit-juice stained and limp, from her shoulders.

She walked naked to the edge of the pool, then dropped down on the side and eased herself in. The warm, silky water enveloped her up to her neck and she began a slow, elegant swim across the pool. She felt rather than saw Ray's eyes upon her and smiled to herself. She loved to display her body; loved the effect it had and the power it engendered.

Flipping over on to her back, she started to float, the golden tips of her breasts breaking the surface of the water. Out of the corner of her eye, she saw movement and within seconds Ray was at her side. He began a lazy crawl across the breadth of the pool and back towards her then stood upright next to her. He was chest-high above the water so that little rivulets of moisture ran down his shoulders, drying very quickly in the heat and transforming into glistening droplets. He looked for all the world like a water-soaked Adonis.

Very gently, he placed his hands underneath her buoyant body, palms upward against her submerged back. His touch was enough to inflame her once again and she reached beneath the water, touching and fondling his penis till it stiffened wonderfully in her hand. She eased her fingers between his legs, rubbing the stretched skin of his balls, feeling for his buttocks and then scratching her nails lightly upwards.

He groaned slightly and moved one of his hands responsively down her back, roughly cupping her bottom, kneading and massaging her excited flesh. He pressed her firmly upward until the damp curls of her pubis emerged from the water and Marissa felt the burning torridity of the sun mingle with her own red-hot heat. They continued to stroke and caress each other, murmuring softly. Soon both were gasping with excitement.

Hurriedly, Marissa turned and swam to the steps at the side of the pool. She beckoned Ray to follow. Her chest heaving with exhilaration, she positioned herself how she wanted him to take her. Facing the edge of the pool, she grasped the metal poles on either side of the steps, letting her body float back into the water.

Ray stood behind her, pushing her legs apart and moving in between them. Marissa stared steadfastly towards the gardens, trembling with anticipation. She could feel his hands on her buttocks, lifting and separating each rounded cheek, then she felt the nub of his penis against her. Wild now for penetration, she rubbed back against him, widening her legs, and all but screamed when she felt him enter. He pushed up deeply inside her, burying his length until she could feel his pubic bone rub on her bottom.

He held her thighs firmly as he began to move, withdrawing entirely at first so that Marissa's vagina contracted in shock, then immediately he thrust straight back

243

in, filling her up once again. Marissa clung tightly to the metal poles, relishing the vigorous intrusion behind her, needles of ecstasy running through her body. She felt weightless in the water, wonderfully at his mercy as he impelled his penis within, gloriously stretching and probing her sex. She never, ever, wanted it to end.

But it had to. All too soon her body betrayed her. A rush of sensation began. Ray was thrusting so wonderfully hard, so wonderfully fast, that she was powerless to delay her orgasm. She closed her eyes tightly as she came, bright, white light flashing behind her eyelids, the throbbing of her sex so sharp that it almost bordered on pain. This was what she loved – lived for. She revelled in the feeling, in the boundless pleasures of her own sensuality. Nothing could compare. Nothing at all.

Behind her, she heard Ray loudly suck in his breath, slapping his hips against her, pressing his fingers hard into her thighs as his own release engulfed him.

Softening her grip on the poles, Marissa relaxed, hazily aware of Ray slipping out of her body. She gently undulated her hips, letting the water seep into her. She felt fabulous, fully sated, and totally at ease – Kelly's return now just a minor blip on an otherwise glorious horizon.

Sighing deeply, she turned to Ray. 'What a wonderful start to the day,' she said, kissing him lightly on the lips. 'Every day should start like this, don't you think?'

'Jesus, yeah!' Ray murmured.

'You're sweet,' she laughed. 'Same time next Thursday?'

'Uh, yeah. I mean, *yeah*. God, yeah! For sure!'

'I'll leave you to get on then,' she said brightly, turning and climbing nimbly out of the pool. She stooped to pick up her discarded gown and, holding it gingerly between two fingers, she wandered fully naked into the house, water still dripping off her body.

Ray got out of the pool, a bemused but elated expression on his face. He shook his head gently, looked disbelievingly towards the house, and shrugged his shoulders. Well, well, who'd have thought it? he grinned to himself.

Then, tunelessly whistling, he dressed very quickly and began to clean the pool.

Marissa skipped through the house, leaving a little trail of water droplets behind her. Up in her bedroom, she went to the window and looked down at Ray, now busy working on the pool. She smiled. A long, lazy, satisfied smile.

After several seconds, she twirled away, turning her thoughts to the day, back again to Kelly.

Damn Kelly! Marissa hated to admit it, but the note Kelly had sent had given her a jolt. It made her realise that Kelly would be back home in no time at all. Thoughtfully, Marissa drummed her fingers on the side of her thigh. She would have to think hard and fast of a way to outwit her stepdaughter. Throughout the past four years, ever since David had died, in fact, she'd had Larry look into all the legal manoeuvres. All of which were hopeless. She'd even thought of contesting the will but Larry had laughed at the idea. Of course, Larry was right. Larry was always right. David Aslett may have been considered foolish in marrying a woman half his age, but he hadn't made a fortune out of being foolish and he'd made damn sure he'd protected his assets when he'd married her. The will was watertight – no doubt about that. Larry had combed through it word for word. But there had to be a way for Marissa to get her hands on the house. Had to be! If not a legal way then maybe something else?

Absently, she twirled around her forefinger a tendril of dark-gold hair, still damp from the pool. She glanced across at the clock. Still only 9.40. Plenty of time to drive into town and let Larry take her to lunch.

Unhurriedly, she showered, washed and dried her hair and lightly made up her face. Then she stepped into her walk-in closet to decide what to wear.

Scanning the bulging rails, she chose a long, cerise skirt,

cut on the bias, that hugged her hips and thighs and flicked out just above her ankles. Teaming it with a very tight, very flattering, black, fine-rib top and black Cuban-heeled boots, she stood in front of the mirror, pleased with what she saw. The tightness of the ribbed cotton emphasised a high, perfect bosom while the skirt showed off the flatness of her toned stomach and the gentle curves of her rounded buttocks.

Throwing her head forward, she pushed her hands through the long, blonde tresses then threw her head back again. Perfect, she thought, pouting at herself as her mass of hair tumbled messily round her shoulders.

Half an hour later, Marissa swung round into the underground car park at the law offices of Aslett, Barris & Associates. She still had the use of her late husband's parking space. Though for how long, once Kelly was back, was anybody's guess, she thought tetchily.

She took the lift up to the sixteenth floor and pushed through smoke-grey glass doors into a large, richly furnished reception area. Annie, the receptionist, was almost hidden behind a high, Italian-oak unit, only her head being visible over the top. Her face split into a wide grin when she saw Marissa. Marissa flashed an equally radiant smile back. When she'd married David, Marissa had thought it prudent to win over his staff and she'd been charm itself in all her dealings with them. 'Hello, Annie,' she said brightly. 'How are you?'

'I'm fine, Mrs Aslett. Thank you for asking.'

'I'm here to see Larry,' said Marissa, resting her hand on top of the high ledge. 'Could you check with Justine if he's free?'

Annie nodded eagerly, only too happy to oblige it seemed. She quickly tapped out numbers on a digital switchboard and spoke briefly into the small mouthpiece of the headset she wore. Then she glanced up at Marissa and nodded again. 'Sure, Mrs Aslett, he's free. Go right on through.'

Marissa smiled. 'Thanks, Annie,' she mouthed as she walked off to the left, down a long, beige-carpeted corridor. She turned at the end into an office where huge, sparkling plain-glass windows looked out over the city. A young woman sat behind a desk, her back to the glorious view. She had straight, even features, mostly obscured behind heavy-framed glasses, and her shiny brown hair was arranged in an immaculate French pleat.

'Hello, Justine,' said Marissa briskly. Justine was Larry's assistant and the one member of staff Marissa couldn't quite gauge. Nothing she could pinpoint. Justine was always polite to her, but coldly, distantly so.

'Oh, good morning, Mrs Aslett,' answered Justine coolly. 'I'll just show you in.'

'That's OK. I know the way,' said Marissa, her clipped, icy tone outdoing Justine's cool one. Marissa breezed past her towards the dark wooden door. She tapped lightly, then entered.

Larry had already risen and was halfway round the desk when she went in. 'Marissa,' he said simply, stooping to kiss her on the cheek. He stepped beyond her to shut the door, dipping his head out first. 'Hold my calls, Justine. Mrs Aslett and I have some business to attend to.'

When the door was firmly closed, he put his finger under Marissa's chin, tilting her face upwards, then he kissed her deeply on the mouth. 'Missed you, babe,' he said, pulling back breathlessly.

'Missed you right back,' purred Marissa. In her way, she had. She looked into his handsome face, feeling the little, prickling charges she always got from being with Larry. Larry Barris exuded power and success in the same way his mentor, her late husband, David Aslett, had. Marissa loved it.

She looked around the office, familiar with the opulence. Nothing had been changed since David had occupied the room. His office, sumptuously furnished, original oils adorning the walls, had been his pride and joy, his private haven from where he'd overseen the smooth running of his business. Larry treated it the same way, she knew.

David Aslett had founded the firm, built it up from nothing, honing and refining it into the esteemed law practice it was today. The practice was sleek, successful, independent – precisely the qualities that had drawn a brilliant young lawyer named Larry Barris to seek employment there.

Nine years ago, Larry, newly qualified and third from the top at law school, had approached David for a job, convincing him he needed a new associate. Actually, David hadn't needed a new associate at all but, impressed with the young man's temerity, he'd taken him on anyway. It had proved a wise decision. Larry was as sharp and ambitious as David himself and, some time later, David had found himself making Larry an unprecedented offer – a partnership, albeit a junior partnership. Larry had accepted at once.

A year later, David had died. He'd been two points from victory in a game of racquetball when a massive heart attack had killed him. It was the one and only time anything had got the better of David Aslett.

Marissa reached up and ran her hands through Larry's thick, dark hair. He grinned boyishly and she traced the little crinkles that formed at the corners of his eyes. Then she sighed wearily. 'I got a letter from Kelly today,' she said. 'Dates, flight times, that sort of thing.'

Larry nodded, stroking the small of Marissa's back soothingly. 'We knew it was coming, babe.'

'We have to do something, Larry,' Marissa said quietly.

Larry let out a deep breath. 'We've been though all this. There is nothing we can do. David secured everything. All Kelly has to do is sign.'

Marissa stiffened. She grasped his hair tightly in her fingers. 'And when she does,' she hissed, 'she'll be the

major shareholder. She'll be your boss. Do you get that?
Your boss!'

Larry tensed. A little vein began beating at his temple.

Marissa tossed back her yellow locks, a look of derision
on her ravishing face. 'You'll be working for a kid, Larry,'
she taunted.

Larry's eyes flashed angrily. She knew the look well. It
should have been a warning.

'You'll never have the money to buy her out, Larry.
Always be the junior partner –'

'OK. Enough already.' Larry's voice was dangerous and
low. 'Enough,' he murmured again, roughly grabbing her
wrists and pulling them from his hair.

Marissa glared at him defiantly, her sky-blue eyes like
ice. 'We'll find a way to work it,' she said, her teeth
clenched together. 'We still got some time, baby.'

Glaring back, Larry held her wrists tightly, moving her
arms out to the sides. His eyes glowered back and forth
between each of hers. Then his gaze dropped to her full,
pink lips, lingering momentarily before moving to the
curve of her throat and travelling hungrily down the rest
of her body. 'Yeah,' he whispered hoarsely. 'We'll find a
way.'

An arc of exultation curved through Marissa's stomach.
Then a sudden weakness suffused her limbs. She stared
deep into Larry's angry, dark grey eyes, then she curled
her fingers back into his hair and drew his head down to
her, kissing him so hard on the lips that she scraped his
teeth with her own. They pushed urgently against each
other, the granite bulge in his groin stabbing painfully into
her navel.

He dipped his head to her neck, raining quick, sharp
kisses as his hands fumbled at the base of her sweater,
trying to pull the clinging fabric upwards. She leaned
away from him, helping him wrest the skin-tight garment
over her head and then they flung it together halfway
across the room.

Larry gazed fixedly at her full, gleaming cleavage. With each of her short breaths, her breasts threatened to spill out of the delicate half-cups of her bra. Quickly, he pushed his big fingers into the lace, dragging each cup downwards so that Marissa's breasts popped out. He squeezed the reddening nipples with his fingertips, tugging gently till the little cones stiffened and stood out proudly. Marissa groaned blissfully and reached behind her back, deftly unfastening the clasp of her bra and shrugging it off down her arms.

Larry cupped her naked breasts, whispering softly. 'Beautiful,' he murmured, pushing them upwards and then squeezing them together. With the centres of both palms, he brushed lightly at her tips, making her want to thrust them forward and rub them wildly against his shirt. Instead, she tipped her head back, feeling her hair tickle the middle of her naked back as Larry toyed with her breasts, his deliberate, faint grazing of her nipples only exciting her all the more.

As Larry loosened his tie, pulling it over his head, Marissa grabbed at the buttons of his crisp, white shirt, frantically unfastening. He eased it off and she ran her hands over his hard, muscled chest, over the soft, dark covering of hair. Their breath was coming sharp and fast, passion so palpable that it hung in the air like a huge, scorching fireball.

While Marissa fingered his nipples and pressed her thumbs hard into his lean rib-cage, Larry bent down, reaching beneath her skirt. He trailed his fingers lovingly up her thighs, inadvertently lifting her skirt on his arm as he straightened up, so that half the garment was upraised.

Marissa's flesh tingled at his feather-like caresses on her thighs. Desperately, she sought Larry's mouth again with her own, pushing her tongue hotly against the roof of his mouth, bruising both their lips with the brutality of her kiss. His searching fingers found the thin elastic at the edge of her panties and he eased his hand fully inside,

stretching the fragile lace as he cupped the globe of her
left buttock, kneading and pinching her satin-smooth skin.
Marissa stifled a moan as he moved to her other buttock,
gently stroking, steadily inflaming her.

'I want you right now,' said Larry, his voice low, their
mouths together.

'Yes,' gasped Marissa urgently. 'Lock the door.'

'No. We'll leave it. No one will come in.'

He swifly pulled up the other side of her skirt, bunching
it roughly around her waist. 'Hold that,' he ordered,
placing her hands on the ruches of material.

Marissa could scarcely breathe, her excitement multi-
plied tenfold by the risk of being caught. They were
directly in front of the doorway. If someone opened that
door . . . if Justine came through with an urgent message
. . . She gasped at the thought, heat searing like a brush-
fire through her abdomen.

Larry was dragging her panties down to her knees. He
pushed her skirt up higher round her waist and then
leaned back, drinking in her exposed flesh. Walking
leisurely behind her, he paused for several long, thrilling
seconds.

'Arch your back for me, babe,' he whispered.

Flushing excitedly, Marissa curved her back, pushing
out her bottom, enjoying every moment of his intense
scrutiny.

'Yeah, that's it. Yeah!' he muttered before circling back
round to the front. 'Jesus, hon, you're perfect,' he said and,
breathing harshly, pushed his hand between her legs,
forcing them apart. Then pressing lightly upwards, he
probed gently till she felt herself moisten his hand.

'Oh yes, baby,' he murmured as he pulled his hand
away, his fingers glistening with her wetness. Marissa was
dizzy. She tightened her hands on her bunched-up skirt,
counting the knobbles on the sleek column of Larry's spine
as he stooped and pulled her panties right off. She was
almost naked now. Only her knee-length boots remained,

and the scrap of material that was her skirt, bunched up round her waist.

Larry's hands wandered over her hips, round to her bottom, across her mons. She began to sway with weakness till he bent his knees and lifted her, carrying her over to his desk. He placed her upon it, frantically clearing it of papers.

'Now! God, now!' Marissa groaned.

'Uh-huh.' Larry's voice was a croak, barely understandable.

He grabbed her hips, pulling her down to the edge of the desk. Then he pushed her legs up high and wide in the air, sliding his fingers gloriously into her shining sex. With firm, circular motions he stroked her, his other hand unzipping his fly and, as he pulled out his penis, Marissa climaxed, her knees jack-knifing in spasm. Fighting not to cry out, she dug her buttocks into the hard, leather surface of the desk, relishing the cool, clammy pressure on her bottom.

In the middle of her shuddering orgasm, Larry pressed his hands on the tops of her inner thighs, pushing her legs even wider apart. Urgently, he thrust into her, leaning forward at the same time to reach for her breasts. He started to move, filling her up magnificently, completely, stroking her insides with his deep, wondrous technique.

Her first, rippling orgasm had barely begun to subside when she felt another surge of sensation, deeper, more profound than the last. With each thrust of his rock-hard organ, darting jags diffused through her sex and navel and buttocks and very soon she climaxed again, arching her back with the force of it, a long, low moan escaping her lips. Larry pressed his forefinger to her lips, hushing her sounds of pleasure but scarcely had he done so when he ground his hips against her, threw his head back and sucked his breath in sharply, endeavouring to silence a cry of his own. He rotated his hips slowly, gripping Marissa tightly round the waist, releasing himself into her as his body shivered and his cry mutated to a drawn-out hiss.

For some time, they stayed in that position, drained and still, neither wishing nor able to move. Gradually, Larry eased away. He placed his hand between Marissa's shaky legs, lovingly massaging the dampness into her small, dark-blonde nest of hair. She closed her eyes in contentment, savouring the soft feel of his fingers soothing the tenderness of her swollen sex.

Groggily she stood, hanging her hands around Larry's neck for support. He pulled her to him. 'The best,' he whispered, a note of wonder in his voice. 'You're the goddamn best!'

'You too!' Marissa leaned heavily against him. She felt too weak to move. 'Let's sit down a while,' she whispered and together they moved across to the olive-green, leather sofa.

Marissa sank gratefully into the cushioned softness whilst Larry smoothed the crumpled band of her skirt down over her hips. He wandered around the room, picking up items of their discarded clothing. Then he replaced his shirt and tie and carried Marissa's clothes to her.

'Leave these off,' he murmured, holding aloft a scrap of black lace. 'I want to know you're naked under there.'

'Sure, honey,' Marissa chuckled, grabbing her panties and pushing them into her bag. She delved further into the bag, bringing out a hairbrush, mirror and make-up and held the little mirror up to the light. Her face stared radiantly back at her, eyes clear and sparkling, cheeks slightly aglow. She dabbed at the smears of her lipstick, applied some more and, deciding she liked the even-more tousled state of her hair, didn't bother with the hairbrush.

'There,' she said brightly, carelessly dropping the items back in her bag and hoiking it over her shoulder. 'Ready for some lunch now, lover?'

Larry straightened his own rumpled hair, then reached to the stand for his jacket. Marissa stood before him, wiping her lipstick from his face and brushing fussily at his lapels.

'Let's go,' he grinned, guiding her in front of him and patting her possessively on the bottom.

The next day, as usual, it was dry and hot in Southern California. A gentle breeze blew in from the ocean and tempered the midday heat. Marissa, hair pulled up into a baseball cap, walked alone along a dusty track. She paused on a ridge, adjusted her wraparound sunglasses, and stared out westwards, across to the distant Pacific.

She had been walking for about an hour. She liked to walk when she had some serious thinking to do. It was a kind of therapy for her. Some of her best-laid plans in the past had been formed in valleys or canyons or on long, wild stretches of coastline. But today, for some reason, she couldn't seem to think of anything beyond last night's supper date with Larry.

It had been a pretty normal date at first. Larry had arrived to pick her up around seven and after a lengthy lovemaking session, they'd driven down to the beach, planning to eat at Quingelli's, a small Italian restaurant right on the seafront that was one of Larry's favourites.

As they ate, their appetites heightened by their energetic lovemaking, Marissa had noticed a tall, dark-suited man pass by their table. He glided by, followed closely by two similarly dressed men, their eyes furtively hidden behind inpenetrable, black shades. The man had walked on a couple of paces, paused, glanced back over his shoulder and then done an about-turn back to their table.

'Good to see you, Larry,' the man had said, holding out his hand. Marissa had immediately noticed the man's ring, a beautiful, crested band worn on his middle finger. The man was very soft spoken, his voice husky and low and strangely compelling. It had an almost mesmeric quality.

Larry, staring out at the black ocean, characteristically post-coitally quiet and lost in his own private world, had looked up, surprised. Immediately, his face had split into his cute, boyish grin. He stood up sharply and firmly grasped the man's proffered hand. 'Johnny. Didn't know you were in town.'

'Yeah, for a while,' the man – Johnny – said. 'With the boys,' he added, flicking his head back at the two men behind.

Evidently already acquainted with 'the boys', Larry nodded hello to them and then introduced Marissa.

Taking Marissa's hand in a chivalrous, old-fashioned gesture, Johnny had grazed his lips against the backs of her fingers. '*Bella, bella,*' he murmured, black eyes glinting and sliding across to Larry with an appreciative nod. Lips still pressed to her fingers, he whispered, 'Larry always did have exceptional taste.'

That dark, unblinking gaze had held Marissa enthralled. She had found herself staring back in utter fascination. Johnny's complexion was dark and gleaming, as smooth and as swarthy as rich olive oil, entirely unblemished but for a shiny, narrow scar that ran the length of his left cheekbone, ending just below his eye. Smooth, black hair was swept back from a high widow's peak. Undeniably, he was handsome. Perfect for the role of the dashing, roguish lead in a 50s Italian film – all white teeth and white shirt and black hair and black suit. Marissa could picture him now, zipping through the streets of Rome in an open-top sports car, cigarette dangling from the corner of his curving mouth.

But there was definitely something else about him, she mused. Something more than looks and glamour. An indefinable quality. There was something vaguely menacing about him.

The man's name was Johnny Casigelli. He had lingered for several moments more, then gripped Larry in a firm, brotherly embrace. 'Come visit me before I leave,' he said, before moving on to the table.

Larry had been silent after that. Marissa had tried to

press him for details, who the man was, how did he know him, but Larry hadn't seemed to want to talk about it. Actually, he'd shushed her and rapidly changed the subject. Getting absolutely nowhere with him, Marissa had turned her attention back to her linguini and reluctantly let the matter drop.

What was really sending her mind into overdrive now was Larry's phone call this morning. He'd called from his carphone on his way to the office and said he'd stop by later, that he had an idea he wanted to discuss. He'd said that maybe there was a way to deal with David Aslett's will after all.

There better had be, thought Marissa grimly. Time was fast running out.

She stared out into the blueness, absently tucking a stray piece of hair back into her cap. Then she turned, stepped off the ridge and began the long walk home.

Later that afternoon, Marissa paced nervously round the living room, a white cordless telephone pressed to her ear. 'Justine,' she said, fighting to keep her voice even. 'Why don't you just tell me where Larry went?'

'Mrs Aslett, I don't know where he went,' answered Justine, sounding equally exasperated. 'He just told me he had to go out to a business meeting.'

'And that's all he said?'

'That's all, Mrs Aslett.'

'OK. Sorry to trouble you, Justine.' Marissa ended the conversation abruptly and cut Justine off. It was like trying to get blood from a stone, talking to Justine, she thought irritably. She'd have words with Larry about him getting a new assistant. Justine's days at Aslett & Barris were most definitely numbered.

Marissa threw the telephone disdainfully down on the sofa and moved across to the big picture window. Gazing absently out at the pool, she nibbled on an immaculately manicured fingernail. Damn, she was getting highly strung! Larry often went out to business meetings and he certainly didn't keep her informed of each and every one of them. Still, there were only five more days until Kelly got home and they seemed no nearer to working out a solution than they had been before. She was beginning to wonder if Larry really was working on a solution at all. If she hadn't seen him with her own eyes, she might just think Johnny Casigelli was a figment of Larry's imagination.

Wandering restlessly up to her bedroom, she roamed around the room, picking up costly ornaments, tossing them idly in her hands then distractedly replacing them. Well, she thought, squaring her shoulders decisively, she couldn't just hang around the house all day, waiting for Larry to show up or get in touch with some news. Better to go out. After all, didn't Larry say leave it all up to him?

Slipping out of her jeans and cropped T-shirt, she yanked a little, yellow halterdress out of the closet and stepped into it, tying it up round her neck. She thrust her bare feet into a pair of low-heeled black mules, then grabbed a brush from her dresser and pulled it energetically through her mass of blonde hair, which she then deftly tied back in a loose, low ponytail. Tendrils of hair escaped and framed the edges of her face, enhancing her pretty, fresh features. Lightly, she glossed her lips to a clear, pale pink sheen then stepped in front of her full-length mirror to appraise the result.

The bottom of the dress just about skimmed the tops of her sleek, brown thighs. Even with low-heeled shoes, her legs looked endless. She did a twirl, cheekily flicking the dress up over her pert, firm bottom to check she'd remembered to put panties on. Larry insisted so often that she left them off, it was beginning to be rather a habit these days. Not today, however. A lacy pair of briefs was flimsily in place.

Entirely satisfied, she turned on her heel and began to fill a large leather bag before running jauntily down the stairs.

'Rosita!' she called from the hallway.

'Yes, Mrs Aslett.' Rosita appeared instantly.

'I'm driving into LA to shop. Probably be gone most of the afternoon. If Larry calls, tell him to stop by later.'

Rosita nodded and pulled open the heavy oak front door.

Marissa got into her black convertible and started the engine. She pushed a pair of sunglasses on to the top of her head and began to back quickly down the long, straight driveway. Rosita, turning in the doorway, made to close the door.

'Be sure and tell Larry to stop by,' called out Marissa from the road, before speeding off in the direction of the freeway.

She drove fast, covering the 40 or so miles in well under an hour. She visited several of her favourite shops, quickly acquiring a number of packages, lingerie mostly, expensive, scant and lacy. Larry's favourites.

Two hours later, she was bored with shopping and decided to head back home.

Speeding out of LA, she rapidly punched in numbers on the carphone. 'Justine,' she barked. 'Marissa. Larry in yet?'

Justine sighed audibly at the other end. 'No, Mrs Aslett,' she answered languidly.

'Did he call in?' snapped Marissa.

'No-o.' Justine sounded suspiciously as though she were swallowing a yawn.

Not bothering with goodbye, Marissa irritably clicked the phone off. Larry sure as hell better have come up with the goods by tonight, she thought, pressing her foot down hard on the pedal. The car instantly accelerated and she raced along the freeway, filtering off to take the coastal route back.

As she drove, the wind coursed through her loosely tied hair, a welcome relief from the beating rays of the afternoon sun and she kept her foot pressed close to the floor, relishing the breakneck speed.

In awe, Marissa dipped her eyes far over to the right, towards the precipitous drops to the ocean. As she looked down at the deep, blue, swirling water, her car so perilously close to the edge, a massive surge of adrenalin assailed her and she gripped the wheel tightly, her knuckles whitening with the force of it.

Without slowing, she rounded a corner, clinging expertly to her lane.

Up ahead, seemingly from nowhere, a vehicle pottered ponderously in front of her. Marissa cursed silently and slammed on her brakes, slowing only just in time to avoid hurtling into its rear. She hovered impatiently behind the car. It crawled along like a little, silver snail, refusing to be hurried by her irascible tailgating. Another bend suddenly loomed into view. Marissa clung dangerously close to the snail's rear bumper, blasting her horn in irritation. The car stuck steadfastly to its torpid pace.

Infuriated, Marissa pulled out. She sped past the car, overtaking blindly on the curve of the bend. Accelerating hard, she drove round the corner, gasping out loud as she careered straight towards an oncoming jeep. Wrenching the wheel to the right, she veered abruptly back into lane, cutting in sharply in front of the snail. The other cars swerved jerkily to the roadside. Horns blaring, they pulled to a standstill.

Excitedly, Marissa drove on, exhilarated by her manoeuvre. Through her driver's mirror, she looked back and saw people out of their cars, shaking their heads, waving fiercely at her swiftly vanishing car. She threw back her head and laughed and laughed. How hilarious! Leaving a trail of havoc and fury in her wake! Her body felt hot and vibrant and alive and she wriggled in her seat as she drove, a strange flush of arousal rising between her legs. Breathing hard, she accelerated more.

Suddenly she heard a siren. She glanced in her mirror

again. A black and white police car was approaching at speed, red and blue lights flashing, garish in the sunlight.

Damn, muttered Marissa softly, lifting her foot immediately and letting her car automatically slow its pace. The car appeared alongside her, gliding up smoothly like a long, sleek predator. Marissa turned towards it.

The lights were still illuminated, swirling lazily now, the siren sounding in a slow, distorted, drawn-out pitch. Marissa caught a glimpse of a black-clad figure, arm extended towards her. A gloved finger pointed authoritatively to the side, ordering her to pull over. Meekly, Marissa complied.

Her tyres crunched on the gravelled surface as she drew up to the right, into a widened area close to the roadside. The black and white followed, stopping some 10 yards behind. Marissa dutifully stayed in her seat, lightly tapping her fingers on the steering wheel. She was still breathing quickly, still exhilarated by the speed and risk of her driving.

Behind her, a car door slammed. Slow, deliberate footsteps ground against the stones, halting suddenly near her car door. Marissa turned her head slightly and fixed her gaze on the thick, black buckle of a belt. Tentatively, she slid her eyes up over a black, uniformed shirt.

'Can I help you, officer?' she asked sweetly, opening her pretty, blue eyes innocently wide.

For a moment the police officer didn't respond. He stared stern-faced down at Marissa, his eyes masked by dark, mirrored shades.

'Ma'am,' he began, 'do you happen to know what speed you were doing?' His voice was cold, without inflection.

'I'm afraid I don't, officer,' said Marissa quietly. 'A-a little fast, I guess.'

'Way, way too fast. Twice the speed limit as a matter of fact!'

Marissa fluttered her fingers to her lips. She dropped her gaze in a look of embarrassment. 'Oh, officer, is that so? I'm terribly sorry. I'm not used to driving long stretches. I guess I just got carried away.'

'You also ran two red lights on the state highway,' he said in a monotone. 'Not to mention that little episode back there. You could have caused a major incident.'

Marissa gasped, biting her lower lip. 'Did I really do all that, officer? It just sounds so awful!'

'You sure did.' The policeman pulled out a notebook from his breastpocket. 'Afraid I'm going to have to write you up, ma'am,' he said, shaking open the book.

'Do you really have to?' Marissa added a slight quaver to her voice.

The officer nodded curtly, his mirrored shades glinting eerily in the sunlight. Marissa looked up at him, trying to see his eyes behind the glasses. His hair was blond and short cropped, she could see that much. And his skin looked smoothly tanned across the forehead and cheeks, but it was difficult to gauge his age and looks with the glasses covering his face.

'Could you at least remove your sunshades if you're going to arrest me, officer?' she asked softly.

She thought she saw a glimmer of a smile. 'Ma'am,' he said, 'I'm not going to arrest you. Just a ticket. On this occasion.'

'Still,' Marissa persisted. 'It'd be polite to take them off.'

This time there was a definite smile. Marissa noted the white evenness of his teeth.

He shrugged almost imperceptibly. 'I guess it would at that,' he answered quietly, pulling off the shades.

Marissa smiled sweetly. His cornflower blue eyes almost matched the colour of her own though tiny lines were forming at the corners of his. He looked 35 or thereabouts. Around the same age as Larry. Good-looking man, she mused, glancing down at his physique. He was tall and broad shouldered and his uniform was sculpted to his body like a thick, second skin, the shirt moulding the contours of his muscles, trousers tight round his hips. His

261

gun holster rested menacingly on one hip and Marissa noticed that the thick, black belt round his waist held his baton to his side within easy reach. Mmm, yum, she thought, armed and dangerous!

'That's better,' she murmured. 'So much more polite.'

She watched him closely as he began to write out the ticket, casually resting her hands in her lap. Raising her arm to the side of her door, she subtly inched her dress higher up her thigh.

'Just a few questions, ma'am. Can I see your licence and registration, please?' The officer glanced up from his pad. His eyes shot immediately to her thighs. Tanned and sleek and utterly exposed. Marissa leaned back in her seat, stretching out like a cat. 'Is a ticket absolutely necessary, officer?' Her voice was no more than a whisper.

His face was deadpan and he reverted to his monotone. 'Yes it is, ma'am.'

Marissa moistened her lips with the tip of her tongue. 'I know I was a bad girl, officer.'

'Yes, ma'am.'

'And I know you should punish me.'

'Yes, ma'am.' His eyes flickered away and he jabbed the nib of his pen down hard on the pad.

'But couldn't you –,' Marissa paused and rubbed her hands languorously over the golden skin of her thighs. 'Couldn't you do it some other way?' Her voice was soft and breathy.

The policeman shifted his weight from one foot to the other. He cleared his throat noisily. 'I'm sure I don't know what you mean, ma'am,' he said gruffly. 'This is correct procedure.'

Marissa popped the end of her forefinger between her lips. She let the tip of her tongue flick over her nail while she lowered her eyelids coquettishly.

'Big, strong man like you,' she murmured slowly. 'Surely you could teach me a lesson!'

The officer watched as she licked at the tip of her finger.

His eyes darted back to her exposed thighs. It seemed an effort for him to drag his gaze away. His Adam's apple bobbed in his throat as he swallowed uneasily.

'Ma'am, if you would just answer some questions.' He focused on his notepad again.

'Big, strong hands too,' whispered Marissa, tracing the back of his hand as it clutched the notebook. 'Bet you could punish me much more with those than with that little ol' ticket book.'

'I –,' began the officer then stopped. He stared at the ticket book then he stared at Marissa. His eyes lingered on Marissa.

Marissa nibbled innocently on her fingernail. She spoke in a sort of a sigh. 'Bet you could spank me so hard with those big, strong hands; so hard that I never run another red light . . .'

His deadpan expression didn't alter. But his eyes still rested on Marissa.

A moment later, he flicked the book shut. 'Follow me,' he said tersely, striding purposefully back to his car.

He pulled back on to the road and Marissa obediently followed, tailing his slow-moving vehicle along the highway. A short distance further on, he turned right on to a narrow, unmade track. They drove for a minute or two, down towards the ocean. Then the track drew up abruptly to a secluded dead end and the officer parked his vehicle parallel to the sea. Marissa pulled up on the inside. She sat in her seat, flushed with excitement.

Silently, he came round to her door, taking her by the hand and leading her back to his car. As they walked, the sun glittered off the water and Marissa had to shield her eyes from the brightness. She lowered her eyes to the ground, concentrating on the officer's heavy black boots.

Opening his car door, the officer seated himself in the passenger seat. His eyes shone brilliantly as he looked at her. 'So,' he said softly. 'You want me to teach you a lesson?'

'Yes!' breathed Marissa.

'Come here then.' He patted his lap gently.

Marissa lingered in the open car doorway. 'How?' she whispered.

'Over my lap.'

She smiled widely. Slowly she leaned down and bent forwards over his lap, resting her arms on the driver's seat. She could feel the slight roughness of his trousers on the tender skin at the front of her thighs. The feeling wasn't unpleasant and Marissa pressed her legs down as she lay across him, weakened by anticipation.

He placed his hand on the back of her thigh, stroking her silky skin. Then, very softly, very faintly, he moved upwards. Tendrils of excitement trickled through her. Through the thin viscose of her dress, he shaped his hand over the curving mounds of her buttocks.

'Fantastic,' he mumbled. Lightly, almost indiscernibly, he patted her. He did it again. Then once more. Too, too gently. Marissa squirmed, brushing her thighs against the thick fabric of his trousers. She clenched her internal muscles tightly, wanting him to undress her, feel her, openly explore her.

The only sounds were the gulls overhead, the lapping of the ocean, the distant hum of the traffic on the highway. His lazy voice joined in.

'It's quite serious what you did,' he said slowly. 'Running red lights, breaking the speed limit, reckless driving –'

Marissa glanced back at him, breathing rapidly. 'I know.'

'I think it warrants quite a punishment, don't you?'

Marissa nodded, her cheeks aflame. 'Yes,' she gasped hurriedly.

His fingers curled at the base of her dress. With one nifty movement, he flicked her dress up to her waist. Marissa heard his intake of breath as he laid his hand back on her behind, those skimpy briefs all that separated her flesh from his.

Leisurely, he moved his forefinger to the waistband of the panties and drew them slowly over her rounded buttocks, pulling them down to the middle of her thighs, baring her bottom completely.

She heard his breath catch again. His fingers lingered in the sliver of white lace now round her thighs. For several seconds, he stared down at her, not touching nor feeling. Marissa's heart knocked excitedly against her rib-cage and she arched her back just a little, displaying herself like a tease.

Suddenly he removed his hand from her panties, raised it up high, and brought it down flat in the centre of her buttocks. 'Ouch!' Marissa yelped delightedly. Her buttock cheeks quivered wonderfully with the impact.

Again, he raised his hand and brought it back down. Then again and again, each crisp, hard slap eliciting a tiny sigh from Marissa. Her buttocks tingled vibrantly. She began to push them up to meet his hand. And as he spanked her harder, the tingles soon grew into a burning sensation, making her insides blaze with arousal.

She wriggled slightly on his lap and could feel beneath her, digging into the fluttering base of her stomach, the huge, hard swell of him. He spanked her faster, Marissa groaning jubilantly at the sharp, stinging contact, and then he began to slow, pausing after each hard slap to squeeze her buttocks together. The keen stinging followed by the vigorous squeezing inflamed her further and she pressed her mons down heavily on to him, feeling his body heat mingle with her own.

As she glanced excitedly behind her again, at the upraised, golden mound of her bottom, now heightened to a deep shade of pink, the officer slid his hand smoothly between the furrow of her legs. He tugged lightly at the soft, blonde fur of her pubis. With each little pull, Marissa's breath strangled in her throat. She opened her legs as far as her pulled-down panties would permit and closed her eyes gratefully as his finger found her clitoral bud. Back and forth, with long, slow, dextrous strokes, he rubbed her. She arched her back to coax him on, her breasts beginning to strain within the tight confines of her dress.

'Please,' she prompted. 'My dress –!'

No further explanation was needed. Still fingering her sex, he reached for the tie of her halter with his free hand and, with one brief pull, he untied it, eased the dress over her shoulders and head, and tossed it carelessly into the back of the car. She sighed with joy as he fondled her breasts beneath her, and stroked her bud from behind her, and soon she was lost in a world of her own, a world of rich, sensual, carnal delight.

As his fingers swirled in her sex, she could feel her moisture seep to the inside of her thighs. He began to work it upwards, over her buttock cheeks, coating the tender skin with her own intimate secretions. Then he began to spank her again, cupping her sore, glistening cheeks after each swift, hard clap. Beneath, his other hand roamed from her breasts to her stomach to her tiny triangle of hair, magically moving downwards, pressing her sex as he continued to spank her.

Marissa writhed over him, enraptured by the stimuli.

Energised yet breathless, she swayed her breasts lightly to and fro, stimulating her nipples on the imitation leather of the driver's seat. She dipped her hips up and down, lifting her head high, consumed by the pleasure he was giving her. She could hear his breathing, quick and rasping, intermingle with the smart, clapping sounds of each incisive slap on her bottom.

For several glorious moments, she was poised on the edge of her peak, curving her back, tensing her muscles, pushing out her bottom. Suddenly it swept over her, releasing her in a gigantic, flashing tide, making her cry out with the depth of it.

As she lay panting across him, the officer ran his hands freely over her body. He tenderly stroked her slender back and, moving to her thighs, he began to edge her panties down her legs, manoeuvring them over her shoes and then tossing them alongside her dress, into the rear of his car.

Marissa let him lift her up. Facing him, entirely nude now, she knelt astride his lap, leaning back against the dash of the car. He cupped her out-thrust breasts, eyes glazed. He was murmuring softly as though awestruck. Swiftly, he reached down to his trousers. Marissa held her breath as he pulled slowly at his zipper.

Suddenly, from nowhere, came a voice. Startled, Marissa jumped. She glanced nervously around her.

There it was again.

'Radio to 714. Radio to 714.'

'Goddammit!' cursed the officer.

Marissa chuckled. Only a radio. The police radio!

'Respond 714. Suspected robbery in progress on Hermosa Boulevard. Request immediate assistance. Repeat, request immediate back-up.'

The officer swore softly under his breath and didn't move.

The radio crackled again. 'Come in 714. Respond 714.'

He groaned, rubbing his hand longingly over Marissa's gently curving navel. 'Excuse me, sweetheart,' he said, leaning forward to pick up the handset. '714 receiving. Attending crime in progress.'

He hurriedly clicked off. 'Sorry about this, sweetheart,' he groaned.

Marissa shrugged. 'It happens, sugar.' She reached in the back for her clothes.

Still running his hands hungrily over her, he helped her dress. Then he walked her back to her car. Opening her car door for her to step in, he gazed at her, his eyes glassy with desire. He groaned again. 'Goddamn robbery! Goddamn criminals!' he muttered.

Marissa smiled. She tugged him down to her and pecked him softly on the lips. 'Thanks for the lesson, officer.'

'Any time,' he said hoarsely. 'I mean that.'

He tailed her back till she was safely on the highway, drawing up briefly alongside. She blew him a kiss and he grinned. A very cute, Larry-type grin. Then he reached into his shirt pocket, replaced his mirrored shades and sped off in a whirl of sirens and lights.

Asking for Trouble

Kristina Lloyd

There's something slightly sleazy about English seaside towns, and Brighton is no exception. In this extract from *Asking For Trouble* the author Kristina Lloyd explores the subterranean world of Beth and her bizarre relationship with her lover Ilya. Somehow he manages to get her to confess her filthiest fantasies, but what she doesn't realise is that he plans to make them reality.

Obsessed with power games and the seedy underbelly of life, Ilya is a once-in-a-lifetime opportunity for Beth to explore her darkest self.

This is a cracking story of sexual obsession and the sleazy twilight world of criminals, whores and low-rent seaside guesthouses. Kristina Lloyd is a fresh literary talent, and her sparky writing takes this Black Lace book into another league of erotic fiction.

Her other title is *Darker Than Love*, a story of Victorian depravity.

Asking for Trouble

*I*lya called on a hot, hot day. I should've known he
would, after everything I'd said about the heat making
me horny.

I'd spent the afternoon down the beach with Jenny,
Mike and some mate of Mike's by the name of Luke, who
we'd met en route. This was my first encounter with Luke
– Luke who I was later to seduce into being my very
casual, far-too-young-for-me lover.

I hadn't intended going to the beach, but the three of us:
me, Jen and Mike, had been in the office, sorting out some
publicity for the club. I employ Jen and Mike – art-school
drop-outs – on an ad-hoc, cash-in-hand basis. Things just
weren't working out that day and so we'd agreed: 'Sod
this. It's too hot. Let's hit the beach.'

And we did. We locked up and ambled down Queens
Road, which was thronging with a freshly disgorged train-
load who were, like us, beach-bound. They were all bab-
bling away, towels and mats poking from their bags, eager
to reach that brilliant blue sea under that brilliant blue sky
which lies, so enticingly, at the foot of the road.

To us hardened Brightonians, Queens Road is an every-
day road; we walk past its shops and offices when it's

miserable and pissing down, when the sky is grey, the sea is sludge and the horizon's completely lost.

But to visitors on hot sunny days that road must scream out: 'Go directly to the beach, do not pass go, do not stop to collect £200.' It's got those street lamps that you only ever see in holiday towns – the tallest street lamps in the world, with white glass balls on ornate black brackets. The road, full of traffic, slopes down to the sea in a series of slumps and bumps, like a gentle big-dipper; and, at the bottom, squashed between buildings, is a slice of the English Channel, shimmering blue and hazy with heat: Mum! I can see the sea!

In the midst of the excitement, we trundled down to West Street, past higgledy-piggledy buildings in any style of architecture you care to mention.

At the bottom, the amusement arcades were all pulsing and glittering, whooping and beeping – trying to outshine the sunshine and saying 'yah boo sucks' to the concrete monsters opposite. But that's Brighton: for all the flowing white grace of its posh squares and crescents, harmony is not something that the town, as a whole, is big on.

Shunning the subway, we crossed far too many lanes of traffic and reached Kings Road. At last the seafront, with its dead fairy lights strung between lampposts and its piers east and west – one bright and brash, its big wheel spinning; the other elegant and derelict, its windows all glassless. The sky was flawlessly blue and the sun was high.

We strolled along the esplanade, glancing beyond the mint-green railings and out to sea, encouraging each other to take deep breaths of the salt-and-vinegar, exhaust-fumed air.

We paused for a while to lean on the railings and wonder exactly where, in that mass of flesh, umbrellas and deckchairs, we might find space to park ourselves.

We were just complaining about the tourists packing out our beach and hogging the tables at our bars down below, when this blond thing in long red shorts roared up on a skateboard. He did a bit of a snaking and turning, then clattered to a halt. He knew Mike, but not, as it later transpired, quite as well as he made out.

When we moved on, he sort of scootered along beside us. When we made our way down the stone steps and joined the milling crowds of the lower esplanade, he followed, chattering away to Mike. And when we drifted past the gaudy stalls with their carousels of postcards, jelly shoes, windmills and special-offer seven sticks of rock for a pound, so did he.

Eventually, we squashed ourselves into a patch on the pebbles. Jen and I continued our meeting in a half-arsed fashion, then we just lazed. Luke hung around for most of the afternoon, bouncing off once or twice when he spotted someone he knew. He went for a swim as well – very brave, I thought, considering all the shit that's supposed to be swilling around in there – and he emerged vibrant and dripping, combing his fingers through tangled wet hair, a beaded thong round his neck, thin red shorts clinging to his thighs.

I didn't really pay much attention to him, except to think: nice face, nice body, could be a model in an Australian-soap or a kids'-TV-presenter kind of way; shame he's such a prat.

It was lethargically hot, with only the merest of breezes coming in from the sea. I lay there, arm across my eyes, top rolled up to bare my midriff, skirt raised high to bare my legs. The heat pressed on my sweat-damp skin. We drifted in and out of conversations.

In the distance, one of the bars played sunny salsa rhythms. Eager kids scrunched across the shingle, chasing and screaming. Gulls wheeled and squawked or strutted near the squatting camps of people, fearless and huge, shaking at litter. Luke brought beer over in plastic glasses. It was almost too much of an effort to drink the stuff.

I was itching to get back home.

I kept thinking, Ah, his hand here, trailing across my belly; his head here, nuzzling into my thighs; his cock here, sliding into my cunt.

Would he be slow and seductive? I wondered. Or rough and hungry? I was greedy for him. I wanted red-hot passion and gallons of testosterone.

I tried to imagine his face, to build up a picture of him from the glimpse he'd offered in his photo. I couldn't do it. I still thought of him as my faceless man.

Perhaps he'd called while I was out. I hoped so, because, while I was at the mercy of him deciding when, I liked to think of him being at my mercy too. He might decide, 'Yes, now's the moment,' and I would be out somewhere, innocently thwarting his anticipation, just as mine had been thwarted by the ending of every day.

I forced myself to stay at the beach until the crowds thinned, the shadows lengthened and the dipping sun cast a burned-gold sheen on the water. We sat for a while, clasping our knees and gazing at the ghostly West Pier – connected to the shore these days by a makeshift jetty because one day soon, so they say, the pier's going to be restored to its dance-hall glory and we're all going to have one rip-roaring, hootin'-tootin' helluva knees-up there.

The evening ahead looked like being a warm one and the others made lazy plans to move on to a bar. I declined and went home to shower.

As I was passing through my living room, towel turbaned around my head, I glanced across to Ilya's flat – a habit I'd quickly formed. I saw movement. He was watching me. I stood for a brief while, unwrapped my hair and rubbed at it, then went on into my bedroom.

The bay window there looks across to two shabbily grand houses, spaced apart by a small row of garages. Behind the garages are the juggled backsides of more houses, with zig-zag fire escapes and black satellite dishes. I closed my curtains. You never know who's looking.

I didn't rush to dress, nor did I linger over staying naked beneath my robe. I tried, best I could, to do the post-shower thing at a natural pace. My skin glowed pleasantly after the day's sun, especially on my shoulders, which were feeling slightly tight – not sore, just tight. I tan pretty easily but my shoulders had just caught. They were a bright ruddy-gold and I slapped moisturiser everywhere before lying on my bed to let the stuff sink in.

It was a hot, muggy evening and the raised windows made no difference.

I waited for the entryphone to buzz. I felt sure he would call soon. He must have seen from his window that now would be a good time, me half-naked and obviously not busy.

But no. So I dried my hair to its usual wavy straggles and swished at clothes in my wardrobe.

After some thought, I stepped into my flimsy, flippy black skirt and buttoned up my pale-blue crochet top. Being kind to my shoulders, I decided against a bra. Slipping on my geisha-girl sandals, I twisted in front of the slightly mottled wardrobe-door mirror. My legs were caramel and my shins gleamed. I was glad I'd put in the hours down the beach.

I looked good, although I wasn't exactly to my taste. Normally I wouldn't be seen dead in such a glut of girly high-street fashion. While I like things that are pretty or flirty or cute, I like them in small doses.

But, tonight, I wanted to be a little girl for Ilya, a sweet submissive miss who would coo inwardly at his swaggering dominance.

My breasts were too evident though. You could see their paler flesh and the dusky pink of my nipples. I reached beneath the crochet web and teased my thumbs over the tips. I smiled to myself, feeling lust tingle as they wrinkled to cones. When I took my hands away, my hardened peaks strained against the blue mesh, threatening to push through the holes.

I quite liked the effect, but I was keen not to look as if I was gagging for it. So I began to rummage in my drawer for a suitable bra.

Buzzzzzz.

Oh hell. My heart slammed. My sex flared.

In a mad panic I wrenched on a plain black bra, buttoning up my top as I went to get the entryphone. Deep breath.

'Hello?' I said questioningly into the receiver.

'Hello,' he replied, muffled intercom voice smiling just a little.

My fingers trembled as I buzzed him in, and I stood waiting at my flat door.

When his lean dark figure rounded the stairs, my stomach contracted with desire. He approached me, smiling – more to himself than in greeting.

He had a beautiful, bony, Slavic face. Just seeing that face made my inner thighs quiver. I didn't stand aside and, as he reached the doorway, he placed a hand on my hip and moved close. Above the V-neck of his grey T-shirt, in the dip between his collar bones, there was a hint of black curling chest hair. I allowed myself to be shuffled blindly into my excuse for a hallway. He was at least a head taller than me.

With a gentle backward kick, Ilya shut the flat door. Then he was edging me further into the hall until I was pressed against the opposite wall. His engorged crotch bulged against my belly and he bent his knees a touch to briefly grind himself into my pubis.

His hand rubbed gently on my side and I could feel its broad strength as he stirred my skirt around the jut of my hip bone. For a long, delicious moment we exchanged a steady gaze, silently agreeing on the need to just look.

His eyes were to die for. They were a deep blue-green, rimmed with black – intense like spilled petrol on tarmac. They were quite definitely not of this country, and they were set deep under dark craggy brows. The skin beneath them had a mauvish tinge. His nose was big and strong, curving like a scimitar. His lips were full and maroon, bruised almost.

I was smitten.

Ilya bowed into my neck and I felt the soft press of those lips there. I tipped my head back. He kissed, ever so lightly. His mouth moved along the stretch of my neck, pulsing damp heat as he licked and sucked. He nuzzled behind one ear. His shorn hair was silky against my skin.

I didn't move. I just let him smear his lips across my neck and throat. He leaned his body into mine and my breasts were squashed beneath his hard chest. A pulse hammered between my thighs. My wetness seeped.

Ilya stepped back a little and, quite calmly, put his fingers to the first little button of my top. He unbuttoned it.

'I called earlier,' he said. He unbuttoned the second. My cleavage was bared. It gleamed with a thin film of sweat.

'I was out,' I replied thickly. I could hardly speak. My tongue felt as it were moving in honey. My throat was in knots.

'I know.' He smiled, eyes down as he undid the third button, then the fourth.

He wasn't slow and tantalising. He was just unbuttoning me with confident efficiency. I marvelled at his cool. It thrilled me utterly and I played up to it, accepting the downward crawl of his fingers with docile passivity. When my top was half-open, he eased the blue crochet from my shoulders and neatly tucked the fabric either side my breasts. My black bra was bared and he scooped a hand into one cup. The feel of his warmth on my flesh made me moan faintly. He lifted one breast free, then the other.

My nipples were bullet-hard. My groin was aflame.

My exhibited tits, half-framed in blue laciness, jutted awkwardly above underwire and rucked-down bra cups. Ilya's eyes trawled lazily over them.

'It was hot today,' he breathed. He spanned thumbs and first fingers below each half-globe and began massaging upward. The callused balls of his thumbs grazed over my nipples and flicked gently at their stiff resistance. Sensation fizzed there and plummeted to my sex, swamping it in humidity. His caress was exquisite, so tender yet so firm.

'Yes,' I whispered. 'It was hot. Very hot.'

'Did it make you feel horny?' he asked.

With the same workmanlike detachment he'd shown in unbuttoning me, Ilya reached for the wavy hem of my skirt, fluffed it up my leg and then, holding the material against my thigh with his forearm, slipped his fingers into the gusset of my knickers.

I moaned. 'Yes,' I said breathily.

'Ah, yes,' he said in a whispered acknowledgement.

His deft fingers split my labia and he drove two deep inside me. He held the position.

'You're very wet,' he said in that deep husky voice. 'Very ready for me.' He teased the forward wall of my vagina. 'That wasn't the plan, Beth. You weren't meant to be ready for me. You weren't meant to be all juicy and full of lust.'

His two fingers churned in my molten hole and he nuzzled into my neck. His lips brushed over my ear. 'You're a horny little bitch, aren't you?' he murmured, his closeness blurring his words. 'I bet you've been ready for ages, haven't you?'

'Mmm,' I said in feeble agreement. Greedily, I pushed my groin toward him, pressing my clit to the heel of his hand and rubbing. He pushed a third finger into me, stretching me apart, and began shunting in and out. His sliding hand pressed back on my bud. I groaned, my pleasure mounting

'You sweet little slut,' he said softly.

I groaned again to show I liked his dirty talk. If it'd been a man I knew saying such things I might have heard only play-acting and cringed at his attempt. But I didn't know him, not in a dull, what-do-you-want-for-breakfast sense, and his words sounded good, unforced. I liked being a horny bitch, a sweet little slut. I liked being cheapened.

I heard the clink of a belt being unbuckled.

'You need fucking,' he said gently. 'You really need fucking, don't you?'

'Yes,' I replied, my eyes closing in bliss.

I heard his trousers drop, felt him step out of his shoes and lower clothes. Swiftly, he dragged my knickers down to my ankles and hitched up my skirt. I opened my eyes, about to suggest the bedroom, but, before I got the chance, I felt his cock between my thighs. With barely a position-seeking nudge, his glans was at my entrance.

'No,' I mumbled. 'Condoms.'

'It's OK,' he cooed. 'It's OK.'

No it's not, I thought, and he penetrated me in one easy glide. His bone-hard length rushed upward, slipping open my wet flesh and filling it.

My cry of protest softened to a moan of delight and my thoughts of big diseases with little names evaporated in a fog of brain-numbing lust. I clamped my muscles to his thick girth, fluttering my pulpy heat around his shaft. He gave a low-throated noise of enjoyment and cupped my arse while I struggled to get rid of my ankle-shackling knickers. Ilya lifted me, pressing me up against the wall.

My sandals clattered to the floor.

I gripped his hips with my inner thighs and then he was fucking into me, slamming up a series of ruthless, measured strokes. Every thrust jolted me, made my tits judder, my feet bounce in the air.

'Jesus,' I gasped, and he crushed his lips to mine, coaxing my mouth wide with a hot, probing tongue. I placed my hands either side of his face then stroked over his head. His close-cropped hair bristled on the up-stroke;

on the down-stroke, oh, it was velvet-smooth, so warm and sleek.

'Tell me a fantasy,' he said, breaking the kiss. He wasn't even breathless.

'Oh Christ,' I said, half-complaint, half-excitement. I couldn't stop caressing the roundness of his skull and I pulled his head close, running my hand up and down, from nape to crown.

Between my dangling spread legs, he pumped steadily. My back bumped and shuffled against the wall. My clit throbbed.

'Go on,' he urged. 'You hot little bitch. Tell me. Imagine we're somewhere else. Where is it? Tell me.'

I struggled to think. Ilya paused, his body held still on the withdrawal, his biceps curving as he balanced my weight. I panted and stuttered incomprehensibly, clutching his wide shoulders.

'Fucking tell me,' he snarled. Then he rammed his cock into me. One. Two. Three.

Three punishingly strong jerks that made my womb quiver, my senses spin. 'Tell me,' he repeated. 'Stop being so fucking coy.'

'Yes, yes,' I gasped.

And as he powered into me, I spluttered out words.

'I like nasty things . . . cheap things. Sleazy. Sordid.'

'Yes,' he hissed. 'More. More.'

He fucked me faster, harder. I felt the tension gathering in my thighs and lapping within.

'I'm going to come,' I wailed.

'No you're not,' he snapped, and he held still, clasping my upper body to his T-shirted chest. Hugging me tight, our groins locked beneath the fuss of my black skirt, he butted open the living-room door.

'The windows,' I protested, as he carried me past them.

'But I'm not at home,' he replied smoothly, somehow knowing where my bedroom was and making for it.

There, carefully, he set me down on the bed edge,

'leaning with me so his prick stayed hilted. The room was shadowy because the curtains were drawn.

Ilya drew back a touch, one foot on the floor near my own, the other on the bed, his thigh supporting my hooked-up leg. I was half lifted from the duvet and I raised my hips further, seeking his thrusts. He smiled down at me and, one-handed, reached back to drag his T-shirt over his head.

A cloud of dark hair covered the scoop of his pecs, fading to sparseness on his hard, flat abdomen. His twinkling eyes meandered over my body, over my wrinkled clothes crushed this way and that.

His nudity contrasted sharply with my thrust-aside garments. He was magnificent and comfortable, while I was strategically exposed, hectic and lewd.

With unwavering control, Ilya ground into me. His thrusts were angled from a low point. He was avoiding my clit, the swine.

'Tell me,' he said kindly. He gave a quick strum of my clitoris with his thumb just to demonstrate that he was the one running the show. Intensity whirled in my groin.

'Well?' he said, his pelvis swinging in long, lazy lunges. 'How sleazy? Do people watch you in your fantasies?'

'Yes,' I murmured. 'Sometimes. Often.'

'Where? What's the setting?' Teasingly, he brushed the nub of my clit once more.

'Oh God,' I wailed, frustrated by the fleeting upsurge of pleasure. I screwed my eyes shut. 'Different places. Please. I . . . strip joints. Squalid, dingy rooms. Tacky pink neon. Me stripping, the centre of attention. Lecherous men. They all want me.'

'I love it,' he growled, his cock plunging, his tempo building. 'What do they do?' He reached a hand out and kneaded one breast. I could sense him restraining his urgency.

'Yes, oh fuck. Different things,' I cried, urged on by his quickening rhythm. 'Sometimes they beckon me over. Or

I sit on the stage, spread my legs. They crowd around me. Stuff notes in my knickers. Someone cheats, stuffs his fingers in my cunt. I groan. I like it. They laugh because I'm so wet. They . . . They say coarse things. They egg him on.'

'Go on, give it to her,' he suggested, his voice rich and husky. 'She loves it, the randy little whore, the dirty little slut.'

'Yes,' I gasped. 'Yes.'

'Give her all your fingers. Someone hold her legs still. Let's see that greedy wet pussy taking all his fingers. Go on, harder. Make her beg for mercy. Make her beg for cock.'

'Yes, yes, yes,' I said in a near-scream.

He rewarded me. Wild and eager, he hammered his prick into my depths, a finger near the root of him rubbing my clit. Ecstasy raced through me, shivering and urgent. It bunched around my core, tighter and tighter, and I howled and cried as my release exploded in one giant, delirious, starbursting orgasm.

Oh fuck.

Ilya thundered on, grunting and pumping. His lips were stretched in a rictus of torment, his head thrown back, his neck corded and taut. On a prolonged groan, he came. I felt the tension in his body and the deep shudder of his thrust, and, to my utmost relief, I didn't feel the gush of him ejaculating.

When he withdrew, I saw the rubber wrinkling on his prick, its teat drooping with liquid. I just hadn't felt it. I guess my vagina wasn't concentrating. Thank God one of us is in control, I thought. He was obviously the type of guy who can distract you with one hand and slip a sheath on with the other. Expertise. I like that in a man.

Ilya snapped off his rubber, then flopped down beside me.

'Words fail me,' he said, harking back to our phone call.

'Mm-mmm,' I replied.

We lay there, silent except for our short, fast breath. No small-talk, no big-talk. Just a meaningless fuck. That was the deal, wasn't it?

After a while, Ilya said, 'I liked your fantasy. Have you got many more like that up your sleeve? Maybe I can help fulfil them.'

Satisfaction had sobered me up and I struggled with a niggling embarrassment.

I wasn't too keen on baring my innermost fantasies. They weren't exactly clean and sweet. Besides, I didn't know if I wanted them fulfilled. I might like the image of being fucked in some graffiti-scrawled toilet, but that didn't mean I actually wanted it to happen. In reality, it would probably be piss-stinking and grim as hell.

So I liked seedy, sleazy low-life, but I liked it where it was: in my head. Ilya obviously didn't. He wanted me to open up so he could make it happen, make my bad dreams come true.

If I'd realised how well suited he was to do that – to drag my dangerous, dirty fantasy down to his dangerous, dirty reality – I might have kept my big mouth shut. But I didn't. Bit by bit, I told him everything.

'Variations on the theme,' I mumbled.

'You mean the sleazy theme?'

I shrugged. 'Suppose so, yeah. I'm not really a Seychelles beach type of girl.'

'I can tell.' He grinned. He rolled on to his side and rumpled my top over my breast, squeezing my flesh through the blue crochet web.

'So what is it about sleaze?'

'Dunno,' I replied. 'Haven't really analysed it. I just like it.'

'But what is it that you like? Have you got a thing about neon or something?'

'No, I just like picturing things where I'm being used, objectified, degraded, that kind of stuff. It's liberating. I'm in someone else's hands. I'm not being me. I'm made cheap. I'm just a thing for sex, a body, an orifice. And fantasy, I guess, is all about –'

'I thought you hadn't analysed it.'

'I haven't. But I'm trying to now.'

'Don't bother,' said Ilya, wearily dismissive. He flopped on to his back and gazed at the ceiling. 'I prefer the visuals. What about rape fantasy? Do you go in for that?'

My pulses gave a shocked little leap. It didn't seem right that a man should speak those words in such a free-and-easy tone, especially after having just cut short my attempts at self-analysis. Well, I knew more about this subject and I wasn't going to let him have his kicks for free.

'Yes,' I said boldly. 'And I don't have a problem with it. Well, not much. I'm not proud of it or anything, but I know it's common. Maybe I've got some deep, primeval guilt about sex. I dunno. I don't think I have, but . . . Yeah, I get off on the idea of, of being forced, of not being responsible. But it doesn't mean I want to be raped. It's just fantasy. I imagine it, so I'm the one in control. My . . . my rapist, he's just a puppet. He does whatever I make him do. It's –'

'Any accompanying visuals?' asked Ilya.

'No,' I said tetchily. I shrugged my top further on my shoulders.

Ilya leant into me again, propped himself on one elbow and regarded me with direct curiosity. 'One day,' he said, 'I'll rape you.'

My heart flipped over. He hadn't listened to a word I'd said. Oh God, what was I doing? Who was this guy? Why was I trusting him with things like this?

Then Ilya smiled, and added, 'If you'll let me.'

My fear sank away and I breathed a sigh of relief.

If I let him, then it wouldn't be rape, would it? It would be me pretending not to want him, pretending to resist, pretending it was violation. It was nothing major. Just a role-play. He was OK. He understood.

'Well, you'd have to ask very nicely,' I replied, trying to lighten the mood.

'Hmm,' he mused, easing back from me a touch and then gazing beyond into nothing. He pushed his hand under the buttoned half of my top and began circling it over my stomach. His touch was absent-minded – as intimate as a familiar lover's or as distant as an executive's playing with desk toys. I didn't know which. Maybe they were one and the same thing.

'What about whoring?' he asked, returning his eyes to mine. 'That's cheap and sleazy. Do you fantasise about that?'

'What?' I laughed. 'About me shivering my tits off on a street corner?'

'With a punter.' He smiled. 'Down an alley. Back of a car. Hotel room. Whatever takes your fancy.'

'Just the one punter?' I said with a sly grin.

He grinned back. 'A lorryload.'

'Yeah,' I drawled. 'I could get into that.'

Ilya crinkled down my bra cups, exposing me again, then trailed his tongue in wet rotations around a nipple.

Shit, I thought. I could seriously fall for this guy.

'So what about a fantasy with one punter?' he murmured.

'Maybe,' I replied. 'If I make him good at using and abusing me. But only when I've finished with the lorryload.'

'Oh, but of course,' said Ilya, smiling up at me.

'What about you?' I asked. 'What are your fantasies?'

He grated his teeth over my crinkling nipple then, holding the tip in a gentle bite, he drew my breast high until I felt an edge of pain. He released me.

'Fucking you up the arse,' he said.

I drew a quiet breath. 'You told me that one on the phone.'

'And?'

'And?' I repeated. 'And tell me another.'

285

Ilya took my nipple between his teeth again and slowly plucked upwards before letting my flesh drop back.

'OK,' he said, pushing my skirt higher and placing a hand on the swell of my mons. 'It's having a whore come round to my flat.' He thumbed strokes across my clitoris. 'She looks just like you. She wears a miniskirt, heels and stockings. Her tits are nearly falling out of her top. Lots of make-up. Tarty porn-style underwear. I make her do whatever I want her to do. I use and abuse her, tell her she's a cheap little slut.'

He looked at me fixedly, those jewel-bright eyes boring into mine. 'Next Friday, if you're free.' He didn't smile, he just kept on thumbing me, a smooth tease that made my clit flesh out.

I gave a little whimper. 'No, I don't know,' I said softly. 'I'm not sure. I might feel daft. It's fantasy stuff. And I'm not wearing –'

'Act it out,' he said. 'Reality's the ultimate fantasy.'

Then a finger slid through the wet valley of my sex to press on the indent of my anus.

I moaned as he massaged me there, spreading my juices over the little muscled ring. And I gasped as he gently eased his finger into my narrow hole.

'Anyone done this to you before?' he asked, driving slowly back and forth, his eyelids droopy with lust.

'No,' I whispered. It was a lie. I'm not that inexperienced but I didn't want to encourage his anal sex fantasy. I wanted to know him better before I even considered agreeing to it.

'Do you like it?' he breathed.

'Mmm,' I murmured.

'What about this?' he asked, and he brought his other hand to my pussy, his fingers swooping into the wet pout of my folds. He gazed down at my face, his buried digits moving in both orifices.

'Ah God, yes,' I groaned, squirming into his thrusts.

And with his thumb, he began rocking my clit, stimulating it until it was a knot of jangling nerves.

'Say you'll be my whore,' he said in a commanding tone.

I eyed his surging cock, traced with thick veins and flaring violently at the crown.

'Fuck me and I might,' I challenged. 'Fuck me hard.'

'Ah, you greedy little slut,' he enthused, disengaging his fingers. Then he began tugging at my clothes, yanking my top up, my skirt down, my bra off. His strength and roughness excited me desperately. In the chaos I lunged to grab a condom from my bedside stash. When I was stripped naked, Ilya flipped me on to all fours.

'Be my whore,' he said, circling my waist with his arm and clasping me tight. 'Or you don't get fucked.' His swollen prick pressed into the split of my buttocks.

'You swine,' I hissed. 'Yes, yes, I will.'

I heard him bite at the foil-packaged sheath. Then his rubbered-up cock nudged and, in one fierce, fluid movement, penetrated me. Again and again he penetrated. He was roused to a frenzy and he just plunged and plunged as if he wanted to fuck me to destruction.

'Hard enough?' he barked.

I gasped yes, no, and clutched the foot of the bed, locking my elbows rigid as he hammered into my depths, sending vibrations to my head. He dropped a finger to my clit and frigged it hard. It didn't take much and, in seconds, I'd hit my peak and I was crying out for him to hurry, to climax, because my body couldn't take much more. It was approaching stupor. With relentless vigour, Ilya ploughed on.

'Come,' I wailed. 'Please, oh God. Come.'

And he did – in his own good time.

We rested. Ilya was a smoker. I listened to him move soft-footed through the living room then rifle through his trousers, discarded in the hall. He shouted for an ashtray. I directed him to the very back of the cupboard under the sink in the kitchen, but he returned instead with an empty Coke can.

It was growing dark. A street lamp shone hazily through the muslin curtains.

As Ilya lay there, contentedly inhaling, I felt serious nicotine cravings for the first time in seven and a half months. Dangerous, I thought; he could make me weaken.

'We need to use a word,' he said. 'If this is going to work, we need a codeword for stop. So if you don't like anything I do to you – not just Friday, at any time – then say . . . say "cuttlefish".'

'Why?' I asked with a slight laugh.

'Because it's a nice word,' he replied. (Oh, how I adored him for that.) 'And cuttlefish are interesting. And I reckon they suit what we're doing. They change colour. They signal to each other.'

'And then they get eaten by budgies?'

'Yeah.' He smiled. 'But I was thinking of the creatures, not their bones.'

He drew on his cigarette.

'Anyway,' I said. 'I meant, Why a codeword? Sounds a bit Special Branch to me. Why can't I just say "no" or "stop"?'

'Slips out too easily,' he said. 'And "no" and "stop" are good words to use when you don't mean them. Cuttlefish is deadly serious.'

'Oh, right,' I said. 'But isn't that what people do who are into S/M and bondage? Safeword, I think they call it. Not my scene, I'm afraid. Too many Goths, too much equipment. And besides –'

'In fact . . .' cut in Ilya. He took a final thoughtful drag on his cigarette then dropped the butt in the Coke can. It landed with a plink and a fizz. 'In fact, let's make cuttlefish truly serious,' he said, exhaling a stream of smoke. 'This isn't a romance or a relationship. It's going to be a sex thing like we agreed.'

I said nothing. He sounded so certain of it.

'So,' he continued, 'let's make it into a bit of a game. What if "cuttlefish" means not just "stop" but "the end, finito"? No discussions. No analysis and future plans. Just "cuttlefish". The end.'

I pondered the implications of this. In theory, it sounded good: an affair that was pure lust with no messy break-up. Wasn't that what I wanted?

'So if I want rid of you,' I said, feigning a cool, cruel heart, 'then I do something you don't like and make you say "cuttlefish"?'

'Yeah,' he said, glancing at his watch. 'Or maybe you just say "cuttlefish". I have to accept. No arguments.' He swung himself from the bed, walked out of the door then returned, fastening up his trousers. 'And vice versa,' he said. 'If I think it's time to move on or whatever, then you have to accept me saying "cuttlefish".'

Seeing all his 'I'm about to leave' moves, I shrugged on my top and did up a couple of buttons.

'I think it's flawed,' I said. 'Supposing you want to . . . or you're doing something I don't like. But I don't want things to end. Then what?'

'Ah,' he said, stooping for his T-shirt. 'Then you have to decide how much you don't like it.'

'But . . .' I faltered. 'I don't know what you have in mind, but my pain threshold's not that high.'

Ilya flexed his chest into his T-shirt. 'Then I have to suss out that threshold, weigh up how much pain you can take,' he said evenly. 'Or how much humiliation or whatever it is. I don't want you to say "cuttlefish".' He smiled. 'Not yet, anyway.'

'Gee, thanks,' I replied.

'Friday, then?' he asked, arching his dark brows. 'Say, ten-ish?'

I nodded. 'Yeah, OK,' I said. 'Friday.'

'Great,' he said, and stroked a quick finger across my cheek. 'Make it good, Beth. I'll see myself out.'

* * *

I had three days to shop for some whore clothes; and three days to try to work out just who – or what – I was getting involved with.

The Houseshare

Pat O'Brien

The central character of *The Houseshare* is Tine, whose glamorous new friends are determined that she should start to enjoy life again after spending a period of time alone. Porsche-driving Sharon is forever flitting about, buying new clothes and having a wild time. In this extract she takes Tine to one of the 'private' shops owned by her father. It's there that Tine is introduced to male pornstar, Red, whose own particular fancy for watersports shocks and arouses Tine like nothing else ever has.

Mixing dirty fun with trust and tenderness is the key to ensuring successful sexual adventure, and this scene shows how it's done.

The Houseshare

The trip down the M1 was uneventful. Tine, because she was petite, was bundled in the rear of the Porsche and was surprised, given the apparent lack of room, at its comfort. Before long she had curled up, her head resting on the cool, soft suede, and dozed. As she drifted in and out of sleep she was amazed at the conversation she overheard. Stevie had commented on the car and, as they entered the outskirts of London, Tine heard the tail-end of a highly technical discussion about the engine performance and gear ratios of various top-range cars.

Sharon was a dextrous and confident driver, weaving in and out of the traffic with casual sureness without breaking her conversation with Stevie. When Tine sat up to peer with interest at her surroundings, she caught Sharon's glance at her in the rear-view mirror.

'Hello sleepy, good timing!'

They parked in a multi-storey car-park. Sharon eased the Porsche into a reserved parking bay, much to Stevie's apparent alarm. Before her passengers could comment, the blonde woman ushered them from the vehicle and shepherded them towards a security cubicle. A young man watched their approach with obvious relish, grinning broadly when Sharon suddenly executed a pirouette before him, her arms outstretched.

'Hello miss,' he said. 'Your dad was here earlier asking if I'd seen you recently.'

'Well, now you can say you have. He's not at the shop, is he?'

'No, he was leaving in the tank,' the man muttered cryptically.

'Perhaps I'll catch up with him.' Sharon waved and led Tine and Stevie on, now mystified but obedient followers.

There was something in Sharon's attitude which forbade inquiry; possibly the defiant set to her shoulders. When neither of her followers sought information her tension seemed to ease and she returned to good humour, pointing out small landmarks as they made their way along Brewer Street into the heart of Soho.

Tine was busily peering into the window of a small bookshop when her companions suddenly disappeared. Sharon returned a moment later to grasp her arm and tug her through a doorway. She got an impression of black lacquer and gold door fittings before she was plunged into the cool, dim interior of a hallway which led through to an up-market boutique. She caught a glimpse of Stevie turning a corner ahead and, following her, stopped and stared as an assistant approached to fling her arms around Sharon.

The woman was incredibly tall; over six foot in height, Tine guessed. She wore an elegant and tailored grey suit. Her red hair was carefully coiffured to hang in a luscious fall over one shoulder and her generous mouth was painted a bright, provocative red.

'Shar! It's been far too long, darling. Your father was here a mere half-hour ago.' Her voice was rich and deep, 'plummy' as Tine's mother would have described it. The woman hurried on: 'We've got in a whole new range since you last dropped by. Would you like a preview? I've got two girls who were here for Richard.' Tine noticed she was smiling at Stevie while addressing Sharon.

Sharon introduced the woman, Magda, as a silent exchange passed between her and Stevie. Tine understood it signified mutual recognition, but of something she could not discern. She dismissed it, and sent a quizzical look at Sharon, who pursed her lips and encouraged Magda to display the new range. The tall woman rung a bell and, at the appearance of a young girl, rattled off instructions which sent her scurrying from the room. Magda followed, disappearing through a solid mahogany door, after urging the trio to make themselves comfortable on the sofas.

The room was elegant. Large, with lofted ceilings, the walls clad in white and gold Imperial wallpaper. The carpet was springy; a massed, soft gold fibre. They settled on tapestry loungers while Sharon explained that her father, Richard, owned the boutique, amongst other things, and that Magda managed the chain and bought the stock.

'Chain?' Tine was determined to suffer Sharon's mysteriousness no longer, reasoning that since she had brought them here, she owed them an explanation.

It emerged that this boutique was one of six. The sister shops were scattered, two on the continent, two in America, and another in Scotland. They were known only by their street numbers, and their clientele was very select. As Sharon spoke, the young woman returned, bearing a silver tea service and bone china cups. They had a choice of freshly milled coffee, the rich vapour making Tine salivate, or tea, its perfume vying with the earthier grounds. The tray also bore a gold-edged menu. It invited the guests to snack, offering an entrée of *paté de fois gras*, Beluga caviar with pumpernickel bread, and *crudités*. The smaller girl was stood patiently nearby and, at Sharon's nod, moved off soundlessly, leaving them to pour their own drinks. She returned minutes later with salvers laden with the delicacies promised by the menu.

Tine was charmed. She helped herself to small triangles

of the rich, black bread and heaped on the cool grey eggs. She closed her eyes softly in appreciation as she popped the morsel into her mouth, savouring the flavour as she chewed with pleasure. Tine wondered if the trays were always kept ready for guests. Perhaps, she thought, the mysterious Richard's visit had something to do with it; the staff would be sure to maintain their professionalism if the boss had a habit of appearing unannounced. But she was sure, however, that this was the sort of establishment one would expect to visit only by appointment.

'You made an appointment!' Tine stared at Sharon. 'That was why your father was here. And we were late because I went to change.' Everything seemed to slot into place: the reserved car parking, their reception at the boutique and Magda's readiness, with models to hand. Tine was hugely impressed and hugged Sharon impulsively.

'How wonderful!' She settled back to enjoy the unexpected and extravagant treat, resolving to simply go along with whatever happened.

Sharon smiled her relief, and draped herself over a *chaise longue*.

'Hang on to your hats, dears!' she warned, as soft music started and the mahogany door swung open to admit two young women. Magda's rich tones introduced the models over hidden speakers:

'Sandy and Cheryl – for your pleasure.'

Tine assumed it was Sandy who led the way over the lush carpet. Tall, dark and very beautiful, her ample breasts were uplifted by a scarlet, cupless basque. Her long, rounded legs were clad in sheer red-tinted stockings, which clung to her thighs with the aid of elasticised, lacy tops. She wore a delicate scarlet thong to match the basque and, when she turned, her generous bum-cheeks trembled saucily. The thread disappeared, with implied promise, between the shivering globes. She moved with languid grace, her eyes warm and half-closed, seeking smoky contact with the prospective customers.

Tine watched in fascination. She had never witnessed such a fashion show, and was equally impressed with the model's professionalism and the blatant sexuality of the outfit. Recognising that her own petite build would not sustain such a creation, she tore her eyes from Sandy to concentrate on Cheryl, a delicate, ash-blonde young woman who appeared to be wearing royal-blue baby rompers. As Tine leaned forward, Cheryl noticed her interest, eased towards her and drew to a silent halt. She slowly turned on her toes allowing Tine a full view and revealing that the outfit was, indeed, rompers. Created in fine, soft leather, they moulded over Cheryl's small breasts then flared into bloomers from the waist. They were gathered high in the thigh with lacy elastic and carefully pleated to fit the crotch. With a naughty smile Cheryl slowly parted her legs. The folds parted to reveal her shaven pubis, pale and softly inviting between the open pleats of the crotchless bloomers. She seemed gratified by Tine's sudden giggle and swift blush, and smiled warmly as she quickly turned and followed her companion out through the door.

In the moment before Magda appeared, Sharon glanced at Tine. The older woman was captivated by the outfit, no doubt imagining where she would wear such an item. She had a faraway expression that Sharon had grown to recognise under her father's tutelage. Sharon made a mental note that, before Tine enquired, Magda would be told to quote only trade prices.

Magda was stunning in black leather. She wore a dominatrix outfit which clove to her like a second skin. Laced at the front, it plunged at the rear to cup under her bare bum-cheeks. Laces spanned her naked back. The muscles of her legs bunched and eased beneath the fine-quality leather and her mons was clearly outlined. She wore thigh-length boots with stark and heavy silver zips. To Tine it seemed an unnecessarily complicated outfit but, as she was working out the practicality of dressing in such a

297

fashion, she noticed Sharon's eyes shining, riveted on Magda as the tall woman sauntered before her.

It seemed that the models were inexhaustible, parading a myriad of complex creations, mainly leather, before the trio. Magda appeared frequently, clad in elaborate, dominatrix styles and looking as if she was thoroughly enjoying her participation. Eventually she emerged in her familiar grey suit and eased onto the *chaise longue* beside Sharon.

'We have introduced something new,' she murmured, 'for interactive viewing.'

Cheryl came through the door, carrying a small leather suitcase. She was followed closely by two young men, wearing only leather posing pouches, and each toting rather larger cases. They assembled before the sofas, busily unpacking and arranging the wares across the carpet. There was a carefully practised order in their movements, the articles revealed and placed in such a way to make them accessible and attractive. On one side, Tine viewed a starburst of dildos and vibrators, ranging in hue from soft oyster to blushing purple. On the other side they scattered a glistening pile of sheer underwear in leather and silk, scraps of pulsing colours which invited investigation and promised pleasure to any seeker who should dig her fingers amongst the delicate fabrics. Fanned before them were catalogues with rich, embossed gold covers depicting elegant models, a single name embossed on the lower right corner: *Richard*.

Once the wares were arranged the models retreated, to pose comfortably on the carpet. They murmured amongst themselves, seemingly oblivious of the company. No doubt, thought Tine as she surveyed them, to enable unembarrassed scrutiny.

The men were certainly as gorgeous as the women. One, olive-skinned, with long, tousled black hair and a suggestion of generous proportions under his pouch, was introduced as 'Tyson'. The other man was slim, lean and pale with a shock of red hair; unsurprisingly named 'Red'. He seemed slightly remote, smiling softly as if enjoying an inner joke, his grey eyes friendly and aware. Tine felt drawn to him, appreciating his mystery and surprising herself with the idea that, were he at her disposal, she would simply like to be pleasured by him. She feared that this was an attitude which would draw criticism, were the genders reversed and, feeling slightly ashamed of herself, she consigned the image to fantasy and concentrated on the sex-toys. Magda was inviting them to take a closer look and Sharon was already fingering each in turn with an experienced air. Far from titillated by the thrumming vibrator now alive in her hand, she seemed to be studying it with the narrowed, calculating eye of the entrepreneur.

Tine watched her with the dawning appreciation that Sharon, most likely the inheritor of her father's empire, had a keen sense of business. The mystery of her rift with her father would remain her secret unless she chose to reveal it. While the blonde continued a muted conversation with Magda, who seemed delighted and even deferential, Tine fingered the pile of underwear. Stevie was leafing through a catalogue and seemed engrossed, her finger marking a place as she slowly turned the pages.

The tiny garments sliding through Tine's fingers seemed ludicrously insufficient to her. In some cases they were mere strings which she turned this way and that to work out how they should be worn. The fabrics were delightful, the fine leathers as soft and crumpling as the satins and silks. She brushed one tiny scrap across her cheek, eyes closed in appreciation of its warm, sheer caress, and imagined the garment nestling against her rift, softly soaking up her juices. Her imaginings stopped abruptly with the realisation that she had overlooked her own lack of underwear, and was presenting the view between her parted thighs to Red. When she opened her eyes to look, he was not there. She felt a warm presence behind her moments before his words brushed softly past her ear.

'This is only a very small selection.' His voice was

gentle, deep and discreet. 'Would you like to enjoy more choices?'

Tine turned to face him and, searching for any sign other than friendly enquiry in his expression, felt relieved when she could trace no innuendo. She glanced at the strewn ribbons of underwear. Delightful as they were, she was neither accustomed to nor particularly attracted by such garments. However, she was entranced by the fabrics and, if more traditional designs were offered in the same materials, she would be tempted. She smiled and nodded, allowing Red to help her to rise to her feet.

It seemed that no one paid any attention as Red ushered her through the mahogany door. Stevie remained engrossed in her pages, Sharon in low conversation with Magda. Cheryl and Tyson relaxed, waiting to be summoned if they were required.

A corridor stretched beyond the door. Red led Tine to the second door on the right, inviting her through with a gallant sweep of his hand and a charming smile. She faced a large room, empty bar the presence of a maroon velvet love-seat which sat solidly on the white pile of a thick carpet. Three white walls gave way to maroon drapes covering the fourth. While stark, the white was not glaring, it was softened by dimmed light which spilled from a crystal chandelier, hung high from the vaulted, ornate ceiling.

Tine perched on the love-seat as Red crossed the room. He moved with grace, his lean, long thighs flexing softly, his shoulders square and relaxed. She could imagine him in a tuxedo, elegant and assured, yet he was not made ridiculous by the posing pouch. She wondered, if he was actually wearing a tuxedo, would she have been as quick to mentally undress him as she was to clothe him in his present, nearly naked state. The thought made her smile, and he saw her expression and returned it as he grasped the cords of the drapes and pulled. They opened to reveal an Aladdin's cave of tastefully displayed underwear and sex-toys. Having revealed the treasures, Red returned to her side, silently examining the panorama with her.

Tine spied a collection of creamy rich satin and lace teddies. Her eyes travelled over black silk lingerie, crumpling soft leather sets in vibrant colours and an artful arrangement of pastel separates. Displayed at the far end was a selection of men's underwear; posing pouches, thongs, penis sheaths and some whimsical silk boxers in primary colours, scattered with heart patterns. She tried to imagine Rupe wearing such items and failed, aware that the lean smoothness of the man at her side was the sort of model the designers had in mind when they produced their sketches.

'It is all image,' she muttered, hardly realising she spoke aloud.

'Any image you fancy?' Red smiled.

Tine nodded. 'The cream teddies.'

Red swiftly removed items from the display, his long, tapering fingers caressing the fabric. As he draped the garments over his arm he turned slightly to her. 'Would you mind a recommendation?'

Tine agreed, intrigued to see what he would produce. It would give her an insight as to how someone else saw her, and perhaps provide a hint on how she should regard herself. Red grasped a handle beside the cabinets which held the colourful leather goods, and the shelves pivoted to reveal hanging rails at the rear. These carried more leather, but all black. Not meant for display, the clothing was not easily viewable and Red selected a couple of garments which he added to those already draped over his arm.

Red swung open two more sets of shelves. One held a selection of sex-toys, and although many were a mystery, Tine's imagination supplied adequate interpretation. She drew nearer and was fascinated at the variety of designs produced for human titillation. Videos were stacked on one shelf. As she scanned them her eye caught the likeness of Red on one spine, entitled *Water Baby*. She reached for the case and turned it over to view the cover. It was Red, or at least a naked, rear view of him, standing in the unmistakable pose of a man relieving himself. He seemed all elegant long lines, tight buttocks and graceful casualness. Unable to avoid it, Tine murmured, 'You are very beautiful.'

She had not thought she would ever hear herself say such a thing to a man. She could not help but compare Red's dark largeness and animal grace with that of her young lover, Rupe. She was drawn to conjoin with Rupe, but Red seemed more aesthetic and her appreciation of him was quite unlike the way she felt about her Australian lover. She longed to touch the redhead, to draw her hands over his almost translucent skin and test his lean tightness under her fingers. He reminded her of a Pre-Raphaelite portrait; heavy, smooth-lidded eyes and a rosebud mouth. She gazed at him with the admiration she would accord a painting by an old master.

Red remained silent, and seemed slightly taken aback by the sincerely given compliment. Then, after a moment, he asked, 'Would you like to see the tape?'

She paused, feeling slightly disorientated. She took in the surroundings, thought of her friends in the other room and grappled with the proposed intimacy of watching Red on video, with him present. There seemed to be no challenge in his tone, more a return of her compliment, a proffering of thanks. It seemed complicit, as if they shared an adventure. She dismissed the notion that he might have shared this experience before.

'Yes,' she answered simply, watching his face. 'I would like that.'

Red beamed, and to Tine it suddenly seemed that he was terribly young, much younger than she had at first supposed.

'There is a viewing room next door. It's only a short movie.' Red looked expectant.

'Okay. The film first, then the clothes?'

'I am at a disadvantage here.' Red gestured at Tine's clothes, then his own near-nakedness. 'Perhaps ... ' His voice trailed off, eyes seeking her permission even as he undid the large, silver safety pin holding the flaps of Tine's kilt.

She stood silently as he eased his hand beneath the open edges, drawing his palm softly upwards along the curve of her hip until he reached the waistband, then flicked open the clasp with his thumb. The skirt fell away while his hand remained at her waist, his thumb now circling softly.

He sighed loudly, spanning her small waist with gentle hands and squeezing softly before reaching for the tape. Then he drew her from the room with him.

He chose the door opposite, ushering her in with the instruction to make herself comfortable and pulled the door closed, leaving her alone in the room. As he turned, Magda entered the corridor, her expression questioning. Her eyes dropped to the video case and held it up.

'She wants to see it.'

Magda kissed him quickly on the cheek, whispering, 'Are you OK with this?' Red knew she had a fondness for him. He rarely interacted with customers in the way in which Tyson was predisposed, and perhaps she was concerned about him. He knew she was aware of his particular interest but in the past she had been inclined to trust his young judgement.

He thought a moment. 'Yes. She's different. There is something special about her.'

'Well, be careful, OK?' Magda told him she had called Richard to alert him that Sharon had arrived. On his instructions she had cancelled two appointments to keep the salon clear of other custom. His clear message was that the staff should endeavour, in every way, to ensure that these visitors left happy.

'Oh,' she said, 'and don't talk prices, OK?' She smiled into Red's eyes. 'This is not business. Think of it as a family matter.'

Red softened, his shoulders eased and a warm light entered his eyes. He hugged her impulsively and dashed into the clothes room, crossing swiftly over to the cabinets and, having chosen an item thoughtfully, he exited the room with pleasurable anticipation.

As he re-entered the viewing room he could see Tine's head above the back of a large, black sofa. He dimmed the lights then slipped beside her after carefully dropping the item out of sight.

Tine sat cross-legged on the sofa and seemed comfortable. This was a much smaller and more intimate room than before. Spotlights in the lowered ceiling cast soft pools of light over the sofa, and a television set and small bar were recessed into one wall. The walls were covered in dark maroon silk and oriental rugs were strewn over a dark wood floor. The sofa was the only place to sit, or lie. Its deep, puffing leather was scattered with bright silk cushions.

Red placed one hand on Tine's shoulder and pressed gently, turning her face away from him. He unbraided her hair then fluffed his fingers though the rich tumble appreciatively, smiling softly as he teased the rippling locks over her shoulders. She looked tiny, her slimness emphasised by the snug black body-stocking. The rich chestnut fall of her hair was shot through with gold beneath the spotlights.

Tine felt totally at ease. She had surrendered herself willingly to this new experience and was avid to see the video, even as she relished Red's careful, planned ministration. It was clear that he was creating an ambience, structuring the hour with forethought. She was not aroused but pleased, the touch of Red's hands gently thrilling but mute.

Red brought her a drink from the bar. It tasted like perfumed water, slightly fizzy and, she suspected, mildly alcoholic. She felt her palate refresh as she sipped, watching him slide the tape into the video slot. He was soon nestling beside her, his eyes fixed on the screen as it came alive, then, satisfied all was in order, he slid to the edge of the sofa, swung his legs up and pulled her to him. She lay with her head resting against his smooth chest and her hips couched between his thighs.

The screen filled with a close-up of Red's face. He looked relaxed as the camera panned away to reveal him seated in a comfortable armchair, wearing a loose, dark sweater and jeans.

'Hi,' said the image. 'I am Red, I am eighteen years old and I am a water baby.' He smiled without apology. 'People often ask about watersports. I show them.' He unwound from the chair and the camera followed him across the room. He stripped, turned and exited through a door. The camera followed, concentrating on his tight bottom.

The view widened to reveal a tasteful bathroom; a champagne-coloured corner bath with gold fittings and a matching lavatory, bidet and basin. Large, fluffy dark towels were piled on the edge of the bath and he wrapped one around his waist, sarong-style, and perched on the edge of the tub. He gestured, waving his hand to encompass the room.

'This is a good place for watersports, the great outdoors even better – as you will see later.' He seemed to be waiting, and before long a woman entered. She peered around in bewilderment at the camera, then at Red.

'I want to use the toilet!' She looked uneasy.

'Hi Andrea.' Red smiled at the woman. He cocked his head to one side. 'Remember our conversation last night?'

He informed the camera that Andrea had asked him about his interest. Their long discussion had persuaded him that she would enjoy helping him to make this movie. He confessed that he had arranged an appointment, then kept her plied with liquids during her half-hour wait. She had been directed to the bathroom when she eventually felt the need to relieve herself.

During this explanation, Andrea stood staring at Red but, as he concluded his introduction, her expression showed that she seemed to be enjoying the idea. There was no doubt Red had researched his subject well, and her surprise was more than compensated by her growing enthusiasm.

'So.' She smiled at Red then grinned broadly at the camera. 'What do we do?'

'You wanted to go to the toilet, didn't you?'

She nodded.

'Then do so.'

Despite his seemingly peremptory attitude, Red radiated warmth. He rose and placed his hands on Andrea's shoulders, before lifting them to cup her face. His eyes assured her he thought her wonderful and, as his towel dislodged and fell away, his erection provided a more clear endorsement. As pale, long and elegant as his body, it quivered in sympathy with her growing need.

'Here, I can help you.' His voice grew deeper, his fingers already undoing her clothing, efficiently stripping away her blouse, skirt and underwear. All the time he spoke softly and persuasively. Her eyes were large and she was passive as she was undressed. Once naked, Andrea displayed a slight, slim build, her sparsely clad pubis bearing out the authenticity of the short, blonde curls tumbling around her forehead.

Red eased behind her and drew her backwards. The camera now held a full view of Andrea, clearly excited, her waist spanned by Red's hands as he guided her. He sat down on the toilet seat, his legs apart, and pulled her back to sit on his thighs. His hands slid forward to part her legs until they rested either side of his. Her quim was now widely exposed to the lens and almost at once her need for relief overcame any reservation about public exposure, and the golden pour began. As his fingers felt the wetness Red cupped her bottom, urging her to rise slightly and bend forward a little. Now the flow was redirected. It ran hotly over Red's erection, coursed down his shaft and tickled over his scrotum before easing into the bowl. He slipped his fingers into the pale cascade and, once Andrea stopped, he urged her from him and rose to face her, tracing his fingertips over her lips. She licked them dry as she watched him suck his fingers with evident pleasure.

Tine moved restlessly against Red. She could feel his excitement as she leaned against him, his rod hard at the base of her spine. His video had produced a surprising response in her and she had become involved and interested, before her own excitement manifested itself. As Tine unconsciously pressed towards him, Red slipped his hand around her, his fingers circling patiently over her mound.

When she squirmed and attempted to edge from him he quickly switched off the tape and allowed her to sit up and face him, calmly awaiting rejection.

'No, it's not that,' she said breathlessly, betraying her arousal but aware of his concern. She recognised the wary look in his eyes. 'It's just that ...' She paused as if embarrassed, and then almost wailed, 'I really do need to go to the loo.'

'Can I come?' Red held his breath.

'Yes, but get me out of this thing!' Tine pulled desperately at the body-stocking, now clenching her thighs. The garment was one piece and she would have to remove it altogether to obtain release.

'Oh no, no.' Red propelled her to the door, swiftly bending to retrieve the item she had noticed him plant earlier beside the sofa, before hurrying her down the corridor. It was the same room depicted in the movie, but Tine had little time for appreciation. Realising she would not make it in time if she stopped to unclothe, she plumped herself firmly onto the seat as the wetness started to seep from her.

For an extraordinary moment Tine felt unable to continue, despite the pressure of her bladder. The leak started then froze; and Red took this as a signal to produce a buzzing vibrator which he pressed firmly into Tine's cleft through the crotch of the body-stocking. He nuzzled the head against her clitoris. The sensation was a painful, sharp intrusion against her sensitive button and she tried to move away.

'Stay with me!' Red demanded, his eyes shining as he expertly wielded the vibrator. He lifted his head and firmly planted his mouth over hers, his tongue rudely filling her mouth. His forceful intrusion surprised Tine and she became torn by sensations. She forced herself to relax into the thrum of the vibrator head and immediately felt the burning pleasure become a hot-centred demand. Her need to urinate became a dull, bloating wash and her lust rose, concentrating on the penetration of his sopping tongue.

She returned Red's kiss with force as she felt herself gush uncontrollably over the buzzing device. Red swiftly withdrew the vibrator and slid his palm to catch her pouring. A surge shot through her and she lifted her hips of her own volition. She felt she was still watching the video but directing her own involvement, as if from a distance. Red's sheer delight in the drench of her hot waters provoked in her a dark desire to soak him and she shot forward.

Surprised, Red tumbled back and Tine crouched over him. She circled her hips so her gush splashed his face and chin and seeped over his neck. The trickles stained his copper curls. Tine peered between her thighs to watch her elixir pool and glisten. The intensity of the image drew her to rub herself to a ringing climax. At last, relieved in all senses, apart from a strange wonder, she tumbled from him and slumped by his side.

Red looked radiant as he turned to face her, studying her with an expression akin to worship. Despite the bizarre circumstances, Tine felt moved, a protective feeling creeping over her. At her age she regarded him as a mere man-child, barely mature and yet his behaviour was so experienced; it produced a conflict in her. She noted that his erection had not subsided. Following the direction of her gaze, Red shook his head, smiling.

'Don't mind that,' he said happily. 'It does not matter.'

Tine felt puzzled, realising that there was much more at play than she could imagine from her previous experience. She had questions but surrendered to Red's evident pleasure following her 'accident'. He peeled the body stocking from her and, while she sat damp and naked on the toilet seat, ran the bath full with water. He lifted her in, laughing at her protests and watched her sink back with a pleased sigh, before he carefully rinsed her garment in the hand-basin. His concentration on the task was absolute. It seemed to Tine that he became involved in a tiny world, concentrating on the sheer fabric which glistened as it slid soapily through his fingers.

His erection had still not died. It remained proud and angry until he rinsed and wrapped the silky fabric in a warm towel, pressing to extract the water. His penis then hung, soft and vulnerable, between his pale thighs.

Tine experienced a moment's regret, wishing she could arouse him again. It seemed that she had not pleasured him, at least not in the manner which she was used to; yet he seemed sated. She realised she would have to revise her perceptions. Not entirely ignorant about 'golden showers', it was not something she could ever have envisaged enjoying. She felt bewildered in the aftermath.

Red was aware of her confusion. He leaned over the

bath, soaping her small form with now friendly hands. His face seemed alight, as if sunshine now filtered through to his world. His touch on her was intimate, complicit and familiar and he soaped between her legs with the same intensity as he had shown while rinsing her sodden garment. His fingers slicked among her folds in the same way as they had slid along the glistening, black fabric.

'It would take too long to explain now,' he whispered, his attention distracted by his task. 'A lot is in the video, and there is a book I would like to give you.' He paused, looking deeply into her eyes with something akin to love, and whispered, 'You were wonderful. All the more because you do not even realise why.'

He explained that, to him, it was like a fabulously beautiful woman not realising she was ravishing, her actions pure and innocent, without vanity or manipulation. It made her painfully desirable. This, he said, was Tine's present to him: in her innocence she had given him the greatest gift. He towelled her dry, helped her into the slightly damp body-stocking and vigorously rubbed her down. The garment dried under his ministration and, as they left the bathroom, it was as if the scene had never occurred; except that Red was gentle, almost worshipping, as he led her back to the showroom. He wound her tiny kilt around her waist and secured the pin.

The teddy she had chosen and Red's recommendations seemed forgotten but she experienced no regret. She no longer felt like shopping. Her head was filled with her recent experience, a pleasant memory still shrouded in questions. Overlaying her curiosity was a strong sense of self-interrogation and a secret wish to experiment more. She returned to the main salon alone.

When Tine re-entered, she knew that the others would be able to tell that something had happened. She was clearly sated, with an embarrassed pinkness to her cheeks, and her smile was tentative while she reassured Stevie that she

310

was okay. She had sat down close beside the dark woman before she noticed the remnants of an obviously explicit interplay.

Tyson and Cheryl were naked, both wearing the pleased smugness of afterglow. Around them were littered the tools which had apparently led to their satisfaction: dildos; handcuffs; creams and limp garments. Tine raised her eyebrows at Stevie, who merely shrugged and smiled. In the far corner of the room, Sharon was engaged in a low conversation with a man. She noticed Tine's return and broke off in mid-sentence to approach, followed by the man.

This, unmistakably, was Richard. Their relationship was betrayed by his eyes, the same startling, violet slants inherited by his daughter. Tine noted they did not seem at all effeminate but she was startled by their keen interrogation.

Sharon hugged Tine.

'Are you OK?' She peered at the older woman's face with a smile.

Tine nodded, suddenly shy. She exchanged a glance with Richard. In his expression lay a wealth of understanding and, for a moment, Tine felt herself laid bare. It was as if she had suddenly grown, moved from ignorance into a state of knowledge. Richard would know Red's proclivities and Tine's uncertainties. His expression assured her that all was well.

He was an elegant man, resting lightly on sprung heels in Gucci shoes. He wore a silk shirt – classic and expensive – and a grey suit. His tanned face was relaxed though watchful. His hair silvered at his temples. Tine believed him to be the most handsome man she had ever seen. It was no wonder, she thought, that he owned this chain of salons; his empathy with them was perfect. Despite his allure, she was guarded after her initial, open response. He seemed to sense her reserve and was courteous and seemingly amused, which hid his intrigue.

As he had followed Sharon to meet Tine, he waved surreptitiously and the models had quickly gathered everything and disappeared. Apart from some mild ruffling of the pile of the gold carpet, the salon was restored. Magda returned to drop a quick kiss on Richard's cheek and proffer him carrier-bags, with a whisper. The bags were gold with woven handles, his name embossed in the bottom right-hand corner.

It seemed the shopping trip was at an end. Tine felt slightly disappointed that Red had not re-emerged to say farewell but she followed the group into the street without comment. A metallic-grey Silver Cloud Rolls Royce sat arrogantly on the yellow no-parking lines.

'This must be "the tank",' Stevie whispered to Tine, unable to keep the admiration from her voice.

Richard must have overheard her, and opened the front passenger door, then beckoned to Stevie who leaped into the vehicle without a backward glance at her friends to see if they approved. Sharon smiled in defeat as she ushered Tine into the spacious rear and followed her as Richard took the wheel.

They did not travel far, but Richard took a circuitous route to allow Stevie maximum enjoyment, talking enthusiastically about the vehicle in response to her questions. He ended up offering her the steering wheel on the drive back to the car park after coffee, which caused Stevie to fall quiet at last, stunned and delighted.

The cafe chosen by Richard for high tea surprised Tine. It was unassuming and not as glamorous as she had anticipated. The staff obviously knew father and daughter, and bustled around until the table was laden with tiny sandwiches, scones, steaming pots of coffee and good feeling.

Tine found herself enjoying Richard's company. He seemed to blend into the group and was self-deprecating and witty, causing laughter and goodwill. He did manage to elicit an invitation to the shared house, including a

312

meal, and Tine grinned at him, recognising the clever manipulation he had used to obtain the offer. He was complicit, smiling back ruefully as Sharon punched him on the arm in jokey frustration.

Stevie stayed mostly silent through the meal, caught up with her proposed treat. She watched Tine, wondering what had transpired at the salon and admiring her appearance. Tine had not re-braided her hair and it swung in heavy chestnut waves around her shoulders. Her dark eyes were alight with mischief and humour as she chatted with Richard. It struck Stevie that Tine was thoroughly enjoying herself. She compared Richard with the raw, dark charm of Rupe and could not avoid thinking that Tine was better suited to the older man. He would provide her with more intellectual stimulation and possessed a depth of understanding not yet available to the inexperienced Australian.

Red, Stevie surmised, was something else. She had observed the young man closely before he had left the room with Tine. He was a specialist, involved in a world beyond the one Tine inhabited; a nice place to visit but she would not want to live there. She figured that, whatever had happened between the two of them had not damaged Tine; the woman was alive with laughter. Stevie suspected Tine was on a voyage of discovery and the richness of her current experiences would lay the foundations for her new life.

BLACK LACE NEW BOOKS

Published in November

VELVET GLOVE
Emma Holly
£5.99

Audrey is an SM Goldilocks in search of the perfect master. Her first choice is far too cruel. Her second too tender. When she meets Patrick – a charismatic bar owner – he seems just right. But can she trust the man behind the charm, or will he drag her deeper into submission than she's prepared to go?

ISBN 0 352 33448 7

BOUND BY CONTRACT
Helena Ravenscroft
£5.99

Samantha Bentley and her cousin Ross have been an illicit item for years. When Ross becomes involved with the submissive Dr Louisa, Sam senses that Ross's true passions aren't compatible with her own domineering ways. Then she reads the classic novel *Venus in Furs*, which inspires her to experiment with being his slave for a month. When Dr Louisa shows up at Ross's country hideaway, there are surprising shifts in their ritual games of power and punishment.

ISBN 0 352 33447 9

Published in December

STRIPPED TO THE BONE
Jasmine Stone
£5.99

Annie is a fun-loving, free-thinking American woman who sets herself the mission of changing everything in her life. The only snag is she doesn't know when to stop changing things. Every man she meets is determined to find out what makes her tick, but her wild personality means no one can get a hold on her. Her sexual magnetism is electrifying, and her capacity for unusual and experimental sex-play has her lovers in a spin of erotic confusion.

ISBN 0 352 33463 0

THE BEST OF BLACK LACE
Ed. Kerri Sharp
£5.99

This diverse collection of sizzling erotica is an 'editor's choice' of extracts from Black Lace books with a contemporary theme. The accent is on female characters who know what they want in bed – and in the workplace – and who have a sense of adventure above and beyond the heroines of romantic fiction. These girls kick ass!

ISBN 0 352 33452 5

To be published in January

SHAMELESS
Stella Black
£5.99

Stella Black, a 30-year-old woman with too much imagination for her own good, travels to Arizona with Jim, her dark SM master. Out in the desert, things get weird, and both the landscape and its inhabitants are more rough and ready than Stella has bargained for. A rip-snorting adventure of sleaze and danger.

ISBN 0 352 33485 1

DOCTOR'S ORDERS
Deanna Ashford
£5.99

Helen Dawson is a doctor who has taken a short-term assignment at an exclusive clinic. This private hospital caters for every need of its rich and famous clients, and the matron, Sandra Pope, ensures this covers their most curious sexual fancies. When Helen forms a risky affair with a famous actor, she is drawn deeper into the hedonistic lifestyle of the clinic. But will she risk her own privileges when she uncovers the dubious activities of Sandra and her team?

ISBN 0 352 33453 3

If you would like a complete list of plot summaries of Black Lace titles, or would like to receive information on other publications available, please send a stamped addressed envelope to:

Black Lace, Thames Wharf Studios,
Rainville Road, London W6 9HA

BLACK LACE BOOKLIST

All books are priced £4.99 unless another price is given.

Black Lace books with a contemporary setting

PALAZZO	Jan Smith ISBN 0 352 33156 9	☐
THE GALLERY	Fredrica Alleyn ISBN 0 352 33148 8	☐
AVENGING ANGELS	Roxanne Carr ISBN 0 352 33147 X	☐
GINGER ROOT	Robyn Russell ISBN 0 352 33152 6	☐
DANGEROUS CONSEQUENCES	Pamela Rochford ISBN 0 352 33185 2	☐
THE NAME OF AN ANGEL £6.99	Laura Thornton ISBN 0 352 33205 0	☐
BONDED	Fleur Reynolds ISBN 0 352 33192 5	☐
CONTEST OF WILLS £5.99	Louisa Francis ISBN 0 352 33223 9	☐
THE SUCCUBUS £5.99	Zoe le Verdier ISBN 0 352 33230 1	☐
FEMININE WILES £7.99	Karina Moore ISBN 0 352 33235 2	☐
AN ACT OF LOVE £5.99	Ella Broussard ISBN 0 352 33240 9	☐
DRAMATIC AFFAIRS £5.99	Fredrica Alleyn ISBN 0 352 33289 1	☐
DARK OBSESSION £7.99	Fredrica Alleyn ISBN 0 352 33281 6	☐
COOKING UP A STORM £7.99	Emma Holly ISBN 0 352 33258 1	☐
SHADOWPLAY £5.99	Portia Da Costa ISBN 0 352 33313 8	☐
RAW SILK £5.99	Lisabet Sarai ISBN 0 352 33336 7	☐
THE TOP OF HER GAME £5.99	Emma Holly ISBN 0 352 33337 5	☐

HAUNTED £5.99	Laura Thornton ISBN 0 352 33341 3	☐
VILLAGE OF SECRETS £5.99	Mercedes Kelly ISBN 0 352 33344 8	☐
INSOMNIA £5.99	Zoe le Verdier ISBN 0 352 33345 6	☐
PACKING HEAT £5.99	Karina Moore ISBN 0 352 33356 1	☐
TAKING LIBERTIES £5.99	Susie Raymond ISBN 0 352 33357 X	☐
LIKE MOTHER, LIKE DAUGHTER £5.99	Georgina Brown ISBN 0 352 34422 3	☐
CONFESSIONAL £5.99	Judith Roycroft ISBN 0 352 34421 5	☐
ASKING FOR TROUBLE £5.99	Kristina Lloyd ISBN 0 352 33362 6	☐
OUT OF BOUNDS £5.99	Mandy Dickinson ISBN 0 352 33431 2	☐
A DANGEROUS GAME £5.99	Lucinda Carrington ISBN 0 352 33432 0	☐
THE TIES THAT BIND £5.99	Tesni Morgan ISBN 0 352 33438 X	☐
IN THE DARK £5.99	Zoe le Verdier ISBN 0 352 33439 8	☐

Black Lace books with an historical setting

THE SENSES BEJEWELLED	Cleo Cordell ISBN 0 352 32904 1	☐
HANDMAIDEN OF PALMYRA	Fleur Reynolds ISBN 0 352 32919 X	☐
THE INTIMATE EYE	Georgia Angelis ISBN 0 352 33004 X	☐
CONQUERED	Fleur Reynolds ISBN 0 352 33025 2	☐
FORBIDDEN CRUSADE	Juliet Hastings ISBN 0 352 33079 1	☐
ÎLE DE PARADIS	Mercedes Kelly ISBN 0 352 33121 6	☐
DESIRE UNDER CAPRICORN	Louisa Francis ISBN 0 352 33136 4	☐
A VOLCANIC AFFAIR	Xanthia Rhodes ISBN 0 352 33184 4	☐
FRENCH MANNERS	Olivia Christie ISBN 0 352 33214 X	☐

-------✂-------------------

Please send me the books I have ticked above.

Name   ....

Address ....

        ....

        ....

        .... Post Code ....

Send to: **Cash Sales, Black Lace Books, Thames Wharf Studios, Rainville Road, London W6 9HA.**

US customers: for prices and details of how to order books for delivery by mail, call 1-800-805-1083.

Please enclose a cheque or postal order, made payable to **Virgin Publishing Ltd**, to the value of the books you have ordered plus postage and packing costs as follows:
   UK and BFPO – £1.00 for the first book, 50p for each subsequent book.
   Overseas (including Republic of Ireland) – £2.00 for the first book, £1.00 for each subsequent book.

If you would prefer to pay by VISA, ACCESS/MASTER-CARD, DINERS CLUB, AMEX or SWITCH, please write your card number and expiry date here:

....

Please allow up to 28 days for delivery.

Signature ....

-------✂-------------------